House of Arsceneaux

SERVANTS OF MORRIGAN: IMMORTAL CREATURES

CATERINA NOVELLIERE

Caterina Novelliere & Connections Across Time, LLC
www.caterinanovelliere.com

Publisher's Note: This is a work of fiction. Names, characters, places, and incidents are a product of the author's imagination. Locales and public names are sometimes used for atmospheric purposes. Any resemblance to actual living people or to businesses, companies, events, institutions, or locales is completely coincidental.

Cover Artwork : BookBrush
Developmental Editing: Magnolia Author Services
Line & Copy Editing: Victoria Ellis of Cruel Ink Editing + Design

EBook ISBN:9781732332782
Paperback ISBN:9781732332799

To Glenn - My real life Evariste

Caitlin DeDanann

The secretary spotted Caitlin coming through the office door.
"Sean's looking for you."

Hearing the principal of the firm was already looking for her,
Caitlin groaned. She came in early to get some work done, not to sit in
another boring impromptu staff meeting. "Tell him I won't be in for
another hour as I have a dentist appointment or whatever type of
appointment sounds believable."

"Considering I am standing behind you and see you are already
here, an appointment of any type isn't believable." Sean Watchous's
voice came from over her shoulder.

"Sean, really?! Do you want the Barringer report on time or not?"
Caitlin turned to look up at her boss. "I can't finish writing it if you
keep summoning the team for random meetings whenever you feel
like it."

"This will take five minutes of your morning." Sean gave her the *I
dare you to keep arguing with me stare* all senior executives learn to
master over time.

"Fine." Caitlin walked into his office and sat down in one of the
ugly gray desk chairs in front of a black desk.

She never understood why Sean decorated his office in such sterile, contemporary colors. He was one of the top attorneys in Virginia. His clothing, home, and cars were all classic and timeless in design. His home had an inviting Old World Tuscan feel to it. His car was foreign, with a horse logo on the hood; it had black leather seats and wood trim. Every suit he wore was custom made in a classic cut, and his high-end, wing-tipped dress shoes always gleamed from a fresh coat of shoe polish. Nothing about him matched this ridiculously modern office in cold tones. It reminded Caitlin of military ships or some weird hospital laboratory room. Maybe he let some interior designer girlfriend riding the boring trend of grays and whites design the space. The click of the door closing stopped her contemplations.

"Caitlin, I have a high-profile client coming in today at ten. I'd like you to sit in on that meeting. If all goes well with it, you'll be the lead investigator assigned to the account," Sean said, settling himself into his desk chair.

"Okay. That's two hours from now and something you could have told me without requesting a meeting." Caitlin doubted that was the reason he called her into his office.

Sean let out a cross between a breath and a *hmm*. His mouth momentarily shrunk to a small, tight line before relaxing again. "I know we've put a lot on your plate lately, and I understand you're trying to wrap up several things before you go on vacation."

Caitlin recognized when Sean was dancing around an issue. "You didn't call me in here to talk about work, did you?"

A sheepish grin tweaked his lips. It didn't quite reach the pale blue eyes of the man who sat back and folded his hands in his lap. "Your grandmother wants you to visit her in England next month."

Caitlin shook her head. She should have guessed by Sean's demeanor that the meeting was more personal in nature than professional. "And why are you the one relaying the visitation request?"

"Because you've been ignoring her calls and emails."

"So I'm just supposed to drop everything going on in life for dear old Gram, who suddenly wants to spend time with her granddaughter after ignoring her for the past twenty years or so?"

"Caitlin, it's complicated. She hasn't been ignoring you." Sean ran a hand through his graying dark hair. "Before you say it, I know how you feel about her. But she's still your grandmother."

"I have a report to write." Caitlin stood and reached for her briefcase.

"Caitlin DeDanann, the report can wait. Sit back down."

The scolding tone caused Caitlin to quickly take her seat again. She hated that, even in her thirties, the little girl in her would quickly do as told anytime Sean's voice took on an angry fatherly tone.

"When your parents died, I promised your grandmother I'd look after you. And I have. I love you like a daughter, Cate. You're also one of my top investigators and project managers. But there are days that Irish temper and stubborn streak of yours tries every ounce of patience I have. Please call your grandmother when you get a chance today. Hear her out and then let me know if you need some time off."

"Fine. I'll call her after our ten o'clock." Caitlin picked up her briefcase and laptop bag. "I need a cup of coffee with how late I was up working on the Barringer report last night since I'm learning to play analyst on top of everything else. Can I get you anything from Amici's?"

"No, I'm good. And thank you for agreeing to call your grandmother. I'll see you in the conference room at 9:55. Don't be late." Sean watched her leave his office before looking at his computer screen.

"THAT WENT SHORTER than I expected, and there was no bloodshed," Esther, Sean's secretary, said, seeing Caitlin come out of the office.

"Oh, I won't forget that you knew why he was looking for me and didn't warn me." Caitlin joked with her. She and Esther had become pretty good friends since she was hired four years ago.

"If he hadn't come up right behind you, I would have covered for you. Everything okay with your grandmother? She called here a little after seven a.m."

"She's fine. She's just mad I didn't drop everything I'm doing to call her back right away. I swear, you'd think she was the Queen of England at times with how she acts. Bossy and mean old lady."

Deciding to quickly check email before going to the coffee shop, Caitlin logged on to her computer. Checking her email turned into just proofreading a paragraph or two of the Barringer report. Glancing down at her watch, the realization an hour had passed and she was running out of time to get coffee before the ten a.m. meeting prompted Caitlin to lock her computer and grab her purse.

She walked down the street to Amici's to get a cappuccino. Not a fan of American coffee, she had been delighted to learn Amici's, a small Italian chain with her favorite brand of espresso, was opening in Merchant's Square.

The spring morning air was cool and crisp, but the sun shining overhead warned the day would eventually warm up into the seventies. Spring in Williamsburg meant a mix of flowers, sunshine, and rain. The commercial area alongside Colonial Williamsburg was just starting to come to life at nine a.m. as William & Mary students headed to another local coffee shop and tourists wandered the small square in search of breakfast.

Amici's wasn't super busy when she walked in. It didn't take long for that to quickly change. A line formed behind her as the second morning rush began. After placing her order, Caitlin waited patiently by a wooden bar toward the center of the shop for her to-go order. She listened to the conversations occurring around her as the barista made the espresso machine whirl and hiss, cranking out espressos and other caffeinated beverages to energize customers for the day. A crabby old grandmother in a nearby booth told who Caitlin assumed was her grandson, "People come to Williamsburg to die. A young person should head to New York or some other big city, then retire in Williamsburg."

A look of shock covered the boy's face as he muttered, "That's morbid." Then he looked over at his mom with an expression that clearly said *do we have to spend all day with this cantankerous old woman?*

Caitlin chuckled at the exchange. She empathized with the boy. Her conversation with her grandmother later would probably take on a similar tone, or she'd get some lecture about family legacy and duty.

"Caitlin!" the barista called her name, setting her cappuccino on the counter and disrupting Caitlin's thoughts.

4

Caitlin picked it up, stirred in one packet of sugar, then started to walk to the door with a lid in her hand.

One of the customers waiting in line turned as she passed him, bumping into her and sending her coffee soaring upward out of the cup.

"Mi Scusi, signora," a baritone voice apologized as a hand settled over Caitlin's.

Amber-colored eyes met hers before Caitlin instinctively arched back to prevent the mini-tidal wave of cappuccino from traveling down her white blouse. The loud buzz of the coffee shop disappeared. Things blurred around her. The only items sharply in focus now were the man who bumped into her, her coffee, and herself. A fleeting sting on her chest made Caitlin gasp. Her hand shifted upward and closer to her chest as if the man magically guided her cup to recapture the suspended arch of coffee coming straight toward her.

Time unfroze once the cup was safely repositioned. Most of the latte-tinted projectiles threatening to destroy her favorite shirt fell harmlessly back into the cup, except for one large blob which made her top finger around the cup sticky. The noise in the room returned, along with the hustle and bustle of patrons drifting in and out of the shop once their preferred beverage of choice had been obtained.

Amber eyes apologized again. This time in English. "I am so sorry. I didn't see you there."

Weirdly enough, only a small amount of foamed milk and espresso splattered on the crisp white material of her shirt, leaving behind a circular patch of tan freckling. Caitlin used the napkin she had grabbed to try to clean off the coffee traveling woven fibers. "No. I should have put the lid on it first. I was in a hurry and haven't ever had anyone bump into me before."

The stubborn stains wouldn't come off her shirt. Great, now she'd look like a slob who can't drink without spilling on herself in front of the client Sean was worried about impressing. She softly swore under her breath.

"I will pay to have your shirt cleaned. Here. Buy yourself a new one on me." The Italian gentleman handed her a fifty dollar bill.

"You don't need to—" Caitlin looked up at the man after he gently took her hand. A zap of electricity traveled between them. Where in the heck had that come from? If he experienced the same thing, he certainly didn't act like it. He didn't even flinch.

"No, cara. I most certainly need to right the wrong I caused." The man closed her fingers around the bill he set in her palm. "A jewel like yourself should never be in a tarnished setting."

"What...?" She started to ask him what type of cheesy pickup line book he had read to utter some crap like that, but the retort caught in her throat. Now that she wasn't focused on her shirt, she took in his appearance. *Damn! He was gorgeous.* Almost unearthly good-looking with the chiseled features of his face, his styled dark hair, and those stunning eyes in their odd shade of citrine. His equally hot, ebony-haired, and blue-eyed companion stared at them with a raised brow. Both men looked like they had just stepped off a page in a fashion magazine, modeling the latest bespoke suits for the year.

Blue-eyes suddenly chuckled then spoke, a posh British accent tinged a deep, almost velvety voice. "Take the cash. He's got plenty of it. And as he more elegantly stated, you don't want to go back to work in a stained shirt, especially if you have any important meetings to attend."

"Well, I do have a few of those today." Caitlin looked at the blue-eyed Brit for a second longer then returned her attention to the Italian. "Speaking of which, I need to get going. Grazie for the new shirt."

"Di nulla, cara," the Italian responded, raking his eyes over her before she turned away.

The two men watched her walk out the front door. While the Italian looking her over annoyed her, their continuing to stare as she left didn't. People blatantly stared at her all the time due to the unique shade of her eyes. Most excused their doing so by claiming they were trying to figure out if she had contacts in or if her eyes were naturally that color. God, the universe, or whatever thing you believe in, must have been in a creative mood the day she was conceived. She had long, flame-red hair with bright lavender eyes. Needing to try and find a shop that might have staff in early to get a new shirt before her meeting in a half an hour, she hurried across the square to one of the clothing shops. Thankfully, the manager answered when she lightly knocked on the door. Taking mercy on her, the manager let Caitlin in to buy a new shirt.

CAITLIN RAN BACK to the office. She had one minute to get into the conference room before Sean would be lecturing her about being on time. Stupid, sun-kissed Italian model guy had to bump into her and spill her coffee. This morning was not off to a good start at all between a ruined shirt and her grandmother. Hopefully, the day would get better.

Esther took her purse and the bag holding her old shirt from her then handed her a pen and notepad.

Caitlin could see Sean speaking with two gentlemen whose backs were to the conference room window. "Thank you, Esther."

"Anytime. Now, hurry up and get in there."

All three men stopped talking as Caitlin shut the conference room door.

"You!" Caitlin blurted, recognizing the Italian from the coffee shop.

He arched a dark brow and offered her a charming smile in response to her loud "you."

Sean politely stood to introduce her. He let the "you" slide rather than inquire about it. "Gentlemen, this is Caitlin DeDanann. She's one of our top investigators and analysts. I've asked her to join us as she will be assisting me with your research into Lagniappe Shipping & Ag. Caitlin, this is Dante Giovanni and Rayne Warwick."

Caitlin politely shook Dante's then Rayne's hands before sitting in the empty chair in between Sean and Dante. "We met at Amici's."

Sean gave the three of them a puzzled look. "Oh?"

Rayne smiled. "We went there for coffee after driving down here from the Richmond airport as we didn't want to impose on you or your staff. We needed to re-energize with taking an early morning flight from New York. Pleasure to meet you, Miss DeDanann. Sean, you were saying our offer should be at least in the three-million-dollar range. That seems high for such a small company buyout."

"Lagniappe Shipping & Ag is easily worth that. Truthfully, you'd probably be low-balling with making that as an initial offer, but it would prompt Arsceneaux to give us some idea of what he might sell for."

Throughout the meeting, something about Dante irked Caitlin. She couldn't put her finger on what it was. The man was polite with perfectly polished manners and clearly knowledgeable in the business world. Maybe she was just pissed about her shirt. It was her favorite blouse, which was most likely brown speckled for eternity now. Every time she looked over at Dante, he'd offer her a warm smile. Her pen tapped against the table, causing Sean to glance over at her a few times as they went over the proposed initial offer contract.

"It would be ideal if someone could conduct an onsite inspection of the company assets and speak with Arsceneaux. We haven't been able to successfully get in touch with him," Rayne suggested, not thrilled with making any higher an offer without having better insight into Lagniappe's current value and portfolio. "The company offices are in New Orleans. We can hire someone local that your firm trusts to go do an audit and inspection."

Sean looked over at Caitlin with a thoughtful expression on his face. "Caitlin is headed to New Orleans next week."

Caitlin's face flushed a bright shade of red. "Don't even suggest it, Sean."

"It would only take you half a day to accommodate Mr. Warwick and Mr. Giovanni's request."

"Oh, because Mr. Italian Underwear Model and Lord British GQ come in here waving a large sum of money under your nose, I'm supposed to give up vacation time to dig into a company these two are only *thinking* of buying?" Caitlin snapped. Now today officially sucked with three bad things occurring. Well, at least all three got knocked out before noon. Didn't the old wives' tale claim bad things only happened in threes?

Rayne and Dante exchanged glances. Surprisingly, grins covered their faces. Almost as if they found things amusing.

Caitlin recognized the *I am going to strangle you the second this is over* tension and forced smile on Sean's face.

"If you'll excuse us, gentlemen. Caitlin, may I speak to you in the hall for a moment?" Sean politely asked, taking Caitlin by the arm.

"Of course, Sean." She stood up. He'd more than likely rip her out of the chair if she didn't, then followed him into the reception area outside the conference room. "I don't want to hear it about business etiquette. I'm a field employee and shouldn't be in these types of meetings anyway."

"I'll address your mouth later. The more pressing issue at the moment is the audit and field inspection. You're the best person to do it."

"Hire someone else."

"It's only half a day, Caitlin."

"You know damn well it will turn into more than that. A site inspection, an operational audit, and full background review into a privately-held, mid-sized international company will take at least a week, and I am not giving up my vacation time. Not this time, Sean."

"How about a compromise? I'll pay for an extra week of hotel and any fees the airline charges for changing your departure date if you handle the site visit."

Caitlin exasperatedly sighed. "No. I work to live, not live to work. I left adjusting and litigation because I got tired of the long hours and having no life, along with constantly being on call."

"You aren't giving up any time off! I'm asking you to delay your vacation for a few days, on my dime. It's not costing you anything. Additionally, it's cheaper for the firm to pay for the one week of hotel, your salary, and airfare fees than to hire an independent party to handle this."

Caitlin knew he'd continue harassing her until she said yes. "Throw in a first-class upgrade and dinner at Masquerades, and you have yourself a deal."

"Done."

"And I get to pick the hotel for the extra week. I'm not staying in some cheap roach motel in a seedy part of town in the interest of cost savings."

"Stay wherever you like as long as it's reasonable. And before you get any ideas, the presidential suite at the Ritz Carlton is not in any way, shape, or form reasonable."

"Presidential suite at The Pontchartrain it is then." Caitlin goaded Sean.

"You're fired if I see that come across on your corporate card and expense report."

Caitlin's jaw dropped in mock horror. "Oh no! Anything but that. And you wouldn't dare, as you'd be the one having to visit dear old Gram to explain why you canned me."

Sean rolled his eyes. "Do we have an agreement? We need to get back in the room and finish the contract review."

"We do."

"I also expect you to apologize for the GQ and underwear model remark before our *two clients* leave today."

"I'm sure they've heard similar comments before."

"Caitlin..." Sean decided it best not to finish the remark. She was already in a bad mood, and clearly, something happened at Amici's with her visceral reaction to Dante. "It would mean a lot to me, if you would swallow your pride this once and apologize."

"I'll think about it."

Sean held open the door for her then swung his hand, encouraging her to go in.

"Is everything okay, bella?" Dante inquired as Caitlin and Sean walked back into the room.

"Fine, and please don't address me as bella. It's Ms. DeDanann, Mr. Giovanni. Other women may find that charming, I don't."

"My apologies, Rosso." Dante leaned closer to her with a come-hither grin on his face. "The new shirt is lovely on you, and the deeper neckline allows the pendant you wear to shine versus hiding it." His eyes drifted down to her chest. "Perhaps men should bump into you with coffee more often."

Caitlin let out a disgusted gasp. He wasn't looking at her pendant. "My pendant isn't anything you'll get to admire, Mr. Giovanni. Sean, I have a ten-thirty, so I'll let you wrap this up." She didn't wait for Sean to acknowledge her.

Annoyed, she left the conference room. Screw apologizing to the lecherous jerk, even if he was good-looking.

Esther looked at Caitlin and fanned herself, mouthing the words "Those two are fine."

"They may look like sex on a stick, Esther, but they're both assholes. Don't be fooled by the pretty packaging," Caitlin said as the room door was still closing. She didn't care if Sean and his "two clients" heard her.

Dante loudly laughed as the door finally clicked shut while Sean looked up at the ceiling praying for the strength not to murder the woman he promised to look after when her grandmother asked him to.

"She hasn't changed a bit," Rayne remarked, watching Caitlin disappear behind a row of cubicles.

Sean shook his head. "Still mouthy and headstrong like always."

Dante found it odd nothing about him or Rayne seemed familiar to her. "Does she not remember anything?"

"Based on her reaction to you in the coffee shop and here, I would say subconsciously she recalls exactly who you are." Rayne struggled to resist the urge to chuckle.

Dante snorted. "She is only mad I spilled her coffee on her."

"You did what? No wonder she's pissed. You ruined her favorite shirt." Sean pinched the bridge of his nose. Things definitely weren't going as originally planned today.

"It was an accident. I turned, bumping into her, and she didn't have the lid on her cup." Dante doubted the coffee incident was that big a deal. "She should be thanking me and singing my praises as I prevented a larger mess by shifting her cup to catch the wayward coffee. The shirt only got a few drops on it. They will more than likely wash out."

"I would say she isn't doing so as you followed up the noble gesture with looking her up and down like a piece of meat. You're supposed to be a savvy businessman, Giovanni. They don't behave that way." Rayne grinned the entire time he spoke. The idea of Dante being business savvy was comical.

Sean glared over at Dante. "Jesus, you did what on top of the remarks?"

Dante shrugged. "It was harmless flirtation. No need to get all protective of the woman, Watchous."

"I told Morrigan you were the wrong one to choose for this. Listen to Rayne here and learn what is and isn't proper business etiquette in the twenty-first century before our next meeting, and before I'm trying to talk Caitlin out of either stabbing you with her pen or filing a sexual harassment suit against you." Sean left the conference room

The Arsceneaux Siblings -

Allister

Allister Robicheaux pulled into her brother's long driveway. Oaks with Spanish moss hanging from the limbs dotted the sides of it and spread out across the sprawling front yard. If one didn't know there was a home tucked back behind the massive four-hundred-year-old live oaks, they would drive right past it. The old two-story house with a wraparound porch and tall, white columns joined on the second floor by large sections of black wrought iron gave the house a stately appearance. While not as grand as the plantation homes on either side of the Arsceneaux property, D'Orme still earned the admiration of anyone who visited it.

Evariste kept the eighteenth-century residence in pristine condition. When he upgraded the historic property with modern conveniences, he was tyrannical with enforcing the need to preserve as many original details as possible. Her brother worked alongside the general contractor and went through several architects to bring the place into the modern age. The general contractor and Evariste butted heads throughout the entire process. There were several days the site supervisor complained that he couldn't work for such a thickheaded and OCD tyrant and threatened to quit. Amazingly, the job got completed, and relatively on time, too.

The large black 4x4 truck parked just slightly ahead of the house confirmed Evariste was home. She heard the side door to the house slam, then the large door of the detached garage slowly descended shut, warning her brother was about to make his planned escape.

"Thickheaded is right," Alli muttered, undoing her seatbelt.

She watched the 'tyrant' throw two fishing poles into the bed of his truck along with a tackle box. Every dang time he didn't want to deal with something Evariste took off to the bayous or the coastline, then he'd pretend to be out of cell tower range, which was absolute whoohockey! He was out of his damn mind to think he was going anywhere but the office today.

Alli got out of her car. "Evariste Arsceneaux, you are not going out fishing! Not with the investigator coming in today and the teleconference with Giovanni Enterprises this afternoon."

The green-eyed, brown-haired man cast her a casual glance over his shoulder and laughed. "The company isn't for sale, at any price, and I pay Alcee a ridiculous amount of money to manage investigators or folks who think they can just make an offer on my company anytime they like. Now move your car. I have a date with some bass and the bayou."

Evariste climbed into the driver's seat of the pickup and stared down at her.

Alli intentionally stood in the center of the driveway and placed her hands on her hips, daring him to run her over. "You're the company CEO. The fish can wait."

The two siblings locked eyes in a hot-tempered Cajun standoff.

"Move, Alli!"

"You'll have to run me over if you want to go fishing."

"Suit yourself."

Evariste closed the driver's side door and started the truck. The hemi let out a loud rumble as the engine came to life. He intentionally gave it some gas.

Allister watched the smirk on his face grow as the engine growled like a threatening beast.

"Don't even think about it, Ev!" Alli yelled over the rumbling truck. Evariste wouldn't run her over, and he had no place to go with her and her car blocking his path.

Evariste

"Sorry, Alli. It's too nice a day to pretend to entertain offers I'm not accepting." Evariste shifted the truck into four-wheel drive and turned the stirring wheel while pressing the gas pedal down. The black 4x4 lurched forward, crushing a bed of purple Louisiana irises before cutting two deep ruts into the manicured green lawn. The oversized tires kicked up the soft brown soil they bared, splattering it all over the driveway and Alli's car.

Noting the look of disbelief on Alli's face, Evariste grinned as he continued past her. Tearing up the yard and massacring the flower bed were a small price to pay for escaping the unwelcome and unnecessary business dealings planned for the day. The grass and flowers would grow back. If not, the flower bed and turf could be replanted. Once he cleared the length of her car, he drove back onto the driveway and continued toward the road.

He looked up at the rearview mirror when Allister shouted his full name. She threw the planner she carried at his truck. A loud whomp confirmed it bounced off his tailgate.

Watching her shaking her head, he laughed. By the way her lips moved, she was cursing him out. He shifted his gaze back to the open space in front of him. The water was definitely calling today, practically screaming for him to come visit it again. It had been six months since he had a day off, and the weather was perfect for catching bass and redfish in the brackish waters around Southern Louisiana. He wasn't about to cancel his plans due to some Italian prick thinking he could wave a check under his nose and he'd randomly sell his company. He'd give up the company when he gave up fishing, which would be never. Both consumed most of his time.

Lagniappe Shipping & Ag had been in the family for centuries. The company was in excellent financial health. He expected to expand his ventures at a nice profit over the next year, too. Neither he nor his partners were interested in selling. Though, he had to give it to Giovanni. The Italian was ballsy to send an investigator down to tour the company grounds and stick their nose where it didn't belong. Alcee was the idiot who offered Giovanni's attorney a tour of the properties and an audit of the company portfolio. Let him deal with whatever poor sap flew into town.

His cell phone ringing disrupted his musings. He glanced down at it to see Allister's name and number flashing on the screen. He ignored the call and turned onto the highway. In another twenty minutes, he'd be on the water, lost in nature, and hopefully forgetting about work and life in general for a few hours. Hearing the phone ring again, he picked it up and shut it off. Today, he wasn't the president, CEO, and founding principal partner of Lagniappe; he was just some Cajun living the outdoor life one can only find on the hauntingly dark waters of the swamps and bayous. Lord knows he had earned a break after the month it had been.

A patch of trees caught his eye as he got farther down the road. Unease churned in his gut the closer he came to them. He should have cut that tree line down long ago, but just couldn't bring himself to do it.

"Not today," he muttered, refocusing on the road. If he didn't have time for Giovanni, he didn't have time for old ghosts from the past ruining his plans either.

New Orleans

☙❧☙

Early spring brought New Orleans back to life after a dreary and unusually cold winter. Now was the time to enjoy all that the city had to offer before the hot, humid summer clutched the area in its unrelenting grip. The midmorning sky was a pale blue, and the sun shone brightly on the Crescent City. Jackson Square overflowed with local artists and fortunetellers setting up for the day. A man painted silver from head to foot took his place on a milk crate outside of the Steamboat Cafe, hoping to get a dollar or two from the tourists starting to enter the square. The smell of beignets and chicory coffee floated on the breeze across Jackson Square and down through the French Market, tempting any passerby to stop for a sweet treat and a warm cup of java.

Caitlin started from her thoughts as the Natchez sounded her horn. The steamboat announced to the city that she was leaving her pier at JAX Brewery to make her first trip up the Mississippi for the day. She laughed at startling so easily at such a familiar sound.

NOLA was still home, she thought as she continued down Tchoupitoulas to the open-air market. Saddened by the fact she only visited her beloved city about once a year now, she sighed. Nouveau Orleans seemed to forgive her departure every time she returned. The city almost whispered to her as if it missed her strolling down Bourbon and Rue

Royale. Truth be told, she missed the city a great deal after moving to the East Coast. Williamsburg was nice and history filled but lacked New Orleans's soul and colorful personality. And the small Virginia town didn't ever call for her to return like NOLA did anytime she left it.

She stopped in front of the first stall in the last building of the French Market. Local farmers with fresh produce and a sea of vendors peddling their various wares to anyone walking by filled the old green and white building. The scent of fresh Pontchartrain strawberries floated from somewhere nearby. You haven't lived until you've eaten a Pontchartrain strawberry. She followed her nose to the table covered in small baskets of the large, red fruit that promised sweet delight to anyone who bought them. Oh, they smelled like heaven itself.

"Caitlin, mon amie! You could never resist those strawberries. You must have a sixth sense that lets you know just when we are at the peak of the season. Girl, you always return at the perfect time to enjoy them," an old Cajun farmer greeted her. "Go ahead, sha, try one. I know you're dying to."

She took the strawberry he offered and savored how it tasted. "Oh, Azard, these are so good!"

She and Azard chatted and laughed as they both enjoyed a few more freshly washed strawberries. Azard befriended her when she first moved to the city and routinely visited the market for fresh seafood and produce every Saturday. Like this section of the French Quarter, Azard kept his charm after Katrina. Sadly, the hurricane reshaped the landscape of the city in more ways than one. Developers moved into the Quarter at the same time they descended upon the demolished suburbs, turning some areas into kitschy tourist shops and trendy restaurants, erasing some of the allure the Quarter offered pre-Katrina.

"So what brings you back to New Orleans?" Azard inquired, refilling the empty spaces on his table with containers of strawberries, Creole tomatoes, and other spring produce.

"I am supposed to be on vacation. Unfortunately, my boss exploited my vacation to do an inspection and audit on some company down here."

"Sorry that happened. What company are you looking into?"

"Lagniappe Shipping & Ag." Caitlin ate another strawberry from the small bucket Azard gave her.

Azard's brows rose; he put down the tomatoes in his hand. "Lagniappe Shipping & Ag? Evariste Arsceneaux's company?"

"Are you familiar with them?"

Azard grinned. "Sha, everyone in the agriculture and farming community is familiar with Lagniappe Shipping & Ag, as well as his daddy's farm, ADL Farms. The strawberries you're munching on come from an affiliate farm owned by Pierre LeBlanc's nephew outside Mandeville. Pierre is also the largest sugar cane producer in Louisiana. That's an old and powerful family whose business you're sticking your nose into. Be careful not to get yourself into any trouble. Evariste doesn't like outsiders sniffing around the farm—or his company books."

Caitlin laughed. "Arsceneaux doesn't seem to like anyone. I can't get the man to return a phone call or email. He hung up on me at least twice after telling me he wasn't selling, then he just let me roll to his voicemail after I tried to call him back."

"That's 'cause you're an outsider. You need to get in with the family or his inner circle if you want the man to give you the time of day."

"I take it you've met Arsceneaux. What's he like? I'd rather not be surprised when I meet him." Caitlin hoped Azard might offer something advantageous she could use to make her investigation go smoother since it appeared she wouldn't be viewed with kind regard once she stepped foot in the Lagniappe Shipping & Ag Corporate Office.

"What's Evariste like? Grumpy with a snarky sense of humor, but smart as a whip, and observant too. Kaw, that man doesn't miss even the smallest thing about people. Don't try to schmooze him or lie to him, sha. He'll have you tossed out on the street in a heartbeat."

"Great. Can't wait to meet him." Caitlin let out an annoyed huff. She knew the inspection and audit would be problematic the moment Sean volunteered her to do it.

Azard chuckled at the way she rolled her eyes. "I wouldn't worry about Evariste too much. Most likely, you won't ever see him. He'll brush you off on Alcee Dugas or his sister, Alli. That's pretty much what he does to everyone outside the family or those he thinks aren't worth doing business with."

A Chance Meeting

Frustrated, Allister called Alcee as she walked through the French Market to get an order of beignets and some coffee from Café Du Monde. "You'll have to handle the field investigator today."

An amused laugh came through the phone's speaker. "I expected that. You should know absolutely nothing comes between Evariste and fishing, not even a multimillion-dollar offer. Did you really think you could convince him to come in today?"

"He's the damn company president and CEO! He should at least review the crappy offer and be there to reinforce the fact he isn't interested in selling."

"Alli, mon amie, Evariste already reviewed the contract and told Giovanni no last week. Giovanni is just insistent. For whatever reason, he's looking to expand his operations into the US, and he thinks the best way to do that is by purchasing Lagniappe. He should have reached out with a client inquiry or as a potential contracting partner instead. Clearly, the Italian isn't that smart, at least not when it comes to negotiating with an Arsceneaux. I will handle everything with Miss DeDanann then call Giovanni and his attorney tomorrow, reaffirming the company is not for sale, especially at that low an offer. Let Evariste enjoy his day off. He's earned some down time. Go get some breakfast before coming in. I can tell by the background noise you're already near Café Du Monde."

"See you in a few." Allister hung up. She hated how Alcee always defended her brother when he was being unreasonable. She missed the old Evariste. The one who laughed and took life in stride, not the temperamental beast of a man who threw himself into work or fishing ever since...

"Can I take your order?" The cashier in the window drew Alli out of her thoughts.

"One order of beignets and a café au lait to go, please."

Once she had food and drink in hand, she started the trek back to the office on Esplanade but cut through the building housing the farmers market to avoid the crowded sidewalk.

"Evariste isn't that bad, sha. He's had a rough go." Azard's voice stood out amongst the others around her.

Hearing him mention her brother's name, Allister halted and looked in the direction his voice came from. Spotting the redhead talking to Azard, she almost dropped the coffee in her hand. It couldn't be who she thought it was, could it?

"Are you badmouthing the competition again, Azard?" Allister smiled as she walked up to the table the woman and farmer sat at.

Azard smirked at the brunette who joined them. "Kaw, alohrs pas, Allister. Just that possede brother of yours."

Caitlin softly laughed at Azard describing Evariste as mischievous. The man certainly was that. "Based on what I've seen so far, I'd add tête dure to your description. My condolences on being related to the man. Allister, isn't it?"

"And you are?" Allister asked, extending a hand to Caitlin.

Caitlin grasped it. "Caitlin DeDanann. I was heading over to Lagniappe Shipping & Ag after I finished up here to meet the infamous Evariste Arsceneaux and learn more about the company."

Allister shook her head in disbelief. "I'll walk with you to the office. Unfortunately, Evariste won't be able to meet with you today due to another matter coming up."

Azard chuckled at Alli's remark. He could guess where Evariste was to avoid meeting with Caitlin. "I heard the redfish are biting with the warmer weather moving in."

Caitlin offered him a five dollar bill for the container of strawberries.

"They're on me today, sha. Just be certain to stop by again before you leave. I want to hear how the new job and Virginia are treating you, as well as your impression of Arsceneaux, or more accurately, your impression on him."

"Stop it, Azard." Allister shot the farmer a dirty look.

ALLI AND CAITLIN walked into the historic building renovated into an office just off Esplanade. A gentleman who looked to be in his late forties with dark hair and brown eyes looked up at the two of them as they entered. A smile slowly spread across his face before he got up and stepped outside his office to greet them.

"You must be Caitlin DeDanann. You look just like your profile picture online. I'm Alcee Dugas, the Chief Communications Officer for Lagniappe. I see you've met Allister, Evariste's sister, and our Director of Community Outreach."

"Pleasure to meet you, Mr. Dugas. I'm looking forward to learning more about your company." Caitlin shook the man's hand.

"Let's go to the conference room to get started, then we'll take you to our warehouse and a few of the farm properties we partner with this afternoon." Alcee gestured toward a hall on his right.

When they reached the conference room, Caitlin set her briefcase and purse down on the table.

"Alcee, before we get started, I need you to sign off on a press release. It should only take a minute. Please excuse us, Caitlin." Allister jerked Alcee's arm and nodded toward the door.

Alcee gave Allister a puzzled look. "A press release?"

"Yes, the one for *The Times-Picayune*. It's got to go out in the next half hour if we hope to get news coverage." Allister hoped Alcee got the hint she needed to speak with him. Now. "We'll only be a minute, Caitlin. My apologies for the delay in starting our meeting on time."

"Take your time. I haven't had a chance to check email this morning, so will do that now since it sounds like we'll be busy most of the day." Caitlin smiled and unlocked her phone screen.

Alcee stepped into Allister's office with her as it was closer to the conference room than his.

"Is she—" Alli started to ask Alcee about Caitlin.

The older gentleman knowingly smiled and raised his hand, cutting off the inquiry. "Why do you think I agreed to the meeting and inspection after Evariste turned it down?"

"This is exactly why Evariste needs to be here, Alcee!"

"Relax, Alli. I have a feeling things will be just fine. He's going to have to come into the office sometime this week while she's here. Now, take a deep breath, and let us do our best to convince Miss DeDanann she has a lot of reasons to want to learn more about Lagniappe Shipping & Ag."

THINGS WENT WELL with the introductory presentation and the warehouse tour. Alcee led the three of them back to the car then drove out to the first farm stop for the afternoon.

Caitlin quietly flipped through the portfolio Alcee gave her as she rode in the front seat beside him.

He caught her staring at several of the old homes they passed. "Do you like historic homes, Ms. DeDanann?"

"I love them. I used to be a catastrophe adjuster and claims litigation manager, so I appreciate the craftsmanship it took to build them. It's a shame so many are being let go with the cost to maintain them or destroyed by hurricanes and floods. It looks like a few of these have been restored recently."

"Several have. Two of the plantations in the area were purchased to be turned into a museum and a bed and breakfast."

Allister grinned in the backseat as an idea struck her. "Caitlin, my family gets together every now and then for dinner at Maison D'Orme. It's a beautiful old home, originally built in the 1700s. The chef there is incredible. He makes some of the best dishes I've ever tasted. Would you like to join us for some made-from-scratch, local fare tonight?"

"Allister!" Alcee's tone held a note of warning with the way he said her name. He shot her a cautionary stare via the rearview mirror.

Caitlin looked at the man in the driver's seat then back at Allister. "I wouldn't want to impose on a private dinner."

"You wouldn't be imposing at all, cher. We'd be more than happy to have you join us." Allister's grin grew to a Cheshire catlike smile. "We tend to eat a little late around here with how long it takes everyone to get over there from work. I hope seven isn't a problem for you."

"Seven sounds great. I look forward to checking out a new restaurant."

Alcee shook his head, not believing the trouble Allister just instigated.

AFTER DROPPING Caitlin off at her hotel, Allister switched to the front passenger seat with a grin on her face.

"You shouldn't have invited her to D'Orme. Evariste isn't going to be happy." Alcee hoped Allister didn't just start world war three with her brother.

"I'll call him and let him know, so he isn't surprised when she shows up on his doorstep. Though it would serve him right with skipping out on the formal meetings today."

Alcee shook his head but softly laughed. "Call him now, so he has time to cool off. Use my phone since he wouldn't answer when you called earlier."

The phone didn't even get halfway through the first ring before Evariste's voice came over the speaker. "Tell me the busybody is bored to tears and on a flight back to wherever she came from."

"Quite the opposite I'm afraid. The lady is thorough in her job and actually finds our business model quite interesting." Alcee could imagine a scowl darkening Evariste's face after hearing that. "Before you hang up, Allister's with me and has some news for you."

"News? What kind of news?"

"Miss DeDanann is joining us for dinner tonight. At D'Orme. I didn't think you'd mind if I invited her since we were planning on a siblings' dinner tonight anyway with Renee and Jeanette."

"You did what, Allister?!" Evariste's voice actually reverberated throughout the car.

"Evariste, it's a good business move," Alcee interceded on Alli's behalf.

"I doubt that. Alli, call her and cancel the dinner invite."

Allister huffed, glaring up at the speaker in front of her. "No, she's flown all this way, is really sweet, and I think you should hear her out."

"Allister Robicheaux! I don't want to hear her out, nor do I need her snooping around my house looking for information to give Giovanni any sort of leverage since he isn't backing off."

"We'll be there at seven. Plan for dinner accordingly." Allister hung up on him before he could chew her out some more.

Alcee laughed at how quickly Alli ended the phone call. "You know he's cursing you to all high heaven right now."

"He'll get over it."

Maison D'Orme

C aitlin sat down on her hotel room bed and again flipped through the portfolio Alcee gave her until she reached the financial statements. She could see what had Dante and Rayne so interested in purchasing the company. It was profitable and projected to become even more so over the next ten years, most likely pushing its value above what they could offer for it. Nothing unusual stood out in the documents she read over on the flight to New Orleans yesterday or in any of the documentation she had reviewed so far today. She could easily green-light the company as a good purchase if the subsidiary farms were well managed and their contracts drafted in a favorable manner.

She picked up her phone and called Sean.

"How'd it go?" Sean inquired, curious to hear what she'd found and what Arsceneaux had to say about Giovanni's latest offer.

"The company is on solid ground and growing. Now would be the time to buy it. I don't see any red flags or anything questionable. The warehouse and trucking operation is well run. The farms they own and partner with are solvent. The only thing I haven't seen yet are the ships and shippers they partner with for exports."

"Do you think Evariste Arsceneaux is interested in selling?"

Caitlin laughed. "Considering he didn't even bother to show up today but had his CCO and Director of Community Relations show me around instead, I would say he's turning down Dante's latest offer—again. Maybe you should go back to Dante and recommend he pursue a collaborative partnership of some type instead of trying to purchase the company outright."

"I could try and suggest that, but Giovanni is stubborn. Once he has his mind set on purchasing a company, he doesn't deter from that path. Call me after you see the ships. In the meantime, I will see if I can incentivize Evariste to meet with you or get Dante to entertain your idea of contracting with Lagniappe for whatever purpose he thinks he needs to purchase the company."

AT EXACTLY SEVEN, Caitlin pulled into the driveway of the property at the address Allister had given her. It didn't look like an open restaurant with only one vehicle parked outside. A man in blue jeans, work boots, and a T-shirt, was on his knees, weeding and planting irises in one of the larger flower beds. She thought it odd someone would be gardening this late in the day, but maybe that was normal in Louisiana, as folks tried to escape the heat and high humidity the afternoons could bring.

"Excuse me, is the Maison D'Orme?"

"It is," the man gruffly answered, otherwise ignoring her presence behind him.

"I'm supposed to be meeting a few business associates here for dinner, but this doesn't look like a restaurant."

The man snorted at the word restaurant. "The chef is late due to having to attend to other matters, so we're not open yet. Posted about it on Facebook, but I suppose you didn't check before coming out here."

"I'm sorry. I didn't think to check the restaurant page," Caitlin politely said. Not wanting to bother the grumpy landscaper anymore, she headed for her car.

The man straightened after hearing her start to walk away. "Miss Robicheaux and her party should be here in a few minutes, along with Chef Gage. You can check out the gardens around back until we open.

They're beautiful this time of year. There's a path leading around the house on the right side of the driveway."

"Thanks. I'll do that."

"I will let Miss Robicheaux know where you are when she arrives."

"Thanks again!"

"You're welcome." The man gave her a polite nod then went back to tending the flower bed.

As she looked for the path, she noticed the pair of tire marks cutting through the yard and the crushed plants he had pulled out laying on the driveway. "Sorry to see someone ran through the yard, and you're stuck cleaning it up. People can be jerks at times."

The man briefly stopped planting and glanced over at her. He sat back on his heels, studying her for a minute, then set back to work without saying a word.

EVARISTE'S PHONE vibrated on the driveway as he patted down the dirt around the last iris he managed to save. Alli's name popping up irked him. She should have been at D'Orme thirty minutes ago. He wiped his hands along the grass, trying to clean the dirt off before picking up the phone.

"You're late, as usual, Alli. And your unwelcome guest is here."

"Rude way to answer the phone, Ev. So what do you think of her?"

A hint of laughter colored his sister's voice as she asked him what he thought of the investigator who shouldn't be at his house. "Her who?"

"You jokin', right?"

Evariste let out an annoyed sigh. "No, Alli, I'm not joking. Get your ass here. I'm not entertaining someone I didn't invite to my home for you."

"Did you even look at her, Ev? Or did you just slam the door in her face and tell her to wait in her car until I got there?" Allister's voice raised as exasperation replaced her earlier humor.

Evariste glanced back over his shoulder to try to get a better look at the woman Allister was so excited about, but she had already disappeared around the house. "I was busy planting flowers, and I sent her

27

around back to wait in the gardens. It's too damn hot for anyone to have to sit in their car."

"You are so damn thickheaded at times, Evariste Gage Arsceneaux! Go around back and take a good look at her."

"If this is one of your or Renee's attempts to set me up with some random woman because you think I'm lonely and work too much, come get your new friend, Alli. I'm not interested."

"I'll be there in about twenty minutes. We'll see if that remains your answer. At least go be polite and say hello."

Evariste shook his head and muttered under his breath after his sister hung up on him. He put the small shovel and potting soil away then rinsed his hands under the cold water of the garden hose on the side of the house. A distinctive blend of flowers and fruit floated on the light evening breeze, halting the turning of his hands under the stream of water. It had been centuries since he caught a whiff of that welcome, familiar scent.

You're imagining things, he scolded himself after the fragrance dissipated as quickly as it appeared. Turning off the garden hose, he slowly inhaled, part of him hoping spring and his nose hadn't been playing tricks on him. When the smell of damp soil, honeysuckle, iris, and grass was all he could identify, mere annoyance grew to raging frustration. He didn't need this crap tonight. Everything the sun and water erased earlier returned, starting to drown him once more: work, the unsolicited buyout offer, and now a nosey investigator wandering his gardens because his damn sister thought it'd be funny to invite her over for dinner.

The perfume of roses and strawberries danced past him again; just long enough for him to determine where it came from: the backside of the house.

"No. Giovanni's investigator can't be—" Evariste snapped himself out of his thoughts. She was dead. Contrary to what others believed, she wasn't coming back, not after three hundred years.

The Garden

L arge oaks and pecan trees lined the pathway to the garden. The
smell of honeysuckle, southern jasmine, and roses filled the night
air as Caitlin neared the main house. Antique gas lanterns burned across
the rear elevation adding to the charm of the old home. The sky was
fading from orange to pink and purple as the sun began to set. She felt
as if she'd stepped back in time entering the gardens.

"You probably shouldn't wander too far in strange places alone this
close to dark," a voice laced with a thick Creole accent lazily drawled,
capturing Caitlin's attention.

"And why is that? Because a girl can't hold her own against a big
strong man like you?" she asked, looking around for the voice's owner.
Her eyes found him only a few feet away. He casually leaned against one
of the old oaks, his back resting against the wide trunk with his arms
folded across his chest. A disinterested and aggravated scowl lingered on
his face.

"I would be more worried about the creatures rumored to come out
after dark in this part of Louisiana than some man leaning against an
oak tree, cher."

"I think I'm capable of taking both the creatures and you."

Now, he surprisingly grinned, shaking his head, and chuckling at her words.

Caitlin recognized the man as the landscaper from out front. "Don't you have flowers to plant?"

"Didn't your mother ever teach you not to talk to strangers?" He moved away from the tree and walked toward her.

"She did, but I'm pretty sure you're harmless. Otherwise, Alli would have warned me about you."

"I might be, or I could be a mass murderer waiting for my next victim after burying my most recent one in the flower bed out front."

Caitlin guessed he was around 5'9" now that he stood directly in front of her. He was a typical Louisiana Frenchman with dark brown hair and average height; the one exception to that being his uncommonly bright green eyes. There was something familiar about him. She tried to place where she had seen his face.

"Something tells me you like roses."

Caitlin shrugged as he stopped in front of her. "Don't all women?"

"May I show you the rose garden then?"

"As long as you don't bite."

The man laughed again, strolling with her around one of the hedges. "I might, especially if a pretty thing like yourself asks me to."

Caitlin rolled her eyes. "Rest assured, I won't make any such request."

"That's disappointing." He held open a gate resting in the center of an arched arbor covered in sweet smelling pink and white jasmine.

Caitlin almost asked if this was his secret garden to murder women in. The dazzling array of colors hidden by the gate banished the snarky retort. A genuine smile graced her lips as she took in the lush landscape.

Roses in shades of lavender, peaches, pinks, blues, whites, reds, and yellows ringed a lawn of emerald-green grass. Hyacinth, irises, and pixie lilies intermingled in the rose garden beds. In the center of the yard was a fountain that softly gurgled as water flowed from the top tier to the crystal pool at the bottom. A rose bush covered in deep amethyst blooms grew a few feet from the fountain.

Caitlin slowly approached the lone plant. It seemed so out of place in the center of the garden instead of intermingled with the other rose bushes. The fragrance from its dark blooms was heavenly. She had never seen roses this shade of purple before.

EVARISTE WATCHED her as she straightened from smelling one of the larger blossoms. The breeze caught her hair and lifted it from her face. A flash of memory produced images of her in the fading sunlight, taking him back to another time. He could picture her in a pale lavender gown that brought out her lovely eyes, turning and smiling at him after smelling one of the newly planted roses. *You're remembering someone else. She isn't the same woman. Let the past go before it buries you*, his conscience cautioned.

"The story I've heard over the years is that the original Arsceneaux who built D'Orme planted this garden for his new bride." He ambled toward her. "The gardens were his wedding gift to her. Each generation adds to it and works to keep the original plants alive."

"What a romantic gesture. He must have really loved her." Caitlin looked around with a new appreciation for the garden.

"Local legend says he adored her. She was the love of his life; his heart and soul." He picked one of the purple roses.

"I can only imagine how much he loved her to give her such an elaborate gift. I'm sure in colonial Louisiana the roses cost a small fortune and had to be shipped in from around the world. Though, this one doesn't seem to be part of the original garden."

Her words startled him. "What makes you say it doesn't belong?" He continued breaking thorns off the rose's stem that he held.

"It's not with the others. It has its own special place by the fountain. Did he buy it for her? Or did someone else plant it later on?"

Evariste spoke softly; his tone strained, almost pain-filled as he answered her question. "He bought it for her. He planted it the day after she died."

THE GREEN POOLS of emotion that met hers when she looked up at him took Caitlin aback.

"He had bought it for her the morning of the day she died. It was a surprise addition to the garden that she never got to see."

"Tragic story. Why'd he choose this rose in particular?"

"From what I've heard, they went to visit some friends in the Garden District holding a party a few days earlier. They had the same type of rose in their garden. She instantly fell in love with its unusual color when she saw it. It's called the..."

"Ebb Tide Rose." Caitlin finished for him.

He absent-mindedly fiddled with the rose he held. "You know your roses."

"No, not at all. The name just came to me." The disturbed expression on his face prompted Caitlin to empathetically take his hand. "I'm sure the woman loved her husband with all her heart just as he did her."

"What makes you so sure?" He placed the rose behind her ear then drew her close.

An odd, almost comforting, scent of soap and soil intermingled with that of the fragrant bloom as they stood not even a half inch apart.

The strong feeling of familiarity with the landscaper returned. Caitlin leaned into him. "I just know."

"How?" His hand slid to the small of her back. His face tilted down toward hers.

"Women's intuition." Caitlin almost couldn't get the words out due to her mouth suddenly being dry. Something just seemed so right about being in the gardens with the grumpy landscaper. She closed her eyes, inhaling the soap and soil combo again. Why did she always find earthy scents so alluring on men? Warmth and tingling spread up her torso from any place their bodies met. Did he feel whatever this connection was between them?

She opened her eyes and stared at his lips, unconsciously wetting her own. The silence they stood in and the short distance between them became unbearable.

"Kiss me," she whispered. The mouth that held her attention shifted from a frown to a grin.

The landscaper chuckled, neither honoring her request nor pulling away. "Do you always ask complete strangers to kiss you?"

"Tell me your name, and we won't be strangers."

Charmed By The Chef

E variste laughed then brushed his lips across hers. It had been a while since he dated anyone, and he was usually the one to make the first move, instigating a kiss versus being asked to give a woman one. Since she didn't pull away, he stole a second kiss. Her lips parted, mirroring the movement of his. The sweet taste of her sparked long dormant, possessive desire. His fingers wound themselves into her hair.

"Caitlin," he groaned her name, breaking off the kiss. His hands trembled as they cupped the sides of her face. He rested his forehead against hers, reminding himself to take things slowly. Hell, the woman didn't know who he was in this lifetime. She might not even be who his heart suddenly insisted she was.

She pressed closer, her lips meeting his for another delightful kiss. He could spend the entire night just like this with her, sharing languid kisses and getting to know the modern-day version of the woman he once loved.

"Caitlin! Gage!" Allister's voice broke the spell the evening cast.

"Damn it," Evariste grumbled, wanting to kill his sister for a second time today. The gravel crunching under Allister's feet cautioned she walked the path leading into the rear garden and yard. What game was she playing tonight? Calling him by his middle name as his friends and business partners did...it must be some stupid game of hers. Has to be.

"Gage? As in Chef Gage? The one who is late and delaying the restaurant opening?" Caitlin eyed the man holding her with a startled grin on his face.

The gate hinges creaked as Alli pushed open the closed gate. She stepped into the garden and immediately noticed her brother's arm around Caitlin's waist and Caitlin's hand resting on his chest. "I see the two of you met one another."

"Sort of." Caitlin continued staring at Evariste. "How exactly did you know my name, chef? Or is it gardener?"

Evariste laughed. "Considering I've been tasked with making dinner for everyone tonight, we'll go with chef."

A confused expression replaced the suspicious one on Caitlin's face. "Wait, are you not a chef?"

"I'm most certainly a chef, the Head Chef, hired by Allister to make your one evening at Maison D'Orme a memorable and pleasurable occasion." He raised her hand to his lips with a slight bow.

Alli shot him a dirty look. "Ignore, *Chef* Gage." She mocked the job title Evariste had given Caitlin. "He can be an ass at times, especially when he thinks a woman is interested in him."

"I'll second that." Another female voice announced the arrival of someone new in the garden.

"Excuse me?" Evariste turned to see his other two sisters walking toward them. "Invite the whole family, Alli?"

"Just those of us that matter," the taller brunette replied with a shrug. "You must be, Caitlin. I'm Renee, and this is Jeanette."

"Nice to meet you." Caitlin politely nodded to the two women.

"I am starving. What do you say we get dinner started, Chef Gage?" Renee smirked as she used her brother's phony job title.

Evariste shot her an irritated glare before mumbling, "Laissez les bon temps rouler, ma petite sœur."

Renee slapped the back of his shoulder. "Don't get sassy!"

"Is something wrong?" Caitlin wondered what caused the sudden tension between Renee and Gage.

"No, dear. Gage just took a liking to you and is mad we won't let him woo you. Not when there are better options around." Renee took Caitlin by the arm, leading her toward the house.

"Better options?" Evariste rolled his eyes, following the group to the house. "Like whom?"

"Azard, as Allister mentioned they know one another from when Caitlin was in New Orleans." Renee paused thoughtfully as they started to walk up the porch steps. "And I believe a certain gentleman who she came to town specifically to see."

Perturbed by the idea of another man dating her, Evariste stopped behind them. "You didn't tell me you were seeing someone, Caitlin."

Caitlin spun on the second step to face him. "I don't recall you asking."

"Most women wouldn't solicit a stranger for a kiss if they are in a committed relationship." Evariste climbed up another step, making their height even. Taking in the familiar incensed glint in her eye, a lopsided grin curved his lips. She had always been quick to put a man in his place when needed. That trait appeared to have followed her into this lifetime as well. Occasionally pricking that fiery temper of hers had been one of his favorite things to do considering what it led to when steered in the right direction.

"A gentleman would have declined any such request from a woman he didn't know."

Jeanette and Allister retreated onto the porch, trying to stay out of the crossfire of the fight Renee instigated.

Evariste could hear Caitlin's heartbeat quicken and sense her distaste for the attack on her character. He probably shouldn't rile her too much until they got to know one another again. "I apologize for wrongly assuming you were single based on the kiss we shared in the garden."

"You're forgiven," Caitlin said, a smile tweaking her lips. "And I'm not dating anyone at the moment. The man I came to see is a business associate."

"Come on you two," Allister called, opening the front door to the house.

Evariste grinned. "A business associate? What line of work are you in, Caitlin?"

"I'm an investigator and project manager for a private law firm. Wow!" Caitlin gasped as she entered the house.

The marble foyer gave way to golden oak floors trimmed with mahogany and cherry wood inlays. A long spiral staircase was on her left. Chandeliers hung from the ceiling and a wrought iron balcony allowed someone to observe those entering the house from the second floor.

"Welcome to Maison D'Orme, cher." He closely watched her reaction to the house for any hint of remembrance.

"Quite the entryway. The detail in the railing and molding is amazing." Caitlin admired some of the molding while running her hand across the oversized banister in front of her. "Is this all original to the house?"

"Most of it. We've made a few updates over time to modernize it."

"You certainly can't tell. Where did you find plasterers who can do this kind of work? Adding plumbing and electricity must have been a nightmare."

"We've lived in Louisiana a long time and have our connections. Most people enjoy the beauty of the house instead of commenting on the construction." Evariste closed the door.

"Sorry. It is beautiful. They certainly don't take the time to build homes with this much care and skill anymore."

"No need to apologize. I'll give you the grand tour of the place after dinner." He took Caitlin's hand, leading her toward the kitchen. "Since the house is reserved for the girls and yourself tonight, come keep me company in the kitchen."

CAITLIN NOTICED the normal furnishings in the home as they walked to the kitchen. "This doesn't look like a restaurant."

"I'm a private chef for hire who apparently hosts dinners in his home." He almost laughed as he kept up the pretense.

The kitchen was certainly a chef's kitchen filled with stainless steel appliances. Top of the line cherry cabinets covered the walls. The center island contained a gas cook top and a sink.

Caitlin sat on one side of the island, watching him stir the shrimp dish he had just thrown together. She noticed the sauce the shrimp cooked in looked thicker than the tomato sauce she typically saw in New Orleans. "Is that étouffée or shrimp creole?"

"Shrimp étouffée. You're in Acadiana out here, which means Cajun cooking. Ya see, sha, we have different cuisines depending on where we're from in the state."

Caitlin smiled at how he thickened his accent. "So are you Cajun or Creole?"

"Both." He poured a glass of red wine for Caitlin. "My mother's family is of Acadian descent, and my father's family is from Saintonge, France."

"Interesting. Normally, I find folks like to say they are one or the other. That explains why your accent fluctuates between Cajun and Creole. I assume you're originally from New Orleans based on what Allister told me about her family earlier today." Caitlin took a sip of her wine.

"You know what they say about assuming things." Evariste pulled a fresh loaf of bread from the oven. "I'm actually from New Iberia. Business brought me to New Orleans."

"Sorry. I guessed with what you said in the garden about this house being built by an Arsceneaux that you grew up around here."

"The house has been in the Arsceneaux family since the 1700s. I didn't live here until I was in my late twenties."

"This is your house?" Caitlin figured it was a family home owned by Alli's parents.

"All mine." He prepared Caitlin a plate of shrimp étouffée with two pieces of bread on the side then fixed himself a plate as well.

"A chef can afford a place like this hosting private dinners?"

"I charge a pretty penny for the use of the place and my culinary talents. I also do a few other things to bring in income. Now, eat your dinner before it gets cold."

"Should we call the others?" Caitlin asked, looking down the hall.

Evariste pulled a beer from the fridge for himself then sat on the stool next to hers. "Nah, they like to vay ya like a bunch of old women in a beauty parlor when they get together."

"Vay ya?" Caitlin wasn't sure what that was.

He grinned at the questioning look she gave him. "It means to gossip or sit around yammering on about something."

"Does Evariste ever show up here for dinner nights?"

Evariste chuckled at the question. "You could say occasionally he does. Alli mentioned something about him having to work late when she updated her reservation earlier today. I believe the words I heard grumbled in the background were 'some presumptuous, Italian asshole keeps trying to buy Lagniappe when it's not for sale.' Alli hushed him before I could ask him to repeat whatever he said."

Caitlin laughed. "Based on that description of Dante Giovanni, the rumors of Evariste being astute and a bit ornery are true."

Evariste smirked and leaned a little closer to her. "Now we both know Azard used the word possede, not ornery, and for the record, possede is a much more accurate descriptor for Evariste Arsceneaux."

"I won't disagree with that." Caitlin watched him bring his beer bottle up to his lips then take another drink from it.

"Were you hoping to meet Evariste?" Evariste couldn't resist making the inquiry as he set his beer down.

"Truthfully, I'm not looking forward to making his acquaintance. He seems like quite the asshole himself based on how many times he hung up on me the past couple of weeks."

"Oh, cher, I'm certain his behavior wasn't anything personal toward you. He's just protective of his company, and this Giovanni guy irritates the hell out of him. I'd bet the two of you would hit it off if you ever find yourself face-to-face with him."

"I highly doubt that."

Evariste opened his mouth to try to persuade her otherwise, but his sisters' loud jabbering as they joined them prevented him from saying anything more.

"Where's our plates?" Jeanette asked, seeing the two of them were already eating.

Evariste nodded his head toward the stove. "Fix your own."

"Isn't that what we pay you for, Chef?" Allister eyed her brother, scooping some rice onto her plate.

"You know where everything is. Plus, the three of you were busy yakking while we were starving."

"You'd be a terrible restaurant owner making your customers serve themselves, Evariste," Renee remarked, picking up a plate.

Stunned by the name, Caitlin quickly looked over at him. "Evariste?"

The girls went silent and stared at their brother as it dawned on them he still hadn't told her who he was.

He finished chewing the mouthful of food he had before offering her a sheepish smile. "Evariste Gage Arsceneaux: chef, landscaper, and CEO, at your service, Miss DeDanann."

Caitlin set her fork down, scowling at him. "How long were you going to wait to tell me you who you really were?"

"Until you were on a plane back to Virginia." Evariste looked her in the eye. "But after getting to know you some, you aren't the nosey, unscrupulous busybody I assumed you were to work for an ass like Dante Giovanni. So, if Renee hadn't slipped up, I would have revealed my full name and actual profession sometime before you left tonight."

Normally, Caitlin would have been mad at being lied to. Tonight, however, she found herself amused instead. "I should have paid closer attention to your picture in the company portfolio today."

Evariste scoffed. "You should have. You're a crappy investigator not to have done so."

"Careful, Arsceneaux, or I'll encourage Giovanni to up the pressure on you to sell."

Knowing she teased him, he flirtatiously smiled at her. "How can such a charming woman work for a jerk like Dante Giovanni?"

"I don't. I work for his attorney, Sean Watchous. So how many Robicheauxs and Arsceneauxs are there in the area, and how are you all related?"

"We're siblings. There's five of us kids in total. Evariste being the oldest," Allister advised, relieved Caitlin wasn't mad about them not telling her who Gage actually was. "We're all scattered from New Orleans to New Iberia. Though we love visiting our oldest brother."

"More like harassing your older brother," Evariste mumbled under his breath before taking a sip of his beer.

"Did you say something, Evariste?" Renee pretended not to have caught what he said.

Evariste eyed his sister. "You heard me."

Renee pointed her fork at Caitlin. "You're dating a grouchy, old man, Caitlin. One might even argue he's ancient and should have turned to dust by now."

"We just met, and we aren't dating." Caitlin said, then looked over at him. "How old are you anyway?"

Evariste almost choked on his food.

Jeannette chuckled at his perturbed expression. "Good question! How old are you, Ev?"

"Ancient, as you said. I'm thirty-seven."

His sisters laughed at his answer.

Caitlin stared at the three of them not sure why that was amusing. "What's so funny about being thirty-seven?"

"My sisters are being stupid. It's an inside joke. Just ignore them."

"How long are you in New Orleans, Caitlin?" Alli politely inquired.

"Two weeks this trip."

"Only two weeks?!" Renee exchanged concerned glances with Jeanette.

Evariste took Caitlin's hand to shift her attention away from his sisters' reaction. "I take it you live out of state."

"I live in Williamsburg, Virginia." She lost herself in the depths of his eyes, which were now a shade of rich emerald.

We will have to see what we can do to change that, a voice whispered in her head causing Caitlin to blush. She could swear Evariste spoke, but he sat quietly beside her. Was she hallucinating now?

Jeanette noticed the pinkish hue of Caitlin's cheeks. "Something wrong?"

"Nothing's wrong. Guess the spice in the shrimp creole got to me," Caitlin replied, not breaking eye contact with Evariste.

"Étouffée," Evariste smirked as he corrected her.

Alli placed her hand on Caitlin's shoulder, breaking the hold Evariste had on their guest. "My brother has that effect on women."

He pinched Alli under the arm, cautioning her to shut up.

"Ouch! Damn it, Evariste!" Alli pinched him back.

"We were under the impression you were a local with how Alli said

41

you and Azard seemed well acquainted," Jeanette remarked, shooting Alli and Evariste a scathing glare that warned they both needed to behave. "Azard told Alli you always visit him when you're in town."

"I do. He's got some of the best produce in NOLA, and this time of year the strawberries he sells are to die for. We met when I used to live in Kenner. I was here for a two and a half years after Katrina adjusting and litigating claims."

Shocked to hear she once lived in the area, Evariste looked over at her again. He had never sensed her presence or crossed paths with her prior to today, even though she had lived so close for almost a year and a half. "When did you say you lived in Kenner?"

"Several years ago now. I lived in an apartment off Loyola."

CAITLIN STAYED another two hours before calling it a night.

Evariste escorted her to her car. "Do you by chance have plans for tomorrow night?"

"Just meeting a couple of old coworkers for dinner. Other than that no. Why do you ask?"

"If it isn't obvious, I'd really like to get to know you better." His arm curled around her, bringing them closer together. "A lot better," he whispered before kissing her.

Caitlin melted into him, returning the kiss. Her head swam when he kissed down her neck then whisked his lips across hers one final time.

"It was a pleasure meeting you, Caitlin. Call me when you're done with dinner tomorrow, and we can meet up for dessert, if it's not too late for you."

"I'll do that." She could swear his eyes glowed as he stared down at her while he opened her car door. "Good night, Evariste."

"Good night, cher. Be careful driving back to the hotel."

She sat in the driver's seat for a moment to stop her heart from racing before starting the car. *Damn that man could kiss!* She wasn't sure what it was about Evariste that made her want him to devour her, but if this kept up, Sean was going to have to assign someone else to the account.

Vampires & Curses

E variste waved after she glanced over at him before starting to pull out. He had to fight the urge to rip her out of the car. An involuntary groan came from his throat as he pictured them entwined in each other's arms on the front lawn. The soft spring grass beneath them and the cool night air caressing their skin with only moonlight to blanket them. Her deliciously purring his name while he delved into her again and again. Thank all that was holy he had the foresight to shut her car door before that image popped into his head. He quickly started for the house while the vampire in him screamed to stop Caitlin's departure and enjoy her as he wanted to.

"Whoa!" Jeanette exclaimed, seeing the fluorescent glow of her brother's eyes and the elongated canines when he turned from shutting the front door.

"What?" he almost shouted, irritated by the way she stared at him

"You're all vamped out. Even after all this time, I just can't get used to seeing you that way."

"Then don't look at me."

Alli glanced up from watching TV, not fazed at all by his appearance. "I have a feeling we'll be seeing this side of Ev more often with Caitlin in town."

"It'd be nice if he'd start acting like a vampire and go seduce her. You've only got two weeks before she leaves," Renee added.

"I agree with Renee. You need to speed up the courtship part of the relationship," Jeanette chimed in.

"And what exactly do you three suggest I do? Sit her down and tell her, 'By the way, I'm a vampire, and my family was also cursed when I was bitten. But it's okay because I'm a nice vampire. I don't drink blood or kill people. I also can walk around in the daylight without turning to ash. One other thing you should know, we were married almost three hundred years ago. Oh, and you're the only one who can break the curse and set my family and me free.' She'd be on the first flight back to Virginia after that discussion. I know I would."

"If you say it like that...." Renee rolled her eyes.

Alli threw a pillow at her. "He's got a point. Between the vampire curse and the inspector sent down here being Ev's reincarnated wife, it is all kinda crazy. What are the odds, after all? Ev, I'm honestly surprised you didn't pounce on her the moment you saw her. There are several times tonight you looked like you would devour the woman."

"If I pounced on her, she's the type of woman who would beat my ass for doing so then head for the hills. We need her help, not to scare her off." He sat down in a recliner, put his feet up on the ottoman, and closed his eyes, thinking back over everything that occurred that day. "Trust me to handle this, dear sisters. I need to take things at the right pace, and she needs to remember the past on her own. Remember what the priestess said?"

"As if I trust 'Tia Dalma' to be the expert on this," Renee snidely remarked, remembering the strange voodoo priestess who appeared shortly after he turned.

Evariste ignored her, but the *Pirates* reference lightened his mood some. The woman had looked like the movie character when she showed up at the door.

"What if she doesn't remember before she leaves?" Alli wondered what the game plan would be.

"We will find a way to bring her back home." He tried to sort things out in his head.

The four sat in silence not knowing what else to say.

He sat up suddenly as Caitlin's comment about living in Kenner rang in his ears. "None of you met her or saw her when she lived in Kenner?"

"Nope. Not once," Alli answered.

Frowning, he stood. "I'm going to bed and will figure all of this out tomorrow."

Searching For Signs

E variste laid a cut stem of Ebb Tide roses on the grave in front of him. He hadn't visited her grave in a few weeks. He'd been too focused on Giovanni's constant pestering and snooping into Lagniappe. The Italian certainly knew how and where to put pressure on someone. After meeting Caitlin last night, he needed to be here, to feel the calming anchor his wife always gave his inner turbulence when confusion and worry churned inside him.

"I am sorry I haven't been here more frequently, mon coeur. Life and work have kept me away. Though, I have missed you a great deal." His fingers reverently brushed the cool stone he knelt before. "Dreamed of you last night. How I wish the dream had been real instead of a distant memory. That you were here beside me still. There is a woman I recently met who has your eyes and hair. Allister brought her home against my wishes. You know Alli and her tenacious nature. Her heart was in the right place with inviting her to D'Orme for dinner, for you see, cher, everyone who has met her thinks she is you. Part of me does too. But the other part of me, is afraid, afraid we are wrong about what we are all seeing. We've been mistaken before; however, in those circumstances there were only hints of you in the other women. This one, this one is virtually identical to you in every way. She even smells like you, and tastes as you did. Forgive me, if that offends you, mon coeur. But I want to be honest with you, I am drawn to this woman as strongly as I was you. When she asked me to kiss her, I couldn't resist."

He gazed at the ground, resting his palm flat against the granite grave. Trying to sort through his thoughts about the past twenty-four hours, he wished she could talk to him from the afterlife. "I'm lonely, cher. No woman could ever replace you in my heart, but I find myself longing for company, and not just a casual encounter any longer. I would want you to find someone to spend your days with if our situations were reversed. As long as the man was worthy of you and treated you right. Give me a sign of some sort confirming she is you, and if she is not, granting me permission to love someone new until we are reunited whenever my miserable existence ends."

"I figured you'd be here when Alli said you were coming in late today," Alcee remarked, walking up behind him and overhearing him ask for a sign or permission to move on. "I'd say she and the universe are giving you exactly what you asked for, but you either can't see it or are frightened of it."

"We've been wrong before, Alcee." Evariste kissed the portrait he commissioned an artist to paint and install on the grave then stood to face his business partner.

Alcee understandingly smiled. "The Fates finally give you a second chance with your wife as promised, Evariste. You only need to seize it. She's coming into the office around one to finish auditing our financials, and I'm taking her to the shipping terminals to tour the ships."

"Are you just handing Giovanni the keys to Lagniappe, Alcee? I can't believe you are giving her that sort of access," he snapped, annoyed at how much Alcee disclosed to Caitlin.

"I am buying you time, Evariste. Once the background check and audit are done, I can do nothing more to help keep Caitlin's interest in you. I also get the feeling she won't disclose half of what she sees, not to mention if she is Madam Arsceneaux returned to us, she will need to know our operations. You always delegated to her when you had to travel or needed assistance making decisions. Don't think I am not aware of you asking for her thoughts in addition to mine and Pierre's."

"You truly believe this Caitlin DeDanann is my reincarnated wife?"

"I do, mon ami. The resemblance they share is too uncanny for her not to be. Not to mention, they have the same first name. The Fates are giving you every confirmation they can of who she is. I reserved the conference room across from your office for her to work in the rest of the week. I'll let you say goodbye to the past, so you can freely embrace the present. See you at the office in about an hour?" Alcee's dark brow lifted as he studied Evariste, waiting for an answer.

Evariste nodded then stared over at the grave that's stone had darkened with age.

Understanding Evariste's discomfort with everything, Alcee patted him on the back then headed to his car.

WHEN HE FINALLY ARRIVED AT the office, Evariste felt like everyone apprehensively watched him. Other than Alcee and Alli who stared at him as he passed Alcee's open door, he more than likely imagined the other employees' uneasiness. They had no clue what was going on in his personal life or what he now had on his mind on top of normal business problems.

Sharon, his executive assistant, smiled up at him once he reached her desk. "Good morning, Evariste. The latest financials are on your desk, Sean Watchous called on Giovanni's behalf again, and I've got a fresh pot of coffee brewing since Alcee said to expect you about now. Should I order lunch in for you?"

He smiled, appreciating Sharon's professionalism and anticipating he'd follow his normal routine of working through the lunch hour behind closed doors. "Thank you, and good morning to you as well. I think I'll play lunch by ear today, but I definitely will take a cup of coffee."

The surprised expression on her face when he declined the lunch order made him chuckle as he walked into his office. Settling into his desk chair, he woke his computer to review and approve the financial report. He only briefly looked up after hearing Caitlin's voice about twenty minutes later. Wondering if he had lost track of time, he looked down at his watch. It was only 12:30; she came in earlier than planned.

She glanced toward his door while talking to Alcee, who turned on the light in the conference room for her.

It was going to be hard to focus on work with being able to see her through the office window. Undoubtedly, that was one of the reasons Alcee picked the conference room he had for Caitlin's temporary workspace. Shifting his attention back to the financials he needed to sign off on, he got back into reviewing them against the company ledgers. He hated accounting and finance, but they were a necessary evil for one managing a company to be well educated on and able to calculate. At least he no longer had to do the books himself.

Once he completed his double checking of the figures and making a few recommended changes to the wording which would be used in the annual report, he signed his name on the signature line and again looked across the hall. Caitlin sat at the conference table, staring at her laptop screen; her long hair was pulled back, so it stayed out of her face as she worked. A pair of reading glasses dangled from her hand, her lips twisted in concentration, giving away her concerns about something she read. He reached over and pressed the button to call Sharon. The intercom beeping drew Caitlin's attention to his assistant's desk. "Sharon?"

"Yes, Evariste?"

His eyes remained on Caitlin. "I see we have a visitor in the conference room. Would you kindly ask Ms. DeDanann to come to my office when she gets a moment?" He grinned, watching Caitlin's head turn toward his door. The redhead pushed back from the table then walked across the hall toward him.

"No need to tell me, Sharon. I heard his request," Caitlin said, passing by Sharon's desk.

His grin turned into a pleased smile when she stopped in the doorway.

She leaned against the doorframe, eyeing him mistrustfully. "You needed me for something, Mister Arsceneaux?"

"I was curious to learn how your investigation is going. I understand from Alcee you toured the farms and warehouse yesterday as well as started your audit of my financials."

"It's going smoothly. I'm quite impressed with everything. You run a tight ship."

"Speaking of ships, I'll be handling your tour of the shipping facilities and one of our ships this afternoon." Evariste could tell he startled her by the way her eyes widened and her mouth momentarily tensed. "Is that a problem?"

"No. Not at all. I'm just surprised after weeks of you ignoring my phone calls and emails requesting a meeting with you."

"Glad to hear you're just surprised versus there being any sort of problem. Before we head to the shipyards, I was thinking we could go out to lunch, if you don't mind. I'm starving and don't want my stomach growling louder than I can speak for the entire afternoon. Masquerades okay with you?"

He loved the second startled look he brought forth in five minutes.

"Masquerades isn't open for lunch." Caitlin straightened, no longer leaning on the doorframe, and took a step into his office.

His smile widened as he stood up and came around his desk. He owed Alcee a thank you for uncovering her favorite restaurant in the city the day prior. "It is if you know the right people." He grabbed his keys then came over to the door. "Shall we go?"

"Sure. Let me grab my purse."

Evariste turned to Sharon while Caitlin went back to the conference room. "Please call John and tell him we are on our way. Also, forward any urgent calls to my cell phone as we'll be out the rest of the day."

"Will do, Evariste." Sharon didn't question him, but by the look on her face, she thought about doing so.

Allister came to her office door as he walked down the hall behind Caitlin, giving him a baffled expression just as confused as Sharon and Caitlin had been. "You're handling the shipping inspection?"

"I've got it, Alli. I know my way around those docks and ships better than you or Alcee ever will." He winked at her as he passed.

Masquerades
⌒⌒⌒

E variste opened the passenger side door of a large black pickup
truck parked in front of the building. A truck was definitely not
the vehicle she expected him to drive.

"Thank you." She stepped up on the chrome running board and
settled herself into the oversized leather seat. The truck rocked slightly as
he shut the door then walked around and climbed in the driver's seat.
"Aren't CEOs supposed to drive beamers or some sophisticated foreign
car?"

He laughed at the inquiry, starting the truck. "Beamers won't tow a
boat or last a month on the farm roads I need to drive. I'm also a man
who believes he should live within his means. An extravagant car is fun
to drive, but other than that, they aren't really practical for all the things
I do."

A soft *mmm* was the only response she could offer. She watched the
colorful balconies and buildings they passed by on the short ride to the
restaurant. She hadn't been able to get reservations at Masquerades due
to the restaurant's growing popularity, and somehow, he managed to
convince them to open for lunch.

"You're quiet today, cher." Evariste cast her a quick glance before he
took a left turn.

"I'm in work mode, and honestly, I don't know what to think about you at the moment."

"You liked me well enough last night."

She couldn't help laughing at the devilish grin he gave her while pulling up in valet parking. "I suppose I still like you. I'm just trying to reconcile the grumpy gardener and chef from last night with the well-dressed businessman I'm seeing today."

His head cocked sideways as if amused. "Which do you like better?"

"I haven't decided yet." She found herself smiling back at him. He was handsome in the charcoal gray suit. A green tie almost the same color as his eyes paired nicely with it and the shirt he wore.

"Well, once you figure it out, let me know." Evariste opened his door as the valet got hers.

"Evariste! Good to see you again." A gentleman greeted them as they entered the empty restaurant lobby.

"John, it's good to see you. Thank you for accommodating such a short notice request." Evariste clasped his hand before giving the man a hug.

"It's my pleasure. You did manage to get a hold of that case of Brunello for me. Now who is this charming associate of yours?" The short gentleman with snow-white hair turned to Caitlin.

"Allow me to introduce Caitlin DeDanann. She's researching the company for a project and is quite the fan of yours. Caitlin, cher, your favorite chef, John D. Fontenot."

A bit star-struck to meet the chef and food historian she had followed for years, she wasn't sure what to say. She managed to sputter out, "It's a pleasure to meet you."

"You as well." John shook her hand. "Well, let me take you two to your table and get back to the kitchen to make sure things are in order for your lunch. The sous chef is already working on the quail eggs and turtle soup."

Caitlin followed John to a private table in the center of the restaurant. Evariste's hand rested on the small of her back as they walked together. John pulled Caitlin's chair out for her, and once she was seated, handed her a menu.

Her eyes skimmed the offerings that changed with the seasons.

52

Everything looked good. Her stomach growled. She heard a soft, deep chuckle across from her. She glanced over the top of the menu to discover a grin quirking Evariste's lips. After settling on a main course, she set the menu down. Evariste's menu still laid on the table, unopened. "Already know what you want?"

"I do, indeed. I'm very much a creature of habit. I hope you don't mind me ordering us the turtle soup and deviled quail eggs to start."

"Not at all. That's one of my favorite dishes here."

A waiter walked up to their table. "Can I get you your usual Sazerac, Evariste?"

"Not today. I'm chauffeuring the lady around. I'll take a sweet tea instead."

The waiter nodded, then looked over at Caitlin. "A glass of wine, perhaps, for the lady?"

Caitlin's eyes drifted to the drink menu, but she reminded herself it was lunchtime. "It's working hours. I should probably have a sweet tea as well."

Noticing the way she briefly stared at the wine list, Evariste grinned. "Go ahead and order a glass of wine, cher. One glass won't impair your judgement. I won't tell Giovanni you had one."

Caitlin snorted, picking up the wine list. "Being Italian, I doubt Giovanni would care. And it's Sean I work for, not Giovanni." After skimming the list, she looked up at the waiter. "I'm not a white wine fan. I think the tempranillo here isn't too overly tannin-y for what I plan to order."

Caitlin looked at the décor after the waiter walked away. She always loved the classic high ceilings and silkscreened or painted walls of high-end places in NOLA. Evariste curiously studied her when her gaze turned back to him after the waiter set their drinks and soups in front of them. They both politely thanked him.

The turtle soup was warm and flavorful, smoothly crossing her pallet, almost like sherry-flavored silk. Evariste certainly had excellent taste in cuisine between this and what he cooked last night. "You are such a strange contradiction."

Evariste swallowed the mouthful of soup he had before responding, "How so?"

"With the way you were replanting those flowers last night, you obviously have no issues with hard work or using your hands, yet run a multimillion-dollar company. And you say you're a man who likes to live within his means, yet, here we are having a lunch that will run you at least a few hundred." Caitlin picked up her wine glass, waiting for him to answer.

One side of his mouth turned up at the inquiry as he leaned forward. "Well, a man has to splurge every once in a while to impress a lady. Since I couldn't have you for dinner tonight, lunch was going to have to do."

Caitlin loudly cleared her throat as an image of her clutching the sheets of a large bed with his head between her thighs flashed before her. His tongue traced the most intimate parts of her. Her body bowed upward in anticipation of more. Snapping herself out of the passionate fantasy that came out of nowhere, Caitlin uncomfortably shifted in her chair.

"Are you all right? You look flushed all of a sudden." Evariste's voice broke through the strange haze filling her head.

"Fine. The spice in the soup must be getting to me." Caitlin tried to justify her strange behavior. She wasn't about to tell him what had popped into her head.

He cynically stared at her from across the table with a glimmer of mischief in his eyes and a slight smirk on his face. "I put a lot more spice in dinner last night."

"Maybe it's the combination of the wine and the soup."

He picked up his sweet tea. Another warm chuckle rumbled from his chest that only worsened the heat spreading through her. "Here. This will help cool you down better than the wine."

"Thank you." Caitlin took a large sip of the cold tea, wishing it was just the Creole seasonings raising her body temperature at the moment. When she looked back over at Evariste, the same intense attraction to him she experienced the night prior returned. "Does this have filé in it?"

"No, cher. It isn't gumbo."

"The tea definitely helped ease the burn. Thank you again." Caitlin offered him his tea back.

"My pleasure, Cate."

The shade of his eyes intensified while he reached for his tea. She quivered from just the brush of his fingers over hers after he grasped the cool glass then pulled it back to him. She briefly contemplated how delightful they'd feel against her bare skin. Another round of imagining being in bed with him struck. In it, his hands cupped her breasts and his thumbs teased her nipples while they kissed before his fingers skimmed her sides. One of his hands settled on the rounded curve of her butt while the other continued down her belly then slipped between her thighs. Her fingers involuntarily curled on the white, linen tablecloth and her breath hitched in her throat as the sensation of an intimate featherlight caress sent a rippling ache through her.

"The scallops and black truffles for the lady, and the cast iron venison tenderloin for the gentleman." John served them their entrees, ending the intense moment of reverie. "Is there anything else I can bring you?"

"Some more ice water for my lovely lunch companion, please. The cayenne in the soup seems to be getting to her." Evariste's eyes remained locked with Caitlin's as he spoke.

"Of course. I'll send your waiter over to refill her glass. Anything additional?"

"No, thank you," Caitlin embarrassedly answered the chef. If she didn't know better, she'd say Evariste was enjoying whatever the hell was happening.

"In that case, bon appetite."

Thankfully, no more erotic thoughts occurred throughout the meal as Caitlin questioned Evariste about his business. She forced herself to focus on gathering information for the report she needed to write. It wasn't until they were leaving and he lightly rested his hand on her back that another jolt of electric yearning traveled straight from where his palm brushed to her core. She stepped forward to break the contact between them while they waited for the truck.

Evariste frowned but let his hand drop to his side.

They rode in silence to the shipyard.

"Are you okay?" Evariste shattered the tension between them.

Caitlin shook her head. "I'm fine. It's...look, it's the whole professionalism thing. I'm not supposed to get involved with someone I'm investigating."

"I understand. Conflict of interest and all." Evariste shut off the truck and exhaled loudly. "Let's get the tour over with, so I can get you back to the office and put some distance between us. The Montrose is in and said we were welcome to come aboard."

"The Montrose?" Caitlin didn't recall the name,

"The Montrose is a Supramax bulk carrier specifically designed to transport produce, sugar cane, and grain. You can't put goods like that on a container ship."

"Why not?"

"I'll explain it on the way down the pier." Evariste got out of the truck and waited patiently for her to join him.

"See those white caps." He pointed to the water just outside the mouth of the inlet as they walked together.

"Yes." Caitlin wondered what they had to do with anything.

"They look small from here, and it's a nice day, so the wind is more than likely causing them instead of large swells. But add in the right chop or a storm and those swells will rock a ship, even one this size. Bulk grain and produce shift if the ship isn't balanced correctly or the grain is mispackaged or misloaded in anyway when the ship pitches. If the rolling waves cause things to shift too much, you not only risk losing the cargo due to product bruising and damage, you risk capsizing the ship. No shipper ever wants to deal with a sinking or capsized vessel. The loss of crew and a ship this size is hard to recover from emotionally and financially, not to mention it creates a PR nightmare and does serious reputation damage. No crew wants to sail for a company that will unnecessarily put their lives at risk. The job's tough enough without throwing incompetence into the mix."

"I take it you've lost a ship and dealt with the fall out."

"A modern ship like the Montrose? I can honestly say I've never lost a bulk cargo carrier. Though the company lost a ship in the 1700s, then one in a hurricane in the 1800s. We also had one jettison its cargo in the early 1800s to keep from losing the ship in a storm. The loss of the galleon in the 1800s nearly did Lagniappe Shipping in. Fortunately, some investments played out in our favor, allowing the company to recover, and our insurance covered the cost of the sunken ship."

"It amazes me that your family has managed to keep the company going for over three centuries. So many companies don't recover from disasters or have that kind of longevity. Your ancestors left you quite a legacy." Caitlin had to admit, she was impressed. The Arsceneauxs must have been sharp and shrewd businessmen. "Why a Supramax over another type of ship?"

"Excellent question. The Supramax carries an adequate amount of cargo to fulfill our larger customer orders while still being versatile enough to sail open sea and access smaller ports, rivers, and locks around the US and globe."

"You seem to know a lot about ships, Ev. Second passion to cooking for you?"

He laughed. "I'm a sailor first, chef second. I grew up sailing. My first job was as a deckhand on a ship. I'm more at home at sea than I am on land. It's also my job to know the vessels and laws of maritime commerce as the CEO of Lagniappe Shipping & Ag. Maritime trade is the oldest part of my business. Farming never really appealed to the founder of the company like shipping did. That came later."

The ship's captain met them as soon as they came aboard. Surprisingly, Caitlin found the ship tour and their discussion more interesting than she thought she would. When it was over, she stood at the rail, staring out into the water, enjoying the salty air along with the breeze blowing her hair. She watched a ship or two navigating their way out to the Gulf while Evariste finished talking to the captain.

"Enjoying yourself?" Evariste asked, stopping a few feet behind her.

"I am. I've always loved the water. It feels like home when I'm near it."

"Grew up on the coast somewhere, I take it?"

"I did. I lived in Northern Virginia most of my life, but we routinely went to the beach or sailing when I was younger. I don't do it as much now with not having a lot of time off." Caitlin smiled over at him. He really did seem comfortable shipboard. The tension that had been in his shoulders while he was in the office disappeared, and he grinned or smiled the entire time they walked the ship.

"We can't be about work all the time, Miss DeDanann."

Caitlin laughed. "Maybe you should tell yourself that, Mr. Arsce-neaux. From what I hear and read, you throw yourself into your work."

"I have to. A lot of people depend on me and the decisions I make. But I still find time to enjoy the simpler pleasures in life every now and then."

The ship jolted, sending Caitlin into Evariste's chest. His arms enfolded her, helping her catch her balance. "A tug is coming alongside to attach tow lines with the Montrose pulling out in an hour. Every once in a while, they bump up against a ship a little harder than intended. Why don't we wait until the lines are attached before trying to disembark? I wouldn't want you taking a fall or twisting an ankle with those landlubber legs of yours."

"Sounds good to me." Caitlin enjoyed how he tucked her in against him when the ship rocked again. Whatever soap the man used was intoxicating as she caught a whiff of it. Her gaze drifted downward to his lips. When her eyes returned to his, she found them partially closed. Their noses brushed before his lips found hers. The kiss they shared was sweet and unhurried. Nothing like the passionate kiss in the garden or before she left D'Orme that made her want to tear his clothes off. "I love the way you kiss me, Evariste."

"What happened to being strictly professional, cher?" He smiled before sampling her lips again.

"Weren't you the one just telling me we can't be about work all the time?" Caitlin made him loudly laugh now. She loved hearing him laugh almost as much as she did the way he so confidently kissed her.

"Touché, Cate. Touché. Come over here, so you can see the lines being attached." He guided her over to the rail of the ship once again. He placed a hand on either side of her. They watched the tug and ship's crews toss lines back and forth to one another.

A weird feeling of nostalgia washed over Caitlin as she watched the tow lines be secured in place, almost as if she routinely observed ship-board activity with Evariste at her side.

"Do you like to fish, Caitlin?" Evariste's voice caressed her ear with the random question.

She glanced back at him. "I suppose. I haven't done that in years either. Why?"

"Just wondered. Maybe I'll take you out sometime. It's my favorite thing to do to relieve stress."

"You really are a redneck Cajun, aren't you?" Caitlin turned to face him again.

"You know what they say; we're outdoorsmen who eat anything that doesn't eat us first," Evariste good-naturedly replied then looked down at his watch. "We should probably get going if I'm going to have you back in time for you to get ready for your dinner tonight. I've enjoyed my afternoon with you, cher."

"You've been a very accommodating host, Evariste. Thank you for lunch and the ship tour."

When they got back to the truck, he pulled her to him. "Since I can't do this when we get back to the office without setting off the rumor mill."

Before Caitlin could ask what he meant, his lips were on hers. Unlike the shipboard kisses, this one was hungry and seeking. She clutched Evariste to her, aching with the same need the kiss conveyed. She groaned as his lips moved to her neck. "What is it with you, Evariste Arsceneaux? I've never met a man I couldn't keep it professional with until you."

"We're kindred spirits, Cate. We both love the water, work too much, and enjoy good food. It's no surprise we find one another attractive. You're beautiful." He squeezed her butt, pressing her tighter to him. "Curvy in all the right places."

"I'd deck any other guy that did what you just did."

"So would I," Evariste whispered, his mouth teasing hers again. "I'd break each of his fingers for daring to touch you."

Caitlin laughed, staring up into emerald eyes. "Possessive much?"

"Only when someone touches a woman I'm dating."

"We aren't dating." Caitlin started to pull away from him.

Evariste didn't let her escape. "What are we doing then?"

"I'm not sure. But I don't date my professional interests." Caitlin forced herself to step back from him.

"Such a shame, especially considering you love how I kiss you. I reserve my kisses for those I'm dating." He opened the passenger door for her. "Get in, Miss DeDanann. Before you end up investigating more about a professional interest than would be appropriate."

Caitlin texted Sean on the ride back to the office.

> Toured the shipping facility and ships. Like everything else, all well run and in excellent condition. Arsceneaux personally escorted me and reviewed the seafaring portion of the business with me today. He reaffirmed he's not selling. Call you later. Heading to dinner with Kevin, Jeanine, and some old cat adjusting peeps.

Tangling With The Past

Caitlin met her friends at a jazz club tucked away on the edge of the French Quarter. They enjoyed hanging out there as it catered to the locals, not tourists. One of the guys sitting at the table whistled loudly as Caitlin walked in wearing a short, black skirt, a red satin blouse, and black heels.

"What's the occasion, Cate? A hot date after dinner?" Kevin Breaux joked, not used to seeing his former coworker dressed as she was.

"Maybe I just wanted to dress up for you guys."

Jeanine laughed and flagged a waiter down for a beer. "Whatever. Tell us who the guy is."

"No one you know." Caitlin opened the menu lying on the table.

The waiter stopped to take Caitlin's order. "What can I get you to drink, ma'am?"

"I think I'll have a mojito tonight." After the waiter walked off, Caitlin looked across the table. "How have you been, Jeanine?"

The two adjusters and two attorneys who made up the former Stafford property claims litigation team caught up over dinner. They laughed as they swapped stories about working together along with discussing old cases and claims. None of them noticed that they were being watched from the back of the club.

Kevin's cell phone rang, stopping the conversation around the table. Caitlin smiled as she listened to him talk to his wife.

"Yes, dear... Sure, I can pick up some pralines...What the fuck type craving is that? Sorry, dear ... I will get the Brussels sprouts too. Love you too, honey."

"Sherry's trying to get Kevin to stop using his favorite word," Jeanine whispered, making Caitlin laugh.

Kevin was well known around the office for how many different ways he could utilize the F word. They always knew when his stress level was high or some outrageous demand was dropped on his desk as he never failed to drop the F-bomb at the top of his lungs while he made his way to one of the senior executive's offices to express how he felt about the whatever set him off.

"Come on, Matt. The old ball and chain says the baby needs Brussels sprouts and pralines ASAP." Kevin rose and threw some cash on the table to cover his portion of the bill. Matt and Kevin were neighbors in addition to working at the same law firm.

"You know Sherry would kick your butt for calling her that," Caitlin said as Matt stood up to leave as well.

"What she doesn't know won't hurt her." Kevin pulled out his car keys.

"Unfortunately, KB is my ride. The wife will probably be calling shortly anyhow." Matt hugged Caitlin goodbye.

"It was nice seeing both of you again. Tell Sherry and Amy I said hello." Caitlin also hugged Kevin before sitting back down.

"Will do." Matt nodded then walked away with Kevin.

Jeanine grabbed her jacket. "I should probably head out soon too. I told the sitter I'd be back by nine."

"Hey, Cate!" Kevin yelled from halfway across the room, causing Caitlin to look up. "Have fun on your date! Don't do anything I would."

"Did I just hear that Caitlin DeDanann has a date this evening?" A brown-eyed and black-haired man sauntered over to Caitlin and Jeanine.

The observer watching in the back of the club noticed how the two women's dispositions turned from lighthearted to guarded when the newcomer walked up to their table.

"You certainly look different without your khakis and polo shirt from your adjuster days, and you aren't in a suit, so you can't be in town to testify in another court case."

"Tristan Dausan, still a jackass, I see." Caitlin turned her back to him so she could continue saying goodbye to Jeanine.

He sat down in the empty chair beside her. "Miss me, Cate?"

"Hardly." Caitlin took another sip of her mojito, trying to ignore him.

"Jeanie, you can run along home. Caitlin and I have some catching up to do." Tristan dismissed her companion.

Jeanine hated Tristan as much as Caitlin did. "Piss off, Dausan."

Caitlin smiled at how Jeanine sat down again. She appreciated the solidarity against the man most of the women in the claims office loathed. "You've got little ones to head home to. I can manage the Dumas here."

Jeanine grinned at the way Caitlin pronounced Dumas. They had used that last name so many times to get away with discretely expressing their irritation at someone in the office.

"Politely calling me a dumbass almost hurts, Caitlin." Tristan smirked and shook his head. "There are quite a few women who would love to have dinner with me. They'd be envious of you having my undivided attention right now."

Caitlin didn't doubt the accuracy of that statement. Tristan was a strikingly handsome man. He reminded her of a power player in the mob with his classic dark looks. The man oozed sexuality; very much the stereotypical romance novel, egotistical, rich, businessman hero who dressed in designer suits and drove a Ferrari. However, there was something predatory about him that always made Caitlin's skin crawl, not to mention the man's ego made him a world-class narcissist. "What do you want, Dausan?"

"Can't an old acquaintance catch up on how a former business associate is doing? Maybe I've just missed having you around the office. Why do I have to want something from you?"

"Cut the crap, Tristan. You never liked me, and I can't stand you." Caitlin's irritation grew with the man who had run off a friend.

Her use of his first name caused him to raise an eyebrow.

THE SHADOW WATCHING the scene unfold moved closer to their table.

"Merde." Evariste recognized the man sitting with Caitlin. She would have no way of knowing he was there, but Tristan would pick up on his presence if he got too close. He hoped he was still hidden in the shadows as he backed up a couple of feet.

A WICKED GRIN spread across Tristan's face as the presence of the vampire watching them settled over him. He leaned closer to Caitlin and stared in Evariste's direction. Then casually brushed her long hair back, revealing the small of her neck to him before speaking. "What I want, Cate, is the chance to sample whatever you were saving for you date tonight." His hand slid from Caitlin's knee to her thigh.

Caitlin slapped his hand off her leg and shoved him away from her. "Don't touch me!"

Tristan gave Evariste a toothy smile as Caitlin stood up, heading toward the front of the restaurant.

Evariste debated between snatching up Tristan and following Caitlin. He chose the latter. Thibodeaux's wasn't the place to confront the sleaze of the vampire community.

Thankfully, Caitlin didn't leave the safety of the club. Instead, she climbed the old, wooden stairs to the second floor where four pool tables took up one side of the open space and an antique bar and small dance floor filled the other side. There were only a handful of customers and the bartender upstairs. She crossed the wooden floor to the pair of open doors leading out onto balcony overlooking Royal Street. Recognizing Evariste silently trailing the redhead, the bartender gave him a friendly nod, continuing to dry one of the glasses that had just been washed in the kitchen.

CAITLIN STEPPED out into the night air and stared down at the street in front of her. Tristan was such a douche. He hated this place. It's one of the reasons the old team enjoyed coming here. If they chose it for dinner or lunch, it guaranteed he wouldn't join them. What in the hell was he doing here tonight? She rested her palms on the black wrought iron rail in front of her, trying to shake off her irritation with Tristan's unwelcome intrusion on what should have been a pleasant evening.

Evariste quietly walked up behind her and gently placed a hand on her shoulder. "I saw what happened downstairs. Are you all right, cher?"

"Fine. Thank you." She closed her eyes, not realizing it was Evariste standing beside her while she worked to regain her composure.

"I'll see what I can do to have the man tossed out of here and banned for life. No one should accost a woman that way."

"Accost?" Caitlin turned to learn who spoke so formally nowadays. Startled to find there was no one behind her, she quickly sat in one of the oversized balcony chairs. Had she imagined the conversation and hand on her shoulder? She must have, or someone slipped something into one of her drinks. That was the only reasonable explanation for hearing a man's voice with no one really there. Not to mention, rarely did anyone notice things occurring around them this day and age between being distracted by smartphones or conversations carried on with friends.

The bartender set a glass of water and a plate of bread pudding and strawberries on the table beside her. "Compliments of the chef for the trouble downstairs."

"Tristan's bad manners aren't the restaurant's responsibility. You don't need—"

"We most certainly do need to. The owner enjoys our reputation of being a safe place for women and men alike. If you need anything else for the evening, come see me at the bar." The bartender winked at her then went back inside.

"TRISTAN!" Evariste caught up with the retreating vampire two blocks away.

Tristan casually looked over his shoulder, stopping halfway down the alleyway. "I suspected she might be your beloved wife back from the dead when she happened to walk into the office a few years ago, but you never came sniffing around. Fortuna seems to have just been biding her time in confirming her identity."

"Stay away from her."

"Or you'll what, Evariste? Kill me? You had your chance." Tristan laughed at the threat as he suddenly stood nose to nose with him.

Evariste warily watched Tristan as the rival vampire circled him. "I swear to god, Tristan. Go near her again, and I will rip you apart limb by limb."

"You couldn't do it then, and we both know you can't do it now."

"It wasn't a fair fight back then. A man versus a vampire. We're on an equal playing field now, and make no mistake, Tristan, you will die if you don't keep your distance." Not wanting to waste any more energy on Tristan, he started walking back to the club.

"Her blood was so sweet on my tongue as I drained it from her."

Evariste ignored the comment.

"Do you know what I loved most about that kill, Evariste? As I was feeding on her, she begged me to stop as she was with child."

"You lie!" Evariste hissed, turning back now and picking up Tristan by his throat. He pinned Tristan to the brick wall behind him.

Tristan was caught off guard by how quick Evariste had become over the years. Never had another vampire in New Orleans confronted him as Evariste did now.

"You didn't know." Tristan sputtered as it dawned on him that no one ever told Evariste about the child. "Ask your sisters; they knew. She found out that morning."

Rage rose up inside Evariste. The kind of rage he hadn't experienced since the day his wife died. The kind that drove man and vampire alike to do things they normally wouldn't. His grip tightened around Tristan's throat. "She never had a chance to tell me, you murderous bastard."

"Watch her, Arsceneaux. After tonight, I am coming for you both when you least expect it." Tristan hurled himself and Evariste into the adjacent wall.

Evariste threw Tristan off him and to the end of the alley. "Your days are numbered, Tristan."

Tristan vanished into the dark night air.

The law prevented random killing between their kind, but he'd find a way around it if Tristan ever came near Caitlin again. Grief tore at Evariste's conscience as images of Caitlin gasping to breathe and covered in blood on the trail between the woods and the cane fields spun around him. Not only was his life forever altered that afternoon, but the damn bastard killed both his wife and child. A child he and Caitlin had prayed for every night. How could no one have told him of the baby?

Playing The Long Game

Sitting alone on the quiet balcony while savoring the warm, decadent dessert erased the hostility Tristan's uninvited presence brought on. Sweet, fresh strawberries paired with whiskey sauce were the perfect cure for Caitlin's foul mood. She walked back into the club, intending to put the empty plate on the bar and ask to speak to the chef so she could thank him for the dessert.

"Let me take that for you." The bartender intercepted her as she stepped inside the doorway.

Spotting Evariste playing pool with someone across the room startled her. The bartender walked off before she could ask to see the chef. She walked over to the pool table Evariste and another man lingered around. "Evariste?"

Leaning over the table and lining up the tip of his pool cue with the cue ball, he briefly looked up at her. "Hello, Caitlin."

He took his shot then straightened. "Small world, isn't it? What are you doing here?"

"This is where my friends and I met for dinner. I was just getting ready to call you." Caitlin was still astonished he had been in the same place she was, and she hadn't noticed him all evening.

"Are you going to introduce me to the lady?" the blond gentleman Evariste was playing pool with asked, giving her a friendly smile.

"Caitlin this is Thib, he owns this fine establishment. Thib, Caitlin."

"Thib? That's a unique name." Caitlin wondered what it was short for.

"You must not be from Louisiana. Thib is short for Thibodeaux." Thib admired the pretty redhead with the unusual lavender eyes who Evariste had come to the club to keep an eye on. "Do you play pool, Caitlin?"

She shrugged. "A little. I'm not very good."

"Well, I am tired of getting my butt kicked and need to get back to the bar." Thib handed his pool cue to Caitlin.

"Before you go, thank you very much to you and your chef for the dessert. It was delicious."

"You're welcome, cher. My, uh, pastry chef was quite upset to learn about you being harassed." Thib grinned and winked at Evariste as he spoke. "Let her win a game or two, Ev. Watch him when you play, Caitlin. Gage can be a sneaky sob at times. Bonne chance."

"Everyone has such colorful things to say about you. Now you're sneaky on top of snarky?" Caitlin smiled at the way Evariste shook his head and started racking the balls on the table for a new game.

"Pay him no mind, cher. Thib's just a sore loser."

"So is it Ev, Evariste, or Gage?" Caitlin chalked her stick.

"Depends on who I am speaking with. I prefer Gage over the other two."

"Gage it is then." Caitlin set the chalk down on the side of the table. "I think I like it better than Evariste anyhow. Evariste is so formal sounding."

Gage chuckled, stepping away from the table. "I'd rather we not be on formal terms, Caitlin. Ladies first."

"If I break, we're going to be here all night. You go ahead and do it."

"You are terrible, aren't you?" Gage teased after she missed a couple of shots.

Caitlin watched him put the fifteen ball in a side pocket. "I warned you that I suck."

"You don't suck. You just aren't taking the time to think about your shots."

"What's there to think about? This is pool, not chess."

"Pool still requires strategy. Here, let me show." Gage walked up behind her. He placed one hand on top of hers which was on the table and the other on her shooting arm. His chin rested on her shoulder as they leaned forward together to examine the various balls scattered across the green felt before them. "Look at your options. Too much green between the cue ball and the three. I've got the side pocket blocked with the thirteen. Your best shot is the four into the left corner pocket. Aim low on the cue ball when you take the shot."

Caitlin lowered the tip of her cue slightly. "Here?"

"Lower." Gage adjusted her shooting arm. His hand brushed her thigh when he helped her draw the pool cue back. He heard her quick intake of breath when his fingers grazed her. Her pulse briefly quickened. He slowly dragged his hand from her thigh to her waist, eliciting a similar reaction. His being a vampire now certainly made their reunion much more interesting. "You're not dressed for playing pool tonight. This skirt has got to go."

"What's wrong with my skirt?" Caitlin impishly asked, enjoying the way his body currently framed hers.

Gage fought back a low groan after she teasingly wriggled that tempting, curved rear end against him. If only she knew how much she played with fire flirting like this. Just that little brush caused him to harden. He pressed a little closer to her, speaking directly into her ear, "It's too damn short. Every guy in the bar is checking out those legs of yours, hoping to see more each time you lean over the table to take a shot. It's downright distracting."

"Doesn't seem to be effecting your game."

Caitlin finally took the shot. She totally missed the cue ball as Gage's fingers traced a line up the sensitive flesh on the inside of her thigh. A low, husky chuckle filled her ear.

"That's how distracting you are in that skirt and blouse. It's taking all I have to focus on the game."

Caitlin moved to the opposite end of the table. "Now that I know that, I'm going to have to find a way to use it to my advantage."

"Oh really?" Amused by how calmly she collected herself, Gage grinned. "I think I've proven I can play through distraction."

Caitlin smirked, leaning low over the table. Her blouse fell away from her body giving Gage a clear view of her breasts. "I haven't even begun trying to distract you yet, Evariste Arsceneaux."

His eyes briefly dropped from hers; when they met her gaze again, he gave his head a slight shake and that sexy grin of his turned into a broad smile. The man really had no shame. She took the shot and sent the three ball into the pocket in front of him.

Gage watched her put two more balls in immediately after the three. "Just remember turnabout's fair play, mon amie. I wonder how well you can play with distraction."

Caitlin focused on the ball in front of her, doing her best to ignore the delightful sensation of his lips traveling the back of her neck while his hands tightened possessively on her hips. Somehow, with heart pounding and heat creeping up her belly, the tip of the stick collided with the center of the white ball, sending the one she really aimed for into a side pocket.

"Nice," Gage rasped, breaking the physical contact between them then moved to the far side of the table to cool the impulse to bend her over the rest of the way and take her right there. The compulsion to claim a lover had never been this strong before. Normally, he could easily control the baser side of his being. He half wondered if he should call it a night. The balls on the table clacked as Caitlin sunk another shot, drawing him out of the internal debate he had with himself.

"I'm starting to think you are lying to me about not knowing how to play pool."

"Just getting lucky tonight, I suppose. Eight ball, corner pocket," She called her last shot dead on.

"I fell for that once long ago. I'm not buying it tonight."

Caitlin laughed, staring directly at him. "If you'd let a girl win on occasion, I wouldn't have to sell it to you twice. Besides, no girl wants to make a guy look bad their first game of pool."

"Excuse me? Make me look bad? Oh, it's on, girlie! Rack 'em up."

Caitlin and Gage played several rounds of pool, staying past closing time. Even with her playing well the rest of the night, Gage thoroughly trounced her. Noticing Thib putting away the last of the cleaned glasses under the bar, Gage took Caitlin's cue stick from her. "Let me walk you back to your hotel."

"Still worried about those things that go bump in the night?" Caitlin watched him settle the stick into the empty space in the rack.

"This isn't Williamsburg, Virginia, Cate. More than you know walks the city streets and wanders the bayous of Louisiana at night."

She took the arm he offered then walked downstairs with him. "Gangsters, ghosts, and gators don't scare me."

"They should, along with all the other ghouls and goblins rumored to run amuck around here."

"My hotel is only a few blocks over." She found it sweet of him to want to make sure she made it safely to her hotel.

"It only takes a second to be pulled off the street into a van." Gage glanced over at the woman strolling beside him. "Next thing you know, the local news station will be running a story about some unfortunate redheaded tourist being abducted then her body found in a swamp a half hour from here."

Caitlin laughed. "You know this isn't exactly a great conversation topic for the end of a first date."

"I suppose it does come off a bit creepy." Gage smiled. "But at least you know I'm concerned about your safety."

"Or you really are a serial killer hoping to lure me in." Caitlin referenced his remark of potentially being a killer and planning to bury her in his flower beds the night prior.

"Well, fortunately for you, I need to wait a few months between murders. Too many torn up flower beds and people associated with me disappearing close together will tip off the authorities."

"You have a dark sense of humor, Gage Arsceneaux." She stopped in front of the Pauger on Bourbon and admired the man beside her. "I had a great time tonight."

"Me, too." Gage looked up at the gold name plate over the old door then the ornate balcony railings above them. "Is this where you're staying?"

"It is. I know it's kind of touristy, but I like to stay in the Quarter."

"Look, I don't want to come across pushy, or like a stalker, or anything, but why don't you stay at D'Orme?" Gage extended the invite concerned about Tristan's earlier threat.

"I wouldn't want to impose."

"You wouldn't be imposing. It will also save you the big bill you'll get after staying here for two weeks. My sisters would love having you around." *Hell, I'd love having you nearby again if you're really who I think you are.*

"Giovanni will be getting the big bill, or at least a week of it. But, I'll think about your offer."

"You had to bring up business after such a lovely evening." Gage shook his head, drawing her against him.

She wrapped her arms around his neck and tilted her face up, waiting for a goodnight kiss. Happy to oblige her, his mouth lightly pressed down on hers, delivering a tender kiss. Anything more would lead him into troubled waters being outside her hotel.

"Good night, sweetheart," he whispered before starting to walk away.

"Gage."

"Yes?" He turned and saw the conflicting emotions on her face. He would wager D'Orme and Lagniappe he was so confident he knew the exact question she wrestled with. "There is nothing else I would rather do than go upstairs and spend the night with you. However, I'm going to do the gentlemanly thing and suggest we wait until you no longer have to debate whether or not we should. I have no problems taking whatever this is between us slowly."

An embarrassed smile emerged on Caitlin's face. "I just don't want you to think I'm like this with every man I meet. And I'm normally a firm believer in not mixing business and pleasure, especially when it comes to getting involved with an executive of a company I'm investigating for a client."

Gage stared into those lavender eyes he had grown to love so much in their prior lifetime together. "Caitlin, cher, I don't think that of you at all."

She started to say something else when he kissed her.

"I'll work on convincing you I'm worth breaking the not mixing business and pleasure rule. My company and I are an open book from this point forward. Investigate whatever you like. Until you are mine again, we can enjoy getting to know one another. Good night, beautiful." Gage ended the conversation and walked away.

"Surprisingly, you're turning out to be quite an interesting man, Arsceneaux. One of the few old school guys left who like to take it slow," Caitlin called after him as he walked away.

He laughed softly to himself, continuing to his truck parked back at Thib's. She had no idea how much effort it took for him to walk away from her or that he conjured those images of them in bed together at lunch. If she did, she'd think he behaved as badly as Tristan had earlier that night.

Siblings & Schemes

On the drive back to D'Orme, Gage contemplated the events of the past few days. Kinda ironic that fate, if there was such a thing, sent his reincarnated wife as Giovanni's field inspector. That certainly wasn't how he imagined them reconnecting. He might have to entertain the prick's offer after all. Or at least for as long as it took to convince Caitlin of their past together.

No lights were on when he pulled into the driveway. His sisters were either out or sleeping. Maybe they finally went home. Gage half-heartedly hoped as he opened the side door off the kitchen. He'd like to bring Caitlin here and spend as much time as he could alone with her.

"Home so soon?" Alli greeted him, turning on the kitchen light as he walked in.

Gage blinked as his eyes adjusted to the bright light. "It's not that early. It's almost three a.m."

After the colorful spots vanished from his vision, he pulled a bowl of grapes and a Gatorade from the fridge. "Shouldn't you be in bed in your own house like the other nuisances I call sisters? You guys aren't creatures of the night."

"Like you are?" Alli pulled out the chair across the table from him. "What the hell type of vampire are you anyways? Up and outside during the day, eating grapes, and drinking Gatorade instead of sucking blood?"

"Good question. I'd like to know the answer to that myself along with a few other things." He popped another grape into his mouth. "Maybe I'm some rare species."

Alli laughed. "Yeah, you only made it part way through the conversion process, so you're stuck in the fruit bat stage; hence the grapes."

"Ferme ta bouche." Gage threw a grape at her, telling her to shut up.

"I take it things went well with Caitlin tonight. It's been a long time since I've seen you grin like you are."

"Mind your business, Alli."

"The way I see it, it's the whole family's business."

"My relationship, my business only."

"Well, you are in a good mood so it must not have gone too badly. However, you're home instead of romancing her. Maybe it didn't go well."

Gage laughed at how she changed tactics. "How do you know I didn't already ravage her and am home to retire to my coffin before the sun comes up?"

"One, you don't own a coffin. Two, if you did, I have no doubt you'd lock Caitlin and yourself in it with a big *do not disturb* sign. I remember how you locked down D'Orme when you first married her. We wouldn't see the two of you for days, and if we tried to visit, the gate guard would tell us, 'No visitors. Monsieur Arsceneaux's orders.'"

"Good old Cleobule. He was a great guardsman. Too bad the curse didn't affect him. He could keep you three troublemakers out of my house so I could finally get some peace and quiet." Gage recalled the first couple of weeks of his marriage and giving that direction. "I need to reinstall that gate over the driveway and put a fence out front to keep you unwanted visitors out."

"We'd just climb over it." Alli stuck her tongue out at him. "Or Daddy would knock it down once he got fed up with you not answering and Momma's complaining about you locking yourself away here."

Gage's expression turned troubled with Alli bringing up their parents. "Do they know she is here?"

"No, we didn't tell them. We wanted to know for sure it was her first, not some woman similar to her. No need to get their hopes up prematurely."

"Smart move that I wholeheartedly agree with. This family seems to be really adept at keeping secrets from one another. Almost disturbingly so." Gage's mood shifted to a darker one as Tristan's words about the baby circled in his head. He gave Alli a hard stare. By the way she suddenly stood, she got the point of his statement. Allister hated confrontation, and there was definitely a fight brewing between them with learning she and the rest of his family hid that he lost a child in addition to his wife.

"Anything else about Caitlin you haven't told me after all these years?" Gage icily asked, halting Allister in the kitchen doorway. It took a moment for her to turn around and look at him again. God, he could smell her fear and apprehension. Her pulse accelerated and the hard swallow she took before speaking sounded like someone banged a drum. Would she really keep lying to him?

"No, I don't think so."

Gage's eyes brightened to a florescent hue as he stared holes through his sister. "Would you like to reconsider your answer? There's not *anything* you've kept from me about Caitlin?" He paused, letting his questions sink in. "There isn't one little tidbit of information the family hasn't shared with me about my deceased wife? This is your only chance to come clean, Allister."

Her face paling confirmed Tristan told the truth. He shook his head, disappointed his own family lied to him after all he had done over the years to make sure they lived comfortably.

"Who told you?" Alli barely got the words out as she collapsed back into the chair she just left.

Gage's world spun out of control again as it had that fall afternoon three hundred years ago. "How could you not tell me? How could you keep that kind of secret from me, Alli?"

"Daddy and Momma swore us to secrecy. They were scared of what might happen if you knew."

"What exactly do they think would have happened? Did y'all honestly think I would never find out?"

"Evariste, you have to understand. Daddy was terrified of what

77

happened to you. He heard the shots you fired at Tristan. Azard, Jasper, and Daddy all ran from the fields to the bayou knowing something was wrong. When they got to the pecan grove, they found you half alive, lying with your head on Caitlin's chest and your arm around her. With blood everywhere, they thought you were both dead until you looked up at Daddy."

Gage closed his eyes; hazy memories of Pierre looking down at him surfaced in the darkness. The sheer horror on Pierre's face twisted Gage's gut as violently as finding Caitlin mauled had. Pierre's face disappeared from focus as the mortal Gage's vision blurred while he slipped into unconsciousness.

"Daddy saw the bites on your neck and shoulder. All he could think of was getting you to someone who could help. He said as soon as he saw the bite marks he knew what you would become. You refused to get up and go with him. You fought him, Azard, and Jasper when they tried to take Caitlin from your arms. It took all three of them to pull you out of the woods. You could barely stand when they brought you through the door. Between seeing you draped across Daddy and Azard's shoulders and Jasper carrying Caitlin's body, Momma started screaming. Roland was sent to find Alcee, which confused us all, as he wasn't a doctor.

"Daddy and Jasper locked you in one of the backrooms not knowing if you would be a danger to the family. We all took turns taking care of you after Alcee arrived and assured Daddy you would not hurt anyone. We all thought that day would have ended so differently. Jeanette and I were with Caitlin when the doctor examined her and confirmed the pregnancy. She couldn't wait to share the news, so she rode out to meet you."

The brother and sister hugged each other; grieving for the lost child and Caitlin.

"Don't hate us, Ev. We were scared you'd go after Tristan before you healed. Or worse yet, kill yourself if you knew. Tristan disappeared out of Baton Rouge after that. How did you find out?"

"Tristan. He's in New Orleans. He showed up at Thib's tonight. I think he's stalking Caitlin again."

Alli grabbed his arm. "Evariste Arsceneaux, go get her. Go get her right now, and bring her here before something happens."

"I hate to say it, but I agree with your sister." A male voice with a heavy French accent made Alcee's presence in the kitchen known.

"I was starting to wonder when you would show up." Gage wasn't surprised by Alcee's sudden manifestation in the doorway. "Tristan didn't know for sure who Caitlin was until he saw me tonight. Apparently, they've known each other for a while through work."

"I think, mon ami, he knew exactly who she was. He was just waiting on confirmation." Alcee disagreed. "That, or it's a large coincidence that he's been watching her since she arrived. Azard saw him lingering around the market, and another vampire spotted him at the airport when Caitlin's flight arrived the day prior. He's tracking her again. We need to know why."

"You don't think she was a random kill for him." Gage always thought Caitlin was in the wrong place at the wrong time all these years.

"Non. How did they say it on the cop show yesterday?" Alcee tried to recall modern-day phrasing. "I think he's got a hard on for you or your lady friend."

Gage and Alli laughed. With Alcee's thick accent and age, the statement just didn't sound right.

Alcee shot them both an annoyed stare.

Allister tried her best to stifle her laughter. "And what were you watching? Doesn't sound like *Law and Order*."

"*Miami CSI.* I don't watch *Law and Order*." Alcee rolled his eyes at her.

Gage coughed, hiding another laugh before it came out. "What do you think, Dugas? Should I go wake her and bring her here?"

"If I were you, I would climb into bed with her and make love to her until she couldn't live without you or you died of exhaustion, then bring her here," Alcee answered with true vampire flare.

Gage shook his head. "One would think as old as you are sex wouldn't be such a high priority in life."

"Sexuality is what a vampire is! We are creatures damned to a soulless existence, sustained on blood and lust alone. Banished from light and the mortal realm. You being the one exception that I know of."

"With me being the one exception, let's try this again. Do I need to go get Caitlin?"

"Zut alors, non! She is safe but bring her to D'Orme soon. Tristan can't enter its doors, so it is the one place he cannot get to her. Then, then, mon ami, you can ravage her in your own bed as much as you like."

"You've been visiting Marie again, haven't you?" Gage knew she was the only creature that made Alcee's sole purpose in life sex.

"Oui! Je brûle pour mon amour. Toujours. Three blissful nights..." Alcee leaned against the wall with his eyes closed, thinking about Marie.

"Spare us the details." Gage cut off any further comments.

"Any ideas on how to get Caitlin's old memories back?" Alli asked the vampire who had saved and guided Gage over the years.

"Amour, Allister. Romance is the only tool Evariste needs."

"Don't get him started, Alli. He's like a drug addict, except for him it's love and sex after feeding off Marie." Gage didn't want her question leading to a tale of sensual vampire exploits from the previous three nights.

Alcee smacked Gage upside the back of the head. "Insolent youth! If you would give into your true nature, your ladylove would be at your side, and we would not be having this conversation right now. Oui, Alli, I have the perfect solution to help your brother get his wife back."

"This ought to be good. Let's hear it." Gage was ready to be entertained by one of Alcee's wild ideas.

"You take her back in time and—"

"In my magic time machine," Gage interrupted, causing Allister to giggle.

"As I was saying before I was so rudely interrupted, take her back in time, to when you first met. Put her in a ball gown and waltz her around the floor while you are dressed in your finest cravat and coat. Then take her on—"

"I got rid of those two centuries ago." Gage cut him off again.

"Shhh, Evariste. I am not finished telling you what you must do. Be quiet until I am done speaking." Alcee recomposed himself after giving Gage a scolding look. "Take her on a carriage ride along the Mississippi with the moon on high. Whisper sweet nothings in her ear while stealing a kiss in the garden."

"How romantic." Alli sighed at the imagery Alcee created in her head.

"And how exactly do you recommend I do that in the age of blue jeans and automobiles? The carriages in the Quarter don't drive along the river anymore, and I am not hiring one to come all the way out here for a scheme that most likely would never work on a modern woman."

Alcee dropped an invitation on the table in front of Gage. "It will work, and you do not need to hire anyone. La Soirée Nocturne à Shadow Oaks is on Friday."

Gage frowned. "A vampire ball? Are you honestly suggesting I take her to the Shadow Oaks where she could end up being someone's hors d'oeuvre?"

"You wound me with your insinuation, Evariste. You and Caitlin attended that ball regularly, and no one ate either of you for hors d'oeuvres."

"That was before I knew who attended that particular ball."

"Oh, Ev, it's perfect!" Alli read the invitation. "Take her. Marie and I can get the proper gown for her, and you still have your suits upstairs. Jeanette and I pulled them out of the donation bin."

"Since he does not need to go shopping for a new cravat and coat, I will send Marie on the morrow to start determining how to make Caitlin tres magnifique!"

"Hold on! I didn't agree to any of this." Gage tried to stop the wheels put into motion.

"She'll love it, Evariste! What woman doesn't love a romantic night out? We'll go with you and make sure she has a great time," Alli said, clearly excited about attending the ball. "Please do it."

"Trust me, mon ami! Have I ever steered you wrong?" Alcee waltzed with Alli around the kitchen. "And before you say it, other than that one time in Baton Rouge."

"Come on, Ev. When has Evariste Arsceneaux not taken advantage of rare opportunities? Isn't that how you're made your fortune over the years?" Alli championed Alcee's cause.

"Fine, as long as it's not a repeat of Baton Rouge." Gage gave in. He most likely fought a losing battle, Undoubtedly, Alli would tell Renee and Jeanette in the morning, and then he'd have all three of them nagging him to go. "And *only* if Caitlin doesn't already have plans. She has to agree to the evening out. I can't drag her out of her hotel to Vacherie unlike others here might do."

"I wouldn't drag her!" Alcee stopped dancing with Alli then teleported behind Gage to loudly whisper in his ear. "I would use the talents Lilith gifted us with to convince her to come to the ball. Seduction isn't such a vile tool to wield for all of us."

"I want my wife to legitimately desire my company, Alcee. She isn't just some random woman I'm interested in."

CONCERNED ABOUT CAITLIN'S SAFETY, he checked in on her one last time before going to bed. She slept peacefully in her hotel room.

"Sweet dreams," Gage whispered, gently brushing away a lock of hair that had fallen in her face.

Maybe I should take Alcee's advice for once. He contemplated undressing and sliding into bed beside her. Resisting the urge to do so, he left a set of keys to D'Orme and a note on her nightstand then returned home.

Girls' Day Out

C aitlin's alarm woke her. The loud, screeching electronica song made her want to throw her phone across the room. Still half asleep, she reached out to the nightstand, searching for it. Her fingers found a set of keys and paper instead of the phone. Had the hotel staff come into her room, leaving the keys and card on her nightstand and she hadn't noticed due to how late she came in yesterday? Confused, she sat up and opened the envelope.

Caitlin,

I hope you slept well. I wanted to extend a formal invitation for you to stay at the Maison D'Orme. You'll find a set of keys with this card. Feel free to come and go as you please.

Hoping to see you soon.

EBA

P.S. My breakfasts are so much better than the Pauger's.

Caitlin chuckled at the PS. She picked up her cell phone and dialed Gage's number.

"Hello?" His voice was raspy on the other end of the phone.

"Good morning. I didn't mean to wake you."

"It's okay that you did." Gage's yawn filled the room when she switched the phone to speaker. "So, what's your answer?"

"I don't know. The continental breakfast is really good here."

"Obviously, you haven't had mine yet. My crawfish omelet puts theirs to shame."

Caitlin could picture him grinning while holding his phone to his ear. "While that sounds tasty, I have to say the beds here are very, very comfortable."

Gage softly laughed. "I can guarantee you will never want to leave mine once you've stayed a night in it."

His inviting tone and thickened accent sent Caitlin's pulse racing. Her lips tingled while she recalled the kiss by his truck at the shipyards. "I may just have to change accommodations then."

A loud knock and someone shouting, "Caitlin, get up, girl!" shattered her fantasy of being in bed with Gage.

Gage groaned. "I can also promise you ruckus like that is absolutely not tolerated at Maison D'Orme. Our guests are carefully screened, and the riffraff are promptly tossed out before they can cause trouble."

Caitlin laughed. "Should I answer the door?"

"I would, or those three are likely to break it down, especially if Marie is with them."

"Who's Marie?"

"She's more of a what than a who. Good luck with them." Gage ended the call.

Caitlin forced herself out of bed and went to open the door.

Renee led the four women into her room. "Good Morning, Caitlin! You need to get dressed. We have a busy day ahead of us!"

"We do?" Caitlin didn't recall making any plans with them as she shut the door.

"Bonjour, Caitlin. I am Marie. We have much to do before Friday." A tall, blonde woman introduced herself.

"Friday?" Now, Caitlin was really puzzled. She didn't have any plans for Friday.

"Mon petite choux, Monsieur Arsceneaux is escorting you to La Soirée Nocturne," Marie informed her. "Stand up straight, so I can see what I am working with."

"La Soirée Nocturne?"

"A ball, at Shadow Oaks!" Alli squealed, excited.

Caitlin jumped back when Marie tilted her face up and began measuring her. "What are you doing?"

"Conjuring my design." Marie continued her inspection of Caitlin. "But I need a few measurements first. You are definitely a nice palette to start creating on. Nous irons au spa for a massage and haircut."

"No haircuts!" Caitlin protested, gathering her hair in her hands.

"My apologies. My English is not so good. I meant trim. I would not cut off tes cheveux. It is too beautiful to do so. Girls, help her pack her bags, so we can get on with the day. The hotel can drop them at the house."

Alli tossed Caitlin a pair of yoga pants and a T-shirt. "Here, put these on."

"Would someone please explain what is going on?" Caitlin almost shouted as Gage's sisters threw stuff into her suitcase and carry-on bag.

"As I said, Ev's taking you to a ball on Friday! And you are going to stay at the D'Orme instead of here for the rest of your trip," Alli reiterated.

"I'm what? I never agreed to do that."

"Isn't all of it romantic?" Jeanette dreamily asked, sitting on the bed.

"I'm sorry to disappoint you all, but I didn't bring any formal wear with me. And I have work to do while I'm in town. Not to mention, your brother never invited me to some ball."

"We're here to do that on his behalf," Renee said.

"Gage is a grown ass man. He can ask me himself, and what if I don't want to attend?"

"Of course, you want to attend! What idiot turns down an invite from a gentleman who is interested enough to indulge a woman in a night of romance and to open his home to her? You also do not have any work to do today. Alcee rescheduled your meeting to tomorrow. Now, get dressed, tout de suite! We have shopping to do," Marie chided her.

"I haven't showered yet. Why don't you guys come back in an hour?"

"Go get dressed!" Alli shoved her toward the bathroom.

"You will bathe in rose-scented water after your massage and hair trim. Just brush your teeth and put your clothes on!" Marie called after her and Alli.

"Trust her, girl! Marie's the best stylist this side of the Mississippi!" Renee yelled as Caitlin shut the door.

Insanity and tenacity must run in the Arsceneaux family. Caitlin almost wished Sean had sent one of the other paralegals or field team members to NOLA instead of her. Who invites a total stranger to stay at their home or drags one out like an old friend on a shopping spree?

Caitlin brushed her teeth and changed clothes, hoping the four women would magically vanish. No wonder Gage hated his sisters at times. If she had such exasperating siblings, she'd get annoyed with them too. Caitlin yanked on her pants and swapped her nightgown for a T-shirt. Maybe she could climb out the small bathroom window to escape the unplanned girls' day out. Weren't there continuous balconies along the backside of the third story? Damn her luck! The stupid window wouldn't open wide enough for her to climb through and escape the four women doing god knows what in her hotel room.

"Are you finished, yet? The car is waiting!" Marie called from the other side of the door. "Honestly, how long does it take you humans to brush your teeth."

"You humans?" Caitlin glanced toward the door. What species did the French woman think she was? Honestly, she encountered the strangest people in her travels.

When Caitlin came out of the bathroom, all of her stuff was packed. Marie was on the phone with the front desk arranging for someone to pick up Caitlin's suitcases and deliver them to D'Orme.

SPOTTING a tray of pastries and fruit near the front desk, Caitlin's stomach growled. She grabbed a Danish as the women rushed her toward the door.

Marie slapped it out of her hand.

"Hey! I'm hungry!" Caitlin snapped at Marie, watching the airborne oblong, fruit-filled sourdough treat sail through the air.

The concierge nonchalantly caught it as it whizzed past his right side.

"Nice reflexes!" Caitlin complimented the man whose only response was a raised brow and a clipped thank you.

Marie scowled, tugging on Caitlin's arm to get her moving again. "I will find you something healthy to eat. We do not need you damaging gowns with sticky fingers when you try them on."

"There are these neat inventions called wet naps and running water that can clean my fingers off. Ever heard of them? Besides, I'm starving, and I wasn't the one who scheduled an impromptu dress fitting."

In a fit of indignation, Marie jerked Caitlin closer, halting the group again as she glared down at her. "You will get lunch at midday. A healthy lunch. This ball requires period costumes. You cannot expect a seamstress to work on only an hour's notice nor do they appreciate customers who are late for appointments as we will be if you keep being obstinate with me. They also do not enjoy customers with frosting-covered fingers who ruin their gowns. Nor do we need you gorging yourself on doughnuts after your fitting so the dress doesn't fit in a few days. Out to the car!"

Marie now steered her through the lobby and to a waiting car.

"I'm on vacation. That's exactly when one gorges themselves on doughnuts or whatever they like!"

DESPITE THE ROCKY START, Caitlin mostly enjoyed the time out shopping and being pampered. She certainly never experienced a day quite like it before. While Marie and Gage's sisters were distracted, she slipped out of the private spa room and called Gage.

"Hanging in there?" he asked, concerned with it being late in the day.

"Mostly. It has been kind of a fun day," Caitlin advised in a whisper.

"Why are you whispering then?"

"Because I'm supposed to be relaxing and cleansing my aura of negative energy or my chakra or something. Marie threatened to take my phone if she caught me on it again today."

"Non, Caitlin!" Marie appeared out of nowhere and ripped her cell phone from her hands. The woman was livid their private meditation session was interrupted. "Evariste, you may speak with her tonight! We are busy at the moment."

Gage laughed before speaking in a mocking tone. "My *apolgeeezz*, Marie. I did not know you were *zo bizzee*. I only wished to *zay elo* to Caitlin and make sure she *iz* okay knowing how *zcaree* you can be."

"I am not scary! And I do not appreciate you mocking me like a child, Evariste."

Hitting Below The Belt

G age looked at his phone after Marie's chastising and the signal going dead. Poor Caitlin would probably never forgive him if she learned he approved Marie's terrorizing of her that day. After another hour in the office, he headed home. Surprisingly, he managed to beat his sisters and Caitlin to the house. He changed into jeans and a shirt to relax for the evening. The women finally walked through the doors of D'Orme around five.

"Hello, beautiful," Gage greeted Caitlin, taking her hand and giving her a kiss on the cheek.

"Did the gowns arrive?" Marie loudly asked as she sauntered into the living room.

"*Zey* are all upstairs." Gage's overdone French accent earned a look of sheer disdain from Marie. "With you taking all day, did you buy out the whole costume shop?"

"The gowns are from a seamstress shop, Evariste, not a costume shop. We are not dressing up for Halloween! You will more than thank me on Friday for my selections. Then, I will be gracious, unlike you, when you offer a groveling apology for your continued antagonism." Marie turned on her heel then marched back out to the car.

"I wouldn't hold your breath on any sort of groveling or apology.

No matter how pleased I am with your selections." Gage earned a second angry glare as Marie reached the open car door.

She rolled her eyes and loudly huffed at him before muttering under her breath, climbing into the backseat of the car.

The driver shook a finger at Gage but laughed at the same time. "The two of you are like overgrown children."

"We're heading out, too. Love you." Alli hugged him. Jeanette and Renee followed suit.

Gage frowned, watching them file out the door one by one. Renee waved then slammed the front door shut. That was unexpected. He figured they'd stay and ply Caitlin with a million more questions or annoyingly try to play matchmaker for the rest of the night with him and the redhead.

"I hope Marie and my sisters didn't overwhelm you too much."

Caitlin smiled. "They were pretty over the top, but I survived. And they didn't leave me much choice about coming here."

Gage didn't want her at D'Orme if she didn't feel comfortable there. "You don't have to stay, Caitlin. I can drive you back to your hotel and explain to the front desk that you were held hostage by a bunch of local terrorists who forced you to vacate your room."

"Nothing's gone as expected this entire trip, especially when it comes to you. I suppose a trial run at a new place with a talented, good-looking chef is just par for the course. Your breakfasts better be as good as the dinner I'm expecting tonight."

Gage laughed, bringing her to him. "Breakfast will be the best you've ever eaten, Miss DeDanann." He sampled those sweet lips which always tempted him. "Although dinner may not be up to our normal standards. It's been a long day, and I don't feel like cooking. Is pizza good for you?"

"Works for me."

"Good. It should be here in about twenty minutes. I ordered an everything along with a spinach, tomato, pepper, eggplant, and pineapple one as Alli said those are the toppings you like."

"Wow. Using your sisters for reconnaissance? You're ruthless, Arsceneaux."

Gage chuckled. "If I was ruthless, I would have left off the pineapple. You know that's a cardinal sin, don't you? Every Italian I know would ban you from entering Italy for at least a decade if they saw you putting pineapple on pizza."

"We're in the US, and I like it. When in Italy, I'll eat as the Italians do." Caitlin rolled her eyes. She should have guessed he'd give her grief with food and drink being near to religion for him. "Purist."

Gage scoffed. "That is Chef de Cuisine to you."

"Are you really or are you just making stuff up again?"

"I'm really a trained chef. I enjoy cooking, so figured why not go to culinary school? I even worked for Fontenot for a while. How do you think I so easily got the reservation at Masquerades?"

Caitlin skeptically eyed him. "How does a CEO have the time to moonlight as a chef and go to culinary school?"

"I'm a man of many talents who hates twiddling his thumbs."

AFTER THEY FINISHED THEIR PIZZA, Gage turned the TV on. Caitlin laid back against his chest as he flipped through channels looking for something to watch. A pirate movie he hadn't seen before popped up. He briefly paused to check it out.

"Oh! *On Crimson Sails*. This is actually decent." Caitlin sat up then re-snuggled into his side. "Not to mention the main character is hot."

Gage snorted, staring at the pirate in dingy clothes with long braided black hair and fake dirt or grime smeared across his face. "You find that attractive?"

"In an earthy way. Not to mention that is Brian Sanderson. He was just voted the sexiest man alive this year. And there is just something about a pirate."

"Women always go gaga over these Hollywood pirates. You wouldn't over a real one. Between the heat, backbreaking work, and lack of bathing for days in those heavy clothes, Captain Whatever His Name Is would more than likely reek, not to mention have horrible breath."

"Funny. I could see you being a sexy pirate after yesterday."

His lips pursed as he gave her a doubtful look. "Oh really?"

"Really." She sat up, smiling. "I can picture you with longer, shoulder-length hair, wearing boots, breeches, and a white shirt billowing in the wind while standing at the helm of a tall ship." She closed her eyes, describing the vivid image in her mind. "Captain Evariste Arsceneaux. That even sounds like a pirate's name."

"Would you sail the seven seas and plunder with me, lady?" Gage deepened his voice and used a mock pirate accent making her eyes open again.

"Absolutely, Captain Arsceneaux." She kissed him then laughed.

"Are you fraternizing with the captain, my lovely first mate? That's a dangerous thing to do with a scallywag of a pirate." Gage teased, delighted by the kiss. "And whatever will the rest of me crew think of said professional lady pirate doing such a thing?"

"Pirates don't have scruples."

"Ahhh...now that's where you're wrong. Pirates and privateers may have had poor hygiene, but they had strict codes of conduct, especially at sea. Though if ye be willing to proclaim us a happy couple, one officially dating, then there'd be no concerns amongst the crew about what we do."

"I'll think about it." Caitlin turned her attention back to the TV.

"Then there be no more kisses for ye here until yer thinkin' is done." Gage noticed how her eyes shifted briefly in his direction and she huffed but didn't acknowledge the remark. Clearly, their conversation was over. He struck out again with getting her to commit.

An hour into the movie, the vampire within stirred, craving the sweet scent wafting up into his nostrils. The longer they sat quietly together, the stronger the scent became. He closed his eyes, trying to ignore the soft percussion of her heartbeat now rumbling in his ears. Predatory instinct slowly took control. He nuzzled her hair then trailed his mouth down to her neck. The sweet, floral smell only grew stronger when his nose passed just under her ear. Her sharp inhale of breath tempted him all the more as he gently grasped her head before running his tongue over that sensitive spot. A honey-like taste filled his mouth. He quickly identified what he was tasting—pheromone powder. Oh, his sisters and Marie hit below the belt doing this! The powder was everywhere on Caitlin's skin, and the same strong perfume in the silken strands teasing his cheek meant they used a pheromone shampoo on her at the salon. He took in the various shades of cooper, bronze, scarlet, and orange intermingled, giving her hair its flame-colored hue before taking a deep breath, letting the tantalizing fragrance seduce his senses further.

"Caitlin, mon coeur," he muttered under his breath before kissing her. His hands slid down her side. She turned her body into his, eagerly caressing his chest and back the longer their kissing went on. His fingers crept up her skin under her shirt. She unabashedly climbed into his lap. Those violet eyes of hers half-closed in a hazy daze of desire destroyed all his self-control. He stripped her shirt off and then ran his forefinger along the edge of her bra before grasping her breast. The soft moan that sounded in her throat urged him on. Her hips slid down his growing erection after he pushed aside the silky material of her bra cup, so his thumb could tease her nipple until it puckered. The heady scent of her arousal mixed with the pheromones brought the beast completely to the surface, but she didn't seem to notice the fangs her tongue periodically scrapped against as they kissed.

Gage teleported them upstairs to his bed. Trying to abate the ravenous craving twisting his gut, he slowly undid her pants then slid them down her legs. She deserved to be pleasured, not just ungratefully devoured by a depraved beast. He gently grasp her calf and kissed the side of her knee, his lips leisurely ascended higher. The sigh that came from Caitlin twisted them into a satisfied smile. Oh, he definitely was going to savor each delicious inch of her. Even if it was a whole new level of hell his immortal soul had to endure.

"Jesus," he growled, discovering the honey-like substance on her inner thighs. His tongue snaked out, sampling the creamy white thigh his hand cradled. It took all he had not to sink his teeth into her soft skin. He hadn't taken blood from anyone before and wasn't going to start with the woman he loved. A husky chuckle escaped his lips just before he pressed his mouth to her; running the flat of his tongue along the soft cotton of her underwear; licking and teasing until he could easily taste her through them. Another violent urge to shift his head slightly and sample the sanguine life-giving fluid from the femoral artery only millimeters away prompted him to move up her body. Her eyes fluttered open and met his as he stared down at her in the dark before his mouth descended upon hers. He focused on kissing her to keep his fangs away from the larger veins now taking on a shimmering shade of lapis blue; the rich, alluring color inviting him to do what he shouldn't. Her breaths came in rapid pants as his fingers probed between her folds while his thumb massaged her clit.

"Gage!" she called out, squirming beside him.

Loving how she bucked against his hand, slick and wanting only what he could gift her, he continued massaging her until a fine sheen covered her skin. The beast in him repeatedly screamed for satisfaction. He again denied it. Damn, he missed moments like this. He could spend hours watching her flushed and nude, lost in pure bliss that his touch created. "Come for me, cher. I want to see that lovely face of yours contort in pleasure from my touching you."

A few seconds later her body stiffened then trembled, a loud cry left her lips.

"God, I want you, Caitlin. You're tormenting me to no end being here." Gage guided her hand down the length of his now painfully throbbing cock. "Tell me what you want, cher."

"You." Caitlin gasped, continuing to stroke him. "I want you, inside me, right now."

That breathy answer and her hands had him almost coming already. Gage spread her thighs apart and settled himself between them. He needed to claim her, to bury himself inside her again and again until their very existence slipped away. "And after I take you? What do you want from me then?"

"I don't know. Snuggles? Does after even really matter at the moment?"

A groan rumbled in his throat. "It matters a great deal, cher. I don't do anything halfway nor am I the kind of man who has one-night stands or casual flings. It's all or nothing, Cate. Now, what's your answer?"

Puzzlement disappointingly replaced the rapture previously on her face.

"I don't, I don't know, Gage. I want you, but beyond that—"

He pulled away from her and rolled out of bed. "Let me know when you figure it out. And keep the damn door locked, so I don't find myself back in this position tonight."

As if door locks would prevent him from entering. He almost laughed at himself for telling her to lock the door.

She sat up after the door slammed behind him. "But I'm in your room."

"I'll sleep in the guest room," he yelled back, pissed he allowed things to go that far. Damn Marie and his sisters for setting him up like that. It was going to be a long night between the relentless erection and denying his carnal nature the meal it endlessly craved the past few days.

He spotted the satin gift bag on the guest room dresser as he entered it. Quickly double checking that the pheromone powder was in it, he swiped it off the dresser with an annoyed growl then walked down the stairs, out of the house, and tossed it in the trashcan outside. The wicked powder couldn't cause him anymore suffering for the night from under the heavy lid and the week-old trash dulling its sweet smell. It would vanish with the other rotting refuse from D'Orme when the trash was picked up tomorrow.

He let out an annoyed sigh after laying down in bed and pulled a sheet over himself. Caitlin's lavender and rose lotion lingered around the room. At least it didn't turn him into a rabid animal. Still, it brought on a pang of loneliness. His mind drifted to thoughts of her lying naked in his bed. The muffled sound of soft footsteps coming down the hallway runner toward the door interrupted the delightful vision. Somedays he found the heightened senses he inherited from whomever bit him a blessing; tonight, they were a curse.

"Gage." Caitlin's voice softly whispered as she rapped on the door. "Gage, are you awake?"

"Yes?"

"I'm sorry for tonight. I didn't mean to upset you."

"You have nothing to be sorry for, Caitlin. You gave me an honest answer." Gage instantly regretted his earlier words. He shouldn't be pushing her so hard. He had time to win her over before she left New Orleans. If he kept acting like a desperate psychopath, she'd most likely get another hotel room and never speak to him again. "We can talk about it in the morning. It's been an incredibly long day, and I don't want to worsen things between us due to being grumpy and tired, cher."

"It's not that I'm not interested, Gage. I like you, but I'm just not..."

The tremor in her voice and the hurt he sensed from the other side of the door only riled him more. He forced aside his anger. He had obviously upset her. "Not *what*, cher?" he calmly inquired.

"Not," Caitlin hesitated, then forced the rest out. "Not long-term relationship material based on how my previous relationships have gone. My ex's have said I'm too picky and demanding."

"Every one of your ex's is a stupid fool to say such a thing," Gage snapped before he could stop himself. He didn't mean to answer in such a harsh manner, but jealousy now mixed with rage and frustration. The idea of any man using or denigrating his wife fueled the flames which were finally calming before she knocked. He took a deep breath and tried again. "I have high standards too, Cate. We'll figure this out, tomorrow, after some sleep."

"Good night, Gage."

Thank all that was holy she didn't come into the room. He listened to her walk back to his bedroom. The master bedroom door quietly opened; the bottom edge of it brushing across the hallway runner. A second or two later, a short click confirmed she shut the door once more as he'd asked her to do earlier. If Marie and the girls hadn't talked her into coating herself in that damn powder, he'd be beside her, simply holding her for the night to reassure her everything was okay between them.

Going Fishing
❦

G age woke shortly before his alarm went off at 4:30. He rubbed the sleep from his eyes, then texted Alcee that he'd be taking the day off. After splashing some cold water on his face, he put on the jeans and shirt he had been wearing last night then quietly headed to the garage. After flicking on the garage light, he started throwing his fishing tackle and poles into the back of his truck.

"What happened that you are running to the water again, Evariste?" Alcee inquired from behind him, making him jump.

"I need to clear my head." He double-checked that he had everything he needed.

Alcee frowned at him in the dark. "You're short your fishing partner."

Gage snorted. "I don't even know if she knows how to fish, and I'm going to get away from her for a bit." He reached into the trashcan and tossed Alcee the jar of powder. "Your girlfriend and my sisters dumped this all over her at the spa yesterday. I could barely control myself last night. I swear one of these days I'm going to send Marie back to wherever the hell she came from for crap like this."

Alcee chuckled after taking the lid off the powder and getting a whiff of pheromone. "I'd wager Renee or Allister was behind this, not Marie. She prefers oil to powder."

"With the way Caitlin's hair is full of the same thing, I have no doubt Marie contributed to the hot mess the four of them made for me."

"The pheromone has more than likely faded by now. Wake the woman up and take her with you. You have less than a week to convince her to be more than friends, Evariste."

Gage glared over at him from across the truck bed. "I can't do that if the vampire is lusting after her. Do you know how close I came to sinking my teeth into her last night, and not in a good way? The ball is off if this is the type of assistance y'all have planned."

"Maybe sinking your teeth into her isn't such a bad thing." Noting the continued icy glare he received, Alcee tossed the powder back into the trashcan. "I'll make a bargain with you, Evariste. You take Caitlin out on the water with you today, and I will ensure no more shenanigans with Marie or your sisters occurs for the rest of Caitlin's time here."

"That's a herculean task to take on." Gage doubted he could make good on that promise.

"Allow me to worry about that."

Gage heard the annoyed sigh from the other side of the truck when he didn't respond.

"Evariste, trust me, mon ami. Time alone with no distractions is what you and the lady need."

He stared at Alcee, contemplating his offer. The older vampire's eyes held his, waiting to see what he decided. Gage shook his head. He knew the stubborn set of Alcee's jaw well. Alcee wasn't going to leave until he agreed to take Caitlin with him. "Fine. You have yourself a deal."

Alcee vanished. Gage steeled himself for waking Caitlin. The damn pheromone better have faded.

Thankfully, the sickly-sweet smell no longer lingered in the air as it had last night the closer he came to his bedroom. He lightly knocked on the door and called Caitlin's name. The sound of sheets rustling caught his ear, but she didn't say anything. On the off chance she ignored his direction to lock the door, he tried turning the knob. He grinned as the door swung open. She had dangerously left an open invitation to him. Thank goodness he resisted any urge to make up last night.

"Caitlin, cher, it's time to wake up." He gently brushed his knuckle across her cheek, sitting down on the bed beside her.

"Gage? What time is it?" she mumbled, starting to come to and glanced toward his nightstand.

"5:15. Come on, we need to be on the water soon if we're gonna take advantage of the morning bite. We miss the early bite and those reds will be damn hard to catch as they run to deep water later in the day."

"Reds? You're waking me up this early to go fishing?" Caitlin groaned, staring up at him now.

Gage chuckled at her quizzical expression. "You said you'd sail the seven seas with me last night. Or are you recanting on that now?"

The smile on her face confirmed she wasn't. "I can't believe I'm getting up for this. You better have some coffee and breakfast in that truck or boat of yours." Caitlin sat up.

Gage pressed a quick kiss to her forehead. "I'll have both waiting for you. Go get dressed. Wear something you don't mind getting wet and dirty."

Caitlin flipped the covers off herself then sleepily slipped out of bed.

Amused by the naked cartoon character only wearing an oversized set of beads and the slogan party naked stenciled below him on the shirt she had on, Gage grinned. She must have gone through his dresser last night to find something to sleep in. His sisters had bought the shirt for him as a joke after teasing him about needing to loosen up and not work all the time during Mardi Gras earlier in the year. He admired her long, shapely legs as she groggily headed toward the guest room. Her hair wildly falling down around her. If he hadn't already called the marina to have the boat fueled up and waiting, he'd be tempted to stay home with her instead.

He made them breakfast to go and filled two thermoses of coffee while he waited on her to come downstairs. He just finished tightening down the lid on the second small thermos when a yawning Caitlin shuffled into the kitchen. "Ready, cher?"

"I suppose so. What do I need to bring with me?"

"Your driver's license, so I can get you a fishing license and whatever else you want to take. I have the tackle and gear in the truck along with food and drink for the day. And as requested, breakfast is packed."

"Then I'm ready to go." Caitlin looked down at the small purse in her hand holding her wallet, phone, and sunglasses.

Gage smiled, picking up the paper bag on the counter and the two thermoses. "Your chariot awaits."

Caitlin chuckled, following him out to his truck. He opened the door for her then handed her the bag holding an egg white, veggie, and avocado breakfast croissant. "And café au lait to wash everything down for the lady."

"Thank you, handsome." She gave him a quick kiss, taking the thermos he held up before he shut the door.

The kiss brightened the dark mood Gage was in. Maybe taking her with him wasn't such a bad idea after all.

Remy

Gage grasped Caitlin's hand, helping her onto the deck of the gently bobbing boat. She put on her life jacket while he started the engine then slowly idled away from the landing.

"Make sure anything loose is put away," Gage cautioned, giving her a second to make sure nothing could fly out of the boat once they were out of the no wake zone.

"Nothing's out." Caitlin enjoyed the breeze against her face as the boat picked up speed. The sky started to lighten. Gage easily navigated shallow waters, heading to his favorite early morning fishing spot. "I'd get lost out here, and you're just flying through the dark like it's no big deal."

Gage laughed. "I've been fishing these waters all my life. GPS also helps."

Caitlin sat on the deck, drinking the rest of her café au lait, and taking in the colorful sunrise as Gage fished. It really was beautiful and peaceful out on the water. She could see why Gage sought refuge here or on the bayous when he needed to escape the problems life and work brought his way.

Neither of them said anything, both lost in their own thoughts. Gage cast out then let the line sink, waiting for that first strike to come in. He didn't have to wait long. Caitlin watched as he set the hook and fought the fish, reeling the line in then letting it run for a bit before working to bring the fish back to the boat.

"Aren't you a lovely catch!" Gage complimented the fish once it cleared the side of the boat. He popped the hook from its mouth.

Caitlin walked over to him as he laid it on a metal ruler. "Does he need to be a certain length?"

"Yep. Reds need to be between sixteen and twenty-seven inches to be kept. This fish is definitely going to be a good dinner tonight. Do you like redfish?"

Caitlin noted the bright red and golden color of fish's scales. "I do indeed. They are pretty fish."

"Yes, they are, and damn good eating, too." Gage carried the fish over to the ice-filled cooler and laid it inside. "Nice start to the day. You ready to fish?"

"I think I'll just watch you for a bit."

"You aren't afraid of getting your hands dirtied by the bait, are you, cher?" Gage teased, rebaiting his hook before casting out again.

"Not at all. I'm just enjoying the morning." Caitlin watched how he let the line slowly sink as he had the first time.

After a few casts and not getting any more bites, he pulled the line in, started the engine, and headed to another nearby spot.

Caitlin hated the awkward tension between them. By the way Gage intently focused on his fishing, he more than likely felt it too. As the boat slowed down, she decided to address the cause of it. "Gage, I'm sorry about whatever I did to upset you last night. I never meant to lead you on."

She noted the frown on his face and heard him loudly exhale. He shut the engine off and tossed the anchor overboard before looking at her again. In just a few days, she had learned to give him time to sort through his thoughts whenever she tweaked one of his nerves.

"I know you didn't, and you don't need to apologize. Hell, I was the asshole last night." Gage stared out at the expanse of blue and green water, trying to get his emotional bearings. He'd had many uncomfortable discussions in his life, but none as disconcerting as the one before them now. Screw it. They were going to have to have this conversation sooner or later. "Cate, there's something you should know about me."

"Okay." Caitlin braced herself for whatever was coming with the strained tone he used. The tension from the night prior returned in his face and shoulders. His refusing to look at her warned it was a serious matter he wasn't comfortable with himself.

"I was married once. Years ago."

Caitlin assumed by his pausing he was ashamed of that for whatever reason. "Divorced?"

"No." He took off his sunglasses, so they looked one another squarely in the eye. "Widowed."

A bit surprised, Caitlin didn't know what to say. How do you respond to a man revealing his wife died? "Widowed? How did she—"

"Murdered." Gage cut off her inquiry. He briefly broke eye contact with her again.

Caitlin instinctively reached for his hand. He gently squeezed her fingers once her hand came in contact with his. "I'm so sorry, Gage."

His chest expanded as he took a deep breath before he looked over at her. "Her death is the reason why I'm an all or nothing guy. Caitlin, I like you, an awful lot. I haven't had feelings this strong for a woman since my wife. Even so, I refuse to be some random vacation fling. I'm too old for that shit. And as much as I want you, if you're just having fun the two weeks you are here, it's better we keep things on the more innocent side than where they went last night. Not pressuring you into anything, cher. Just trying to put the brakes on before either of us gets hurt or does something we'll regret a day or two later."

"I understand. Since we're sharing things, it isn't that I don't want to date you. It also isn't just the whole unprofessionalism aspect either, Evariste." She hated how his brows slightly rose in surprise; his lips tucked inward before leveling out in a straight line as his jaw re-tensed and his gaze turned toward the water. "If you can't tell, relationships and I, well, we just don't work. Thought I had found the one and the asshole dumped me for a job promotion."

"A job promotion?" Evariste quizzically stared at her. "You mean you broke up due to him wanting to pursue a new job somewhere else or his company relocating him someplace if he accepted the promotion?"

"No. I mean exactly what I said. My ex had the choice of either continuing to date me, and by doing so, be passed over for an executive position or dump me and become a VP. The company didn't relocate him at all. He just couldn't continue to date a subordinate, even one he intended to marry."

"And the bastard chose the job over you after proposing?"

"He did. At least we hadn't gone down the aisle. A divorce would have been much messier than a breakup. I quit my old job as I couldn't stand to see him around the office. I moved back to Virginia after Sean hired me. You don't want to be the rebound guy having to deal with the baggage a breakup like that one created."

Stunned, Evariste shook his head. "How long has it been since that happened?"

"Four years." Caitlin frowned, thinking about how Sean warned her Liam was a douchebag, but she figured Sean was just being the overprotective guardian he had always been with any guy she dated. He and Gram seemed to compete with one another in who could be the first to scare off whoever she dated. But Sean pegged Liam accurately in every one of his complaints about the guy. She had been either too blind to see it or just didn't want to.

"Rebounds usually don't occur that far out after a breakup." Gage thoughtfully stared at her. "I think I'm safe from being one, and even if I'm wrong about that, I'm willing to take the risk. If you can put up with a grouchy, at times temperamental workaholic who prefers fish and the sea to people, I'm damn good at getting things to work that didn't for others. Not to mention, my superpower is making things last —like Lagniappe Shipping & Ag. My ideas also transformed Thib's from being on the brink of ruin into the most successful jazz club in the city. Just imagine what I could do for you, *if* you'd give me a chance."

Caitlin laughed. "You're such a humble guy, Evariste."

"I'm not bragging, cher, just trying to prove a point." Gage grinned, his eyebrows raised as he waited to see if she would give him the chance he hoped for.

"Think you can teach me to fish?" Caitlin picked up one of the large rods he had laid down on the side of the boat.

"If I could teach Renee to cook, so she quit burning ice cubes when we were younger, I think I can teach you how to cast a line and bring a fish to the boat." Gage stood behind her, unhooked the artificial lure from the small loop holding it in place, reeled up the slack then settled the rod handle in her hands. "You're a hell of a lot smarter than my sister and a fast learner."

Caitlin laughed as he helped her cast out. He wrapped his arms around her waist, instructing her on how to tease the line just right while slowly reeling in to tempt any nearby fish to bite.

ONCE THEY CAUGHT a limit of reds, Gage turned the boat back toward the marina.

"Are we in salt water or fresh with where we are?"

"Out here, we're in brackish. Salt takes over about a half hour's run south, just past the salt marshes. It starts turning to fresh water when we get to the marina."

"Is that why you didn't take the boat that's in the side garage?" Caitlin tried to learn a little more about Gage's interests.

"That's a bass boat, cher. While it can handle brackish waters, it's designed for fresh. This one is called a center console boat and is designed for fresh and salt water fishing. If the reds weren't biting here, I would've run into the Gulf for some offshore fishing to try and catch them."

"So, you have two boats?"

"Three. The bass boat, this one, and a john boat I take out in smaller bodies of water when I'm just perch fishing."

"No pirogue?" Caitlin brought another big smile to his face.

"I'm impressed you know what a pirogue is. And I have one of those too, but it needs some repairs made to it. It's in the old barn at D'Orme."

Caitlin watched a crane fly up from the tall reeds they passed. "Fishing seems like an expensive hobby."

"It can be."

"I still don't get you, Evariste." She looked back over at him, grinning and enjoying being behind the console with the wind in his hair in jeans and a T-shirt. A total contrasting picture to the stern, well-dressed businessman she had seen in news articles and online photographs before coming to New Orleans.

"What's there not to get? I'm a pretty simple, straightforward guy." Gage slowed the speed of the boat to clearly hear whatever her answer was.

"No, you're not. It's like someone threw a grumpy, worldly elitist, a redneck, and a foodie into a blender then turned it on, and out popped you. One minute you're a cold, shrewd businessman who likes dining at five-star establishments and lecturing folks on their choice of pizza toppings, the next you're a crazy Cajun, grinning away while driving a boat over the waterways of Louisiana at sixty miles per hour."

Gage loudly laughed at the way she described him. "Welcome to doing business in the South. You'll meet a lot of men like me if you hang around down here long enough. And while I'm a bit OCD about things and have particular tastes, I'm not an elitist. I think you'll discover I'm far from it the more you get to know me."

The marina came into view as the boat glided around a gently curving bend.

"Need any help?" Caitlin asked, not sure how she could actually help Gage out as he tied the boat to the dock.

"I've got it, cher." He straightened after giving the rope a final tug then kissed the woman standing beside him. "Why don't you head back to the truck while I unload the cooler and a few other things?"

"You sure?"

"Positive. My keys are in the console by the steering wheel. Go get the AC running, so we don't have a steamy drive home."

"A steamy drive home sounds fun." Caitlin pulled his keys out.

Gage looked back over his shoulder at her. "I thought we agreed to keep things PG until we figure out where this is headed."

"Making out and heavy petting doesn't cross into the R or NC-17 realm from what I understand."

"Go get your ass in the truck before you start something that gets us both in trouble again."

Caitlin laughed at how he grinned before double-checking that the lid of the cooler was locked shut. She started up the dock toward the parking lot. A loud hiss stopped her cold. One of the largest alligators she had ever seen blocked the entire end of the dock. A second hiss warned her that she wasn't making it to the parking lot.

"Gage!" she shouted, not knowing what to do.

GAGE SPUN around with the panicked way she called his name. He looked slightly ahead of her and saw the angry alligator. He grabbed the cooler and jumped from the boat, slamming the cooler down on the dock as he whistled and yelled at the alligator. It took a few steps forward. Its tail lashing back and forth when it did. Gage slammed the cooler down harder so the bang it made traveled the length of the dock.

"Come back to the boat, cher. Right now," Gage calmly instructed before shouting and stomping his feet again.

When Caitlin turned and ran toward him, the alligator followed.

Gage caught Caitlin around the waist and heaved her into the boat then turned to confront the alligator stalking her.

"Don't you even think about it, Remy!" Gage bellowed, waving his arms at the old alligator that enjoyed periodically terrorizing folks when they pulled into the marina.

The alligator actually froze in place but opened its mouth, uttering a cross between a grunt and hiss. Gage kept his eyes on Remy as he reached into a side locker on the boat. "Go on, get out of here!"

Caitlin watched Gage coolly confront the alligator as if he did such a thing every day. Amazingly, the alligator didn't attack and actually backed up a bit.

"Remy, so help me. You better get off the damn dock right now."

The gator took a couple rapid steps forward, grunting and bellowing at Gage. The loud click of a round being loaded into place drew Caitlin's eyes down to the rifle he held. She hadn't even noticed he had pulled a weapon from the compartment until now with how flustered the encounter with the alligator left her.

"Don't test me, you cantankerous overgrown lizard. I'll turn you into a pair of boots like I did Emile when he got uppity."

The alligator barreled forward. The loud crack from the gun being fired made Caitlin jump. Gage cleared the chamber then set up a second shot should he need it. Thankfully, the gator flopped down dead on the dock a few feet from Gage.

A game warden and one of the marina staff ran down the dock toward them.

"You all right?" the warden asked, staring down at what was Remy.

"Fine. He went after the lady and me." Gage lowered the rifle then handed it to the warden.

"I saw the whole thing, Evariste, and was headed over to shoot him myself since he was openly going after you two. No need to turn over the gun. Though, I do have to issue a warning for shooting him out of season, but you don't have to worry about going to jail today." The warden returned the weapon to him.

Gage chuckled. "It was easier for a man to protect himself before all these regulations."

The game warden smiled and nodded his head. "Just be thankful I know you well, and my word carries some weight with the boss. Otherwise, I'd be hauling you in. A hundred and twenty days behind bars isn't the end of the world, but it isn't a picnic either."

"You'd really throw someone in jail for fending off an alligator attack?" Caitlin couldn't believe the game warden would do such a thing. "I'd understand doing that if he had been poaching, but in this case?"

"Ma'am, state law is pretty strict about these matters. Normally, someone shoots an alligator out of season, and without a tag, they're getting fined and going to jail. But with me confirming old Remy attacked two people who did nothing to provoke him, Evariste won't be seeing the inside of a cell."

"She's well worth the jail time, Brian." Gage winked at Caitlin as he spoke.

"I can see that. Ma'am." The game warden tipped the brim of his hat to Caitlin before turning to face Gage again. "I'll let you get back to unloading. Steven, help me drag this carcass off the dock."

Gage picked up the cooler then walked with Caitlin over to his truck.

"I can't believe that just happened, and that someone named the alligator. Why would the owner let it hang around the marina if it was aggressive?"

"Oh, Remy's been here a long time. He didn't use to be aggressive, but he's gotten more and more testy the older he's gotten. Today is the first I'm aware of that he didn't just run someone off from any spot he suddenly thinks is his. Ignace would have had him removed if he had any prior incidents of being aggressive toward folks. There was another gator that ruled the roost before Remy named Emile. Ignace hired me to shoot him after he ate a patron's dog then went after another boater during hunting season. I kinda felt sorry for Emile. If I was a gator, I would have eaten the annoying chihuahua running around and yipping nonstop at me too. People should know to keep little dogs on a leash anytime they're near brackish or fresh waters where alligators lurk."

"You have the same personality of a grumpy, old gator at times. Thankfully, you can't eat anyone," Caitlin remarked without thinking as he tossed the cooler and fishing rods into the truck bed.

"Oh, let me assure you, I can most certainly eat someone." Gage pressed her back against the side of the truck, lowering his voice. "I just do it in a more pleasurable fashion."

Caitlin laughed as he lightly bit her neck.

"Agree to date me, and I'll demonstrate exactly how expertly I devour a woman."

"Didn't you just remind me we weren't going to hop into bed with one another anytime soon?" Caitlin locked her fingers together against the back of his neck.

"No, that isn't what I said. I said I'm an all or nothing kind of guy who doesn't like one-night stands. If you're willing to give dating a professional interest a try, I'm willing to pick up where we left off last night."

"Kiss me and convince me you're worth compromising my job."

The mischievous smile on her face made him regret setting the boundaries he just had with her. Thinking of how she purred his name while lying nude in his bed the night prior, his mouth crashed down against hers. His tongue forced its way between her lips. She pawed at his shoulders, returning the hungry, bruising kiss. She groaned in response to his knee parting her legs.

"I'd fuck you right here with the whole world watching if it would convince you that I'm worth dating." Gage pressed into her, letting the bulge in his pants confirm he would. "Christ, Caitlin, I know we got off to a rocky start with the business dealings, but if you can't see how badly I want you, how much I adore you—Hell, I was willing to go to jail for you a few minutes ago—no amount of kissing can make you see what you don't want to."

No, her body screamed when he pulled away from her then walked around to the driver's side door. She panted, leaning against the truck, trying to get a grip on her raging hormones. She hadn't been so damn hot for a guy since college. All it took was one kiss and she wanted to rip his clothes off. Images of her doing exactly that then climbing on top of him and grinding herself against him until they both came played like an erotic film behind her closed lids. The rumble of the truck starting followed by the whirling buzz of the window her head rested against rolling down jarred her out of the daydream.

"You wanted a steamy car ride home. I hope hot and bothered is close enough, cher." Gage smirked as he looked over at her. "That's the best I can offer a woman with a 'professional interest' in me. I don't believe in dipping my pen in company ink."

"You really are an asshole, Arsceneaux." Caitlin climbed into the truck and slammed her door shut.

"I prefer to consider myself someone who drives a hard bargain. Technically, it's called principled negotiation, Miss DeDanann."

Caitlin snorted, side-eyeing him. "More like adversarial negotiations. You're only going after what you want, giving no consideration to what my end goals or needs might be."

Gage laughed. "Trust me, cher, I've got a good idea of what the end goal is and am more than happy to take care of *all* your needs. You're the one trying to strong arm me by staring up at me with those purple doe eyes of yours and begging me to give you kisses anytime we're alone together, not caring at all that you'll break my poor heart in the long run by forgetting about me after you go back to Virginia. Based on that, I'd say it's you being one-sided about things."

"First off, I don't beg, I ask. Secondly, I wouldn't forget you."

"Oh, you wouldn't? Elaborate a bit more on that for me."

"You've definitely made this the most unique trip I've ever taken to Louisiana. If it wouldn't go to your head, I might say you were the highlight of it, but I don't want to make that ego of yours any bigger."

"The highlight of it?" Gage's grin widened to a pleased smile.

"Well, considering I've been auditing and conducting onsite inspections of your company assets instead of enjoying some downtime, along with being tortured by Marie and your sisters, it wouldn't take much to stand out this past week."

Gage laughed and shook his head. "Ouch! That actually stung, Cate."

Second Thoughts

"Ahhh, you're smiling. Taking her fishing yesterday was exactly what you need, non? Just wait until Friday evening after the ball." Alcee grinned, waltzing with an imaginary partner as he walked into Gage's office.

Gage shot Alcee a skeptical look. "I enjoyed my time with Caitlin yesterday. I'll give you that one, but I'm not so sure about going ahead with the ball."

"It is a bit too late to back out now. The arrangements have been made, and Marie will be furious if she doesn't get to bring her vision to life."

"Marie is your problem, not mine." Gage went back to proofreading the proposal he was working on.

"As you don't care about Marie, what about disappointing Caitlin? Surely she is looking forward to the event."

"Truth be told, she isn't sure what to think about it, and I don't think she'd care if I opted to stay home with her instead."

Confused by Evariste's sudden change of heart, Alcee sat on the edge of Gage's desk. "Does she not want to go?"

"Alcee, she has no clue who she was, and I've got reservations about exposing her to those who might say something which spooks her."

"We can manage anything someone might say or that she might overhear, Evariste. And give the vampire community more credit. They know what happened to her and about the curse. They also have a healthy amount of respect for you and your position. If they mentioned anything, it would be something subtle to determine if she's really returned to you. Their words or the location may very well spark her memory."

"Respect." Evariste snorted at that. "The former planters loathe me for being a Northern sympathizer and my anti-slavery sentiments. The others respect me out of fear due to how I've dealt with the rabble in our community when needed. That isn't exactly being respected. I won't comment on vampire subtlety. And what if Tristan has the audacity to show up?"

"So you have a few vampires who snarl and gossip behind your back, Evariste. We all do. Many in the community support you and consider you a friend. You would see that if you got out of the office more. They would have never elected you to the Council if they thought ill of you. As to Tristan, he wouldn't have the nerve to show his face there, not with it being held at the Shadow Oaks. There will also be security present should he attempt something as stupid as confronting you or going after Caitlin."

Allister heard Alcee mention security as she passed by the office door. "What's going on?"

"Evariste is having second thoughts about attending the ball with Caitlin."

Gage let out an annoyed sigh. He didn't need Alli ganging up on him as well. "I'm finally making progress in winning her over. I just don't want anything to jeopardize that."

"We'll all be there to ensure that doesn't happen, Ev." Alli smiled at her brother. "And if need be, I've got another jar of pheromone powder at the house. Maybe we can put it on you and see if she'll take the bait, since it appears you didn't."

Gage threw the stress ball on his desk at her. "Keep that shit out of my house, Allister Robicheaux. I'm still mad at the group of you for that nonsense. When does Jude get back into town so he can keep you away from D'Orme?"

"Next week. You've only got to put up with me tormenting you for another week." Allister stuck her tongue out at him.

Gage laughed and shook his head. "So I may actually get one week of quiet to spend with Caitlin before she leaves? Thank god for small favors."

"Speaking of Caitlin, where is she? Her things aren't in the conference room." Allister glanced across the hall to see if she had missed Caitlin, but the room was as dark as it had been before her meeting.

"When I left the house this morning, she said she was going to get some work done there and then go visit with some of her old coworkers. I can't drag her everywhere I go as much as I'd like to. I'm sure I come off controlling and creepy enough with everything that's gone on this week. Throw in the torture you and Marie put her through the other day, and I'm surprised she hasn't gotten on a plane back to Virginia."

Allister lobbed the stress ball she caught earlier at Gage. "She had fun with us. If anyone is going to run her off, it's going to be your grumpy self. Don't even get me started on how unromantic taking a woman fishing is, or even better, your couyon butt shooting an alligator on the dock."

"What's wrong with dat, sha?" Gage laughed at the glare Alli gave him before disappearing down the hallway.

Alcee chuckled then looked over at Gage. "What's this about shooting an alligator?"

Gage shook his head, wondering how Alli even knew he had shot Remy. He hadn't told anyone about doing so. "Remy went after Caitlin and me on the docks. He won't be doing so again."

"Oh, Evariste"—Alcee's shoulders shook as he laughed—"at least you're giving Caitlin an honest taste of life with you."

CAITLIN SAT at the dining room table with her laptop when Gage got home that evening. She was on the phone with someone. He assumed her boss with her talking about the Montrose.

"Hello, beautiful." He kept his voice low as he spoke then kissed the top of her head, bringing a smile to her face. She mouthed the word hello to him. Giving her some privacy to wrap up her call, he headed upstairs to change out of his work clothes. He grinned at how her eyes followed him across the room.

When he came back downstairs, she was just getting off the phone. "What counteroffer is Giovanni going to annoy me with tomorrow?"

"I have no idea, but he had several questions about your shipping operations. I did let them know I'd be busy most of the day tomorrow and had plans for tomorrow night. I also mentioned that Sharon told me your calendar was booked solid, so it might be better to call you on Monday with any new offers."

Appreciative of her trying to keep any work-related matters off his plate over the weekend, Gage smiled, going to the fridge to get something to drink. "And you call me devious for using my sisters to learn what type of pizza you like. I wanted to talk to you about tomorrow. We don't have to go to the ball if it's something you don't want to do. You won't hurt my feelings if you'd rather stay home and watch crappy pirate movies or do something else."

"*On Crimson Sails* isn't a crappy movie, and I'm fine going to whatever this cosplay ball is. It sounds like fun."

"I question your definition of fun as much as I do what you consider a good movie."

Caitlin rolled her eyes, closing her laptop. "You just don't like that I think the main character is hot." She smiled at him as he shut the fridge then strolled toward her with a drink in hand. "What do we do at this ball anyway? Go around biting necks? I've never been to a 'vampire' ball before."

"Neck biting might get you into some trouble, unless it's me you're nibbling on. I don't recommend you do that or anything else weird like hiss at people. Just be you and behave as you would at any other type of ball. In case you haven't ever been to a ball, proper behavior is quite simple. We dance, drink, eat hors d'oeuvres, socialize, that sort of thing. It's like any other formal event, besides the theme of the evening."

"Good to know. Last thing I need to do is to offend a supposed vampire. Wouldn't want to end up floating in a bayou somewhere after being someone's midnight snack."

"You wouldn't end up in the bayou, cher. Everyone knows you'd just disappear as vampires destroy the carcass of their leftovers to keep suspicion away from them. We're smarter than you humans." Gage jokingly growled, pulling her to him then lightly bit her on the shoulder.

Caitlin laughed, tilting her head and closing her eyes when he nuzzled the spot below her ear and lightly kissed her there. "I tried looking up the Shadow Oaks but couldn't find it online anywhere."

"It's a private property that isn't open to the public. The owners keep it off the internet search results, which isn't easy to do nowadays."

"A private property hosting a ball?"

"That's not uncommon around here. I think you'll find it a beautiful location based on your reaction to D'Orme. Since we have a formal event tomorrow night, what do you want to do this evening?"

Caitlin settled her arms on his shoulders. "Curl up on the couch with you after some of that delicious étouffée of yours."

"I suppose I can make you some étouffée again, but it'll have to be crawfish this time as I need to get some more shrimp."

"That's fine. I like crawfish better than shrimp anyway."

"A man can't ask for a better woman than one who loves crawfish over shrimp. You're a true Creole at heart, cher." Gage let his hands drift down her back as she leaned into him then pressed her mouth to his.

Caitlin's phone rang interrupting their kiss. They both glanced down at it.

"It's Sean. I probably need to answer."

"What you need to do is set boundaries with that boss of yours. Working hours end at five, mon coeur." Gage stole one more kiss from her then went to make dinner.

"You're one to talk," Caitlin called after him before answering the phone.

Gage chuckled, pulling out a pan.

TAKING advantage of the mild weather, they enjoyed dinner outside on the back patio.

"So what else did you do today besides giving Giovanni more ammunition to irritate me with?"

"I did the tourist thing. I drove out to River Road and toured the plantations. Every time I visit one of them, I struggle with the contradiction each one offers a visitor. On one hand, there's an elegant, rich life for the wealthy, white landowners in a stunning house. The grounds are always beautiful with the Louisiana landscape and the manicured gardens. On the other, a dark and difficult existence for the enslaved peoples working in the fields and mills. I can't even begin to imagine what it would have been like to live here back then. Or how one develops the lack of heart and conscience to keep enslaved peoples, fellow humans, squished into tiny shacks when not out in the field. All to justify maintaining a wealthy lifestyle and avoiding paying a fair wage to laborers."

"I imagine the cause of that was a lot of cognitive dissonance and greed." Gage set down the glass he had just taken a drink from. "While most say we shouldn't judge the sins of the past based on the morality of the present, a slaveholder's ability to dehumanize another human is disturbing, regardless of when you live. Slavery was a vile institution that thrived too long around here."

"You sound like my old history professors with the not judging the past on the morality of the present. By your remarks, I take it your ancestors didn't own slaves? That surprises me considering Lagniappe's ties to agriculture and D'Orme isn't your average house."

He deeply inhaled then slowly let the breath out. This certainly wasn't a discussion he thought they'd be having over dinner tonight. "No, cher. The Arsceneauxs did not ever own an enslaved person. They probably seem like an oddity in that regard, and I understand your assumptions in thinking they may have with what you see of my home and company. My family arrived before slavery was established in Louisiana. As it gained a foothold in the state, the man I'm named after got himself into quite a bit of trouble speaking out against implementing the *Code Noir*. While the Arsceneauxs did own some land, it wasn't enough to make them members of the planter class, especially as the planters began consolidating properties in the early 1800s.

"And don't lose sight of the fact there were other people present in Louisiana besides the wealthy planters and the enslaved people when you consider the state's history. Freedman, indigenous people, poor

117

whites, newly-arrived immigrants, the working class, the middle class, and those with some money, but not quite enough to be considered elite, or the frowned upon *nouveau riche*. Not to mention, this is one of the states in the South where there were several wealthy black slave-owners and interracial relationships even when the law outlawed them, which all compound a lot of the racial and socioeconomic issues we still struggle with today. Louisiana is a strange, complex place in that regard. It always has been."

"Your ancestor sounds like an interesting guy to go against the grain." Caitlin sat back in her chair, studying him.

Gage didn't know what to say. With the way she stared at him, she was passing some sort of judgement on his actions in the past. That bothered him more than her digging into Lagniappe prior to their meeting did. "The majority of my ancestors' income came from maritime trade, not agriculture. As you probably already know, the farming part of my business came much later on in time, not during the heyday of cotton and plantations. I'm not saying the Arsceneauxs didn't have some sort of complicity in the whole plantation economy as they did transport raw goods from the plantations to Northern marketplaces and overseas, but from what I understand, the men in my family firmly believed a man should be paid for his labor. That belief and their maritime roots kept them from engaging in slave ownership. Not to mention, the brutality of the shift to chattel slavery sickened my family member who witnessed the change in the codes based on the letters he left behind and the documented run-ins he had with the planters."

"You're getting a bit defensive about things you had no control over. The past is what it is. All we can do is learn what not to do from it. And I'm not judging you or your family's decisions. As you said, being in the South there's a lot of complexity anyone living here faces. I'm just startled by what you told me. That and hearing folks think there's a curse on D'Orme when I stopped at the gas station on the way home has me contemplating why Louisiana is the way that it is."

Gage shook his head and laughed. "Let me guess, you stopped at Meche's to fill up."

"How'd you know?" Caitlin asked, surprised he named the gas station.

"Landry loves telling that story to anyone who will listen. He's probably seen your car around here and was just dying for you to stop in so he could tell you all about the supposed ghosts and dark things that happen at D'Orme." Thinking about the last time he and Landry ran into one another, Gage chuckled. The man had thrown a bucket of holy water on him in addition to waving some voodoo charm around to cast out the evil spirit possessing him. It took all he had to control his startled reaction to finding himself suddenly waterlogged. He didn't want to scare the poor old man by flashing fangs or snarling at him, especially when Landry's intentions had been good. Landry had sheepishly apologized and handed him a towel after he realize the holy water and old voodoo ritual didn't make him mortal again. "I'm curious to hear what new embellishments he's added to his tale."

"He actually didn't say much to me. He just told me to be careful with the curse over the place and gave me this to ward off any evil spirits." Caitlin fished a small leather pouch that looked like a tiny purse hanging from a braided leather necklace out of her shirt. She gently pulled it over her head and handed it to Gage. "I put it on to humor him since he was so adamant I do so."

"A gris-gris." Gage smiled, flipping open the flap to discover an engraved stone. "With a protection stone no less. Landry must've really taken a liking to you to give you this."

"Why do people think D'Orme is cursed?"

A *mmmm* came from his lips as he studied the engraving on the stone. "Back in the eighteenth century, shortly after D'Orme was built, the lover of one of my ancestors was found dead on the property, and he was mauled by what was most likely a black bear the same day. Amazingly, he survived. Since both events occurred so close together, the story of the property being cursed and haunted took off like wildfire."

Caitlin's eyes widened in surprise. "There are black bear around here?"

"Oh, yes. You don't see them often, but they're definitely here."

Vague Recollections

⟨∾⟩

Marie arrived early in the morning as Caitlin, Gage, and his sisters sipped coffee and finished up breakfast around the dining room table.

"Today, we transform Caitlin from a mere mortal into a goddess," Marie announced, walking into the room. "Ladies, get your things. A day of magic and artistry awaits!"

Gage brought Caitlin's hand to his lips with a wink. "I think you're already a goddess. No transformation needed."

Caitlin smiled. "Thank you, mon beau."

"Shoo, Evariste!" Marie waved her hand at Gage and pulled Caitlin to her feet. "She will be yours later. You and Alcee may get ready in the downstairs guest room. The upstairs will be off limits as I do not want you seeing *ton ange* until she is ready."

"My suits are in my bedroom."

"I will send Jeanette down with them. Alcee will be here shortly."

"My house. My rules. Evariste *wanz* to *drezz* in *zhe* comfort of *iz* own bedroom and will do *zo*!" Gage needled Marie.

"Fine! But no peeking when we return. You are always so difficult!" Marie exasperatedly muttered, following the girls outside with Caitlin trailing behind her.

Caitlin turned and mouthed the words, "Help me."

Curious to see if he could converse via telepathy with Caitlin, he silently responded, *Sorry, you're on your own. Monsieur Evariste only pushes Marie so far.* The startled look on Caitlin's face confirmed he could do so.

"You know Marie could smite you for mocking her." Alcee materialized in the hall beside Gage.

Gage laughed. "Some days I wish she would."

THE DAY FLEW by as nails were done, legs were waxed, and facials completed. Caitlin enjoyed a few minutes of quiet, soaking in a hot bath Marie had drawn for her. The bathroom smelled like the flower garden where Caitlin first met Gage due to the rose oil added to her bath water. It had been months since she was this relaxed and her head clear of any work-related thoughts.

"Time to get dressed!" Marie appeared beside the tub with a large fluffy towel and robe, spooking Caitlin.

"You just gave me a heart attack, Marie. I hate how you walk around so quietly." Caitlin dried off, put on the robe, and sat down in the chair Marie directed her to. Marie and another woman painstakingly hand-curled her long, red hair into loose ringlets. As they finished the curls, a third woman she didn't know entered the room with a corset and hooped skirts.

"You weren't joking when you said a ball. I thought you meant a formal dinner, not the real thing." Caitlin eyed the corset and skirt. "Didn't women pass out from those things?"

"They are custom fit to your sizing, and non, you will not pass out. These are modernized versions." Marie assured her she would be fine.

Alli and Renee laced up the back of the corset for Caitlin.

"Too tight?" Renee asked before tying the last knot.

"Amazingly, not too bad."

Caitlin balanced herself on their shoulders as she stepped into the hooped skirt they held. Marie raised and laced the hoops so they would stay in place. She finished styling Caitlin's hair then applied her makeup. The excitement grew on Marie's face while she worked.

Caitlin wondered what she looked like, but Marie forbade her from looking in the mirror.

"Ready for the gown?" Renee asked, once makeup and hair were complete.

"Oui." Marie helped Caitlin remove the robe she wore over the corset and petticoats.

"This is beautiful! I love the color," Renee cooed after lifting the lid off a box labeled Caitlin and discovering a burgundy gown.

"Good, as that is your dress." Marie turned to one of her stylists, giving her an order in French. "It was a decoy should your brother get nosy. This is Caitlin's gown."

The ladies turned to see Marie's assistant carrying a lavender and cream ballgown from the wardrobe.

Alli recognized the dress. "Oh, Marie. Evariste is going to freak out."

"He will not freak out. He will fall in love all over again." Marie and her two assistants carefully pulled the gown over Caitlin's head and smoothed out its long skirts. "Alcee, I need the finishing touches!"

A black velvet jewelry box appeared in Marie's hands.

Caitlin couldn't believe what she just witnessed. How in the world did a box materialize out of thin air? "Did that just...?"

Marie ignored the half-spoken inquiry, raising the lid of the case.

"How did you get those out of the safe?" Renee whispered, seeing the necklace and earrings.

Marie took the necklace from the box. "I have my ways."

"They are gorgeous." Caitlin admired the ornate pearl and amethyst necklace and earrings. "Are they real?"

"Yes, dear. They are on loan to you tonight." Marie fastened the necklace as the girls hung the earrings on Caitlin's ears.

"One final detail." Marie slid a diamond ring onto Caitlin's left hand. She ignored the simultaneous gasping from Gage's sisters.

"You are a vision, Caitlin." Marie beamed proudly as she turned Caitlin to face the mirror.

Caitlin reached up and gently touched the large amethyst hanging from her throat. For a moment, an image of her doing the same thing in a dream flickered in the silver glass surface before her.

The Reason Why

❦

A lcee and Gage waited for the women in the foyer.

Gage adjusted his cravat and tugged his shirt sleeves from under the cuffs of his jacket. "I look ridiculous."

"You look fine. She always found you fetching in that outfit."

Gage scoffed but said nothing else. Alcee loved seventeenth and eighteenth-century fashion.

Alcee watched Gage fidgeting with the buttons keeping the oversized cuffs of his jacket secured. "Relax, Evariste. It's not like you are getting married again. You're merely taking the lady out dancing."

Gage looked in the hall mirror a second time and ran a finger under his collar. "This thing is as uncomfortable now as it was then."

Alcee laughed at the eighteenth-century gentleman standing beside him. "That is because you are wearing the real thing, not some Hollywood recreation."

The emerald and diamond ring in his reflection caught Gage's attention. It was a gift from Caitlin for their first wedding anniversary. On his right hand, he wore a gold signet ring bearing the Arsceneaux family crest. The ring was handed down each generation to the first-born male of the family. He didn't know exactly how old it was, but it predated him.

"I hated going to these damn things," he grumbled, brushing some lint from the black gentleman's cloak laying over the back of the couch in front of him. Why had he let Alcee talk him into this?

"You used to go all the time, and as I recall, you always enjoyed your evenings out." Alcee chuckled before taking a sip of the cognac he had been drinking.

Gage shook his head when Alcee offered the sniffer to him. Alcee set the glass down and helped Gage with his cloak.

"The only reason I ever attended these things—" Gage stopped mid-sentence as the sound of skirts rustling came from behind him. It had been centuries since he heard that particular sound in his home. He turned, his eyes following Alcee's gaze to the top of the staircase.

"Is waiting for you at the top of the stairs," Alcee whispered when Gage stared dumbfounded at what he saw.

Caitlin– as she was in May 1708. He was not Evariste, the President and CEO of Lagniappe Shipping & Ag, any longer. He was once more a shipping merchant and new landowner starting up a small business in Louisiana. Caitlin had been the daughter of a British commodore in Colonial Virginia. She stole his heart when they met in Norfolk. A few months later, he brought her to Louisiana as his wife. Tonight became their wedding day all over again. She was beautiful in the lavender and cream gown she had chosen to get married in. Seeing she even wore the pearl and amethyst wedding set he and a jeweler in New Orleans designed to match her gown, he disbelievingly stared at the woman fate brought back into his life. How in the world had Marie restored that gown and gotten those jewels out of his safe?

A fierce pride swelled in his chest as he ascended each step toward her. She was most definitely his lost wife back from the dead. Back in his arms where she belonged. He would do anything to ensure she remained at his side for the rest of his days.

Caitlin smiled nervously when he stopped before her. Impulsively, he drew her against him; his mouth found hers, not caring that all eyes rested on the two of them. Her thoughts of suddenly wanting to stay home alone with him, letting things lead where they may, fueled his desire to win her heart back. He resisted the temptation to grant her unspoken wish.

"Enchanté, mademoiselle," Gage whispered. "You are truly a vision from my dreams."

Alcee coughed from the bottom of the stairs. "I believe we have a ball to attend."

Marie and Alcee exchanged knowing glances. By the way Marie's eyebrows raised and her satisfied grin, the woman silently proclaimed victory in yet again, successfully bringing together two individuals perfect for one another.

Alcee bowed to the creature he claimed as a lover, giving a gallant flourishing of his hand as he did so. *As always, your work is perfection, mon trésor. May it make Evariste as content a man as I.*

Oblivious to Marie's gloating, Gage placed Caitlin's hand in the crook of his arm and escorted her down the stairs. Reaching the foyer, he raised her hand to his lips. Noticing the diamond ring she wore, he smiled. She had happily taken his last name when he first slid that exact ring onto her finger. Thinking of their wedding night, his lips lingered on her knuckles. He might have to concede on his requirement of being moved from acquaintance to boyfriend.

Caitlin's heart missed a beat with the way he briefly stared at her before he turned her hand to kiss the inside of her wrist. She gasped from the tip of his tongue grazing across the valley blood flowed through just beneath her palm.

Her sudden intake of breath caused his eyes to meet hers again. *La chasse commence.*

"What?" Caitlin asked.

The confusion on her face at the third time of hearing his voice in her head over the past week brought a smirk to his face. "I didn't say anything, cher."

Alcee chuckled beside them. "Shall we go?"

"We definitely should. After you, beautiful." Gage broke the spell he entrapped Caitlin in then opened the door.

As they stepped out onto the porch, Caitlin stared up at him again. "Gage, are you okay tonight? The intensity in your eyes..."

Gage smiled at the inquiry and how her voice drifted off. "I always stare that intently at something I'm determined to have. I'm surprised you hadn't noticed the way I look at you before now. And I'm more than okay. In fact, this is the best I've been in years. I was just imaging that my ancestor who built this house must have been as entranced by his bride as I find myself with you tonight. Twice now, you seem like a beautiful phantom stepping through time to grace my undeserving self with your presence."

Flattered by the compliment, Caitlin shyly looked away. Her cheeks tinging a light shade of pink. "Thank you. You're rather handsome in period dress yourself."

"Come on, you two!" Alli yelled from the car after they lingered on the wrap-around porch.

Gage shot her an annoyed glare. "As usual, you ruin a perfect moment with your impatience, Alli."

"Whatever." Alli rolled her eyes, scooting over as Caitlin and Gage finally came down the steps and toward the car.

Shadow Oaks

❧

The car rolled to a stop on the road in front of Shadow Oaks. Caitlin had driven past the property many times before, but never knew what was hiding farther back behind the large gates. She always thought it was most likely another old plantation. With Gage mentioning that it wasn't, she was curious to see what building greeted her. Haunting notes from a cello and violin drifted into the car when Gage opened the door then helped her step out on the grass.

A massive building that reminded her of a European palace or villa spanned out in front of her. Ornate arches and columns spanned the two and a half story structure. Was she in Italy or Louisiana?

Gage chuckled beside her. "I had a feeling you'd be impressed."

"Impressed is an understatement. I'm trying to figure out what I'm looking at. It's like the New World and Olde World collided in the design of this place. How old is Shadow Oaks?"

"The construction of it began in 1718 and completed in 1740. The property was damaged by both a fire and hurricane in 1850, so sections of it were rebuilt in a different style after the Civil War. That's probably why you can't identify the architectural style."

She found herself drawn to the property engulfed in a mix of moonlight and warm flame coming from lanterns hung in the trees and lining the walkway. People of all shapes, colors, and sizes dressed in elegant costumes filled the yard and milled about on the stairs leading up into the building. More were being dropped off alongside them as Alcee and Gage assisted Alli, Jeanette, Marie, and Renee with getting out of the car.

"Ready to go inside, cher?" Gage offered her his arm with a charming smile.

She slid her hand into the crook of it, then walked with him on the red paver path under a tangled umbrella of oak tree limbs. The distant music became livelier as more stringed instruments joined the initial two she could hear from the road.

Gage politely nodded and acknowledged people he recognized while they made their way inside.

Absorbed in the sights and sounds of the evening, Caitlin didn't notice the way people stared at her and Gage, nor did she pay much attention to whoever Gage politely greeted once they stepped through the front doors. Old gas lanterns and chandeliers lit the interior. "It's like traveling back in time."

"Yes, they really go all out for events like tonight," Gage agreed beside her.

Once they reached the coat check, Gage handed his cloak to the attendant. Rid of the unnecessary and heavy jacket, he placed his hand on the small of Caitlin's back to escort her to the ballroom.

"What was this place originally? It's huge to have been a home."

"It started out as a government building similar to the Cabildo in New Orleans then had a stint as an inn."

"How is this not a museum or a tourist attraction? The frescoes on the walls are incredible. I haven't seen anything like them in the U.S. They alone would be worth an entry fee to help fund the upkeep of the place." Caitlin stopped to admire one of them.

"The owner works extremely hard to keep it off any tourist trails or maps. It serves a special purpose in the local community." Gage waited patiently beside her while her eyes skimmed the walls.

She turned her head back toward Gage and noticed they were by themselves. "We lost the others."

"No, we didn't. This way, cher." Gage gently pressed his hand into her back, guiding her through the mob of people in the hall. "Alcee always reserves a table in the back corner of the main ballroom."

STRAUSS'S WALTZES enraptured couples gliding across the dance floor. Tables full of people framed in the open space. The crowd seemed to part for them as they made their way to the table Alcee, Marie, and Allister sat at. Gage politely pulled out a chair for Caitlin by the dance floor.

Alcee noticed her fascination with everything going on around them. "Your first ball, Caitlin?"

"I've never been to anything even remotely like this. How often do these go on?"

"Twice a year. One during Mardi Gras and this one later in the spring. Evariste tells me you were born and raised in Virginia. They are definitely more conservative than us Creoles up North. Did you grow up in Williamsburg?"

"No. I grew up in Alexandria, just outside DC. I've lived a few places after graduating college, even in New Orleans. After a career change, the firm I worked for moved their offices from Norfolk to Williamsburg."

"Evariste and I used to go through the Port of Norfolk on our travels to Williamsburg. We rarely made it north to DC."

Caitlin didn't catch the old reference to the city of Norfolk in Alcee's statement. "Really? What brought you to Williamsburg?"

"Commerce. Our transport team brings sugar to Virginia. We also buy peanuts and soybeans to sell here in Louisiana. Once the sugar and molasses are offloaded, we bring the Virginia crops we bought here through the port of New Orleans."

"I'm still surprised you guys use ships for domestic deliveries. I'd figure you'd use trucks this day and age. Isn't the risk and cost of sending things via ship more expensive?"

Alcee set down the Sazerac he held after taking a sip of the strong liquor. "Depends on the nature of the goods we are moving. We select rail, road, or sea based on whatever product we are hired to transport.

Agriculture and shipping have always been big business in Louisiana. I have no doubt they will continue to be well into the future."

"Your usual, Madam Arsceneaux?" An elderly gentleman interrupted them, handing Caitlin a glass of red wine then walked off.

Alcee smiled at the shocked expressions on Caitlin and Gage's faces.

"He's confusing you with Evariste's grandmother." Alcee tried to explain what had just happened, giving Caitlin a reassuring pat on the knee while winking at Gage.

She caught the fleeting scowl Gage shot Alcee. Before she could ask what the scowl was about, Alcee leaned a bit closer to her and spoke louder as the orchestra began another song.

"The Arsceneaux men appear to have similar taste in women. Maybe what features they are attracted to is genetic. Evariste's grandmother looked a lot like you when she was in her youth; she had long, red hair as well. However, she did not have your lovely violet eyes. She died a few years back. Jean, the man who brought you the wine, was quite infatuated with her, and absolutely heartbroken when she married Evariste's grandfather. Poor Jean. He must be in his eighties now and is still managing to host these events."

"How sweet of him to remember what she liked to drink. What was her name?" Caitlin took a sip of the wine, feeling sorry for the old man.

"Jeanette," Alcee said as Gage said, "Lena."

"What? Which is it?" She eyed both of them as if they had each grown two heads.

"Your grandmother. You would remember her name better than me." Alcee deferred to Gage.

"Lena Jeanette Arsceneaux." Gage merged the two names, hoping it sounded believable. "The family often called her Lena, while others who didn't know her as well called her Jeanette. Similar to many friends calling me Gage while my family calls me Evariste or Ev. Would you like to dance, Caitlin?"

Nice explanation, Alcee complimented Gage, raising his glass up in toast to Evariste before sampling the Sazerac again.

No more family history tonight. Gage shot Alcee a quick glare before he led Caitlin to the center of the dance floor.

"I'm not sure if this is a good idea. I have never danced like this."

Caitlin hesitantly took Gage's hand while he placed his other hand on her waist.

"It's a simple waltz, cher. Just slide your feet and let me lead you."

She nervously moved with him as he directed.

"Look up at me," Gage gently scolded when she glanced down as they took their first couple of steps together.

"I-I'm sorry," she stammered, embarrassed, as she stepped on his foot again.

"Trust me, Caitlin. Quit trying to lead. That's why you're stepping on my feet. Relax. You can do this. Just feel the pulse of the music." Gage's voice was almost hypnotic.

Caitlin stared into his eyes and pictured the two of them gracefully dancing across the floor together. Her confidence in her ability to learn how to waltz grew with each step they took together.

Tension slowly fled her body. She relaxed into Gage's palm resting lightly against her back, and unconsciously fell into a natural rhythm, moving in sync with him.

Gage grinned. "Much better, beautiful."

MURMURING BROKE out in the crowd of onlookers lining the walls. Too wrapped up in the moment, neither Gage nor Caitlin noticed the attention they drew. Several couples stopped dancing to turn and stare at the pair as whispers of Evariste Arsceneaux returning to the La Nuit Soiree flitted about the ballroom.

Pierre and Helene Leblanc, Gage's stepfather and mother, entered the room as only a handful of couples remained on the dance floor.

An old friend stopped Helene in the doorway. "Who is the woman Evariste is dancing with?"

The inquiry baffled her. "Evariste hates balls and isn't seeing anyone. He wouldn't be here tonight."

"What's going on?" Pierre asked, noting the look on his wife's face.

"Isn't that him dancing with the woman in the lavender gown?" The woman pointed toward the dance floor.

Surprisingly, their son indeed attended the ball and waltzed some woman across the marble floor.

Helene doubted her eyes as she took in the woman's long, copper hair and fair skin. "Pierre, is that who I think it is?"

Pierre recognized Caitlin in Gage's arms. "I believe it is." Pierre laughed and shook his head. "Kaw, Evariste Arsceneaux, you sneaky son of a gun."

Helene tapped his arm with her fan, warning him to watch his language.

Pierre smirked at his wife. "That boy of yours is ever full of surprises. I wonder how long he's been hiding that girl away from everyone."

"Momma, Daddy." Gage politely acknowledged them as he and Caitlin twirled past. His mother's tightly drawn lips and narrowed eyes warned he was in trouble for not saying anything to them about finding his wife again. In contrast to his mother, Pierre grinned ear-to-ear as he shook his head, then softly laughed.

"Your parents are here?" Caitlin tried to pick them out of the crowd as Gage spun her again.

"They are. I will introduce you after the waltz is over."

When the music stopped, Gage politely bowed to Caitlin before leading her from the floor. Caitlin fanned herself with a lace fan as they made their way back to Alcee's table. The hooped skirts were heavy to move in and hot. How did women wear them and dance all night long in the past?

"Evariste?" Gage's mother stopped them before they reached the table. Helene was short with brown hair that had hints of red in it.

"Momma, may I present Caitlin DeDanann? We recently met in New Orleans."

"Nice to meet you, Mrs. Arsceneaux." Caitlin extended her hand to Gage's mother, who loosely took it before quickly dropping it. Not sure what to think about that, Caitlin turned to his father. In contrast to Gage's mother, Pierre was tall with gray hair on his head and speckling the dark beard on his face. "It's a pleasure to meet as well, Mr. Arsceneaux."

Pierre firmly grasped Caitlin's hand. A warm, broad smile accompanied the handshake. "Likewise, but I'm a LeBlanc, and so is Helene now. While Evariste calls me Daddy, I am actually his stepfather."

Helene looked as if she had seen a ghost as she gazed at Caitlin.

Pierre gently tugged on Helene's arm after noticing her reaction to Caitlin. "Come on, cher. Let's leave the two of them alone to enjoy their evening."

"Did I do something wrong?" Caitlin asked, as his parents walked away.

"Not at all. Why?" Gage appreciated Pierre's tact in heading off a potential dramatic episode that was on the verge of occurring based on his mother's expression.

"Your mom looked shocked. Like I had done something to upset her."

Gage gave her a deadpan expression. "You forgot to curtsey and say 'how do you do' as they did in the eighteenth century. We'll learn you right one of these days."

Caitlin smiled as he started to laugh. "Don't be a jerk. I want to make a good impression on your parents since we're dating."

"Are we now?" Gage's smile widened. "I'm delighted to hear I've finally moved from professional interest to boyfriend. Maybe wearing this itchy, uncomfortably stiff shirt was worthwhile."

"I would say it was a worthwhile investment. The crawfish omelets and crepes the past couple of mornings definitely aided in changing my mind about dating you."

"I'll alternate between crawfish omelets and crepes every morning we're together then. To make sure the crêpes are as sweet as those kisses of yours, I'll follow the seasons: strawberry crêpes in the spring, peaches in the summer, blackberries and cherries in the fall, ending with pears or satsumas for the winter." Gage's voice lowered the closer his face came to hers before their lips finally met. The tender kiss slowly deepened. Gage caught her lower lip gently in his teeth, thinking about how delectable each of those filings would taste sampled from her skin.

NOTICING porcelain points before Evariste's upper lip fell concealing them as Caitlin and Evariste stared at one another, Alcee smiled. It wasn't often Evariste openly displayed his vampiric nature.

"Your eyes seem so much greener tonight, brighter almost," Caitlin remarked, enchanted by the man holding her.

"It must be the lamplight in here." Gage downplayed any shifts in his eye color. "In the warm flicker of the flame, you are utterly radiant, cher."

Alcee snorted, drawing a chiding glance from Gage. *You will have to reveal what you are sooner or later, mon ami.*

Gage ignored Alcee. Tonight was about winning back Caitlin, not anything else. After accomplishing that, he would find a way to explain what he was and their past. "Your wine glass is empty. Would you like a refill?"

"Yes, please."

"Stay with Alcee, and I will be back in a minute." Gage gestured to the chair beside them then glanced over at Alcee. "And you behave." He picked up Caitlin's wine glass then ventured over to the bar.

Stirring The Pot

Caitlin lost track of time as the evening went on. Alcee made her laugh with his over-the-top personality and French accent. She mastered the waltz after being whisked around the floor multiple times by Gage and Alcee. She searched for Gage as she danced her fourth round with Alcee. He was standing near the rear doors of the ballroom, speaking with two other men. His head turned in their direction as if he knew she was looking for him.

Alcee didn't miss how she smiled and slightly lowered her face when Gage gave her a polite nod, acknowledging he caught her staring at him. "Ahhh. You are in love, mon petite chou."

"I wouldn't say that. Evariste and I just met, Alcee."

"That does not mean anything. The heart does not tell time like we do. You absolutely glow whenever Evariste gazes at you."

"Are you always such a romantic, Alcee?"

"Oui. I live for romance. Love is what makes the world go round."

"Marie is a lucky woman."

"Be certain to remind her of that the next time you speak with her. Now, let me get you back to your beau before he gets jealous of me compromising too much of your time this evening."

"My beau? You watch too many movies, Alcee. Gage also isn't the jealous type from what I've seen so far."

Alcee tossed his head back and roared with laughter as they stopped dancing. "You do not know Evariste well yet. He would be at your side in a heartbeat if another man expressed an interest in you. Look at him, cher. He is watching every move you make. The man is besotted with you."

"Besotted? You really love to overexaggerate things, Monsieur Dugas."

"You doubt me? Let us test my theory." Alcee searched around the ballroom for one of the other vampires who might come across a rival for Caitlin's attention. He spotted the perfect suitor, Ethan Metoyer. The good-looking vampire was slightly younger than Evariste and was flirtatious but respectful.

"Alcee." Ethan acknowledged Alcee as they approached him, but his eyes rested on Caitlin.

"Ethan. It is always a pleasure to see you again."

"And who is this tempting morsel?" Ethan raised Caitlin's hand to his lips.

Caitlin quivered as he kissed her knuckles, holding eye contact with her. There was something absolutely virile about Ethan, and he definitely knew it based on how he grinned at her. The man's hazel eyes were entrancing set against light brown skin and curly black hair.

"Caitlin this is Ethan Metoyer. Ethan, Caitlin DeDanann."

"An absolute pleasure to meet you, Miss DeDanann."

Alcee grinned at the way Ethan discretely raked his gaze over Caitlin. "Watch this one. He's a silver-tongued devil."

"Don't believe a word Alcee says about me. None of it is true." Ethan flashed her a sensual smile. "He's just mad I beat him at the card tables the last ball, mon bijou." He turned her hand, running his finger along the underside of her wrist before slowly bringing it toward his mouth.

Gage suddenly stood next to Caitlin. He yanked her hand from Ethan's grasp and settled an arm around her waist, possessively drawing her against his side. His actions declaring Caitlin off limits to anyone but him. "Ethan, I see you've met Caitlin, *ma petite amie*."

Startled to see Evariste at a vampire function, Ethan slowly straightened. "Arsceneaux? It isn't often you grace us with your presence. Is this mortal flower truly here with you?"

"She is." Gage's glare warned the vampire to take another step back from Caitlin.

"Pity. If you change your mind about Evariste, ma belle, ask Alcee for my number." Ethan grinned at Gage then walked away.

Gage shot Alcee an accusatory look. *What are you playing at endangering her like that? Ethan was about to sink his fangs into her wrist, and you were going to stand there letting him do so.*

"And you doubted he was besotted," Alcee whispered to Caitlin then raised his voice to address Gage. "Bête jalouse!"

"Protective, not jealous." Gage disagreed with Alcee's calling him a jealous beast.

"Whatever term you like, Evariste," Alcee said, then strolled off, grinning.

Gage's narrowed eyes followed the older vampire across the room. Alcee extravagantly bowed to him after reaching their table, then laughed and shook his finger at them. Marie joining him ended the round of taunting.

Claiming His Wife

"Let's go walk the grounds." Caitlin drew his attention back to her.
Gage guided her out the rear exit and onto the lawn behind
the house. He shared the history of the property as they walked
together.

"With the way you talk about this place, I'd say you knew the original owners and their business well. But, of course, that isn't possible."

"I have a good memory for facts and local stories." Gage hadn't realized how much he allowed himself to slip into the past tonight. If she hadn't made the remark, he might never have been aware he had done so.

"That type of recall probably comes in handy with running a company."

"At times." He shrugged, stopping and looking around them. Weirdly, no one else was out exploring the rear gardens on such a nice night. Only three vampires engaged in conversation lingered on the rear steps of the building. The crowd present tonight seemed to prefer milling around the front lawn and inside instead.

"This place is deceptive just like the lush landscape around it." Caitlin walked over to a bench surrounded by a small group of trees.

"Deceptive?" Gage settled himself beside her.

"It's beautiful and secluded, and lulls the visitor into a false sense of a fantasy past that didn't exist. It's actually a rather romantic location, especially lit up by lantern light as folks in period costume grace the grounds. Very similar to how the bayous and trees draped in Spanish moss can make you feel whenever you look out at them." She reached up and touched one of the long tendrils of moss dangling from the branches above them. "The wetlands and swamps appear so peaceful, almost magical at times, giving you temporary amnesia so you forget the predators that lurk there. Then when you fall in love with the place and least expect it, you get eaten by an alligator or mauled by a bear. It makes me wonder what dark secret this place holds for the owner to keep it off public radar."

Gage laughed at the comparison, drawing her into his side. "Have no fear, cher. I won't let an alligator or bear eat you. After all, I'm the evil, cursed descendant of some poor soul. The creatures of the bayou are terrified of me."

"After what you did to Remy and Emile, who can blame them?" Caitlin loved the lopsided grin and crinkles around the corners of his eyes that appeared as he chortled again. "Whoever owns this place must have spent a small fortune restoring it after fires and hurricanes. It amazes me that folks like you manage to keep these old properties in fairly good shape when mother nature and time work against you. Truthfully, the perseverance of anyone who continually lives here amazes me with how disaster prone Southern Louisiana is."

"That's just part of life here. You make peace with the fact that you can lose everything at the whim of fate. Louisiana has always reminded the rich and poor alike of how futile it is to resist the forces of nature. But we Cajuns and Creoles are stubborn and stay anyway. Part of me actually appreciates that aspect of living here. It makes me thankful for what I have. It really wasn't that long ago when disease ran rampant due to poor sanitation and mosquitoes. The heat and humidity suffocated anyone working outdoors. There was no escaping brutal summer days either. AC didn't exist, and once it did, it was a luxury to have installed for decades. You just endured what you had to. And hurricane season, hurricane season brought storms the like many of us had never seen. Homes, livestock, barns, wagons, ships, anything one built or accumulated washed away or ripped apart by hellacious winds."

"Then why stay? Or for that matter, what was the allure of coming to such a hostile place if you had the choice not to do so?"

Caitlin stared up at him, patiently waiting for an answer. The genuine curiosity in her eyes brought on a pang of longing. His heart screamed, *Remember me, cher. Please. I need you to.* He gently ran his thumb across her cheek, a sad smile briefly curving his lips. "There were undoubtedly many reasons people still came to the New World. Land, adventure, military service, a chance to become something greater than Europe's social structure allowed. Or possibly trying to outrun one's past."

"Which of those do you think brought your family here?"

"Maybe now I'm guilty of romanticizing the past, but I'd like to think a new beginning and the opportunity to be something greater brought the first Arsceneaux to Louisiana's shores."

Caitlin let out a soft laugh. "Romanticizing the present and the past seems to be what this entire night is about. What else would people dressed up as vampires on a historic property be doing?"

Gage chuckled. She wasn't far off the mark in that observation. He brought her here for that exact reason. If only she knew she sat amongst the predators she mentioned in her earlier comparison, not humans masquerading as some imaginary creature. That the secret of the property she wondered about was it was the meeting place of the local Vampire Council and offered sanctuary to their kind when it was needed. One day he'd be able to tell her the truth about Shadow Oaks and the reason why Landry had gifted her the gris-gris. "Vampires can romanticize just about any location with their nostalgia for everything ancient. Their strong sense of sensuality can even lead them to justify hedonistic orgies in a mausoleum or church. They can be quite the theatrical, carnal beings at times."

"You almost sound like you believe they really exist."

"Anything's possible." He whisked his lips across her temple.

She leaned back against him as they sat in silence, taking in the serene evening. A field of freshly planted corn and sugar cane sprawled out into what they could see of the horizon before them. The moss hanging from the branches above them almost curtained them from the wandering eyes of the ghosts who roamed the grounds. A full moon cast a glow over their private resting spot.

Caitlin laid her head on his shoulder and looked up at the silver orb above them. "This is going to sound as outlandish as vampires being real, but sometimes, I think I was born in the wrong century."

Curious to know what prompted the remark, Gage asked, "Why do you think that?"

"I don't know. There are times when I visit certain places and they seem so familiar, like I've been there before, especially here in Louisiana. The music, the people, the food; they all speak to my soul or some strange subconscious part of me. Now, I sound like the crazy one."

"No. You don't. Some people are just old souls. Trust me, when you live in Louisiana long enough, I can assure you, you'll hear much stranger remarks than someone experiencing déjà vu." Gage hoped her past self now reached out from deep within.

"Not meaning to brag, but I think I pull off eighteenth-century dresses rather well."

"Yes, you certainly do, cher." Gage smiled, his eyes drinking in the woman for the millionth time that night. He wanted to tell her she had lived in Louisiana three centuries ago, to remind her of their life together, to come clean about what he was, but he knew he couldn't, not yet anyway. "If ghosts and vampires could be real, maybe you did live a prior life here."

"Maybe so. If we had met back then, do you think you would be interested in me or would I be too independent for you?"

"Interesting question." She had asked a similar inquiry the night they met in Virginia. Though at the time, it was more a snarky deterrent of unwanted attention and mocking a gentleman at the dinner they attended than an actual question as it was tonight. His smile widened, recalling the shocked expression on the man's face after she posed it to the men seated around the table. "Even in the 1700s, I didn't want a docile wife. I wanted a woman with a mind of her own and a passionate spirit. Most likely, I would have pursued you relentlessly until you agreed to marry me."

"Even in the 1700s?" Thinking he misspoke, Caitlin laughed. "You mean even if you lived in the 1700s."

"If I met you, Caitlin, in any century, I would want you just as I do now."

His face drifted toward hers until their lips met. The ember of their past love at last sparked into a shared inferno, consuming them as the night stoked an ancient allure between them. The more they kissed, the more frenzied their yearning for one another became.

"Take me home, Gage."

The breathy request sent every drop of blood in his body straight to his loins. He'd been praying she'd ask him that from the moment they arrived. His lips brushed her bare shoulders causing her breath to catch in her throat. "Take you home?"

"You know what I'm asking."

He lightly nipped his way across her collar bone to her neck. The way her body quivered from the warmth of his breath against her skin roused the vampire's licentious nature. "Are you sure that's what you want me to do?"

Caitlin gasped as he cupped a breast he freed from the bodice of her gown. His thumb strummed her nipple, teasing soft flesh until it warmed and hardened before capturing the perky nub begging for his attention between his lips. Her fingers splayed on the back of his head, pulling him closer.

"Evariste Arsceneaux, if you don't—" Caitlin moaned from the sting of his teeth grazing her skin until his tongue swished out, easing it.

Gage lifted his head from her chest, a knowing smile and lifted brows taunted her as his thumb once more took over the caressing his tongue had been doing seconds ago. "If I don't what?"

Another soft moan escaped Caitlin's lips. "If you don't take me to bed and satisfy me this instant, I'm on the next flight back to Virginia."

Gage laughed at the hollow threat and the bedroom eyes she now stared at him with. "I better get you home then."

MAKING GOOD ON HIS PROMISE, he teleported the two of them to the car Alcee hired for the evening.

"I hate these freaking skirts," he grumbled, pushing aside layers of lavender and white to caress the legs hidden beneath them.

When the car rolled forward, turning onto the highway, Caitlin glanced around wide-eyed and twisted her torso away from his. "How did we—?"

"Don't worry about how we got to the car, cher." Gage's seeking fingers delved into the soft apex between her thighs. "Focus on what we're doing, on how good this feels."

The hand not under the skirt gently cupped her face bringing her attention back to him. Her lips slightly parted while her eyes fluttered shut. He stifled the escaping passionate cry his stroking elicited with a kiss. The soft sounds and groans coming from within her throat as their tongues dueled with one another paired with how slick and ready she was for him brought a feral growl from his chest. If it was a longer ride to D'Orme, he'd undo his pants and take her then and there with how his cock throbbed, pressing against the material restraining it.

The car slowed, warning they were nearing D'Orme. He threw the driver a quick tip before helping Caitlin out of the car. His hands trembled as he unlocked the front door and hit the alarm button on his key fob to turn off the alarm.

He had barely locked the front door again when Caitlin reached for him. Their mouths hungrily meeting while he yanked off his jacket and dropped it on the floor. He pinned her against the foyer wall, his fingers dragging her skirts upward.

"Caitlin," he groaned her name in protest as she undid his belt and seized a hold of him, stroking him until his own body shuddered. He had wanted to make love to her, slowly, all night, but need churned to fervor. He had to be inside her. Now. The tip of his cock easily slipped into her wet sheath. They both groaned as he pushed deeper into her, lifting her slightly then taking her against the foyer wall. He thrust slowly at first, losing himself in the long-missed, welcoming warmth of his wife. Pent up desire turned to lust as the vampire within demanded more. He slammed himself into her, wanting to conquer the stubborn part of her that still held back from him, to physically convince her she belonged here, at his side, and nowhere else.

"God, yes, Gage!" Caitlin cried out, her fingers digging into his shoulders with how hard he took her. She wrapped her legs around his waist, eagerly meeting each thrust of hips.

The crash of a painting on the wall beside them bouncing off its hook then falling to the floor cooled Gage's emotions some. "So I don't have to replace anything else we might knock off the walls, let's go upstairs."

After what seemed like only climbing one step, they were in the master bedroom. Caitlin's gown and the hoops underneath it collapsed to the floor. Gage lifted her out of the pile of satin, linen, and lace. She unbuttoned his shirt then her lips skimmed across his bare shoulders before leaving a trail of gentle kisses down the center of his stomach.

Gage moaned as her lips unexpectedly closed around him. He watched the flame-red waves of hair undulating around his waist and brushing his thighs. After a few minutes of indulging himself, he crooked a finger under her chin, halting the divine brushing of her tongue against him. "Stop, cher."

Once she was on her feet, he spun her so he could unlace her corset. It only took a few seconds for him to pull the laces free of the hooks and through the rounded eyeholes.

"You seem to know your way around a corset and petticoats. With as many knots as Marie tied the lacings in, I'm surprised you can get them off," Caitlin said after the corset joined the rest of her clothing on the floor.

"I would rip the damn thing off you if I needed to." Gage gently pushed her backward on his bed. "My god, you are beautiful."

His eyes roamed her body in the moonlight. Her throat and shoulders progressed into two perfect white orbs tipped with peach buttons. Full and curvaceous hips led to long legs. Gage saw her reach to remove her necklace.

"Leave it on."

He smiled as her fingers drifted away from her neck. He had dreamed of making love to her like this for so many nights. Tonight was no longer a dream or distant memory. His wife lay in front of him. He

145

climbed onto the bed, settling himself between her thighs. Both of them moaned as he slid inside her. He slowly moved against her, savoring the feeling of finally being one after so many centuries apart.

Caitlin lost herself in each intense ripple of pleasure Gage created. His hands and lips seemed to be everywhere as their bodies danced together. She cried out his name when she came. He lightly kissed her cheeks, allowing her to be swept away by the torrents of desire tearing through her. When her pulse slowed, Gage thrust into her again, giving into his own need. She zealously matched the tempo of his hips, rolling hers so she pulled him deeper inside her.

"I love you, Evariste," she whispered, lost in the euphoria of lovemaking.

"I love you, Caitlin Arsceneaux. Always have and always will." Gage shuddered, erupting inside her.

The Morning After
〜

Caitlin snuggled closer to Gage, resisting the waking world and not wanting the blissful night to end.

"Good morning, beautiful," Gage rasped, not quite ready to greet the new day.

"Good morning, handsome." She gazed up at him from his chest.

He smiled, admiring the amethyst orbs that captured his heart the second he met her. They were such an unusual color, especially for a flame-haired woman. "Are you hungry, cher?" He kissed the top of her head. "I believe I promised you a crawfish omelet or crêpes."

"I am, but not for an omelet or crêpes." She propped herself up on one arm and ran a finger down his chest.

Gage chuckled as he rolled her underneath him. "I am more than happy to take care of that type of hunger as well."

After another round of lovemaking, both showered then went downstairs for breakfast. Caitlin smiled as they walked past their shoes, Gage's jacket and cravat, along with the painting that now had a broken frame in the foyer on their way to the kitchen.

"I hope no one tripped over our stuff if they came back here last night."

"It would serve them right with as much as they won't let me have a little privacy lately."

"I guess if they did, everyone will know what happened between us. We weren't exactly quiet on top of the mess here."

"I hope you aren't having second thoughts about us, cher."

Caitlin laughed. "Not at all, but there's probably a better way to announce our relationship than clothes scattered across your house."

"We can pick that mess up after breakfast. I'm starving."

Caitlin smiled the whole time they cooked together. She dressed in the long, white shirt he had worn last night. Gage wore a T-shirt and a pair of boxers as he taught Caitlin how to make a crawfish omelet.

"Ready for the flip?" he asked, helping her pick up the pan.

Caitlin grinned at him. "I always mess this up."

"This morning you won't. Ready?" Gage didn't wait for an answer, tilting the pan downward then flipped his wrist, so the omelet turned over. Once the egg and ingredients settled perfectly into place, he brushed his lips against her temple. "See, cher. You just needed someone to teach you how to do it correctly."

"Allo?" Alcee called from the front door, spotting the shoes and clothing cast across the foyer. He shook his head and carefully stepped over the broken chunks of picture frame.

"In the kitchen!" Gage yelled as he handed Caitlin her breakfast and started to make himself an omelet.

Noticing that Caitlin wore Evariste's shirt, Alcee grinned. "I take it the two of you had a good night after the ball?"

Caitlin laughed at his question. Gage smiled over at her before stirring the contents for his omelet.

"Crawfish omelet?" Caitlin offered Alcee a bite of her breakfast.

"Non. Merci for the offer, ma petite. I just came by to make sure the two of you arrived home safely after you disappeared. Allister stayed with Marie and me last night, but the others returned home."

"Really?" Gage said, surprised that Alcee allowed Alli to stay in his house, which was more like a museum than a home.

"I thought you might like some privacy." Alcee now saw that Caitlin still wore her wedding ring as she drank her orange juice. "You also left these at Shadow Oaks last night." Alcee set Caitlin's fan and Gage's forgotten gloves and cloak on the kitchen table.

"Thank you for grabbing them, Alcee. I need to give Marie the fan, jewels, and gown back today. Please tell her thank you for letting me borrow them." Caitlin picked up the fan and played with it.

Alcee frowned. All those items belonged to her and Evariste. He had hoped the ball and an evening with Evariste would prompt the return of her past. For a moment, he thought that might have occurred with the wedding ring on her finger. "Actually, they belonged to Evariste's grandmother. You need to return them to him, not Marie."

"Were they really your grandmother's?" Caitlin asked, looking over at Gage.

Her question caught him off guard. He hated lying to her about his "grandmother." Gage stirred the contents of the frying pan, unable to look her in the eye. "Yes. I thought they would make last night memorable for you."

"We must be pretty close in size. I could swear the dress was made for me with how well it fit," Caitlin nonchalantly commented, taking another bite of her breakfast.

Alcee and Evariste exchanged glances, not sure how to react to her statement.

"You are burning your omelet," Alcee warned Evariste who was now lost in thought.

"Merde." Gage quickly flipped the omelet onto a plate.

Silence filled the room as he sat down to eat.

"Is everything ok?" Caitlin worried about the strange tension in the air.

Gage gave her a charming smile. "Everything is fine. Why don't you go get dressed since you're done eating? I'll take you out to the farm, so you can see how my family raises sugar cane since you mentioned being interested in learning more about the farm last night."

Alcee watched Caitlin quickly kiss Evariste before going to dress. He didn't miss the longing in his friend's eyes as they watched her disappear down the hall. "Je suis vraiment désolé."

"For what?" Gage played with the food on his plate.

"For being so certain the ball would unlock her past, and that not happening." Alcee sat down at the table.

"Not your fault. I also wouldn't say nothing happened last night. While she doesn't remember yet, we had some interesting conversations that lead me to believe it is only a matter of time before I have my wife back. I also like the woman she is in this lifetime. She's beautiful, smart, and successful. I would be happy with her as she is."

"Undoubtedly you would be, but could you deal with her growing old or her dying, if you didn't return to a human state during this lifetime with her?"

Alcee's questions irritated Gage. "I would consider myself exceptionally fortunate to spend this lifetime with her and to watch her grow old. That's how marriage and loving someone works, Alcee. Let's take this one day at a time and see what each day brings. I still have faith she'll eventually remember; hopefully, when she does, she'll break this damn curse we're all under."

A First Drink

❦

Caitlin's last week in New Orleans went by too quickly. Gage enjoyed rediscovering the wonders of the city and the surrounding areas with her. He appreciated how his family welcomed her back into the fold and carefully censored stories to ensure no one shocked her by sharing too much about her prior life. It was going to be pure hell on him to come home to an empty house after she went back to Virginia.

They spent her last night in Louisiana secluded away together. He took the house phone off the hook and shut off their cell phones then set them on the dresser. "I want no interruptions tonight. No contact with the outside world. I refuse to share you with you flying out in the morning."

He strode to the bed, taking in the vision of the woman waiting for him to join her.

"I'll be back in a month for a conference."

"A month is too long. Even a day away from you will feel like an eternity to me."

For the first time, Gage completely lost control of the beast within as they made love. The vampire broke free and refused to be caged again. Caitlin's pulse thundered in his ears. The thumping tempo tapped temptingly against his lips when his face rested against the crook of her neck. The sweet, floral smell of the lotion on her skin paired with the more heady scent of her arousal drove him over the edge. He had to taste her, to claim her, to bind her eternally to him. His teeth sunk into soft, warm flesh. His body tremored from the welcoming feel of muscle giving way for his canines, then moist warmth meeting his tongue, mirroring the way her body embraced his cock when he drove himself into her. He groaned, biting down deeper, drinking the sweetest elixir he had ever tasted. Caitlin cried out, climaxing. Her legs wrapped around his as her fingers frantically pressed his face into her neck. The soft whimpers and pants coming from her brought him to the brink of insanity. He pounded himself into her, continuing to drink; only heightening the euphoria they both experienced from his feeding. He never wanted to stop lapping up her blood with the feral pleasure it gave each of them. Every sip, every flick of his tongue bringing more across his palate, intensified the wildfire coursing through him.

"Gage!" Caitlin screamed his name, her nails frantically raking his back as she experienced another orgasm.

An animalistic growl left his lips when he finally threw his head back from the intensity of his own release and the merging of their two souls.

He gently rubbed a thumb across the marks he left on her neck, closing them. "I didn't hurt you, did I?"

"Not at all. You're quite the lover, Gage." Caitlin smiled, her hand drifting down his chest. "Every time we make love I enjoy it, but tonight, tonight was incredible"

"Even when I—?" Gage couldn't bring himself to admit what he had just done, especially to a woman he cared about.

"When you what?"

The way Caitlin stared up at him confused shared she didn't have a clue that he drank from her. How was that possible? He assumed all this time humans would know when they were fed upon. "Got a little rough near the end there."

"That was the best part. I've never orgasmed like that before. I'm going to miss the way you kiss me."

"Just the way I kiss you?" Gage brushed his lips over hers.

"And how you touch me." Caitlin kissed him again. "Then the way you make love or fuck me."

They both laughed before sharing another kiss.

"Truthfully, Gage, part of me wishes I wasn't going home."

Gage grinned at her confession. D'Orme was her home, not Virginia. Something inside her now recognized that. "Good. That means you'll keep your promise to come back in a month."

"I have to come back. Between the conference and Giovanni being hell-bent on buying Lagniappe, I'll undoubtedly be delivering another offer on your company for him." She ran a finger across his pecs.

"Then I'll keep stringing Giovanni along and make any discussions or offers contingent on you conducting regular on-site negotiations, declining any such discussions via the phone or online conferencing. So he has to use you as an intermediary."

"You're devious, Evariste. But I like it, especially if it means more nights in your arms."

Gage caressed her forehead with his thumb, admiring her in the moonlight. "You can always quit your damn job and move in with me, then you can spend every night in my arms."

Caitlin smiled, settling her hands on his shoulders again. "Always pushing for the next thing you think you want, Arsceneaux?"

"You know what they say about the outcome of never taking chances or going after the things you want," Gage whispered, lowering his face back to hers.

GAGE LAID AWAKE, watching the woman sound asleep with her head on his chest. She really hadn't noticed what he had done, which relieved and puzzled him at the same time. He debated waking her and revealing what he was. What was the worst that could possibly happen if she learned he was a vampire? If he confessed he needed her to stay with him, to help him make business decisions, and to ease the nightmares he continually suffered from by sleeping beside him every night. Her presence the past two weeks had actually erased the night terrors which routinely robbed him of a peaceful night's rest. God, he needed his wife back.

The thought of her looking at him horrified prevented him from doing any of the things he contemplated. He wasn't willing to lose her again. He'd wait until the right time, when he could ease her through whatever reaction she may have to the news and their new relationship was on more solid ground.

He reached over to the nightstand and opened a pouch containing a pendant given to him by the same voodoo priestess who prophesied Caitlin's return and his salvation. She had instructed him to give it to Caitlin for protection against the darkness that would reawaken and seek them out. They had to be unified to overcome the darkness. When he asked the priestess what exactly the darkness was, she refused to elaborate any further. Tristan had to be what the priestess referred to as the darkness. Nothing else threatened Caitlin. He would do everything he could to keep Tristan away from her.

The sandman finally won the battle he waged against the vampire refusing to sleep. Gage drifted off with the pendant still in his hand.

THE ALARM WENT off way too early. Caitlin stirred beside him, but instead of waking fully, she nestled closer into his side.

"Caitlin, cher, we need to get up, so you don't miss your flight." Gage groggily whispered, rubbing her shoulder.

Caitlin groaned, hugging him then stretched. "Do we have time for breakfast?"

Expecting that question, Gage chuckled. "Yes, cher. We've got time. I wouldn't send you back to Virginia on an empty stomach."

"Do we also have time for...." Caitlin's hand drifted down his belly and under the covers.

"I more than factored in plenty of time to make love this morning to ensure you wouldn't forget me."

The smile Caitlin gave him promised she wouldn't.

THINKING about the better days ahead with his wife back in his life, Gage smiled while making Caitlin one last breakfast. Her phone rang. By the way she answered, it was her boss.

"Don't talk too long, cher. Your breakfast will get cold," he murmured in the ear her phone wasn't held up to then brushed his lips across her forehead.

"Who was that?" Her boss's voice raised, clearly coming through the speaker.

"The hotel chef. He was kind enough to arrange an early breakfast for me this morning." Caitlin grinned as she answered the inquiry.

Gage chuckled at what she told her boss before she quickly ended the call. "Worried he might make further inquiries?"

"No. I just want to enjoy my breakfast and the little bit of time I have with you this morning." Caitlin picked up her fork.

ON THE DRIVE to the airport, her hand rested on his anytime it was on the center console between them. Stopping in front of the terminal, Gage leaned over and kissed her. "I hope you have a pleasant flight, Cate. I'll be counting down the days until you return."

Caitlin smiled, squeezing his hand. "Me, too."

After handing her bags to the attendant at the curbside check-in, Gage pulled the pouch out of his pocket. "I have something for you."

He settled the white and yellow gold filigree pendant around her neck then secured the clasp for her.

"It's beautiful, Evariste. I can't take this."

Her use of his first name made him smile. "Nonsense. You most certainly can and will. It's a very special gift and has been in the family for a long time. Alcee swears it brings the wearer a lifetime of love and good luck." Gage straightened the round medallion, so it rested on the center of her collarbone.

"Well, in that case, I'll happily wear it. Thank you." Caitlin hugged him.

"You better get going." He kissed her one last time and whispered something in French that she didn't understand. He watched her until the glass doors closed behind her.

Alcee walked up behind him. "You're really letting her go?"

"What choice do I have? She'll be back in a month. If I waited three hundred years for her, I can manage a month apart. You're up early."

"Never went to bed. I also wanted to be certain that one didn't cause you any trouble." Alcee pointed out Tristan standing in a group of people several feet away.

Gage scowled, not liking the fact Tristan loitered around the airport. "If I didn't need to move my truck, I'd tell the stalking bastard good morning. Hire someone to keep an eye him and dig into his affairs. I want to know why he's so interested in Caitlin, now and in the past."

Return To Williamsburg

⟡

aitlin's first couple of days back in Williamsburg were hectic. Two new projects came in, which Sean put under her oversight. She managed to avoid a face-to-face with him for two days. The email summoning her to the office meant she could either come see him willingly or he'd be showing up on her doorstep to discuss Lagniappe Shipping & Ag. Deciding it was better they deal with things in his office rather than her living room, she packed up her laptop and headed into work.

"Welcome back!" Esther cheerfully greeted her. "I can't wait to hear all about your trip."

"She'll fill you in later." Sean caught Caitlin's arm, walking in behind her and led her to his office. "Why have you been avoiding me?"

"I haven't," Caitlin denied the accusation, sitting down, knowing this wasn't going to be your typical five minute debrief. "I was unpacking, buying groceries, and catching up on emails, so I could focus on the hot mess you dumped in my lap with those two new suits, on top of my work on Lagniappe Shipping &Ag."

"With Arsceneaux suddenly opening the door to us, he won't take up so much time anymore. Any idea why he had a change of heart?"

"No. I would assume it was more Alli Robicheaux and Alcee Dugas's doing than him having a change of heart. He's a pretty stubborn guy and definitely doesn't like anyone sticking their nose where it doesn't belong, including me. I still think Giovanni needs to move on. I get the feeling Arsceneaux won't sell at any price."

"Every man has his price." Sean grinned. "It's our job to figure it out. Keep digging into Evariste and the company to see if there might be any little thing we could use as leverage to bring him to the negotiating table."

Caitlin let out an exasperated sigh. "Fine, but I'm telling you now, we won't find anything."

"With business done, want to tell me about this chef you met?" Sean eyed Caitlin, finding it out of character for her to randomly hook up with a man on vacation.

"No, as you'll run and tell Gram about him, getting her all worked up when he and I aren't even serious yet."

"You were at the man's house and he was making you breakfast when I called you three days ago. I would say that is the starts of something serious."

"How do you know where I was?"

"The check out date on your room invoice. It isn't hard to guess where you stayed after that, especially with him whispering in your ear and the kiss I heard. You spent over a week with someone you hardly know?"

"Not exactly, and as for the relationship, it's the start of let's see what happens. You better not breathe a word about him to Gram. The last thing I need is her showing up here planning a wedding prematurely or you interrogating the guy and spooking him off. When it turns serious, I will tell you about him. Until then, he's none of your business. I'm a big girl now. You don't need to keep acting like my father."

Sean chuckled. "I will never stop acting like your father, Cate. Whether you like it or not. I made a promise to him and your mother to watch over you. Gram regularly reminds me of it too."

A WEEK of twelve-hour days wore on her. She sat down with a microwavable dinner for lunch and read emails as meetings left her little time to keep up with her own workload.

"Caitlin?" Esther walked up to what was quickly becoming Caitlin's designated desk.

Caitlin groaned, wondering what meeting she was being pulled into now.

"What does Sean need?" Caitlin asked, turning in her chair.

"Lucky for you, nothing. These came for you a little while ago, and the delivery guy made me promise to give them to you as soon as you were out of your meeting." Esther wheeled around a cart containing a massive arrangement of red roses and large, white lilies.

"Oh my. They're beautiful. Thank you for bringing them over." Caitlin inhaled the pleasant fragrance coming from the flowers. The strong, sweet scent of the white oriental lilies intermingling with the nuanced musk of the roses took her back to the garden at D'Orme and lazy mornings in bed with Gage.

Sean walked by with Bill, one of the other partners in the firm, and saw the flowers. "Guess Arsceneaux really took a liking to you. He won't return my or Dante's calls but will drop a couple hundred on an arrangement for you. Better tell him about that chef you're seeing."

"They're from the chef, not Arsceneaux."

Sean snorted at her denial. "I don't know many chefs getting paid well enough to send women such expensive flowers."

"He's the head chef of a five-star establishment. They get paid rather well." Caitlin earned a second cynical look from him.

Sean went back to talking with Bill as the two continued on to the conference room.

"Whoever this new man of yours is in New Orleans, he is a keeper. Those are gorgeous," Maria, one of the paralegals, commented over the cubicle wall.

"Yes, he certainly is." Caitlin smiled as she pulled out the card.

Thinking of you. D'Orme isn't the same without you here.

Gage

Arrangements like this warranted a phone call, not a quick text. She pulled out her phone to thank him for the flowers.

Gage answered on the first ring. "I take it you got the flowers."

"Yes, I did. Thank you for sending them. They made my day."

"I'm glad they did, cher. You've sounded stressed the past couple of nights when we've talked. I thought they'd make you smile. I hate to cut this short, but I'm walking into a meeting."

"Not a problem. I'll call you tonight."

"Caitlin." Gage stopped her from hanging up. "Tell Esther I said thank you for bringing them to you. Bill is driving her crazy with all the schedule changes as well. Je t'aime, ma ange."

He hung up before she had a chance to respond. How did he know Esther dropped off the flowers and that Bill was driving them all crazy with these two new projects implementing?

Caitlin walked over to Esther's desk. "By chance, did you speak with Gage earlier?"

"Who's Gage?" Esther thought Caitlin had finally snapped underneath all of the pressure from the past couple of days.

"Evariste Arsceneaux. His family and friends call him Gage."

"So you're family and friends now? Is that allowed?" Esther quipped with a smirk. "You know Sean suspects the chef and Evariste are one and the same? You aren't fooling him any."

Caitlin acted as if she didn't hear what Esther said. "I'm sorry Bill and Sean are making your day crazy as well."

"Pssh, I'm used to the craziness that happens around here. Though thank you for caring. I am looking forward to seeing how this business rivals to lovers relationship of yours turns out."

Caitlin laughed and shook her head. "We've never been rivals, but I am pushing company policy a bit. That is exactly why I'm sticking to my story of dating a chef from New Orleans, and I expect you to do the same if Sean asks you anything about my personal life. Out of curiosity, what did the delivery person look like?"

"An old gray-haired lady."

"Thanks." Caitlin tried to figure out how Gage managed to know the things that he did.

"Before Sean sucks you into another meeting, are we still on for the Preservation Society event tomorrow night?"

"Yeah. By the time we get out of here, we won't have much time for dinner. Wanna eat at Kings Arms since it's near the Governor's Palace?"

"Sounds good to me. I'll book us a table." Esther started to type in the website address of the reservation platform.

Sean's door opening and a familiar voice sounding behind her caused Caitlin's upper body to twist slightly while she tried to get a better look at whoever spoke.

"Thanks, Sean. I appreciate the advice, and will definitely check out La Tienda while I'm in town."

The smile on Caitlin's face vanished as Tristan Dausan strode toward her.

"Don't worry, Cate. I'm not here for you." Tristan leaned closer, biting the air.

Caitlin flinched at the sound his teeth made as they snapped together. Her fingers wrapped around the pencil lying on Esther's desk.

"Going to stake me, sweetheart?" Tristan almost dared her to try.

Fear paralyzed Caitlin in place. Tristan's breath surfaced goose-bumps anywhere it warmed her skin. The tip of his nose moved threat-eningly along her hair. "Evariste marking his territory with trinkets now? Tell him it won't completely keep the monsters at bay."

Without realizing it, she slammed her fist and the pencil toward Tristan's chest. An amused chuckle and his fingers tightening around her wrist, halting her swinging arm, made her aware of what she had just done. "Careful, Cate. That's foreplay for men like me."

"You're a disgusting pig, Tristan." Caitlin jerked her hand free.

"I'm not the one suddenly throwing themselves at someone." Tristan riled her more. "Unfortunately, I'm headed back to New Orleans this evening. Otherwise, we could see where this might lead."

"I should have rammed the pencil straight through you," Caitlin snarled back at him.

"So feisty! Maybe I should change my flight, so I can spend the evening putting you back in your place, Cate."

"Fuck off, Tristan. Why are you even here?"

"I'm taking care of a last-minute request for a client that needed to be carried out in person and decided to stop in to tell Sean hello."

"I wasn't aware you two knew one another." Caitlin glared at him. "Sean normally doesn't slither around in the sewers with ambulance chasers like yourself."

Tristan loudly sucked in air between his teeth and put a hand over his heart. "Ouch. Always such a vicious little thing, DeDanann. And for the record, I've never been an ambulance chaser."

"You may need one if you keep talking to her like you are." Sean inserted himself between the two of them. "I believe you were leaving."

"See you around, Cate." Tristan winked at her then walked out the door.

"First, Giovanni, and now running in the same circles as Dausan? I'm starting to think I need to find a new job. Giovanni I can sort of understand, but a low life like Dausan, Sean? The firm's sunk to an all-time low if we're working for assholes like him." Caitlin couldn't believe Sean would represent or collaborate with Tristan on any project or suit.

"No need to start filling out job applications. I'm not a fan of Tristan Dausan either, and we aren't representing him or associating with him in any professional manner. His 'stopping by' shocked the hell out of me. The last time I saw him was across a federal courtroom when I won the Haydel case. How do you know him?"

"He was one of the company litigators for Stafford when I ran their catastrophe team. I hated being an expert witness on his suits. He's the one litigator who always creeped me out during prep or anytime I was alone with him. Not to mention he's a complete douchebag that's always hitting on women. He almost ruined my dinner with the old crew in New Orleans. Thankfully, a bartender noticed him harassing me and tossed him out of Thib's."

The tips of Sean's ears turned red and his jaw clenched. His eyes locked on the door as he looked over Caitlin's head to see if Tristan was still there. "Harassing you to the point he was thrown out of a restaurant? The stupid prick better be thankful I didn't know about this until now. Esther, call security and ask them to ensure Mr. Dausan vacates the premises. I also want one of the guards to see Caitlin to her car when she leaves this evening."

THANKFULLY, there was no sign of Tristan when Joe, one of the office security staff, walked her to her car. Hopefully, there were a thousand or so miles between her and Tristan with his saying he had a flight out that night. An hour after she had been home, Sean called offering to take her out to dinner, claiming it was to finish discussing a few things about the Jameson file, but she knew it was really because he didn't want her out and about alone tonight. Her spat with Tristan worried him, even though he denied it did.

"Dinner sounds good." Caitlin accepted the offer. It had been a while since they hung out together as friends versus boss and employee. "La Tienda?"

"Sure. I'll be there in ten."

They casually discussed work over tapas and paella for most of the evening.

Halfway through dinner, Sean smiled at her, refilling her wine glass. "So, tell me a bit more about this chef sending flowers to my office?"

Caitlin laughed. "Plying me with wine then peppering me with questions isn't going to work tonight, Watchous. I already told you what you need to know about him. His name is Gage. He's a chef at a long-standing establishment in Louisiana. And as you've seen with the flowers, he's sweet and charming when he wants to be."

"How'd you meet Mr. Sweet and Charming?" Sean eyed her from across the table.

"He's the chef who cooked dinner for Alli and me when she invited me out to dinner the first day I was at Lagniappe Shipping & Ag."

"Mmm, I had forgotten Allister invited you to dinner. What was the name of the restaurant again?"

"None ya business." Caitlin laughed as she said the Southern phrase Evariste periodically tossed out when folks asked him a question he didn't want to answer.

Sean raised a brow and let out an aggravated sigh. "As long as he treats you right, Cate. That's all that matters."

"He does, Sean. I think you'd like him. He's different from most guys I've dated."

"Different?" Sean waited for her to elaborate on that.

"He keeps to himself and isn't ladder climbing like Liam. In fact, he's rather down to earth, and a weird combination of worldly and redneck."

"Redneck?" Sean laughed at the way she described her latest beau. "Are you trying to convince me the woman who hates cowboy boots, the outdoors, and country music is suddenly dating some Cajun from the swamps of Louisiana because he made you breakfast in bed one morning? You really don't want me to figure out who the chef is to be telling such tall tales, do you?"

"Oh, Sean, you'd understand why I've had a change of heart if you ever ate one of his omelets. And I know you won't believe it, but we even went fishing together, at it's-too-freaking dark-thirty in the morning, and I enjoyed it."

"Fishing? You went fishing? Is that a euphemism for something I should be scolding you for doing?" Sean almost didn't believe his ears.

"No, we actually went fishing. I caught two redfish, and Gage cooked them for dinner that night. He also shot an alligator that came after me when I got off the boat."

"Saints preserve us. You really are falling for this guy. Gram is going to have a stroke when she hears this." Sean smirked and shook his head.

Caitlin threw a piece of bread at him. "You promised you wouldn't say a word to her unless things got serious."

"By the way you're ohing and awing over the alligator slayer, things are heading that direction. Can't wait to meet him. Does he at least have his front teeth?" Sean chuckled as he spoke.

"Nope, and that gap between his lateral incisors allows him to do such amazing things with his tongue." Caitlin overdramatically closed her eyes before loudly swallowing a mouthful of red wine.

"La, la, la, la!" Sean covered his ears with his hands. "I don't want to hear about what he does with his tongue, Caitlin DeDanann, or any other part of his body."

Caitlin laughed at how he tossed back the wine still left in his glass and shook his head. "Then stop asking questions and picking on me."

"It's my job to pick on you, Cate, and to thoroughly screen whatever man you're dating to try to keep you from dating losers, not that telling you a guy is a worthless piece of trash ever worked. But I have to at least attempt to honor the promise I made to Gram and your parents."

New Experiences

 ⟋⟍

Caitlin called Gage after Sean dropped her off at her apartment.

"Hello, beautiful." His voice cheerfully greeted her. "Have a good rest of the day?"

"I did for the most part." She could hear the clicking of computer keys in the background.

"For the most part?"

Caitlin sat down on the couch and pulled a blanket up over herself. "Are you still at the office?"

"I am. I've got a few things to catch up on since I spent most of last week with you."

"It's almost ten o'clock, Gage. Ever heard of working from home?"

Gage chuckled before speaking. "I do that, too. But don't feel like lugging the paperwork home with me tonight. Now, tell me what happened for you to say your day was good, for the most part, instead of it being fabulous after getting flowers from the handsome man who adores you."

She smiled at how he described himself. "Why is it guys think flowers or jewelry cure everything that ever upsets a woman?"

"Are you telling me they don't?"

The mock astonishment in Gage's voice made her laugh. "You're such a smart ass. The flowers were the highlight of my day. Surprisingly, there was only one brief blip after getting them that tarnished my afternoon."

"Hmmm...and what was the blip?"

"Tristan Dausan waltzing out of Sean's office like he owned the place."

The periodic clacking of keys in the background stopped. She could almost see Gage staring down at the phone laying on his desk with an angry look on his face.

"Dausan? The piece of shit who got himself tossed out of Thib's for bothering you and your friend?"

The way Gage almost growled out the inquiry warned he wasn't happy to learn Tristan was in Williamsburg.

"Yep. Thankfully, he wasn't in the office long and is flying back to NOLA tonight."

"Did he happen to say why he was in Virginia?"

"Something about a last-minute request from a client having to be done in person." Caitlin looked over at the flowers she had brought home now sitting in the center of her coffee table. They made her apartment smell like D'Orme. "I told Sean about what happened at Thib's. If Tristan's smart, he won't step foot near Sean or me again anytime soon."

A loud huff came through the phone. "No one would ever describe Dausan as smart, except for himself. I have an odd request to make of you, cher. The necklace I gave you, please wear it for me the next couple of days, even when you're sleeping. Promise me you'll do that."

"Sure, I guess I can do that." She almost asked why but decided against it.

"Because I'm a superstitious fool at times. Blame my Creole nature for that. While I know it's probably only an old story, it makes me feel better knowing you're wearing something from me that is supposed to ward off bad luck."

Caitlin smiled, running a finger over the filigree pendant she wore. She hadn't gotten around to taking it off for the day. Now she wouldn't be anytime soon with the promise she just made Gage. "How do you do that?"

"Do what, cher?"

"Know what I'm thinking, even when I don't say it."

"Good businessmen learn quickly how to read people. You're an open book to the right reader. And you're quite possibly my favorite piece of literature to read."

Her eyes involuntarily closed and she bit her lower lip in response to the sensual familiarity suddenly in his voice. No man had ever compared her to a book in a manner that made her long for his fingers to run down her body as they would a page before it was turned.

"If only I were there, mon coeur. They'd trace every line on your body then my tongue would etch each word into your soul. We'd get lost in the narrative together, authoring our own tale. My quill diving into your well, scrawling word after new word into your flesh, slowly building a world crafted exclusively for us, playing with pacing and tension until plunging us both into climactic ecstasy. I'd revise each word, each sentence, again and again until it was perfectly written just for you."

The growing ache between Caitlin's legs made her shift on the couch. "Never thought I'd find writing so arousing. I wish you were here."

"Do you? Put the phone on speaker, then take off your night gown."

"What?" she squeaked, her heart almost jumping out of her chest. Had he really just said what she thought he did or was she hallucinating?

"You heard me, Caitlin. I'm not a man to leave his lover wanting and unsatisfied. Now, please, do as I asked."

"I've lost my ever-loving mind when it comes to you." Caitlin hit the speaker phone icon then pulled her nightgown over her head. Her hands shook and she swallowed hard before climbing back onto the sofa. She had never in her life contemplated phone sex with someone. It had always seemed like a cheesy idea to her.

"It won't be with me, cher. I promise." Gage perceptively chuckled.

That earthy baritone laugh only worsened the heat gradually spreading throughout Caitlin's body. The slight brush of her fingertips against her thigh as she sat down ignited it now. Anticipation engulfed every fiber of her being while waiting for Gage's next instruction.

"Lay back, close your eyes, and imagine me with you. Think of the contrast between the cool velvet of the couch against your back and my warm hands caressing your skin. The scruff along my jaw tickling your neck then me rubbing my cheek gently along your collar bone and shoulder before I nip at your neck."

A sigh came from Caitlin's lips as her fingers traced along her clavicle envisioning exactly what Gage asked her to.

"Run your fingertips ever so lightly between your breasts then down your belly as you would my back. Let them travel over the cotton of your panties. Stop after making one circle between your legs, gently teasing yourself, but no more than that."

Caitlin softly moaned when her fingers brushed against her core, confirming she did as instructed.

"Good girl, cher. Now slowly bring those fingers upward until you reach your breasts." He paused and waited a few seconds before speaking. "I want you to trace small circles around those lovely nipples of yours until they harden."

"Gage," Caitlin breathed his name as she now saw him gently taking a hard nub between his lips. Her fingers mimicked the way he suckled then teased it, twisting and rolling it with his tongue and teeth. She unconsciously grasped her other breast doing the same.

"Oh, cher," he crooned breathily as if he whispered in her ear. The damp heat between her thighs immediately intensified. It seemed as if he was there, dragging one of her hands back down her body; his fingers gently guiding hers against herself. She wantonly tossed her head from side to side, massaging herself; soft gasps and cries of pleasure fell from her lips.

"Jesus, Cate. You have no idea how hearing those sounds you're making right now is torturing me." His voice took on a strained tone when he spoke again, "By how damp those panties are, you're more than ready for me. Slide them off, so you can rub that clit and pussy just as I would."

Almost as if in a trance, Caitlin hurriedly did so, anxious for waves of red-hot desire to once more wash over her. Flesh tingled and sang— her fingers easily sliding against her slick core. Listening to Gage's every instruction, she brought herself closer to orgasm. By the way Gage groaned and his breathing grew labored, he was partaking in the same guilty pleasure she was.

"Gage, are you?"

"Oh, cher, I most certainly am. My cock is in my hand twitching and agonizingly hard, knowing you're picturing me fucking you as you get yourself off. Though my fingers could never match the feel of that sweet, warm body of yours. How wet you get for me, allowing me to perfectly slide in and out of you."

They both moaned together.

"There's nothing more pleasurable than your cock inside me, Gage." Caitlin more rapidly strummed the swollen button above her opening.

"In that case, slide two fingers inside yourself, Cate."

Another throaty moan escaped her lips as she did as requested. A cross between a growl and groan came through the phone's speaker.

"I want to hear you come, cher. I know you're close. Don't hold back on me."

Visions of him driving himself into her as his thumb massaged her clit flooded her head. She could feel his body moving against hers, his girth filling her as her fingers never could, the tip of his cock perfectly stroking her G-spot with each thrust of his hips. She bucked against her hand, drawing her own fingers in deeper.

"That's it," Gage's voice rasped from somewhere in the darkness Caitlin lost herself in. "I love being inside you...how perfectly you fit me...the way your pussy clenches around me."

Blissful tension built within Caitlin like the tight coiling of a cord, threatening to delightfully snap with each new pluck at its taunt center. Deliciously torturing her and Gage alike. She didn't want whatever this erotic connection to Gage was to end.

"It won't ever end, Caitlin. I'm never letting go of you again," Gage rumbled in a vacillating tone.

His promise of never letting go tore a loud cry from somewhere deep inside Caitlin. "Gage, this—oh my god!—this is exquisite. I've never..."

A brief moment of shyness or maybe some weird self-reproach at openly masturbating with a lover prevented her from completely losing herself to the enthralling rhythm of her fingers and Gage's voice dancing with such vivid imagery in her mind.

"Damn whatever guilt is creeping into that pretty head of yours. Let go of it. This is supposed to feel better than everything else, and it gets me off thinking of you pleasuring yourself since I can't be there to do it for you. Now, come for me."

Her inner world exploded, her body doing exactly as he commanded. Her back arching and a satisfied scream escaping her lips.

Silence filled the room as Caitlin drifted back to the couch from wherever her soul had gone. Her breathing gradually slowing to a normal pace.

A soft chuckle sounded from the phone lying beside her. "Finally back with me, cher?"

Caitlin let out a short laugh. "I'm here. I never imagined phone sex could be so close to the real thing."

"With the right partner, it can be.But I'd much rather have you here, so we can explore all the fun, sinful things you like to do together."

"You really are something else, Arsceneaux. Always full of surprises" Caitlin sighed. He was so different from the other men she dated.

"I'm definitely not like any other you previously dated, and I intend to keep you on your toes as long as we're together. Next time, I'll have you turn on your camera, so I can watch too."

"Oh hell no." Caitlin couldn't believe they had done what they had tonight. There was no way she was doing something like that on camera, not even for Gage. Who knows what pervy hacker might be watching them. The last thing either of them needed was for footage of an intimate moment to be posted somewhere in the dark bowels of the internet.

Gage laughed. "Well, at least we've established where your boundaries are. As much as I'd love to stay on the phone with you all night, I need to um, clean up, and get back to work."

"I guess I'll talk to you tomorrow then."

"Pleasant dreams, cher."

"Gage, thank you for the, the new experience." Caitlin blushed as she spoke.

"You're most welcome. Stop blushing like some guilty Catholic school girl. There's nothing wrong with enjoying a little self-love every now and then. And don't open what I just ordered for you with anyone else nearby."

"What'd you order?"

The devious chuckle she heard made her smile.

"Something that should help you really enjoy new experiences when you need them."

"You're a bad man, Evariste Arsceneaux. Get back to work, handsome, so you can go home and get some sleep. I know you've got your weekly staff meeting at eight tomorrow. Maybe you should consider moving it back to ten." Caitlin grinned, waiting to hear his response.

"I'm going to have to if you're sticking around. Eight a.m. is definitely too early a start if I'm staying up most of the night with you on the phone or in person. Good night, cher."

THE INTIMATE MOMENT with Caitlin and his work should have distracted Gage from the unease growing within him once again. He sat back in his chair, trying to figure out why Tristan had gone to Williamsburg. Was he really there for a client or was he stupidly provoking another fight between them? The investigator trailing him had mentioned Tristan disappearing two nights ago but hadn't said a word about him getting on a flight anywhere.

Worried about Caitlin, he picked up his cell phone, scrolled through his contacts until he found Alcee's number then hit the call icon.

"You never call me at this hour unless there's a problem. What's on your mind, Evariste?" Alcee answered the phone.

"I talked to Caitlin a little while ago. Tristan showed up in her office out of the blue today."

"Pardon, mon ami? Did I hear that correctly? Tristan was in Virginia?"

Gage scowled. It wasn't often something caught Alcee by surprise. "He claimed to be there due to a request that needed to be handled in person. I'm not aware of any business dealings of his or any possible client of his who has an interest in anything in Virginia."

"All of his business interests are here, Chicago, Los Angeles, and New York. I can go back through the copies of his rolodex and calendar his secretary secretly copied for us to confirm that. I'll also check with Fabien to see if we overlooked something. It's odd for Fabien to have missed a commercial flight reservation. He's been closely trailing Tristan and keeping an eye on his affairs since Caitlin left as we asked him to do."

Troubled by the fact Fabien either didn't know about the flight or chose not to report it to Alcee, Gage leaned back in his chair. "Do you trust Fabien, Alcee?"

"With my life. He's one of us, Evariste, and he hates Tristan almost as much as you do."

Gage frustratedly sighed. "Then this was a spur of the moment trip, or Tristan knows we're watching him. Are there any vampires in Williamsburg who can watch over Caitlin while we figure out what Tristan is up to?"

"Oui, I have a contact or two there. One of whom is close to her already. I'll let him know about her and Tristan's history and ask him to ensure it doesn't repeat."

"Merci, Alcee. I'll not lose my wife now that I'm so close to having her back."

"Rest assured, Evariste. The individual I'm about to call won't let Tristan get anywhere near her again."

Artistic Mysteries

C aitlin and Esther walked from the office to The King's Arms
tavern for dinner. Both casually chatted about life while they ate
colonial fare.

"Any idea what this private donor might have given the Preservation
Society?" Esther asked while they waited for their bill.

"No idea. Considering the exhibit's in the Governor's Palace probably some furniture or artwork linking to some founding father."
Caitlin normally looked forward to the Historical Preservation Society
events, but tonight, she just wasn't into it.

The firm had recently become a sponsoring member of the Historical Preservation Society. She and Esther were the employees Sean
appointed to represent the firm at board meetings and other events. He
and Bill only made appearances at the more prestigious fundraisers and
annual gala.

Caitlin's level of enthusiasm didn't improve once they stepped
inside the Governor's Palace. She tried to force a smile, but her mind
kept wandering back to another building built a decade before the
reconstructed property in Williamsburg. She missed Gage and the
welcoming oaks of D'Orme. Being in an eighteenth-century building

with people dressed in period garb only made her loneliness worse as the environment conjured visions of the vampire ball.

"Girl, you've got it bad to look so depressed tonight," Esther said, after catching Caitlin staring out the window at the gardens behind the home.

"Got what bad?" Caitlin didn't catch whatever Esther hinted at.

"Feelings. You're moping like a heartbroken teenager today. You're missing Gage, aren't you?"

Caitlin smiled at her co-worker. "I'm not heartbroken at all, and yes, I'm missing Gage. For whatever reason, the guides in costume and being in a colonial building are making me think of him."

"That reason's called love. One of these days you're going to have to admit you've fallen for him. Sean's going to flip when you turn in your resignation to move to NOLA."

Caitlin snorted at the idea. "You sound like Alcee, and I'm not rushing into things. I learned my lesson with Liam."

"Liam was a selfish prick. We all tried to warn you. Evariste, while a tyrant when it comes to business, seems like quite the gentleman when it comes to you. Flowers, phone calls, text messages. The man genuinely cares about you and is trying to ensure you know he does."

"Or he's a crazy love bomber who will disappear in a few weeks," Caitlin joked.

Esther rolled her eyes. "I'll be sure to share that at your wedding reception. That'll make a great toast opener. Caitlin, in complete denial of her feelings, told us all Gage was a crazy love bomber. But love bombing turned into something more after he didn't ghost her: a life-time commitment which we are delighted to be here to celebrate today."

Caitlin loudly laughed, earning them several shushes from the group they walked with and an angry glare from one of the docents.

She only partially listened to their tour guide as they made their way into another room. A new painting on the far wall caught her eye. From where she stood, it looked like the governor of Virginia was with several other men in period dress. As she crossed the room to get a better look at the artist's subjects, two of the men's faces grew more and more familiar to her.

She recognized Gage and Alcee. There was no doubt in her mind as to the identities of two of the men in the painting as she studied their features. The artist even captured the emerald and diamond ring Gage wore on his left hand and the gold signet ring on his right.

"That's impossible," she muttered, continuing to stare up at the painting. She glanced at either side of the painting and below it to see if there was a placard offering some type of description about the work. Surprisingly, there wasn't.

"Excuse me." She stopped one of the volunteers working the event.

"Yes, ma'am?" the gentleman politely responded.

"Can you tell me who the men are standing with the governor?"

"I believe I can as the collection came with a journal inventorying all the pieces. We weren't able to get all the placards up before the exhibit opened tonight. If you'll come with me." The volunteer walked over to an antique secretary's desk then flipped open a dusty, leather-covered ledger.

Esther joined them at the desk. "How old is that ledger?"

Curious to learn more about her family history after her parents died, Caitlin had enlisted Esther's help with creating a family tree. She could have emailed Gram but decided against it as she got the feeling her grandmother didn't particularly like her father. Based on the short, clipped answers Gram offered whenever Caitlin asked about him, she probably didn't have his family history. Between Esther and herself, they managed to overcome several roadblocks in their genealogical research. Caitlin had a strange knack for finding pieces of family history that professional genealogists they reached out to couldn't or were rumored to have been destroyed in some calamity or another. She used to joke that her ancestors talked to her and showed her where to look after one genealogist swore a marriage certificate and a birth certificate for a particular couple's children manifested itself out of thin air.

"The collection dates back to the 1699. Ah, here is the information on the painting." The volunteer turned to the page with gloved hands and laid the ledger flat on the desk so all three of them could read it. "The painting is of Lieutenant Governor Alexander Spotswood and four business associates from Louisiana. He was contracting with them to purchase sugar for the colony. The four gentlemen are Evariste Arsceneaux, Pierre LeBlanc, Jude Robicheaux, Alcee Dugas, and the fourth just has initials, A.A.B."

Esther started at the name. "What are the odds that this Evariste Arsceneaux is related to the current one?"

Just as startled as Esther, Caitlin smiled at the universe surprising her with another reminder of Evariste in Williamsburg. "I would say pretty good. Lagniappe Shipping & Ag actually started in the 1700s based on the company documentation and my discussions with Gage."

The coincidence of Caitlin dating the descendant of one of the men in the painting tickled Esther. "How cool! You can tell Gage his ancestor is on display in Williamsburg."

"I will definitely be mentioning it."

The volunteer followed her when she went back over to the painting. They stood together, staring up at the men made of oil paint and brush strokes.

Caitlin absentmindedly played with the pendant around her neck. The resemblance of Colonial Alcee and Evariste to the present-day men was uncanny. Gage's stepfather was named Pierre LeBlanc. He easily could have been a younger version of the man she met at Shadow Oaks. Who were Jude Robicheaux and A.A.B? And why did A.A.B. only have initials instead of his name spelled out? "Is there any other information about the men in the journal?"

"None. You may want to ask your friend in Louisiana about the painting. If he is related, it would be nice to get a statement from him along with some history about his ancestor to include in the Society's records." He took a step backwards after noticing the pendant around her neck. "If that is all you needed, I have to get back to giving tours."

"I'm good. Thank you for your help. Is it okay if a take a picture of the painting?"

"Sure. Just be certain not to use a flash when you do."

She snapped a quick couple of pictures then scrolled through them on her phone to make sure they came out okay before continuing on through the exhibit.

CAITLIN TOSSED and turned in her sleep. Dreams that seemed more like actual memories than unconscious imaginings filled the night. In them, she was married to Gage and just found out she was pregnant with their first child.

D'Orme – 1715

"PLEASE WAIT for Evariste to come home." Jeanette repeated her earlier plea for Caitlin not to meet Evariste on his way back to D'Orme.

Gage's two sisters followed behind her as she stepped onto the front porch. A groom stood waiting outside the door with one of her horses.

"I will be fine, and the good news can't wait until tonight." Caitlin descended the steps then swung into the saddle. "The two of you worry too much about nothing."

"Caitlin, a woman in your condition should not be riding as you do. You took a fall from Gambit when a rabbit spooked him a few weeks ago. The last thing you want is to be bucked off and risk losing the baby, not after how long it's taken for you to conceive," Allister stated, concerned.

"That is why I am riding Sahara, not Gambit." Caitlin gathered the dapple gray mare's reins in her hands.

Alli and Jeanette both cringed at the thought of a pregnant Caitlin riding her favorite horse. The big black monster was an unpredictable beast, but Caitlin adored the horse anyway.

It was a gorgeous autumn day. She rode astride instead of sidesaddle, which she was certain Allister and Jeanette found just as imprudent and unladylike as her continuing to ride after finding out she was pregnant. She never could understand what was so scandalous about a woman doing such a thing. Her lavender day gown more than covered the majority of her legs. Also, going against the tradition of the day for women to keep their hair styled and pulled up, hers hung freely down her back. She waved goodbye to her sisters-in-law as she eased the horse into a canter, leaving the yard. Lost in thoughts of the future, she rode across the headlands and past two of the main cane fields. She slowed Sahara's pace as they entered the woods alongside the bayou.

Something hard struck her in the chest, knocking her from the saddle. She groaned as she sat up; her head throbbing, her back sore, and her butt smarting from hitting the ground so hard. Sahara stood a short distance from her. The mare squealed and snorted with nostrils flared. What spooked Sahara to the point she still showed the whites of her eyes? And what tree limb had she ridden into? That was the only reasonable explanation for what happened. When she looked around, none of the tree branches were low enough to have done such a thing.

After a dazed moment, Caitlin climbed to her feet and spoke softly to the nervous mare. "Easy, Sahara. Whatever it was is gone now. Come here, girl."

A hand wrapped around her throat as something flung her into a nearby oak. She gasped for air and tried to pry the fingers of whatever held her loose. The hands on her neck felt human; however, what she saw was an animal of some sort.

"Please. If you understand me, I am with child. Please, release me." She frantically tried to free herself as the hand constricted, cutting off more of her air supply.

The beast sinisterly laughed. "Beg again for your life and that of your child, woman."

Using all the strength she had left, Caitlin kicked the monster in the groin. It released her and howled in pain. As soon as she realized its hands were no longer around her throat, she ran. The creature followed and caught a fistful of her hair then heaved her backwards. He yanked her hair downward until she was on her knees in front of him. Her head forced back and her throat bared. She shrieked as its teeth tore at her flesh.

"Your blood is sweet, my dear."

Even in a daze, Caitlin felt around her for something to use as a weapon. Her fingers found a fallen limb behind her. When her attacker came at her again, she swung it at him. The stick broke across the beast's face with a loud snap. It stood still as blood trickled down a pale cheek. It smiled and tasted its own blood on its fingers.

"You will pay dearly for that, Madam Arsceneaux."

Caitlin stared him down as he approached. She didn't know what else to do. There was no way she could outrun him.

"I smell your fear." His voice danced around her. "Beg for mercy, and I will take your life quickly."

"I won't beg for anything."

As soon as the words left her lips, the beast sprang. His teeth ripped through skin and muscle again.

Two gunshots echoed through the woods and the bayou. A flock of ducks flew up from the water and several birds soared up from the trees. The monster howled when the bullets lodged in its back.

She could see Gage riding toward them. A pistol in his hand. He dropped the reins of the galloping horse and reloaded the weapon to take another shot. A moment later, another burst of smoke and flame flared from the gun's muzzle. The beast released her when the third bullet entered its side. Without the monster holding her, she couldn't stay upright. She collapsed onto the ground and stared up at the sky, watching the bright white clouds drifting overhead. The thumping of her heart in her ears slowed.

Gage flung himself from the saddle and ran to her. "Caitlin!"

She heard her name being called but couldn't do more than mouth his name. Her tongue no longer seemed to work. Air refused to travel her vocal cords as she tried to force sound out. Gage's face blocked out the sky as he leaned over her.

"Caitlin, Caitlin, look at me. Look at me, mon coeur," Gage frantically demanded, cradling her in his arms.

"Evariste." She smiled and placed her hand against his cheek.

"We will get the doctor, cher." He yanked the shirt he was wearing off then placed it against her throat and applied as much pressure as he could without choking her. The blood flow wouldn't stop. He briefly lifted it to get a better look at the wounds. No one could survive the damage done to her throat. It was only a matter of time before she would be gone. Hot tears streamed down his face despite his best efforts to give her hope in her final moments.

"Gage," she finally forced out his name then mouthed the words, "I love you."

"I love you, too. I love you, too, Caitlin." He kissed her forehead and gently rocked her. She closed her eyes; her breaths shallower and farther apart. "Let go, cher. I will be lost without you, but I can't stand to watch you suffer."

Her hauntingly beautiful lavender eyes stared up at him again. They widened in horror as her assailant stood behind her husband.

Gage didn't have time to turn around to see what frightened her. Something sharp pierced his shoulder. He cried out as burning followed by excruciating pain from the ripping of muscle traveled the length of his upper shoulder. Once the jaws locked on him loosened, he let go of Caitlin to face his attacker.

Caught between the land of the living and the dead, she watched her husband fight for his life. The beast fled as the sounds of approaching voices and running feet moved in on them. Gage managed to crawl to her. He briefly held her face between his hands then collapsed on top of her. The world went black for the both of them.

D'Orme – Present Day

"CAITLIN!" Gage shouted, waking himself from a dead sleep. Dazed, he sat up in bed and looked around to get his bearings. Seeing the digital alarm clock along with his phone on the nightstand, he was safely at home in the twenty-first century, not fighting off Tristan in the woods. Taking a couple of deep breaths, he leaned back against the headboard.

"You're okay, Evariste. You're at home," he said, shaking off the horrible memory of holding Caitlin's lifeless body. Prior to tonight, he never knew how Tristan attacked her. He always assumed it was a quick feeding that he happened to ride up on, not the long moments of suffering she experienced. How could he have dreamed about what happened prior to discovering the monster mauling his wife? Seeing the past or the future wasn't anything he had ever done before. Vampires couldn't see such things. Visions were the realm of witches, holy men, and oracles. Vampires could only recall what they themselves had lived through. In the three hundred years that he walked the earth, he never had such a dream. Why did he have it now?

"Merde!" Realizing the dream couldn't have been his, he scrambled for his phone.

CAITLIN WOKE IN A COLD SWEAT, gasping for air. Her phone ringing caused her to jump. She grabbed it off her nightstand.

"Are you okay?" Gage asked the second she answered.

Surprised to hear his voice, she laid her head back on her pillow. "I think so. I just had the craziest nightmare."

"Can you tell me what it was about?"

"I died, from some animal attack in the woods a mile or two from D'Orme." Caitlin glanced over at the alarm clock. "Why are you calling me at three in the morning?"

Her question caught him off guard. He wasn't sure how to answer it. "I felt like something was wrong, and you needed me." Damn, he should have been prepared with a better answer. He would have asked the same thing if she called him at this hour.

"Other than bad dreams, I'm good. Can I call you tomorrow, or um, later this morning?" Caitlin started to fall back to sleep.

"Sure. Sorry for waking you. Are you certain everything is all right?"

"Everything is fine. I'll talk to you later today. Love you," she mumbled, passing back out.

"Sweet dreams, beautiful."

GAGE HUNG UP THE PHONE. Something was definitely wrong. That nightmare didn't come out of nowhere. He debated catching a red-eye to Norfolk or Richmond. Between the Baton Rouge and New Orleans airports there was bound to be one headed to Virginia.

Alcee appeared at the foot of his bed. "She is safe, Evariste."

"No, she isn't. I just dreamed of Tristan attacking her."

"She's only remembering. You are getting worked up over nothing, mon ami."

Wrestling with a sense of foreboding which screamed that he needed to get to Caitlin, Gage flipped the sheets off himself and started to get out of bed. "We'll have to agree to disagree on this one."

Alcee teleported in front of Gage. "Go back to bed, Evariste. Now isn't the time. You'll frighten her."

Drowsiness dulled Gage's anxiety, beckoning him to slumber once more. "I'll remember you did this, Alcee. If anything happens…"

Try as he might to resist whatever spell Alcee cast, he fell back onto the bed and succumbed to it anyway.

Tracing Family Lines

ᕊᕥᕒ

C aitlin gave up on sleep. The dream and the painting bothered her. She showered then got dressed. Deciding to try to solve the mystery of the painting, she did another online search for Gage and Alcee. Nothing too unusual came up. She saw the same news articles about the company, some press about donations they made to local organizations, and other random news. A few stories popped about Gage's sisters and their husbands. Jude Robicheaux? Caitlin started at the name of Alli's husband just below a photo of them together. *What the hell? Another descendant of the men in the painting? Maybe the families that started Lagniappe Shipping & Ag together kept the wealth to themselves by intermarrying?* Caitlin cringed at the thought. Gage and his family wouldn't engage in a virtually incestuous relationship like that for money. There had to be another explanation.

Hoping to solve the mystery of A.A.B. and confirm her suspicions about the founders of the company, she retraced her earlier steps in researching Lagniappe. Typing in the company name surfaced pretty bland results of a repetitive paragraph or two about the company's history and details of the services Lagniappe Shipping & Ag offered. With the company being privately owned, a lot of their business dealings weren't publicized. They met the legal disclosure requirements, and that was about it. State business records, the Better Business Bureau, and the Chamber of Commerce all showed the company had a good business rating and was financially stable. Maybe a Lexis Nexus search at work later might pop something more.

"What are you hoping to find? You've already dug into Gage and his company," Caitlin asked herself, yet something urged her to dig deeper; the painting, Lagniappe, and the two men from this century were definitely interrelated.

About 7:30, Gage texted her good morning.

She smiled, picked up her phone, and texted him back; she wished him a good day, then headed to the office.

Her mind kept wandering back to the painting in the Governor's Palace throughout the weekly project meeting with the firm's principal partners.

Sean stopped her as they walked out of the meeting together. "You okay? You seem distracted this morning."

"Fine. I just didn't sleep well last night. Thanks for asking, though. I'll have the Jameson information on your desk by noon today."

"Great. I'm headed down to the courthouse. See you later this afternoon." Sean smiled at her before she made her way back to her desk.

Try as she might, that painting and the initials A.A.B. kept popping into her head as she tried to type the Jameson report. *Who in the hell was A.A.B.? What were his ties to Lagniappe or the other men in the painting?*

"Get it together, Caitlin. You can deal with those questions after you get Sean the Jameson file," she scolded herself. A three-hundred-year-old painting and some dead men shouldn't be bothering her so much, especially considering the pile of papers on her desk that needed her attention in the present. Last thing she needed was to find herself unemployed in the future.

Even being distracted by the night prior, Caitlin managed to finish up the Jameson report. It wasn't her best work, but it would do. She looked at her watch: 11:45 a.m. *Report done on time and as promised!*

Sean was still in court arguing a breach of contract case. He wouldn't be back for a few hours, if at all today. She tossed the report onto his desk then closed his office door behind her. The rest of her day was clear of meetings for a change, so she headed to the Governor's Palace to see if they had any records on the mysterious A.A.B.

Thankfully, her friend Annette was the volunteer working today. "Annette, I'm helping a gentleman whose ancestor is in that painting put together his family history." The lie rolled off her tongue much smoother than she anticipated it would. "Two of the men are business associates or relatives of his, but this one"—Caitlin pointed at the stranger—"is a bit of a conundrum. Gage isn't sure who he is and doesn't recognize the initials he is identified with in the journal. However, we think they're related to one another. Would it be possible to go back through the ledger to see if anything else might help identify Mr. A.A.B.?"

"Sure, it's slow right now. Come on in the back." Annette smiled, happy to help her out.

Unfortunately, they couldn't find anything about A.A.B. anywhere.

"You could try William & Mary or the Louisiana State Archives," Annette suggested. "It may be a long shot, but you could also try using ancestorysearch.com to find some information for your friend. More and more old records are being scanned and put online every day. Crowdsourced family stories can be a gold mine of information when trying to put together a complicated history, you just need to verify the truth of them to make sure they're accurate. I am sure with the work you do, you know how to do that."

"I hadn't thought about ancestrysearch.com. Thanks for the suggestion." Caitlin debated if she wanted to snoop into things that much. Going that route seemed like an invasion of privacy. Then again, Gage said he and his company were an open book. She could review whatever she liked. After returning to the office, she opened her laptop and typed in Ancestorysearch.com then logged into the account she hadn't used in a few years.

"Here goes nothing." She created a new tree for the Arsceneaux family.

The afternoon slipped by as she clicked on blue feather after blue feather, following a convoluted trail of historical documents and reviewing partially completed family trees.

Every generation seemed to have either an Evariste, Gage, Pierre, or Alcee in it. That wasn't uncommon for Creole and Cajun families. Names were often handed down generation-to-generation following French custom. She wrote down notes about sources to investigate later and what records were allegedly destroyed. Several trees mentioned an old Catholic records archive burned to CD and put together by a priest for the first families who settled in Louisiana. She'd do an online search to see if she could purchase a copy of it anywhere. The firm had several old computers with CD drives to view various contracts and legal documents on. She could also probably get someone to transfer the information onto a thumb drive for her.

Predictably, she couldn't find many old photographs or tins of the Arsceneauxs, LeBlancs, or Dugas. She did find a few recent pictures of Gage and Alcee at various events they attended.

"Ancestorysearch.com? What are you researching on company time?" Sean's voice came from behind her.

She briefly glanced up at him. "Arsceneaux and Lagniappe Shipping & Ag. All the normal searches we use didn't turn up anything concerning or particularly useful for gaining any sort of negotiation leverage. This is a last-ditch effort to try to make sure we covered all bases. Otherwise, Giovanni is going to have to accept that the company isn't for sale."

"Clever to do this kind of search. I wouldn't have thought of it." Sean hated to admit it, but he was impressed with Caitlin's resourcefulness. "If you've got a minute, I have a few questions about the Jameson file."

Caitlin closed her laptop to make sure she gave Sean her full attention as he sat down across from her.

OVER THE NEXT FEW DAYS, she continued her search of electronic historical records. Gage's family tree had multiple gaps that didn't make any sense. Both his first ancestor and Alcee's seemed to pop up out of nowhere in Louisiana. Neither were on any ship manifests or listed as military members on the old militia records. When she searched the LeBlanc and Robicheaux lines for more clues into Gage's ancestor, the program showed Gage and his sisters to be cousins, not siblings. How does that happen?

She scoured the Louisiana State Archives and New Orleans online archives for any additional information. There was only one entry in either one referencing an Evariste Arsceneaux in the colony of New France in 1701.

Only one state record was available after several generations for review in the archives? That can't be right, even with most records being kept at the local churches or parish level. She couldn't find a mention of either family in most of the census records between 1701 and 2013. There was no way a family as old and well off as Gage's got overlooked on a federal census.

She picked up her phone and dialed the archives. No one answered, so she left a message requesting information on how to obtain a copy of the one document she did locate.

Setting Boundaries

⌒⟳⌒

G age, Alcee, Alli, and her husband, Jude Robicheaux, sat around a table in a private dining room eating a late lunch at Renaud's— John Fontenot's newest venture. John was kind enough to let them use the small, private dining space since they were having a working lunch.

Fabien, the blond-haired and hazel-eyed vampire investigator Alcee routinely hired, knocked on one of the French doors, interrupting the business dealings going on around the table. Alcee motioned from him to enter. "Evariste, Tristan's back in town."

Gage pushed his chair back and threw the napkin from his lap onto the table. Anger openly surfaced the vampiric features normally hidden from human eyes. "Where is he?"

"The Heights. By the way he's throwing Benjamins around, he either earned a big retainer or someone's paid him off for that trip to Virginia."

"Virginia?" Allister's gaze shot to Gage. "Is Caitlin okay?"

"She's fine." Gage forced the statement out through gritted teeth. The unspoken accusation in her eyes brought Gage's simmering rage to a boiling point.

Brother and sister glared at one another as Gage stepped away from the table.

"I told you not to let her leave Louisiana, Evariste! I knew something bad was going to happen if you did, but your stubborn ass wouldn't listen."

"Don't start with me, Alli! I'm handling the matter, which you know nothing about."

"Evariste, you're not thinking straight. Don't do something—" Alcee tried to warn Gage not to act rashly.

"The last time I ignored his antics around Caitlin, she ended up dead," Gage snapped. "That isn't happening again."

A slew of French curse words left Alcee's lips after Gage disappeared from the room.

"What exactly is going on?" Alli asked, worried about Gage's vamping out and Alcee's reaction to it.

"Tristian went to Williamsburg and paid Caitlin a visit. Your brother wants his head for that. Come on, Jude. Let's go make sure Evariste doesn't get himself killed." Alcee clapped the back of Jude's shoulder.

Alli pulled her cell phone out of her purse. "I'll call Daddy in case you guys need help."

"It's better you let the vampires of the family handle this. We don't know what sort of injury you merely cursed ones could suffer if this escalates," Alcee said, stopping her from calling Pierre.

Jude shook his head and stood up. "I'll see you at home, cher." He brushed a quick kiss across his wife's cheek then sent himself to The Heights with Alcee.

THE BARTENDER at The Height's recognized the two latest vampires to poof into the strip club in the past five minutes. He jerked his head toward a black door on his left. "He's in the VIP lounge."

They walked into the room just as Evariste ripped Tristan from the chair he sat in and pinned him against the wall.

"Ladies, clear the room," Gage dismissed the two strippers who had been entertaining Tristan.

The virtually naked blonde and black-haired beauties quickly scampered out of the door. Being human, neither wanted to get caught up in whatever was about to happen between the vampires.

"You hardly leave your office or house, Evariste, and now you're patronizing strip clubs?" Tristan smirked at Gage.

"I warned you never to go near my wife," Gage growled, tightening his grip.

Tristan gagged but still sputtered out a laugh. "Is that what this hostility is all about? I had no idea your precious ingénue worked at Langley and Associates. I was only there settling an estate for a client and stopped by to tell her boss, Sean Watchous, hello. I haven't seen Sean since he left the DA's office to practice corporate law. Now get your damn hands off me, Arsceneaux. Or I might just file a grievance with the Council for one of their members behaving in such a manner toward another vampire."

At the mention of involving the Council, Gage released Tristan.

The cocky vampire stumbled after falling two feet to the floor, but quickly righted himself then ran a hand through his hair. "I'd start being more worried about Sean hanging around your wife if I were you. There were quite a few pictures of the two of them on vacation together and at other non-work-related events in his office. I'd say the two are rather close to one another."

"Sean's never harmed her. This is the last warning you're getting, Tristan. I catch you following, stalking, or doing anything that remotely whiffs of threatening her again, and I'll have your head as a trophy on my wall. Council approval or not."

Tristan snickered at the threat. "An upstanding vampire like yourself would never get crossways with the Vampire Council. You're too good to do anything that would draw their ire or violate the law."

Gage snarled, taking a menacing step toward Tristan. Surprisingly, Tristan actually moved back in response to it. "When you're the Council Chair, you get to set the law and determine the punishments for those who break it."

The smug smile on Tristan's face vanished hearing what Gage said.

Gage grinned, displaying his fangs in a silent warning for Tristan to watch himself going forward. He looked over at Alcee and Jude. "Let's go."

"Sharon, get Sean Watchous on the phone," Gage said, walking past his secretary. Alcee and Jude followed him into his office.

"You have nothing to worry about when it comes to Sean." Alcee closed the door behind them, worried about why Gage had asked Sharon to call Sean.

"I'm not worried about Sean. I'm ensuring he understands I will rip his arms from their sockets if he ever lets Tristan Dausan into his office again."

"I have Sean on the line one for you." Sharon's voice came over the intercom.

"Thank you, Sharon," Gage calmly replied then picked up the receiver.

"Evariste, think whatever you're about to say through before uttering it," Alcee cautioned, watching Gage press the button for line one then raise the receiver to his ear.

Jude groaned and rubbed the bridge of his nose. No one could reason with Gage other than Caitlin when he was this pissed off. "Evariste, mon beau-frère—"

"Sean." Gage scowled at Jude and Alcee, but his voice was calm and friendly as if he wasn't fuming at the moment.

"Hello, Evariste. What can I do for you?"

"Well, to put it frankly, I'm concerned about continuing negotiations with Langley and Associates. I pride myself on the fact that Lagniappe has always had an excellent reputation for trustworthiness and delivering on any promise we make to a client. If the day ever comes that someone else were to take ownership of my company, I would hope they'd want to continue that same legacy."

Hearing the angle Gage was playing to ensure Tristan was kept at arm's length from Caitlin, the tension left Alcee's shoulders. He and Jude sat down in the chairs in front of Gage's desk.

"Rest assured, Evariste, you have nothing to worry about. Giovanni Enterprises and my firm share that same reputation. May I ask what brought on this sudden concern of yours?" The slightly higher timbre of Sean's tone gave away his surprise at Gage suddenly questioning company values.

"Tristan Dausan and I ran into one another a little while ago. He mentioned he was an associate of yours. In fact, he just returned from Virginia, and while he was there, he stopped by your office to say hello."

Jude quietly laughed at how Evariste made it sound like Tristan and he casually bumped into one another.

"Tristan has no relationship, professional or otherwise, with Langley and Associates or Giovanni Enterprises. Prior to yesterday, the last time I saw Dausan was six years ago in a federal courtroom in Lafayette." Sean paused, allowing time for his words to sink in. "I hope that eases your concerns, Evariste."

"Partially." Evariste tactfully steered the conversation in the direction he wanted it to go. "They'd be completely relieved if I were to receive confirmation of no professional ties in writing and a confidential addendum to Giovanni's latest offer stating that for the first five years after the sale of Lagniappe all company officers must be voted as approved for hire by the Board and all majority partners prior to their hiring, not just presented for review. Furthermore, Alcee Dugas must approve any new legal counsel retained during that same time period to ensure the continuation of the company's outstanding reputation."

"That's a rather odd thing to request."

"I don't think it's that unreasonable a stipulation to be added to an agreement for the sale of a company as old as mine. I also want to legally ensure Tristan Dausan's name is never on Lagniappe's payroll. Are you aware he was tossed out of Thibodeaux's for harassing Miss DeDanann while she was here in New Orleans?" Gage tested Sean to determine how close he and Caitlin really were.

"Caitlin brought the matter to my attention yesterday after Tristan left the office."

"I would hope, Sean, that you and your firm would take steps to ensure an event like that one does not repeat. Employee safety is always top of mind for me when I consider business ventures, and I wouldn't want my employees routinely put at risk by engaging with a predator like Tristan Dausan."

"Careful, Evariste. While not your legal counsel, I do want to caution you that it's one thing to express concern over a situation or individual, but anything beyond that borders on defamation."

Gage let out a loud, mocking laugh. "Defamation requires a statement to be false. I'm willing to stake my reputation and my company's on every word I just uttered being true."

"You'll have an email in your inbox by the end of the day confirming Tristan has no ties to Langley and Associates. I'll also discuss your request for the addendum with Dante. Is there anything else I can do for you?"

Evariste smiled; Sean's clipped diction confirmed the attorney got the point of the call. "Tell Miss DeDanann to stop staring at you with such a startled expression on her face and she owes me a thank you for ensuring Tristan won't be stepping foot into any of Langley and Associates' offices ever again the next time we see one another."

"I don't need to tell her anything. She's been sitting here listening to the call the entire time, as I believe you requested she partake in all conversations a few weeks back. As you can see, we are both men who honor our agreements, Evariste. Have a good afternoon."

Gage finally sat down after hanging up the phone.

"Well, at least you didn't threaten to dismember him." Jude broke the tension hanging over the office.

Gage grinned. "Caitlin would be furious with me if I did such a thing. She and Sean are friends in addition to being boss and employee."

Jude shook his head. "You're putting that attorney through an awful lot of work for nothing. He's going to be furious whenever you tell him you aren't selling for stringing him along so long this last go-round."

Gage chuckled. "I'm sure Giovanni pays him well for his time, and it'll be the Italian who's angry with me running up his bill then having a change of heart."

Conflicts Of Interest

"Caitlin, can you take the lead in reviewing the property damage modeling and codes for Baton Rouge, similar to what Travis proposed for Biloxi? Sean suggested you for the task as you'll be headed down there in a few weeks and have some connections from your Katrina days still in the area." Bill drew Caitlin back into the conversation occurring around the table.

"Sure. I'll be happy to. Are you thinking of litigating against the developer or the company that manufactured the materials?"

"It's starting to look like the developer cut corners and didn't follow code when the neighborhood was built rather than a materials defect. Though I will take whatever information you can find on the manufacturer just in case that turns out to be wrong," Bill advised.

Travis leaned over and whispered to her as Bill continued on with the investigation and litigation strategy. "Good luck with that. Baton Rouge's modeling hasn't been updated in months, and you know damn well the mayor is connected with this development. He is going to drag his feet on any records requests you make."

"I can handle the corrupt politics Louisiana thrives on." Caitlin grinned over at her coworker. "There's always a legal way around them."

Caitlin's phone went off as the meeting ended. Expecting one of the vendors on the Jameson case to call, she answered it.

"I understand you're looking for information on the Arsceneaux family." A gravelly male voice came through the receiver.

"Yes, I am. I'd really like to review anything you may have on an Evariste Arsceneaux in Louisiana. He arrived sometime in 1701."

The man on the other end of the line chuckled. "Is there another than the first?"

The stranger's reply made Caitlin uneasy. "Who is this?"

"Someone with a common interest in the Arsceneauxs. Check your email."

Three loud beeps came through the phone and the call ended banner flashed on her screen.

Not sure what to think about the caller suddenly hanging up, Caitlin stared down at her phone. An email notification immediately popped up. She was almost nervous to click the mail icon to read whatever was sent to her. Mustering the courage to do so, her fingertip tapped the white envelope to open her email. At the top of her inbox, a bolded subject line of **Evariste Arsceneaux** held her attention. The only thing in the body was an attachment. There was no return email address in the sender's line. How could someone send her an email without using some sort of identifying sender's address?

"Everything okay, Caitlin?" Sean asked, worried about how she stood in the center of the hall staring at her phone.

"Fine. Just trying to view an attachment that for whatever reason won't open." Sighing, she finally looked up at her boss and friend. "I really need to look at whatever this is. Can you tell Bill I will be a few minutes late to the next session?"

"Bill and that email can wait. Step into my office." Sean opened his office door.

"Sean, I'm fine."

"The look on your face says otherwise. Now, sit."

Caitlin huffed, but she did as requested. "Really, Sean, nothing's wrong. You don't need to worry about me."

Sean sat down in the chair next to hers. "The hell I don't. Caitlin, I pretty much raised you after your parents died. I know when something's wrong. You can talk to me about whatever you've gotten yourself into."

"I haven't gotten myself into anything. I've been putting in long hours with all the things you've stacked up on my plate."

"Bullshit, Caitlin DeDanann. You may get away with lying to your grandmother, but you don't with me. Something's definitely going on. You come dragging in here the past several days, rumors are floating around that this Chef Gage you're seeing is actually Evariste Arsceneaux, and you looked like something was going to reach out of your phone and grab you. The only time I can recall you looking like death and acting like you are now is when you were convinced a monster, who supposedly lived under your bed, was attempting to steal you away whenever you fell asleep."

Recalling how she had screamed one night and Sean came running into her room with a baseball bat in hand, Caitlin smiled. "There are no monsters reaching out from my phone, just as I now know there wasn't one living under my bed. I'm not getting much sleep lately and am trying to juggle things here at work."

Sean frowned. "Why aren't you sleeping?"

"I'm having nightmares about being killed by some vampire-like creature in Louisiana. I have no idea what's causing them, and weirdly, I am married to Evariste Arsceneaux in every single one."

An audible, irritated breath escaped Sean as he shook his head then stared her in the eye. The tips of his ears turned red, warning the mention of being married to Evariste confirmed the dating rumors for him. "God damnit, Caitlin. You really are dating Evariste, aren't you?"

"Yes." She didn't even try to deny she was any longer.

"Fuck. No wonder he is demanding you be present at all negotiations and offer meetings. That also explains why he is suddenly returning my calls and the demand for an addendum to keep Tristan away from Lagniappe. He's protecting you, not his company." Sean ran a hand down his face before looking at her again. "Now I don't know if I should be more concerned about these nightmares or pulling you off the Lagniappe inquiry. Dating the man you're investigating is a serious conflict of interest for the firm."

"You don't need to be concerned about either. I'm not a little girl anymore. The nightmares are only dreams that will go away. And you don't need to pull me off the investigation. It's done. There's no dirt or any kind of leverage to be found on Evariste or the company. Giovanni's out of luck. Time to suggest a partnership offer versus a buyout, as I suggested a few weeks back."

Sean took her hand in his. "Cate, a mhuirnín, I will always be here for you. We were family before I was your boss. If you've gotten yourself into some sort of trouble, ask for help. That's what I'm here for."

Caitlin suddenly hugged him.

Sean chuckled, giving her a squeeze. It had been years since she had hung onto him so tightly. "Now, I am really worried."

"I swear, I'm not in any trouble, Sean."

"If you say so." He smiled after she pulled back from him. "See you at the three o'clock with Arsceneaux?"

"Only if you don't mind an investigator banging the competition a client is trying to buy out being on the call."

Sean rolled his eyes. "No more comments about whatever you and Arsceneaux are doing in your free time. I run a respectable shop here. And for the love of God, call Gram when you get a chance, since you still haven't done so. She's been reading me the riot act every few days after I promised you'd call her."

CAITLIN SAT down at her desk to view the email that had prompted Sean to call her into his office. On the laptop, the attachment opened, taking up the entire screen. She slowly scrolled through each page, reviewing the individual documents consolidated into a large PDF. The first was a French land grant for the Maison D'Orme. The second was an old census record from the *Early Families of Louisiana Collection*, along with some documents on sugar cane farming that referenced the LeBlanc, Dugas, and Arsceneaux families. Nothing too earth-shattering. So how exactly did Robicheaux and A.A.B. fit into the picture? Caitlin ran her finger across the trackpad again to pull up the last document. It was a death certificate from 1715 for a Caitlin Arsceneaux.

"What the...?" She reread the certificate to make sure she hadn't mistranslated it or the woman's name. It was written in French, and she hadn't used the language since college almost fifteen years ago now. She shook off the strange coincidence of her name matching that of the wife of the first Evariste Arsceneaux. If she died in 1715 with no children, who was the woman that birthed the rest of the Arsceneaux line? Evariste must've remarried.

A second email came in as she contemplated where she could look to figure out who the second wife might have been.

> In case you are wondering, there was no second wife, and there is no other Evariste Gage Arsceneaux. They're all one and the same.

To hell with work. She needed to figure out what these emails were about and who was sending them. Her hands shook as she clicked on the printer icon then packed up her laptop.

Caitlin stopped at the secretary's desk and skimmed the travel schedule for commercial airline flights and the destinations of the private jets the firm chartered for the month. She found a private charter leaving for Baton Rouge in two hours. Fortunately for her, there was an empty seat on the manifest, and she knew the pilot. If she left now, she could just make the departure. "Esther, please cancel my meetings for the rest of the week. Tell Bill and Sean I'm taking a couple of personal days."

"Everything ok?" Esther asked, concerned. Caitlin rarely took personal days, much less personal days without any notice.

"It will be. Have a good one!" Caitlin said, dialing the travel coordinator's number to request she be added to the passenger manifest for the flight to Baton Rouge. Once she got to her car, she texted the pilot about being a last minute add to the passenger list and that she was en route to the airport, not to leave without her.

THIB AND GAGE sat in the jazz club, going over some new contracts for several artists who wanted to perform at Thib's club.

Gage couldn't shake the feeling that something terrible loomed. He tried contacting Caitlin several times, but she didn't answer her phone. When he finally called her office, Esther advised she was in meetings the majority of the day; she'd give Caitlin the message to call him back as time permitted.

"Something wrong?" Thib asked when Gage rested his forehead in his hand with his eyes closed.

"Didn't get much sleep last night." Gage shook his head and picked up the contract he had been reading again.

Thib frowned. It was more than that. Rarely did anything distract Gage when the man focused on business or financial matters. "Jude mentioned your scuffle with Tristan when he and Alli were in here the other night."

"Eh, Tristan isn't bothering me anymore. We've got eyes on him and Alcee has someone he knows watching out for Caitlin in Virginia." Gage crossed out a clause he didn't like in the proposal he held. "This is problematic and presents a liability to you. The singer's manager should know better than to put some crap like that in a contract. Don't accept this clause in anything you sign."

"Thanks." Thib didn't even look at whatever Gage crossed out. He set the contract aside. Evariste's out of character behavior was more worrisome than some agent slipping an unreasonable demand into a contract. "So what's really eating at you, Ev?"

"I don't know. Life in general?" Gage's eyes met Thib's. The frown on Thib's face shared that Thib didn't buy the I don't know. Gage let out an irritated breath. Maybe it would ease his nerves to talk about things. Thib always offered some helpful advice in the past when it came to personal matters. His fellow vampire should've been a councilor, instead of a club owner. Lord knows Thib didn't have the savvy Evariste or Alcee did when it came to negotiating contracts or managing a business. "Caitlin isn't answering her phone, Giovanni is being a pest with wanting an answer on his latest offer, and my gut is telling me there's more to whatever Tristan was doing in Virginia. I've got Fabien digging into things, but since I do things the legal way, it takes time to get information."

Gage's palms hit the table with a loud whomp. He leaned back in the chair and studied the pattern in the tin ceiling tiles above them.

"Someone who isn't a regular client of Tristan's financed his trip and paid him a large sum of cash for handling whatever he did in Williamsburg. I want to know who and why. I'll sleep better once we have that information."

"You're stressing yourself out over something that is most likely nothing. And you make yourself a burr in someone's ass when you're pursuing a business deal, it shouldn't surprise you Giovanni is being the same way. As to Caitlin, she's probably just busy. From what I saw when she was here, the poor woman is hooked on you but hasn't quite figured that out yet. She'll call you back."

Uncovering The Past

C aitlin headed to D'Orme as soon as she had the keys to her rental car. She needed to know what was going on. Those records couldn't be real. Someone was playing a sick practical joke on her with that death certificate. Her money was on Tristan being the culprit behind everything. It seemed like some shady crap he would pull. Not to mention, his random stopping by the office. Maybe he swiped her business card off the front desk when he was leaving to get her current email. She only needed to figure out why he would do it. Clearly, he didn't like Gage with the remark about Evariste marking his territory. He must've seen her and Gage out in town together one day during the last week of her trip. Otherwise, he wouldn't have known the two of them were dating.

Her thoughts shifted away from Tristan and back to the emails. The claim of there only being one Evariste Arsceneaux sent her mind into an even more chaotic spin. Her reasonable side screamed she was being irrational about everything. Though that tiny, faint voice inside from earlier stood firmly against the storm of reason repeating see this through. There's something here you need to know.

"You're a crazy woman to hop on a plane and come down here instead of just asking Gage about everything," she muttered to herself.

Nerves heightened the inner conflict between reason and irrationality taking place the closer she came to D'Orme. She pulled off the interstate and turned down the farm road that passed in front of the historic Arsceneaux property.

She stopped at Meche's for gas. Her phone vibrated on the dash as a text came in. Figuring it was Esther or Gage, she picked it up to see what they needed. An image of her and Gage dancing together at Shadow Oaks popped up.

> The Mortal & The Monster: A Vampiric love story.

A short five digit code at the top of it meant it was auto sent from someone.

"This crap really isn't funny anymore," she said, trying to think of who may have sent it while putting the nozzle back into the pump and screwing the gas cap back on.

She swore she heard a deep laugh from behind her. Turning, she didn't see anyone. *As if the day couldn't get any stranger, I'm imagining things.*

"Caitlin!" Landry came running out of the shop; a cross and some other amulet held up in his hand. He waved it around her while chanting something in Creole.

"What in the world are you doing?"

"Warding off the darkness trailing you." Landry panickedly raised his talismans again. This time facing the wooded area behind the gas station. "Get yourself to D'Orme and don't take that pendant off. It's more powerful than the gris-gris I gave you."

"Darkness trailing me? Landry, have you been drinking?"

"Cher, I know it sounds crazy to an outsider, but there's one hell of a powerful vampire stalking you. He's watching us right now, but ol' Evariste will keep him at bay. Go home. Right now, while the talisman holds *le vampire* here. The spell won't last long."

Caitlin looked in the same direction Landry did but didn't see anything. "There's nothing there."

"Oh, he's there. He's a sneaky bastard, cher. Go on, now. Get yourself to sanctuary at D'Orme."

To keep from upsetting Landry further, Caitlin got in the car. *Voodoo, vampires, and disturbing emails. What the hell have I gotten myself into? And what did Evariste Arsceneaux have to do with all of it?*

A jolt of fear then loss cascaded through her as she passed one of the larger clumps of trees lining the road. Shaking the disturbing emotions off, she slowed the car and pulled over alongside the trees. She left the engine running as she stared at the oaks and pecan trees. Long grass and scrubby bushes grew up between them. The same tiny voice that battled with her sense of reason returned, whispering that the spot hadn't been overgrown as it was now. Once upon a time, a path cleanly wove its way through the large old oaks; their lower limbs trimmed so one could easily pass under a canopy of green on foot or horseback. A vivid mirage of the wolf-like creature that attacked her in her nightmare sprang forward from the darkened space between the trees and through the windshield. Her foot instinctively slammed down on the gas pedal. Gravel and dirt flew up from squealing tires as she whipped out onto the rural road again.

"Get a grip!" she scolded her reflection in the rearview mirror, straightening the rental as its backend still fishtailed from peeling onto asphalt so quickly. This wasn't like her. Never had she been afraid or bothered by weird things like horror movies or local legends. Then again, since meeting Gage, she wasn't exactly her old, normal, analytical self. The strange rounds of déjà vu regularly returned after years of being gone. A newfound sense of sensuality awakened in her that hadn't been there with any other man, including Liam. Now this crazy paranoia driving her to do ludicrous things like fly to Louisiana on a whim threw itself into the chaotic mix of change. Was she too young to experience a midlife crisis? Or was this the beginning stages of one?

The turn signal seemed louder than normal as she pulled onto the gravel portion of the driveway leading up to the main house. Two looming wrought iron gates now blocked her path when they hadn't a few weeks ago. Gage had said he installed the gate in the interest of privacy after some reporters drove by and he caught another set of curious trespassers in his driveway one night claiming to just want to see what the house they could barely make out from behind the trees looked like. But now she wondered if that was the truth or merely an excuse to cover up something else.

She entered the gate code he had given her. Chains clinked and the clamor of metallic pulleys disturbed the spring air while the two panels of black lines and swirls topped by gold fleur-de-lis's swung apart, ominously welcoming her back to D'Orme.

The black 4x4 Gage drove wasn't in the driveway. He was most likely still at work with it being midday. The house was dark and the garage door down. Part of her hoped the girls would be there or her key wouldn't work as she slid it into the lock. Maybe it would be better if she didn't give into the urge to investigate matters. One of the SIU investigators who trained her on various ways to follow her gut if she suspected fraud used to joke that she needed to develop a healthy sense of fear when deciding to revisit a loss site. She could almost hear Scott lecturing her to do the same now.

Caitlin gave the front door a gentle push inward. "Hello? Anyone home?"

No one answered. She had the place to herself.

After quietly closing the door, she walked down the hall to Gage's study and rummaged through his desk drawers. No paperwork, photographs, ledgers, or anything of a personal nature were in them. There also wasn't any sort of documentation relating to Lagniappe Shipping & Ag to be found. A notebook holding passwords rested in one of the drawers she pulled open. After finding what appeared to be the main one for the desktop, she logged into the computer. Like the drawers, it didn't have any type of helpful records stored on its hard drive. The only thing slightly interesting she could find was Gage's email box. She skimmed the subject lines of the emails then clicked the link for the sent box to view whatever was in there. They were all fairly mundane business communications.

"Where do you really keep your personal records, Evariste? I know they wouldn't be in the corporate office." Caitlin scanned the room for any signs of a file cabinet or something that he might store them in.

Look upstairs! Her subconscious guided her.

She climbed the grand staircase and went down the hall. To her left, were the master bedroom and two other rooms she hadn't been in. On her right, were the guest rooms. She chose to go left. The first room door was locked, but the door to the second opened, revealing an upstairs study with dark wood furniture. Floor to ceiling built-in bookshelves spanned two of the walls. A massive brick fireplace with an elaborate hand-carved mantel took up the far wall, and the remaining exterior wall consisted of two large windows framed by burgundy velvet drapes. Now this looked more like a space Evariste would use as an office. As she entered the room, she noted a large oil painting of the Maison D'Orme hung in a gold frame. A small, gold placard on the bottom of the frame read 1714.

She could swear she heard Gage's voice explaining he moved the office upstairs so he could be closer to her and the children they were planning for when he needed to work late. Lack of sleep the past couple of nights had to be making her imagine things. They never had any such conversation.

Sitting down in the oversized leather chair behind the antique desk, she ran her fingertips across the polished wood. They certainly don't make furniture like this anymore. How old was the desk?

The hand cut inlays decorating the top were gorgeous, along with the carved sides and legs. When she gently tugged on one of the larger drawers, it held fast, confirming it was locked shut. She felt along the underside of the desk, hoping she'd find a key or hidden latch that unlocked the drawers. Her fingers discovered a small switch hidden on the underside.

"It's now or never," she whispered and mustered the courage to flick it toward herself. A small drawer on the left side of the desk popped open, revealing an antique key. She quickly stuck the key in the first of the two large drawers. The lock turned, and the drawer seemed to slide open on its own.

Caitlin nervously looked around before pulling files from it and setting them on the desk. The documents in the files grew older the farther back she went in the stack. The oldest were written on parchment paper. Each one was dated with some year in the 1700s. Worried she'd damage them, she only touched the corners of each document she reviewed. All referenced an Evariste Gage Arsceneaux. She guessed he must have come from old money or a powerful aristocratic family in France to own all the things he did, and for the King to grant him land in the New World. The business and land grant documents noted Evariste not only owned the land D'Orme was built on, but also several nearby properties and two ships: one sloop and a galleon. Business logs and various identification documents filled the other folders.

She found a death certificate for Evariste Gage Arsceneaux from 1780. His age was listed as a hundred and ten when he died. That wasn't normal for colonial Louisiana. Most of the early settlers died much younger. As she went through the rest of the files, she found multiple birth and death certificates for an Evariste or Gage Arsceneaux. The first name alternated with the middle one every other generation. She didn't find any marriage certificates or parents' names on several birth and death certificates.

"You didn't come out of thin air Gage Arsceneaux." Caitlin pulled out two more files, hoping to find information on his parents. Pierre LeBlanc and Helene Boudreaux's names repeated on several of the birth certificates. None mentioned a prior marriage between Helene and anyone with the last name Arsceneaux. If his mother was a Boudreaux and Pierre a LeBlanc, who was Gage's father for him to have the last name Arsceneaux?

A closed wooden and leather box in the back of the second drawer caught her eye. She lightly blew off some of the fine dust covering the top of it before flipping the lid onto the desk. Several old photographs and tins rested inside it. After putting the files neatly back in the drawer, Caitlin sorted through the contents of the box. She expected to see various generations of Arsceneauxs and family friends. Instead, the photographs contained the same people but in different time periods for almost two hundred years. On occasion, an unfamiliar face would appear in a photograph.

"Who in the hell am I dating? A time traveler?" Caitlin gently placed the pictures back in their box for safekeeping. When she started to put the box away, she noticed a leather portfolio crammed back behind where the box normally sat. She almost missed it in the shadows of the drawer with its dark brown leather being coated in dust and it being firmly pressed back against the far end. Whoever put it in there must not have wanted it to be discovered. *Or they didn't want to see it again,* her subconscious continued its pricking of her nerves.

Caitlin slowly untied the old leather bindings then unwound them from the metal button they clung to, sealing whatever was inside the pouch from view. She flipped over the first document that was backside up so she could read it. It was the original of the death certificate from the email. Her name scrawled in elegant calligraphy leapt off the page at her. It may as well have been a hot coal singeing her fingers tips with how quickly she dropped it. She pushed herself back from the desk, debating running out of the house and never coming back. Her heart pounded in her ears and her hands shook.

"It's not you. It can't be," she chanted over and over, forcing her body to bend and her hands to retrieve the parchment from the floor.

As she lifted the leather portfolio to put the death certificate back inside it, a small painted image fell out. Pale lavender eyes stared up at her from the tiny canvas. A startled scream left Caitlin's lips as she recognized the face they sat in the center of as her own. She sprinted down the stairs and yanked the keys out of her purse. Whatever was going on, it wasn't funny. Her phone suddenly vibrating in her jacket pocket scared the hell out of her.

She unlocked the car door as she answered it.

"Find what you're looking for?" the same voice from that morning asked before she even said hello.

"Who is this?"

"It's better you never know, and trust me when I say don't leave without talking to Evariste. The last time you left D'Orme in an all-fire rush it didn't turn out so well."

Call ended popped up on her phone before she could ask what the caller meant by that. A loud, feral growl from up the road conjured images of the wolf creature again. Not wanting to find out if the thing was real or not, Caitlin went back in the house. *That haint blue porch ceiling better keep whatever growled outside.*

Her phone vibrated again. This time Gage's name and the picture she had put in her contacts for him popped up. She let it go to voicemail.

Needing something to calm her nerves, she poured herself a glass of wine then hit the voicemail icon on her phone. "Hey, gorgeous. Just checking on you. You sounded like you were upset in the message you left earlier. Hope things are okay. I'm worried about you with these nightmares you're having. Call me when you get a chance, cher."

Noticing the picture of her and Gage sitting together on the porch swing at his parents' house on the refrigerator door soothed her frazzled state. Alli had taken it after Gage asked her to. That had been such a nice, relaxing afternoon. She slid the magnet off the photo and studied the smiling guy in it. "I hope like hell you can explain whatever is going on, Evariste Arsceneaux. As I'm starting to think I'm crazy or you really are some time-traveling mass murderer."

The Truth Comes Out

T he day went from bad to worse when Gage pulled up his driveway. He still couldn't get a hold of Caitlin. Sean had called him to ask if he had spoken to her at all today as she had missed a meeting prior to theirs at three o'clock, and she wasn't anywhere to be found in the office. She also didn't answer her phone anytime Sean called her. He hadn't ever heard a hint of concern in Sean's voice about anything in their previous phone discussions, but it certainly colored every word Sean spoke today. The attorney openly worried about her disappearance.

Now, there was a strange car parked in front of his house. No one was supposed to be at D'Orme. His sisters had gone on a trip. Pierre was planting for the upcoming season, Alcee was at the office, and Caitlin was somewhere in Virginia. How in the hell did his unannounced visitor get past the new gate?

The front door opened slightly as he started to put his key in the deadbolt. It had been locked and firmly shut when he left that morning. He rarely set the alarm system with living so far outside the city and never having a problem with intruders due to the stories locals told about the Maison D'Orme being haunted and cursed.

Normally, he could tell if another vampire or human were inside the

210

house. This afternoon he couldn't identify what was in his home. Papers being rustled upstairs ignited his temper. The intruder was rummaging through records no one outside the family should know about. After grabbing a pistol from a hidden drawer built into the hallway closet wall, Gage leapt to the top of the stairs. He flicked the safety off and rested his finger on the trigger before stepping into the room, centering the barrel on the figure sitting in his desk chair.

Recognizing the mane of red hair and the violet eyes locked on him, he lowered the gun. "Caitlin?"

She held a glass of wine in one hand and a few faded papers in her other.

"What are you doing here?" Relieved there wasn't a thief or worse in his home, he quickly laid the pistol on a table by the door. "Why didn't you call me and let me know you were back in town?"

"I hadn't planned on being here. Who exactly are you?" Caitlin's voice had an edge to it when she spoke.

The negative energy she projected warned Gage to be cautious.

"Let me rephrase that." She scattered the papers she held across his desk. "What are you?"

"Caitlin," He wasn't sure what to think of the woman who confronted him. Something changed in her, and she definitely wasn't happy.

"I'm waiting for some sort of explanation."

"A man who loves you very much," he spoke softly, trying to soothe the fear and anger he sensed in her. "And has done so, for a very long time."

"Men don't live to be three hundred years old!" she snapped, coming around the desk. "Or am I getting my dates wrong? My French isn't the greatest, and this is hard to read." She held his birth certificate up to him.

He took the document from her. "Cher, I can explain all of this."

"Let's hear it then, Gage? Or is it Evariste? Are you even an Arsceneaux?"

He resisted the urge to reach out and touch her after noticing the tears welling up in her eyes. "I am both men, and yes, my last name is Arsceneaux. My full name is exactly what I told you when you first asked me it, Evariste Gage Arsceneaux. I was born in France, in 1670, and came to Louisiana in 1701. I designed and built the Maison D'Orme shortly before meeting the love of my life. A woman I have loved for over three centuries. I've waited so long to see you again."

"That's not possible."

"I'm telling the truth. You know I am. I can read your thoughts, cher. All of your emotions, too. And you believe me. Even if you don't want to say you do."

"What exactly are you?" she asked in a voice barely a whisper as she stared up at him.

"I think you already know."

Panic rose in her again. Gage hated how she was afraid of him. That was the last thing he wanted. "I could never hurt you, Caitlin. You have nothing to fear."

"You're a vampire. Like the thing in my dream." Caitlin wobbled on her feet, trying to rationalize everything. "Aren't you?"

"Of some sort."

"Who's the woman in the painting?" Caitlin held out the miniature portrait she found in the leather pouch.

Gage looked down at the painting she set in his palm. There were so many days he had sat and stared at it after Tristan killed her. Giving up hope of her ever returning almost a century ago, he banished the beloved image he used to carry in his jacket pocket each day to the desk drawer. "You, cher."

Her eyes rolled back. Gage caught her as her knees gave out.

Dear god, not again! He hoped she only fainted from the shock of the truth. "Caitlin, answer me."

He settled her into his desk chair then lightly patted her face, trying to bring her back to consciousness. Her breathing grew shallow. He placed his fingertips against her wrist. Her pulse grew fainter with each second that passed.

"Alcee!" Gage shouted, summoning the older vampire.

"This better be important, mon ami. I was..." Alcee complained, aggravated that Gage interrupted his afternoon. Discovering Gage kneeling beside an unconscious Caitlin, he stopped speaking mid-sentence.

"She's dying." Gage glanced up at the older vampire. "You said all that would happen is she would remember. She wouldn't be hurt."

"That is how it should have been. I swear, Evariste, no harm should have come to her. Quickly, tell me what happened." Alcee joined him beside Caitlin and began examining her for anything unusual.

"I came home, and she was waiting for me. She went through my desk. I started explaining everything. She collapsed after I confirmed I was a vampire."

"That was it? Did she remember anything about you or say anything strange?" Alcee desperately tried to determine what brought on the woman's weakened state.

"Stranger than finding out she's dating a three-hundred-year-old vampire that she was once married to?"

"There has to be something else. Think clearly for a minute about every interaction you've had with her recently."

The only unusual thing that occurred recently as far as he was aware were the nightmares she was having. "As you know, she dreamed of her death. I swear I was in the dream with her the first night it happened. I saw each second Tristan attacked her. I experienced each scratch and bite she endured, Alcee. Her fear, her pain, it was my own."

Alcee doubted that type of shared experience could happen. "Shared the same dream? That isn't possible. That only happens if..."

Guilt wrenched Gage's gut. "I fed from her."

"Pardon? Did you just say you fed from her?" Alcee couldn't believe what he was hearing. In all the time he had known Gage, he had never taken blood of any sort. "Evariste, feeding binds her and you. She definitely shouldn't be unconscious if that is the case. She'd have your ability to heal."

"I know that. Alcee, I can't explain what happened. One minute I was making love to my wife, the next minute, my teeth were in her neck, and I drank from her. I only drank for a few seconds. Is she turning into one of us?"

"Merde, Evariste. You should have told me about the blood bond immediately. And non, she is not turning into one of us." Alcee lifted her hair and examined the nape of Caitlin's neck. He jumped up and cursed after seeing the birthmark that now revealed itself. "The glamour..."

Alcee's reaction to whatever he saw didn't calm Gage any. "Glamour? What is going on?"

"She will be fine."

Alcee started speaking in an ancient tongue Gage didn't know. A woman appeared in the room. She had long, gold hair and emerald-green eyes. She dressed in a green gown with gold Celtic bands around her forearms. Alcee gestured to Caitlin as he and the woman spoke.

The woman knelt alongside of Caitlin. A warm golden glow surrounding the woman illuminated the room. She whispered something in her language while placing her hands on either side of Caitlin's face.

Alcee restrained Gage when Caitlin's heart stopped.

"She's killing her!" Gage hissed, fighting against Alcee's hold.

"Non. She is giving her life. Trust me."

"She's dead, Alcee!" Gage cried out in a rage with losing his wife for a second time.

The woman leaned over Caitlin's body.

"She will live, Evariste. Morrigan, the woman tending to Caitlin, protects her. You have nothing to fear. You must let Morrigan heal her." Alcee tried to ease the suffering that besieged the vampire he mentored.

Gage recognized the name. "Morrigan? The goddess?"

Alcee released Gage. "Oui, the goddess of Earth and War."

Caitlin woke and spoke to Morrigan in the same Gaelic tongue Morrigan used. She took Morrigan's hand. A golden ethereal glow slowly outlined Caitlin's body.

"Caitlin is a healer like Morrigan," Alcee explained, in awe of the power radiating off the two women.

"What?"

"A healer. A human with the ability to heal the sick and comfort those in pain."

Gage sensed Alcee held something back. "I know what a healer is. I have known several. What aren't you telling me?"

"Shhh! I am trying to listen, and my Gaelic is poor at best."

"Come." Morrigan motioned for Gage to join her and Caitlin. The goddess smiled and whispered something to Caitlin. She placed her hand on Caitlin's forehead then gently closed her eyes with two fingers.

"Take care of her, Evariste. I am entrusting you with a precious gift." Morrigan laid an unconscious Caitlin in Gage's arms, then vanished as quickly as she appeared.

Caitlin opened her eyes. "Evariste?" She stared up at him, the baffled expression on her face conveying she almost doubted he was real.

"Oui, mon coeur?" He clasped one of her hands then brought it to his lips, thankful she survived whatever had just happened.

Her free hand reached up to touch him. A smile erased the confusion on her face after she rested her palm against his check. "Je t'adore, mon beau."

"Je t'aime, cher. Je t'aime de toute mon âme," Gage whispered the words he had always responded with anytime she told him she adored him in the past then kissed her. He clutched Caitlin to his chest, silently thanking Morrigan for returning his wife to him. "No more leaving me, cher."

"Never again, Evariste." Her arms wrapped tightly around his shoulders. "Never again."

Alcee grinned at the reunited lovers. Deciding it best he depart now that Caitlin was okay, he vanished from the room.

Two Sets Of Eyes

$\mathcal{C}$ aitlin looked around the master bedroom, seeing it with completely new eyes. The furniture was almost the same, though the colors of the curtains and the bedspread had changed. The hand-woven rugs they bought together still covered the wood floors. She opened the double doors leading to the master bath. Everything seemed so familiar but different at the same time due to the modern upgrades.

A large garden tub filled the far corner of the bathroom. She turned on the faucet then sat on the tub's edge, watching the water rise. There had been many nights when she and the two servants they hired to help around the house filled an old copper tub that originally sat where the garden tub was now. The copper monstrosity cost Gage a small fortune to import from France and was quite the oddity in the area. But Gage loved indulging in a hot bath whenever he could, and she enjoyed soaking with him. He often told her the tub was well worth the price he paid for it as it gifted him good health and time with his wife. There were so many evenings where they'd sit across from one another discussing the events of the day.

Caitlin undressed, then slipped on the satin robe Gage bought her the last time she was in New Orleans after she complained that she left her robe in Virginia.

With it being late in the evening, the moonlight transformed their bedroom, taking her back in time. She gently pushed open the French doors leading to the second-story balcony. The smell of roses and honeysuckle floated on the breeze into the room. Cicadas and frogs serenaded her as she gazed out into the darkened countryside. There were no nearby neighbors or lights to invade the privacy and incredible views of the fields, bayou, and woods that D'Orme offered.

GAGE CAME UPSTAIRS, bringing a bottle of Malvasia and two glasses with him. He halted in the bedroom doorway, taking in the scene which greeted him. Moonlight outlined her silhouette on the balcony. He would often find her enjoying spring and summer evenings in the same spot where she now stood, wearing only her robe or nightgown, when he arrived home late after working at the shipyard in New Orleans or helping Pierre on planting and harvesting days. *God, that was a sight he had missed seeing every night.*

Hearing the bath water running, he set down the wine and glasses, then checked on how full the tub had gotten. Water just kissed the porcelain rim. After shutting off the faucet, he poured them both a glass of wine.

He walked onto the balcony, extending one of the glasses he held to Caitlin. "What are you thinking about, beautiful?"

"Everything." She took the glass he offered and sipped from it. The sweet liquid was perfect for a summer evening. Memories of the night he introduced her to the wine brought a smile to her face. "How familiar everything is, and yet, how different it is at the same time."

"Almost three centuries have passed since the last time you were at D'Orme as my wife."

"Your wife," she repeated the words. They sounded strange, so foreign, rolling off her tongue. "It's as if I'm two different people living in the same body."

"In some ways, you are." Gage slid an arm around her. He frequently struggled with reconciling his age and all that he had seen compared to the average person as well. "The young woman I married lived in the 1700s, while the one I am holding is a successful, independent twenty-first-century woman. I love them both. In many ways, they are one and the same."

"I'm not so sure about that. They feel like two very different women in love with the same man. It's so strange to see through both sets of eyes."

"I understand more than you know. The Gage Arsceneaux standing in front of you differs greatly from the Evariste you married. You will grow more accustomed to the dual viewpoints as time passes."

"What are you really, Gage? You don't act like a vampire."

He sighed, not really having a good answer for her. "One of the damned, I guess."

"And what exactly is one of the damned? A ghost, a cursed soul, one of Anne Rice's vampires?"

He chuckled. "I wouldn't compare myself to any of her characters."

"You weren't kidding about being some type of vampire."

"No, I wasn't." Growing uncomfortable with where the conversation headed, he walked back into the bedroom.

"Where are you going?" Caitlin called after him.

"To take a bath before the water gets cold. Want to join me?"

He undressed, then settled himself into the tub, trying to relax after the stressful evening.

Caitlin strolled into the bathroom. "You haven't answered my question."

"I did answer your question. I told you I was going to take a bath."

"That is not the one I want an answer to." She sat on the side of the tub, shooting him an annoyed glare.

"Don't get grumpy with me, cher," he lightheartedly warned, his eyes opening a sliver then closing again.

"What are you going to do about it if I am?"

He jerked her into the tub with him. "Care to challenge me again?"

"My robe!" Caitlin stood up and examined the soaking wet material.

"If it's ruined, I will get you another." Gage tugged on the robe so it slipped from her shoulders then threw it toward the walk-in shower.

"You want to know what I am?" He gently pulled her down into his lap. His lips lingered against hers in a soft kiss. Getting lost in the unique eyes of the woman who finally remembered their past, affection overtook the playfulness in his expression. His voice warmed as he murmured, "I'm a vampire, very much in need of your love."

"Show me," Caitlin whispered, still not quite trusting what her eyes saw.

"What more proof do you seek, woman?" Gage placed her hand on his erection.

She laughed, slowly running her fingers up the length of him. "Not that. I meant your fangs or something vampirish."

"My fangs?" Gage repeated incredulously. *Of all the damn things she could ask to see.* "If that is the proof you need." He offered her a devilish come-hither smile. His eyes burned brightly between desire and letting his darker nature out to play. "Satisfied?"

Caitlin couldn't believe she hadn't noticed the four elongated canines previously. Shock faded to childlike curiosity. She gently touched one tooth. Still doubting they were real, she pressed the tip of her finger against the porcelain pointed bottom of one, pricking her finger. Her body jumped from the sharp stick.

The tantalizing taste of blood filled Gage's mouth. He briefly closed his eyes, savoring the sweet flavor that always made him crave more. He opened his eyes to see her quickly jerk her hand back then she watched the growing red bead on her skin. Her uninjured hand reached for the washcloth lying on the tub's edge after a stray burgundy stream wove its way down the side of her finger.

"Allow me." Gage brought the finger she stared at back to his lips. He gently sucked on it before his tongue snaked across the injury, stopping the bleeding.

Caitlin quivered, her core liquifying from just the light stroke.

"You weren't lying," she mumbled, still mesmerized by his appearance and running her thumb across his lower lip to reveal the canine-like fangs again.

"I'll never lie to you, Caitlin. Now that you know the truth, there's no need to," Gage promised, amazed that she didn't run or scream as others did when the vampire emerged.

Her mouth pressed against his; her lips separated and her tongue drew his inward. Tonight, she devoured him, greedily tasting and teasing. He groaned as she straddled him, taking him inside her then slid her hips along his until she sheathed every inch of him. The man and the unholy creature he had become would never tire of how incredible it was whenever their bodies joined; her soft, slick warmth encompassing his cock. Their lips routinely locked, exchanging breaths and passionate pleas while sharing their love for one another.

"I don't care what you are, Evariste. I've missed you," she whispered, her hands resting against his shoulders while she slightly lifted herself out of the water then brought her body down his again. "I've missed this. I never want to be without you again."

"Nothing, and I mean nothing, will ever separate us again, cher." Gage curled dampened red locks around the fingers of one hand then groaned, grasping her hips with the other. He leaned back against the tub, letting Caitlin take him at any tempo she pleased.

CAITLIN LIGHTLY TRACED the four scars on his neck and shoulder when they laid in bed together after their bath. "Is this where you were bit?"

"That is the one spot which scarred." Gage momentarily remembered the pain from the bite when her fingers brushed his skin. "The vampire who attacked us bit me several times on the neck and shoulders."

"There aren't any bears around here, are there? You tell that story to hide that vampires exist and to scare people away."

Gage chuckled. "There most certainly are black bears roaming the woods and bayous in the area, just as I told you. Only they never attacked any ancestors of mine."

"Do you drink blood?"

"Not usually. I prefer food and eat just like a human does."

"You go out in daylight, which vampires aren't supposed to be able to do. I guess being afraid of crosses and not being able to walk on sacred ground is all Hollywood fiction, too?"

"I'm afraid so." Gage grinned, thinking of how strange he must be when compared to the fictional vampires on the silver screen. "All old wives' tales made up to keep humans away from our kind."

Her mouth twisted in a puzzled fashion, giving away that she tried to sort through her returning memories and all that had happened in 1715. "Are all of your family members vampires?"

"No, just me and Alcee. But the girls, Pierre, and my mother were affected by what happened to me. A voodoo priestess visited the family about a year after the attack. She claimed to be sent by an oracle to deliver a message. She said we were all cursed to live forever by an angry ancestor. I, in particular, would be trapped between the world of the living and the dead, but fate did not want me to go on that journey alone. The only thing that could free us from this curse was your return, and only the Fates could decide when the time was right for us to meet again."

The idea of being that old and waiting so long for some prophecy to fulfill was incomprehensible to Caitlin. "So, you've stayed in Louisiana all this time, waiting for a woman who might never return?"

"At times, I doubted your return. I'll admit I grew angry waiting and periodically gave up hope, but even then, part of me always believed you would eventually come back to me." Gage ran his thumb across her cheek, his restless soul at peace for the first time in years now that the weight of the secret he carried was off his chest.

"The history you've seen. The birth of our nation, the Civil War, the hurricanes."

Gage smiled at how her eyes lit up. "I lived through it all. We can talk more about things in the morning. We've both had a long day."

Caitlin laid silently beside him as he soothed her arm. "Gage?"

"Hmm?" he answered, almost asleep.

"How many other women have there been after me?"

Stunned by the question, his eyes reopened and he looked over at her. "I've never loved another."

"You honestly expect me to believe that? For the past three hundred years, a man, no, a vampire, didn't have any other lovers in his lifetime."

"Believe what you want." The doubt in her voice aggravated him. He really didn't want to have this discussion their first night back together. "Now, go to sleep."

He ignored the feel of Caitlin's eyes on him in the darkness, hoping that she would let the matter drop, even though he already knew she wouldn't. The sheets rustled and the mattress rocked as she shifted position to rest her hand on his chest.

"If what you said is true, your life must have been incredibly lonely. I wouldn't wish that on anyone."

"It was," he honestly said, looking over at her now and deciding to tell her more than he probably should. "Most women don't handle the truth as well as you are. The one or two who stuck around after finding out were more fascinated by the vampire side of me than anything. None of them saw me as a man worthy of spending their life with as you do."

A twinge of jealousy riled Caitlin. "So, there were others?"

"Hundreds. Ten a night sometimes. So many blissful orgies. And once our carnal appetites were sated, I drained them of their blood and stole their souls."

She hit him with her pillow. "Don't be an ass."

He laughed, throwing the pillow back at her. "Isn't that the answer you expected?"

"No, I was thinking more like two or three. Like in those movies when a vampire has a soul but doesn't want to get close to anyone. Then he meets a handful of women he can't resist."

Gage laughed again. "Why couldn't I just be dark and moody, and want to spend eternity alone?"

Caitlin rolled her eyes and flipped onto her side, looking away from him. "Forget I asked."

"Don't go to sleep angry, cher." Gage propped himself up on one arm. "That's never good to do, and you don't want to make your vampire boyfriend mad." He teasingly raked his teeth against her exposed neck.

"Keep it up, Evariste, and I'll stake you."

"You wouldn't stake me. You enjoy all the wicked things I do to you too much to vanquish me." He lightly nipped her shoulder, pressing himself against her and tucking her hips into the curve of his lower body. His voice, deep and husky, whispered in her ear, "Je t'adore, ma petite amie. Tu es mon âme soeur. Only you hold my heart. The others just stemmed the loneliness while I waited for you."

Loving the lilting cadence the old Louisiana accent created every time he used it with that bedroom voice of his, Caitlin smiled. "C'est vrai?"

"C'est vrai, mon coeur."

Rude Awakenings

❦

"**E**variste Gage Arsceneaux! It's almost noon. You've missed two meetings and a conference call!" Someone flung open the bedroom curtains, letting sunshine fill the room and waking Caitlin and Gage. "We've been calling you all morning after Sharon told us you didn't show up at the office."

"Allister!" Gage barked while reaching for a sheet to cover himself and Caitlin.

"You would think a three-hundred-year-old vampire would know the importance of running a business right and answer his damn phone when someone calls." She turned and now saw Caitlin in bed with her brother.

"And I would hope, after all this time, my two-hundred-and-ninety-three-year-old sister wouldn't barge into my bedroom as she just did. Get out!" he growled at her, the vampire side of him on full display after the rude awakening.

"S-S-Sorry, I didn't know Caitlin was here." Alli ran out of the room and slammed the bedroom door shut behind her.

Caitlin laughed at the way he glared at the closed door. "I thought ruckus like that wasn't tolerated at Maison D'Orme."

"It's not." He still couldn't believe what his sister had done. None of them had barged into his room like that since they were kids.

"Put the fangs away, Gage. She was worried about you." Caitlin turned his face toward her then kissed him good morning. "Is it really almost noon?"

He glanced at the clock on the nightstand. "Unfortunately. Remind me to call a locksmith this afternoon. I'm changing all the damn locks and deleting her gate code to keep that from happening again."

"I can't believe we slept through the phone ringing all morning."

"We didn't. I turned the ringer off and shut off the cell phones. I didn't want to be disturbed last night now that you know the truth."

Caitlin draped a leg over his waist and traced a line down his chest. "Or were you afraid one of your hundreds of girlfriends might call?"

"They only have my work number," Gage teased, rolling her underneath him.

"Evariste!" she shrieked as he playfully pretended to bite her shoulder and tickled her.

"THINK ALLI IS STILL HERE?" Caitlin asked as she dressed after taking a shower.

"She left right after closing our door." Gage pulled a shirt on. "Though I'm sure it's only a matter of time before she is back with reinforcements."

Caitlin laughed. "You mean Renee and Jeanette?"

"Those two, my mother, the townsfolk with pitchforks and a torch or two, all for my biting her head off this morning. She won't come alone to face the beast."

"Hopefully, she won't be back for a while. I still want to learn more about the man I used to be married to."

Disliking the idea of her framing their relationship in past tense, Gage frowned. "Didn't you already ask me a hundred and one questions last night? What more do you want to know?"

"Everything. Were you always a shipping merchant? Who is growing the sugar cane in the fields alongside D'Orme?"

"Sugar cane is Pierre's business, and he's the one planting the fields alongside D'Orme. I only experimented with farming here and there. And you know I'm still in the shipping business as I was back then." Gage watched her brush her hair. He almost envied the bristles being submerged in scarlet tresses then gliding down the soft, silken strands. The color and feel of her hair against his skin were two of the many things he loved about Caitlin. He resisted the urge to run his fingers through the now knot-free mane of red. Doing so would lead to another round of lovemaking and both their stomachs were growling. Food needed to come before other carnal pleasures at the moment.

"Do you still own all the land you used to?" she asked, drawing him out of his wandering thoughts.

"Most of it. I sold a few acres here and there over the years."

"Why does Giovanni want your company?"

Gage shook his head. "I don't know. You'd have to ask him."

"Out of morbid curiosity, did you ever fight in the Civil War?"

Puzzlement at that question clouded his face. "Briefly. Why?"

"Just curious." Caitlin shrugged, as if the question was no big deal.

He doubted that inquiry came solely from curiosity. For her to ask such a specific question, there was motive behind it.

Catching his frowning, Caitlin smiled over at him. "How about the Revolutionary War?"

"Didn't concern me, and I was busy trying to survive here at the time. The Civil War affected my business in addition to battles occurring in my backyard, forcing me to become involved in it. Believe it or not, I try to avoid conflict when I can. Most vampires do the same."

CAITLIN NOTICED Gage staring at her as they ate breakfast. The downward tilt of the right side of his mouth, his creased forehead, and his eyes taking in every movement she made meant the man contemplated something. "Why are you looking at me like that?"

His lips finally quirked into a grin. "I expected you to be a bit more perturbed this morning. You're taking everything in stride like it's an everyday occurrence to learn vampires exist and you are the reincarnated wife of one. I wasn't prepared for that."

Caitlin shrugged. "Weird things have happened to me all my life. Yesterday, I was pretty freaked out. Now, I'm more curious than anything. But I won't pepper you with questions. I know you need to get to work."

"No work for me today. Things can wait until I know you're really okay. If you're done eating, I'd like to show you something that will help answer all those questions you have." He offered her his hand.

Caitlin took it and followed him back upstairs.

They stopped in front of the locked door of the room next to the office. Gage unlocked it and pushed the door open. Antiques, clothing, paintings, books, weapons, and other historical items filled the space.

"Wow!" Caitlin looked around, unsure of what to think. The large room could have been a museum dedicated to only exhibiting his many identities.

"My life is here for you to see."

She walked over to the wardrobe and sorted through the clothing from various time periods hanging in it. The suit he had worn to the vampire ball a few weeks ago made her smile. She gently pushed it aside to discover a familiar brown coat and matching vest from the eighteenth century. Hazy memories of him wearing the combo with a cream-colored shirt flitted before her eyes. His long, brunette hair tied back with a dark ribbon. "You used to love wearing these."

The soft laugh from behind her caused her to smile over her shoulder at him.

"They were my favorite jacket and vest long ago."

Caitlin ran her hand over the gray and gold officer's jacket that hung in front of her. "A Johnny Reb. I should have known with where you live."

"Union spy. I always believed in country first, state second. Being a Yankee sympathizer made me even more unpopular than being a vampire did. My actual uniform is behind the gray one."

"I can imagine. Northern sympathizers weren't treated well during the war or after in the South." She recognized the emblem on the dark blue jacket, then glanced over at the matching wide-brimmed hat and sword lying on a bookcase next to the wardrobe. "You were cavalry?"

"For a time." Gage watched her pick up the soft leather riding gloves he had worn then inspect the collar devices and awards on his jacket.

"Sheridan's division when he took command of the cavalry for the Army of the Potomac. And this pin means you were part of Grant's staff." Caitlin couldn't believe Gage managed to keep what he was a secret after being in such a high-profile position. Then again, several women managed to hide their gender for a few campaigns. Perhaps it was possible for a vampire to hide his immortality if injured in battle.

"I'm impressed you know that."

"What was Grant like? Or did you not report directly to him?" She looked again at the Confederate uniform and noticed the Northern Virginia emblem on the buttons. "You infiltrated Lee or Longstreet's ranks?"

Surprised again, Gage smiled. "Longstreet's. I stole the uniform when I escaped from a prison I got locked up in after an uppity colonel figured out what side I was really on. As to Grant, I met him a few times. He was a contradiction in many ways. Introverted, more humble than most, and stuck to his values. Took him some time, but he became an excellent commander. Never would have figured you for a Civil War fanatic."

"I'm not. My parents used to take me to battlefields and military museums when I was little, before they...." Caitlin noticed a bullet hole surrounded by some dark staining on the left side of the jacket. Either Gage or the man who originally owned it had been wounded.

"Before they what?" This was the first she'd mentioned her parents in this lifetime.

"Died. They were killed in a pretty bad car wreck when I was young." Caitlin looked back at the jacket, fighting the sudden sense of loss washing over her. She caught the saddening of Gage's expression before she looked at the jacket again.

"I'm so sorry for your loss, cher."

"Thank you, but I've made my peace with it. It was a long time ago." She discovered a folded letter inside an inner jacket pocket. Curious about it, she carefully unfolded the old parchment.

"You fought at Gettysburg?" she asked as she read the dates and battles in the letter serving as a makeshift service record that was written to accompany the dead soldier home.

"Technically, my great, great, great, great grandson died at Gettysburg. I lied about who I was when I got stuck in a skirmish there after escaping. He only saw action on the first day before being unfortunately killed. His father fought as a union calvary officer in Virginia, Georgia, and Louisiana before being killed. The war sadly tore the family apart with father choosing the North and son the South."

"I guess one of the benefits of being a vampire is the ability to stage your own death so that the corner can't tell the difference."

"It's more a pain in the ass than anything. Always having to cover up things and find creative ways to end one mortal identity then begin another so people don't catch on to what you are."

"Is that the reason why you live up to the reputation of being the elusive, grumpy CEO?"

"Partially."

"Partially? What other reasons do you have for sequestering yourself in the office or D'Orme?"

"Caitlin, cher, I've lived on the fringes of two worlds since being bitten. Neither of which truly accept me for amazingly similar reasons. Your death also devastated me. I lost more than my mortality when I lost you. Work is how I coped with that loss."

The doorbell ringing interrupted their conversation.

"Your sisters?" Caitlin figured the girls returned to see if she remembered who she was.

"No. I'm not sure who it is." Gage didn't recognize the person ringing the doorbell. This was the second time in twenty-four hours that he couldn't identify if friend or foe was at D'Orme. He scowled, wanting to know why that was.

Caitlin followed him downstairs. When Gage opened the door, a tall man with graying dark hair and blue eyes smiled at them.

Caitlin recognized their visitor. "Sean?"

Gage stared at her, startled by the name she uttered. "You know this man?"

"Yes. He's an old family friend and my boss. Sean Watchous, Gage

Arsceneaux. Gage Arsceneaux, Sean Watchous." Caitlin shot Sean a puzzled look. "Sean, what are you doing here?"

"I wanted to make sure you were okay. Esther let me know you left for Baton Rouge in quite a rush yesterday. After our talk and finding this on the printer, I figured this is where you were headed." Sean held out the death certificate she had printed. "It really isn't like you to take off on an impromptu trip, Cate."

Caitlin took the paper from him, debating what to say. "So you fly to Louisiana to check on me?"

"I've been worried sick about you. You didn't return any of my calls or my texts. If I could've gotten a flight to Baton Rouge or New Orleans sooner, I would've been here last night. The earliest one I could get was this morning. You know your grandmother would kill me if she learned you randomly took off somewhere and I didn't track you down to make sure you were safe."

"Gram is crazy." Caitlin smiled at the mention of her grandmother. "I'm fine, Sean, and I'm sorry. My phone must've died last night, so I didn't get your messages. I'll make sure I charge it this morning." She cast Gage a quick glance. He guiltily grinned over at her with this being the second unexpected incident of the morning turning off the phones had caused. She took a breath then continued, "With Bill asking me to investigate the development case in Baton Rouge then a personal situation coming up, I thought it best I get a jump on things. Gage kindly offered to let me stay here since Baton Rouge is only a twenty-five-minute drive from D'Orme."

"A personal situation? Is there something I can do to help out with that matter?"

"No. The situation's been resolved. But, thank you for the offer and your concern."

Sean pointed at the paper she held. "Care to explain that?"

"Genealogy research." Caitlin shrugged as if it were nothing. Sean's knitted brow and the hard stare he gave her screamed he didn't believe her.

"May I come in, Cate? We need to talk about a few things."

"How did you know she was here?" Gage interjected before Caitlin could respond. Sean wasn't mortal if he needed an invitation to enter the house. Gage pushed Caitlin back from the door and placed himself in between her and Sean.

"Relax, Evariste. I'm only here to speak to Caitlin, not to harm anyone."

"If you were harmless, you could freely step through that doorway," Gage retorted, his canines now showing and the shade of his eyes deepening to a rich, vibrant green.

"Gage." Caitlin grabbed his upper arm, not wanting him to hurt Sean, but not certain if she could trust the man who raised her any longer. Gage wouldn't behave like he was if Sean wasn't some sort of threat.

Alcee materialized behind them. "He works for Morrigan. Let him enter, Evariste."

"Morrigan?" Gage eyed Sean but cleared the entryway, giving Sean room to step into the foyer. "Please, Sean, come in."

Caitlin almost asked why Sean needed to be invited in then remembered vampires needed an invitation to enter a home. "Don't tell me you're a vampire? That would certainly explain a lot."

"I'm not a vampire like your two new friends here. I'm a guide. There's a spell on the house that keeps all immortals out."

"A guide?" Caitlin hadn't ever heard of such a creature before.

"An immortal soldier and your appointed guardian. Morrigan charged me with watching over you. The goddess isn't fond of her family members or healers suffering any sort of harm," Sean briefly explained what he was.

"Healer? As in laying of the hands type people?" Caitlin tried to understand what Sean implied. No one had ever called her a healer before.

Sean looked around the opulent home Gage managed to hold onto for three centuries. He didn't look forward to the discussion about to occur. "Some healers do that. Your calling is slightly different, Cate, which is why you are attracting so much immortal interest."

"What exactly is her calling?" Gage asked, leading the group into the living room.

"For now, to save your soul, vampire."

A name suddenly popped into Caitlin's mind. "Who is Cassius?"

"Tristan Cassius is the vampire who killed you," Alcee casually remarked as if they discussed the weather.

"Alcee!" Gage threw his hands up, giving Alcee a disbelieving look, clearly conveying the message of what are you thinking to speak so bluntly?!

Caitlin reached for her throat. She shuddered when her fingers came in contact with her skin. Something drew her back in time. Air suddenly left her lungs. She wheezed, struggling to breath then collapsed to the ground. She stared at the blood flowing down her favorite day dress, which was a slightly paler hue of her eye color. The beast's face came into focus when she looked up at him. The reverberation of two gun shots rang out, much louder than she recalled happening the day of the actual attack. Once again, she saw the rage and horror on Gage's face as he rode toward them, reloading and firing again.

Caitlin knew the creature's eyes. "Dausan."

The three immortal men stopped talking as she whispered the name.

A sudden sensation of reeling backward at a mind-numbing speed brought her back to her present-day self. *What the hell had just happened?*

"Dausan? As in Tristan Dausan?" Sean recognized the name. "The attorney from Lafayette?"

"He's the thing from my nightmares," Caitlin mumbled. "It had his eyes."

"Caitlin, cher, that wasn't a dream." Gage now understood why she had become so quiet. She had flashbacked to her death. He comfortingly took her hand in the two of his, hoping to ease the unavoidable blow the truth would deal her. "It really happened that way."

Horrified, she yanked her hand from between his and took a step back from the three people she thought she knew fairly well until today. "You weren't my boss when I worked with Tristan, Sean. You said you hardly knew him."

"Would you recognize me better as this gentleman?" Sean changed into the senior Vice President at her old employer, James Gillard.

Astonished by what he had done, Caitlin's eyes widened. "You can change your appearance?"

Sean returned back to his normal self. "If I need to. I have been with you a very long time, Cate."

"Is this what you really look like?"

"Most of the time," Sean casually said as if shapeshifting was a completely normal occurrence.

"Most of the time? What do you really look like?"

Sean frowned but took on his natural form.

Caitlin gasped at how the perfectly human-looking, modern businessman transformed into a tall, fit being with silver-streaked, long, dark hair, and elongated ears. His eyes paled to an opaque hue of aquamarine. He looked like an overgrown elf in the book of Celtic fairy tales her grandmother had given her as a child. "You're a fae."

"Partly," Sean drily replied.

"That's why Gage didn't meet Caitlin when she lived in Kenner." Alcee realized the guide shielded her from anything mystical, including Gage. "You blocked the energy around her."

"Morrigan was concerned when Caitlin moved to New Orleans. I had strict orders to keep her hidden, so I glamoured her." Sean confirmed Alcee's assumption was correct.

"You what me?" Caitlin didn't follow.

"Glamoured, it's a type of spell that changes a being's appearance or hides one's abilities." Sean gave her an empathetic smile. "Tristan shouldn't have ever been able to find her. I'm still confused as to how that happened."

"Either he got lucky or you aren't very good at your job." Gage took a jab at the guide.

"Careful, bloodsucker. I kept you away well enough." Sean shot back.

This was all nuts, but deep down, Caitlin knew everything being said was true. "What does Alcee mean by blocking energy so Gage and I couldn't meet?"

"I keep the nonhuman things away. Unfortunately, that included Gage until the time was right."

"Keep the nonhuman things away?" Caitlin's temper flared at the claim.

"Caitlin, remember to assume positive intent." Sean slipped back into his managerial self, trying to weaken the storm about to be unleashed.

"Assume positive intent? Take that stupid philosophical crap and stick it! All three of you act like this is a normal conversation. Am I the only one who thinks the world has gone crazy? I'm standing in a room with two vampires and this guide thing. I was married to one of them in a past life. There is something stalking me that I used to work with, who also killed me three hundred years ago. And you! You say you keep the nonhuman things away? I've seen ghosts since I was a child. You aren't doing too well with keeping the nonhuman things away!" She stared at Gage now. "I don't even know what to say or think. I'm sorry for the loss of your wife, but I am not her, Gage, at least not anymore."

Gage set a comforting hand on her arm. "I know, cher. We both have changed so much since then. I also understand the confusion and anger you are feeling."

"Caitlin, mon amie—" Alcee started to approach her.

"Stay away from me!"

Puzzled by her reaction, Alcee's shoulders lifted as he turned to look at Gage and Sean.

"Cate, it's going to be okay. What you're feeling right now is perfectly normal and expected," Sean soothingly said, keeping an eye on her. "Try to remember that all three of us in this room care deeply for you and would never intentionally hurt you."

This must be a lot for you to take in. Give it time. You'll come to grips with it, Gage's voice sounded in her head.

"I don't want to come to grips with it," Caitlin responded aloud. "I want to wake up from this strange dream to find out I ate or drank a bad combination of something. That I'm dating a normal guy, and my boss is just my boss, who is back in Williamsburg, not here."

Gage reached out to her again. *I wish I could make it a dream for you. I wished for the same thing in those early days after you died.*

Caitlin blinked back the tears blurring her vision. *I'm so sorry you went through this too, Evariste.*

Gage embraced her. "You have nothing to be sorry for. You can't control any of this."

"Telepath?" Sean asked Alcee.

234

"Oui, but he rarely uses that gift," Alcee said, surprised he didn't notice the silent communication between Gage and Caitlin before.

"Cate, call Gram. She can explain everything to you."

"Gram? Why would she be able to—"

"Morrigan is your grandmother, Caitlin," Sean cut her off. "Call her name. She'll answer."

"Just say her name?" Caitlin doubted she could spontaneously bring her grandmother from England to D'Orme by simply saying her name.

"Yes. She's waiting for you to do so."

Frustrated, Caitlin let out an annoyed breath then mistrustingly spoke her grandmother's name, "Morrigan."

The goddess appeared in the room, creating another shock for the men standing around Caitlin. "Hello, Caitlin. I've missed you, *a leanbh.*"

"Gram?" Caitlin wasn't sure she should believe her eyes when her grandmother appeared looking the same age as she was in flowing green and gold robes with golden hair. The last she had seen her Gram, the woman had silver hair and crow's feet crinkling the corners of her eyes, but she always carried herself with the same regal bearing this goddess did.

"I know this is confusing for you. But the time has come to know who you are. You need to remember the past."

"I need to remember?"

Morrigan smiled. "In due course, all will be revealed."

"I did not summon an oracle. I summoned a goddess, a family member, to speak plainly with me." The words coming out of her mouth shocked Caitlin. *Since when did she speak that way?*

Sean cringed. Had any other spoken to Morrigan in such a blunt manner, they wouldn't still be breathing.

Pleased by her granddaughter's brusque tone, a smile curved Morrigan's lips. Subconsciously, the old Caitlin, the survivor and fighter, remained within the modern woman. "As you wish. Be forewarned, you may not like what you learn. Ask me the questions you seek answers to."

"Am I the woman Gage waited for?"

"Yes. Come look in the water, medica. Seeing always worked better than words when you were angry." Morrigan directed Caitlin to a crystal clear stream suddenly running an inch from her feet.

Caitlin glanced around. They were no longer in the living room, but in a rich wood, dark green grass and moss covered the bank on either side of a stream. The flowing surface oddly shimmered here and there as sunbeams struck crystalline water. She slowly knelt on the bank. Images of Gage and her emerged in a rippling circle. They laughed as they rode along a beach somewhere. She guessed Grand Isle by the surroundings. The beach shifted to their wedding at D'Orme then Gage grieving at her grave. Her second life surfaced, and she saw herself as a child speaking to a Union Army officer when she visited Gettysburg. In her teenage years, another ghost visited her, an eighteenth-century gentleman clad in brown pants, matching vest, and white shirt in Sean's Virginia home. The face of the two men overlapped, revealing Gage's face. He was her ghosts? "How is this even possible?"

"Echoes in time crossing paths," Morrigan explained. "Different centuries, but souls recognizing each other in those rare, fleeting moments where past and present overlap. As you can see, you and Evariste have never really been far apart."

"Does he know?" Caitlin wondered what Gage saw at those moments.

"Ask him later." Morrigan helped her up.

"What does Tristan want from me?"

"You have special gifts as one of my descendants, Caitlin. The one he works for desires all your gifts. Tristan himself desires your ability to reach out through time, beyond the realm of the living, and to speak with those that passed." Morrigan wished she had asked about the prophecy from the voodoo priestess instead. She could not reveal more than Caitlin inquired about.

"I stopped talking to ghosts once I turned sixteen. How would Tristan know I could do that?"

"He can sense your power, just as Evariste feels when you are near."

"How do I stop him? How do I set Gage and his family free? What happens if I do?"

"Trust your instincts when the time comes to manage Tristian. They will guide you. As to the curse, that is a much more complicated matter.

We will have to wait and see what the Fates choose to reveal. In the meantime, remember how powerful you are, your name should remind you if you find yourself forgetting."

"My name?"

"Your last name, DeDanann, is a shortening of Tuatha De Danann. It means of the folk of the godess, my family, and all those who serve our cause. Ask Sean to share more when you are ready to learn your true ancestry." Morrigan kissed the top of her head then disappeared.

Caitlin returned to the living room.

Alcee glanced in Caitlin's direction. "A daughter of Morrigan. No wonder she sent Sean to watch after you."

"A what?" Gage asked, unsure of the significance of that.

"Cate is a direct descendant of Morrigan herself. Her granddaughter," Sean clarified things. "If Tristan finds a way to siphon her abilities, he not only takes on the healer traits, he inherits some of Morrigan's powers."

"The last thing we need is a psychotic vampire with a direct link to a goddess of war." Gage could only imagine the hell that would break loose if Tristan gained any more power. The vampire was ambitious to the point the Vampire Council kept a watchful eye on him and periodically reminded Tristan of his place to keep him in check.

"He won't get one," Caitlin spoke up, a new sense of confidence setting in along with a slight thrill at the idea of conflict with Tristan. "He failed the last time trying to harvest those abilities from me. He will fail with whatever he is plotting now."

Sean scoffed at her statement. "Quite the claim coming from a woman on the verge of a meltdown a few minutes ago. You are just learning who you are. Do not make the mistake of trivializing your enemy. There is more than Tristan you are facing."

Not having considered Tristan might have allies, Gage frowned. "Who else is involved?"

"We are working on figuring that out. When I can share more, I will."

Caitlin's brow rose; her lavender eyes locked on Sean. "You instigate today with the words 'there is no other.' Yet, aren't prepared to share everything you know that could help Gage and me?"

Sean grinned at the way she cynically stared down her nose at him and the slight cocking of her head. Now, she looked just as Morrigan did when the goddess disapproved of or doubted something. "Instigated? I don't have any idea what you are talking about."

"You're the only one in the room who has my internal work email address. The only one who could have possibly emailed me my death certificate and the deed to Maison D'Orme. The state didn't have any records on file as they were all destroyed by a fire in 1780 when the local church and courthouse burnt down."

Gage uncrossed the arms folded over his chest. "Someone emailed you the deed to D'Orme and your death certificate?"

"And called me to tell me there were no other Evariste or Gage Arsceneauxs. They're all one and the same." Caitlin's eyes narrowed, still locked on Sean. "You knew I'd come here."

"It was time for you to, Cate," Sean confessed to the email and the phone call. "Especially after you saw the painting in the Governor's Palace."

"What painting?" Gage demanded, fearful someone endangered his loved ones. "I own all the Arsceneaux and LeBlanc paintings predating the Civil War."

"There is one hanging in the Governor's Palace in Williamsburg of you, Alcee, Pierre LeBlanc, Jude Robicheaux, the colonial governor of Virginia, and someone with the initials of A.A.B. I saw it when I attended a preservation society event," Caitlin confirmed the painting's existence.

"One of you parlor tricks, guide?" Gage almost spat at Sean. "Such a painting was never commissioned. By creating it, you place her, along with all of us hiding here in Louisiana at risk."

"I had nothing to do with that painting showing up. It caused quite a bit of concern for Morrigan and me knowing what it would trigger. Hence the phone call and emails. You were supposed to be with her when she remembered who she was, Evariste. Since you weren't, the past manifested as nightmares in her sleep. Do you really think I would put a woman I raised and care about through such trauma?"

"You two fighting isn't helping matters." Alcee halted the escalating argument then turned to Caitlin. "Do you recall who the artist was or who owned the painting?"

"No, but it was donated with a bunch of stuff from a private collection. There was a journal one of the society members used to look up everyone in the painting."

Sean took a deep breath. "Where was the journal, Cate?"

"On the desk in the governor's office." She closed her eyes, remembering standing next to the volunteer as he read the entry. For a fleeting moment, she was in the room watching the scene unfold. She saw Sean in the crowded hall.

"Good. Concentrate on where we are," Sean said, needing her to hold the vision longer.

She heard herself asking if there was any more information on the Louisiana men in the journal.

"None," the volunteer said as she turned back to the painting.

Caitlin touched the pendant around her neck, staring at the painting. Time stood still as she scanned the room, looking for anything unusual. She wasn't sure what she was looking for, but her intuition told her she'd find something there. A shadow caught her eye. It morphed into a man.

"Sean, the fourth man in the painting! He's here," she alerted the guide, startling Gage and Alcee.

Alcee realized what was happening with Sean no longer present in the room. "Mon Dieu! She's channeling the past."

"Get Gage." Sean made his way through the crowd toward the shadow. "But don't let go of the vision. We need to identify whoever that shadow is."

"How do I get Gage?"

Sean wasn't sure what to tell her. "However you always conjured him up. I could never stop it from happening."

"I don't know how those times happened, and they were mostly when I was asleep." Caitlin shook her head, somehow rewinding the scene.

"I can come to you, cher." Vampires could teleport a short distance when needed. Joining Caitlin wherever she was in time shouldn't be much different a process. Though, he'd be lying if he ever said the thought of time travel didn't scare the hell out of him. He focused on Caitlin then jumped to her location. Glad things worked as he hoped they would, he let out the breath he had been holding. Standing beside her, he searched for a shadow but didn't see one that stood out. "Where is he?"

"There." Caitlin pointed at an odd-shaped form in the corner of the room.

The empty form once again gained human features. "I see you, Evariste!"

The vision shattered, sending Caitlin, Sean, and Gage back to D'Orme.

"Do you recognize him?" Sean hoped Gage did.

Alcee didn't like how pale Gage had become. "Tristan?"

"Much worse," Gage remarked, coming around. "Antoine Bonin."

"Bonin? It cannot be. He died long ago." Alcee doubted Bonin lived.

"It was definitely him in the painting and in the room. Tristan must be his lackey." Gage grimly stared at Alcee. The gods help them all if Bonin returned from the dead.

"Antoine's definitely your man." Sean handed the open journal he held to Alcee.

Alcee read the name of the painting's initial owner. "Merde!"

"Who's Antoine Bonin?" Caitlin asked, puzzled by why the two vampires seemed so disturbed.

"One of the most deranged and powerful vampires in the history of Louisiana," Alcee answered her.

"Also my grandfather," Gage added. That explained how the painting was so well fabricated.

Caitlin vaguely recalled Gage discussing his family history around the time they were married. "Your grandfather? The one who died shortly after arriving in Louisiana?"

"Appears he didn't die." Gage looked at Alcee.

"Two vamps in one family. Someone wasn't happy about you all coming to Louisiana." Sean earned a scowl from Caitlin and Gage.

"Well, at least we know why Tristan was in Virginia." Alcee showed Gage the sticker on the underside of the journal's front cover.

"Donated by Tristan Dausan on behalf of a client who wishes to remain confidential," Gage read the label aloud.

"The devious bastard wanted us to connect the dots. That's why he stopped by my office." Sean frowned at the blatant provocation playing out.

"You're giving Tristan too much credit. He isn't smart enough to come up with such an idea on his own. It's my grandfather baiting us." Gage handed the journal to Sean. "Alcee, have Fabien start researching everything the Vampire Council has in the archives on Bonin. I want to know how he managed to hide the fact he was still alive from all of us this long, and find out where exactly he is now. Keep who knows about this to a minimum. God knows what chaos will erupt in the vampire community if word of Bonin's return leaks before we can advise the council of it."

"Evariste, I will ask Morrigan what I may share from the High Council records should any information we have assist you in locating him." Sean wanted to ensure Caitlin was kept safe.

"Thank you, and you needn't worry. I have the resources to protect my wife," Gage said, grateful to have a new ally in the brewing fight.

Caitlin worried if anyone discovered someone had taken the journal, they'd have more than a mysterious vampire to deal with. "Sean, put that back before anyone notices it missing."

"Yes, ma'am." Sean turned and took a couple of steps forward.

"Wait! Before you go anywhere, did you send me this?" Caitlin turned on her phone and showed Sean the text and picture she received.

"No." Sean handed Gage Caitlin's phone, hoping the vampire might know who did.

Gage stared down at the picture of him and Caitlin dancing. "This was sent to get my attention. Antoine or Tristan was at the ball."

Alcee noted the fear hidden underneath Gage's angry expression as he took the phone from him then read the picture caption. "Antoine most likely. We'll find him, Evariste. Before he can do any harm."

"Now I really need to get this back and alert Morrigan to matters here. Evariste, I trust you've got the watch going forward. Actually, you've probably always had it with as many times as you two have found each other."

Sean's comment perplexed Gage. "Caitlin only recently remade my acquaintance."

"Hardly! How do you think I knew she could do what she did today, Major? Remember Fredericksburg?" Sean laughed, disappearing.

"Major?" Alcee waited on Gage to explain whatever Sean hinted at.

"I thought I saw Caitlin in Fredericksburg." Gage recalled how he dreamed of her there. The pleasant dream was so vivid he swore it was real when he woke the next morning to the unpleasant rumbling of cannon fire. Plumes of artillery smoke had blended with thick fog, gifting him a few extra moments of reprieve before the bloody field engagement began. He had seen enough death that day to last a lifetime. Now death may once again be making himself an unwelcome guest in Gage's life. "We need to warn the rest of the family. Bonin may target them as leverage to use against me."

"Stay with Caitlin. I will alert Pierre and Jude." Alcee turned to depart. "Did you ever invite Antoine to D'Orme?"

"No. He died before it was completed."

Exchanging Vows
ᏮᏉᏉ

Gage picked up his car keys after Alcee disappeared. "Come on."

"Where are we going?" Caitlin grabbed her purse and phone, following Gage out the door.

"To the Quarter. We need to remedy a problem."

He drove like a madman into the city, not saying a word.

"Tell me about Antoine," Caitlin ended the silence due to needing a distraction from Gage's crazy driving.

"There's not much to say about him. He's a ruthless killer with no conscience. He even scared the Vampire Council to the point they ordered his execution." Gage kept his eyes on the road as he spoke. "No one's heard of him since then until today."

"And he's your grandfather?"

"Unfortunately." Gage turned into the Quarter.

"Remind me to come to the Quarter with you more often. I can never find a parking spot like this one," Caitlin remarked as he navigated the backstreets and parked just outside Jackson Square.

Gage got out of the truck and opened her door. "We can come to the Quarter as often as you like. This way." He led her toward St. Louis Cathedral.

Not sure what to think when he opened the church doors, Caitlin shot him a puzzled look. "What are we doing here?"

"Meeting someone."

"Can you even go into a church without bursting into flames?"

"Apparently so." He grinned and blessed himself with holy water.

Caitlin laughed, watching him do so. "Suicidal tendencies?"

"I've always been a risk taker."

A priest standing near the front row of pews recognized the man approaching him. "Evariste! Nice to see you again."

"Father." Gage shook the priest's hand. "I have a request to make of you."

"As long as it's legal, name it." The priest hesitantly smiled, noting the dark mood Gage was in.

"Marry us."

"What?" the priest and Caitlin said in unison.

"Marry us. Right now."

"Son, the Church stopped performing marriages on short notice about a hundred years ago."

"Father, I know that, but this is an urgent situation. I really need you to make an exception to current protocol."

The baffled priest tried to comprehend what was possibly so urgent. "You're a bit old for this, Evariste, but I need to ask, is she pregnant?"

"No!" Caitlin snapped, dumbfounded by the priest's intrusive question.

"Father." Gage shifted to Creole for the rest of whatever he had to say.

Caitlin didn't catch everything with as quickly as he spoke. The minister looked at him wide-eyed, then walked up the steps to the altar and opened the Bible resting on it.

Caitlin shook her head. "No way."

Gage roguishly grinned. "The priest is waiting, Caitlin."

"Does he really think he is going to marry us?" Caitlin whispered when the priest gestured for them to stand in front of the altar.

"Yes."

"Aren't you supposed to propose first?"

"You already said yes." Gage kept his voice low as his grin turned into a smile.

"In 1708!" Caitlin exclaimed, startling the priest.

The priest cleared his throat, hinting for them to make up their minds.

"Are you telling me you don't want to be my wife in this lifetime?" Gage asked, slightly surprised she acted as she did.

"No, not exactly. I would just like a little more romance and some time to think about it. You know, date for a while, then you get down on one knee. I buy a white dress, the whole nine yards."

"I promise you will have all that later. You married me before after only a two-month courtship."

"And look how that turned out. I died seven years later!"

"Were you happy for those seven years, Caitlin?"

"Yes."

Gage took her hands in his. "Do you no longer believe I am the man for you?"

"That isn't the point, Evariste! This is too damn fast for modern me."

"Your grandmother approves of us wedding."

"My grandmother is a bit crazy if you hadn't noticed. Hell, she used to fly around as a crow to scare men she didn't like into thinking they were dying."

"Is there a problem, Evariste?" the priest asked, noting the flustered look on Caitlin's face.

"No, Father. She's just nervous and needs a minute."

Caitlin shook her head. "I need more than a minute. This is crazy!"

"Make a deal with you. If you find you're unhappy after six months of being married, we'll get a divorce. Now, Caitlin DeDanann, may we get married?"

Caitlin's brows rose and her mouth dropped open then closed. "Fine. I expect you to honor that promise if I ask for a divorce."

"I've yet to break any promises to you." Gage grinned, guiding her up the stairs to stand before the altar.

The priest smiled and began reading in Latin. Unexpectedly, Caitlin found she understood him even though she hadn't studied Latin a day in her life.

"I do," Gage answered the priest in English after the priest paused and looked at him.

A second later, the priest stared over at her.

"I do." She couldn't believe the words just came out of her mouth. Gage slid the diamond wedding ring she wore to the soiree onto her left hand. Someone else seemed to take over her mind as she spoke her vows and slid a gold band onto his ring finger. Memories of their previous wedding flashed before her as the priest announced them to be man and wife.

"Merci beaucoup," Gage thanked the priest before signing the marriage certificate. He watched Caitlin slowly sign her name beside his.

CAITLIN STARED down at the diamond ring on her hand as they drove back to D'Orme. *Sean is going to kill me for getting married like this.*

"He didn't kill you the first time. He won't kill you this time either," Gage said as they turned into the driveway.

"The first time?" She didn't recall eloping or a rushed marriage before.

"We didn't exactly wait until we came to Louisiana last time. I married you with your supposed father's blessing in Norfolk prior to the big event at D'Orme. Although, after meeting Sean today, I suspect he was posing as your father back then. The two men certainly look a great deal alike."

"I've eloped twice now?"

Gage laughed. "Much more willingly last time, cher. You thought it was incredibly romantic. We had the captain of the galleon we sailed to Louisiana on marry us then. At least we married in a church this time."

Caitlin gasped. "I wouldn't do that."

"Hate to tell you this, but it was your idea. I proposed and planned to come back to Virginia to marry you. You didn't want to wait and insisted I take you with me. I couldn't compromise a lady of your standing by taking you with me unwed. To head off any scandals, we married on the ship as she pulled out to sea. My mother was the one who was angry about the impromptu wedding. She was very unhappy to learn I brought a bride home from Virginia. We had a proper wedding a short time later. We didn't even have wedding bands when we married on the ship." Gage smiled as he recalled the details.

She groaned, now remembering the shipboard wedding. "We used two brass rings from one of the smaller sail riggings."

"Selective memory fading away?"

Several cars were parked in the driveway when Gage turned into D'Orme.

"Looks like we've got a full house. I take it Alcee put out the alarm on Antoine."

"No more talk about Antoine tonight. We will worry about him tomorrow." Gage got out of the car. "Madam Arsceneaux, your castle awaits."

"So it does, my dark prince." Caitlin took the hand he offered, then walked up the porch steps with him.

"Shall we stir up our subjects waiting inside?"

Before she could answer, Gage kicked open the door and swung her into his arms.

"Can a man not have some privacy on his wedding night?" he shouted, carrying Caitlin into the house.

The group of guests stood dumbfounded as he set Caitlin down then kissed her.

"Damn it, boy! Your mother is going to be livid that you've done this to her twice," Pierre's voice boomed as he walked from the kitchen to the living room. "With the same girl, no less." Pierre hugged Gage then his daughter-in-law. "Welcome to the family, cher. Again."

Caitlin noticed the food and drink set up in the dining room. "Alcee didn't put out a warning about Antoine."

"No, he will do that tomorrow. He and I planned tonight earlier today," Gage confessed, looking around the room.

She had been with him all day and only saw Alcee when Sean rang the doorbell. "When?"

"After Sean's visit, I enlisted Alcee's help in getting permission from your grandmother to marry you in this lifetime. Once Alcee confirmed I had her support and approval, all I had to do was tell Alli my plans. I sent her a quick text saying we were getting married this afternoon. With how she and my sisters gossip, the news spread like wildfire."

"You're lucky I said yes."

Gage grinned. "Fortune favors the bold, or so they say. I was willing to wager your last name would be Arsceneaux by this evening, or I'd gladly endure the embarrassment of telling everyone I got a little overeager in my assumption you'd say yes."

After dinner and cake, Caitlin sat in the living room, chatting with Gage's sisters. She periodically beheld the ring on her hand to remind herself that she was indeed married. Something she never planned on doing after several failed relationships.

ALCEE JOINED Gage on the back patio. "She is handling all of this rather well."

"Caitlin's always been a remarkable woman." Gage watched his wife through the window. *Things were finally as they should be.* A smile tweaked his lips in reaction to the serene scene of Caitlin and his sisters laughing at something.

"She's powerful, Gage. You saw what she is capable of today with Sean and her retrieving the journal."

Alcee danced around something. Gage stared into the glass of Grand Marnier in his hand. "Say what's on your mind, old friend."

"Antoine will be more careful this go round. I do not think Tristan will be the one who comes for her. He was too sloppy with his assignment last time."

Gage sipped his drink, his eyes still on Caitlin. "I've thought about that myself tonight."

"Your grandfather is one of the most powerful and vindictive vampires I know, Evariste. Don't underestimate what he is capable of," Alcee warned, concerned Gage didn't realize what a formidable enemy he faced.

"I won't," Gage reassured his friend before heading inside.

"Drinking her blood didn't work last time."

Alcee's words froze Gage in the doorway. His back stiffened at the thought of Bonin harming Caitlin. He once more took in his smiling wife. His mother now sat with Caitlin and his sisters. He'd be damned if he'd let anyone ruin the happiness that returned to their lives. Hell would freeze over before Bonin, Tristan, or anyone else for that matter hurt the women in his family again.

"Evariste, we've both always suspected Tristan wasn't the only vampire to attack you that day. Bonin's actions the past few weeks confirm he was there, and he's most likely your sire. I don't know what he has planned, but he is the only vampire besides Lilith I know who has the power to create a curse like the one on your family. A man who would damn his own flesh and blood will stop at nothing to claim what he is after."

"That's the main reason for the rush wedding. He can't enter D'Orme, and I don't plan on allowing my wife to leave the safety of the property alone."

"Good luck with that!" Alcee recalled how Evariste tried that before. If 1700s Caitlin didn't take kindly to being escorted everywhere, present day Caitlin wouldn't like it any better.

Unwelcome Surprises

G age absentmindedly played with Caitlin's hair while she slept
soundly beside him. Had Bonin orchestrated everything in 1715
as Alcee suggested? He mentally reached out into the night, searching
for any energy trace of Bonin or Tristan.

They are not here, several voices whispered as he walked the temporal
plane, checking out Bonin's old haunts.

We will help you watch, another vampire promised him.

Rest, Arsceneaux. We stand guard, a second one ordered. *The
Council is as concerned as you are with Alcee sharing Bonin might be
alive.*

Merci, mes amis! Gage thanked the other vampires before ending
his search.

He was grateful for his friends and allies throughout the ranks of
vampires in Louisiana and the spell of protection the voodoo priestess
had placed on D'Orme. Bonin couldn't bypass that mystical barrier.

THE NEXT MONTH WAS QUIET. Almost worrisomely so. No further
revelations about him or Caitlin, nor trouble from Bonin and Tristan.

Gage went to the office for a few hours to ensure everything was still running smoothly.

"I thought I saw some sparks between you and Caitlin when she was here. Congratulations on your marriage!" Sharon, his secretary, greeted him as he walked in the door.

"Thank you, Sharon." Gage picked up his mail and continued to his office.

"Whoa! Did I just hear the words congratulations on your marriage?" Sid, one of his partners, asked, peering inside Gage's office doorway.

"And apparently, no one, not even Alli and Alcee, warranted an invite." James, the company attorney, joined Sid at the door.

"It wasn't exactly planned, gentlemen. It was a rather spur-of-the-moment kind of thing." Gage read one of the more interesting pieces of mail that came in while he was out.

"When Sharon said Caitlin, did she mean the redhead from Langley and Associates?" Sid asked.

"Yes."

"Talk about heated negotiations. You must have given her some tour of the shipyards." Sid chuckled, amused that Gage was now married to the woman who he had done everything he could to avoid meeting.

"Are we on track for Friday?" Gage gave Sid a pointed stare, shifting the topic of conversation. He trusted Sid and James, but they had no idea what he was. No need to put humans at risk by sharing too much information, especially humans who worked for him.

"Sounds like the honeymoon was short-lived." Jim shifted the portfolio in his hand.

"You two are worse than my sisters."

Sharon brought him his morning coffee.

"Thank you, Sharon. I appreciate it."

Gage added cream and sugar to the coffee then stirred it, grinning over at James and Sid. "The honeymoon is still ongoing. She's amazing, and if we didn't have a hard and fast deadline on Friday morning, I wouldn't be here. I'd be working from home again. Since the two of you appear to have nothing else to do, let's get to work, so I can get home at a reasonable hour. I'll even be a nice boss and cut the entire office loose an hour early."

Around 2:00 p.m., Sharon walked into his office, interrupting the team of three who were putting the finishing touches on their next project proposal.

"Evariste, your sister's on the phone. She wants to know what time you think you'll be home."

Sid and James laughed at the cynical expression on Gage's face.

The last time his sisters had called the office with that question, he came home to a full-blown makeover mess. Every woman in his family had invaded his house for a girls' afternoon out.

"At least it's not the wife calling already." Sid patted Gage on the back, remembering how pissed Gage was when he came into work after makeover day.

"That's what concerns me. I think we've got enough done to call it a day." Gage wanted to get back to D'Orme. His sisters inquiring about his return home was rarely ever a good thing. "Which one of my sisters is on the phone?"

"Renee and Allister."

Gage frowned. No good would come of whatever the girls were up to. "Both of them? Tell them to expect me promptly at four-thirty."

"Yes, sir." Sharon walked out of the office and relayed the message.

Alcee's tall frame took up the doorway after Sharon left. "Before you head out, we just received another offer from Giovanni."

Gage shook his head. "The Italian is really getting to be a pain in the ass with these continual counteroffers. Call Giovanni and Sean, tell them I have given the last three offers careful consideration and my answer remains firmly not interested. If Giovanni still doesn't get it, tell him hell will freeze over before he sits in the CEO's chair at Lagniappe Shipping and Ag. I don't want to hear from him again."

Alcee, Sid, and James all chuckled at Gage's response.

"He's got the girl, Alcee, so there's no need to keep playing the game with her employer," Sid said with a smirk.

Gage ignored the remark. "Thanks for all your hard work on the Metairie proposal. I say we all call it a day, as I need to make sure my house isn't being destroyed or redecorated."

NOTHING SEEMED TOO OUT of the ordinary when Gage pulled up in the driveway. His sisters' cars were there, along with his father's truck.

What is Daddy doing here? It was planting season. Pierre would normally be in the fields at this time of day. He heard Pierre's voice coming from the rear of the house but couldn't quite make out what he said. Gage tossed his keys and briefcase on the front porch swing, then walked around the side of the house to investigate things. As he came around the corner, he saw his dad and his sisters, but no Caitlin. A loud neigh from his right drew his attention.

"Where did that come from?" Gage demanded, walking up to Pierre and his sisters.

"Where did what come from?" Pierre smiled, pretending not to know what Gage referenced.

"That." Gage pointed at the horse and rider loping along the edge of the yard.

Pierre furrowed his brow. "That? That is your wife."

"I'm not talking about Caitlin. Where did the horse come from?" Gage watched the Friesian Caitlin rode as she turned it for another pass along the grassy border just before the manicured landscape shifted to wild grassland then plowed field. The black gelding reminded him of Gambit, the first horse he bought her. She begged him for that wild beast the second she laid eyes on him, and like a lovesick fool, he had purchased the stallion who destroyed two stall doors, one barn door, more fences than he could count, and would go for random excursions in the neighboring properties' fields.

Alli smiled. "Daddy and Caitlin went to the livestock auction this morning."

"You let the two of them go to a livestock sale? Allister, we don't need a barn full of horses again. I don't have time to take care of the property as it is." Gage wanted to strangle her. He intentionally had gotten rid of the horses and didn't have any pets so he could work any hours he needed to in the office. Last thing he needed was to be rushing home to muck out stalls or fill an empty food dish, not to mention he didn't miss finding various items or furnishings randomly destroyed by small teeth or large hooves.

"I needed some help picking out a few animals for the farm. Caitlin always did have a great eye when it came to cattle and horses," Pierre said.

"Yes, she does. That obviously hasn't changed," Gage complimented his wife's most recent acquisition now that he could better see the features of the Friesian and how smoothly his gait flowed. Caitlin slowed the horse to a walk.

"And a horse gives her incentive to stay nearby," Pierre justified the purchase.

"I suppose a horse is better than a puppy who will eat the sofa, but still, Daddy." Gage stopped himself from saying something that would upset his stepfather.

"We can always get her one of those too." Alli smirked as Gage glared at her, his lips curling to bare his fangs.

"Stop being grumpy." Renee nudged him with her elbow, his old riding boots in her hand. "You're going to need these."

Gage warily took the boots. "And why is that?"

"We told her you'd take her on a guided tour of your and the LeBlanc's land when you got home."

Gage set the boots down. "Hard to do that without a horse."

"We thought about that, too. She picked one out special for you." Pierre stepped aside so Gage could see the second horse groomed and saddled, standing with one leg cocked and eyes closed, dozing in the afternoon sun a few feet away.

"Merde," Gage growled, approaching the second unwelcome surprise of the day. The horse raised its head. Clear, curious, wide brown eyes studied him. Gage gently stroked the horse's muzzle as he looked the animal over. The bay definitely wasn't some random hack for pleasure. By his lines and height, Gage guessed he was a young thoroughbred, probably racing stock at that. "Do I want to know how much I am out?"

"Consider them a late wedding present."

"Care to join me for a ride, Evariste?" Caitlin called to him with a beaming smile on her face. The Friesian she rode snorted as she stopped him a few feet away.

"After I change."

"I've waited all afternoon for you to get home. Most gentlemen ride in a coat and slacks. That hasn't changed over time. Or are you stalling as you've lost your riding skills, Major?"

Gage grinned up at her. "I can assure you, madam, I haven't lost any of my *riding* skills."

Caitlin laughed at the emphasis he placed on riding. "Prove it, Evariste."

The Friesian pawed at the grass and backed a step or two; softly whickering to the bay as if to ask, 'You guys coming? We're ready to go.'

Gage handed his coat and tie to Pierre, then rolled up his shirtsleeves and unbuttoned the first two buttons on his dress shirt. "You are going to regret issuing that challenge." He swapped his dress shoes for the boots he had set down.

"Catch me if you can!" Caitlin rode off as he swung aboard his horse.

Gage lightly tapped the thoroughbred's sides with his heals. The horse jumped forward with the physical cue and the loud yah from Gage, tearing off after the Friesian who had a slight head start.

Renee shook her head, watching Gage chase after Caitlin. "Those two will never change."

"I hope not. I haven't seen Evariste smile this much in years. Well, it's time for us to go." Pierre rounded up his daughters.

CAITLIN'S LAUGHTER floated back to Gage on the same wind that caught her hair. The Friesian she rode galloped across the flat cane field. Gage checked his horse's pace as he came up on her. This used to be one of her favorite things to do. He gave the bay looser rein, pulling alongside her. They raced up the headland, then turned into a second cane field, thundering down their old course. Both urged on their horses. The winner would be whoever reached the far end first.

A rabbit shot out from the cane stalks, spooking Caitlin's horse. She kept her seat as the horse reared. Gage slowed some to make sure she didn't fall. Once the horse's front feet were on the ground again, Caitlin spurred him forward, prompting Gage to take advantage of the slight lead he held. The bay he rode reached the end of the cane field several feet ahead of Caitlin. Gage dropped the reins and punched the air with a closed fist while shouting, "Yes! Victory!"

"Any doubt left about my riding skills, cher?" he asked as Caitlin trotted toward him

She rolled her eyes, halting her horse alongside his. "You would've lost if it wasn't for that rabbit."

"If that's what you need to tell yourself."

They turned the horses in the direction of the barn, leisurely riding back home.

Enjoying riding with his wife, Gage mischievously smiled. "As I recall, I won the last race as well."

"Jumping from your horse and knocking the other rider to the ground doesn't count."

"I had a sworn duty to keep you from crossing enemy lines. I didn't hear you object to my methods."

"Sworn duty!" Caitlin repeated in mock anger. "Did you make love in the pouring rain to every woman you caught crossing a battlefield?"

"Only the ones who looked like my wife. I thought you were a dream. Have mercy on me, cher. I was a long, long way from home fighting a war and hadn't touched a woman in almost a hundred years. How could I resist you?"

Thinking of their passionate encounter, Caitlin closed her eyes. She could feel the warmth of his skin against hers after she yanked off his shirt. The cool rain falling from the sky hitting her face. Her lips tingled from the ferocity of his kisses. Her arms hooked around his waist and shoulders when he finally joined their bodies. Neither one of them caring about anything other than how desperately they needed one another. Like crazed wild, licentious creatures, they made love in the middle of some farmer's field. The thunder drowning out their cries and moaning. Caitlin came back to the present. "Hard to believe that actually happened."

"After that memory, let's get back to the house."

"Only an outdoorsman when at war, Arsceneaux?"

"A gentleman doesn't take his wife in one of his fields. Too many people could find us naked and in between the rows in the twenty-first century or we'd get run over by one of the tractors. It is planting time." Gage chuckled, cueing his horse to canter now.

THE SOUND of a child laughing distracted Caitlin. She looked around but didn't see anyone. It must have been a child on a neighboring property. The laughter came a second time from her right.

"Ma Mere!" the child's voice called in between sessions of song and laughter, moving closer to her each time.

Caitlin now noticed a little boy weaving his way in and out of the bordering tree line as he played. She stopped her horse. Where had he come from?

"Ma Mere!" the child called out again for his mother.

Was he real? Caitlin wasn't sure if there was a child lost on D'Orme's grounds or if he was a ghost from a different time.

A FLOCK of mourning doves flew up around Gage. The bay shied when they did. The birds cried out, "Beware! Beware!" A crow cawed in the distance, echoing danger neared. Dread rolled like a thick fog over the field. Perturbed, Gage glanced over his shoulder. Caitlin no longer rode a few feet behind. Where had she gone?

"Caitlin!" Gage shouted, turning his horse. He spotted her riding toward the trees dividing his property and Pierre's. If she had heard him, she showed no signs of acknowledgment. She neared the edge of the property. Now he heard the child's laughter. He spurred his horse into a dead run, praying he reached her in time.

"HELLO?" Caitlin called to the child who jumped when she spoke.

"Bonjour," the little boy shyly returned the greeting. He wore brown trousers tucked into small, polished brown boots and a white linen shirt. Surprisingly, he had the same dark hair and green eyes as Gage. His head periodically popped out from behind a tree he hid behind once he realized Caitlin talked to him.

Caitlin stopped her horse. She didn't want to scare the boy away.

"Are you lost?" Her question caused him to peer out her again.

"It's okay. I won't hurt you," she spoke softly, slowly sliding a foot out of the stirrup, intending to dismount.

"Don't!" Gage stopped her, suddenly sitting behind her on the Friesian. He reined the horse backwards away from the trees.

The little boy started to cry and extended his hands toward Caitlin. "Ma Mere! Ma Mere! Ne me laisse pas seul!"

"A child crying for his mother, Antoine? This is a despicable new low for you," Gage confronted the boy.

"Antoine?" Confused, Caitlin glanced back at Gage.

"My grandfather's full of deceitful tricks."

The boy morphed into a middle-aged man. "Comment ça va, Evariste?"

"Unimpressed by your antics," Gage responded, circling the restless Friesian and keeping his eyes on his grandfather.

"Easy," Caitlin whispered, patting the horse's neck as it reacted to the growing tension in the air.

The man dryly laughed and changed forms again. "Now is that anyway to speak to your dear old grandfather when all I wanted to know was how you and your lovely bride are faring." Long, brown hair a slight shade darker than Evariste's reached the older man's shoulders. His eyes changed from brown to blue then back to brown as he stared at them.

Dressed in black and carrying an ornate walking stick, he reminded Caitlin of the vampire cosplayers who hung out in Jackson Square. All he was missing was a top hat and wire rimmed sunglasses to complete the Bram Stoker ensemble.

"As my grandson has forgotten his manners, please allow me to introduce myself—" Antoine moved slightly to his right, coming closer to them.

"I never expected Evariste's terror of an ancestor to be such a tacky cliché," Caitlin cut off whatever Antoine started to say.

Antoine's jaw clenched. His eyes turned icy. Gage half expected him to leap through the invisible barrier separating them.

A slow, sardonic smile spread across Antoine's face. "As no formal introductions are needed, why don't you extend an invitation to your new grand-père, so we can get to know one another better? Once I enter D'Orme, I will show you how far from cliché I truly am."

Gage laughed, then spoke in Creole, "I will die before you get near her again."

"You should have died the first time I was near her," Antoine snarled. "I will come for her, Evariste. If you get in my way again, make no mistake, my bite will do more than turn you."

Antoine vanished in a burst of gray smoke.

"Promise me you will never, under any circumstances, invite anyone or anything to D'Orme that you don't know very well," Gage said, riding toward his horse.

"I promise." Caitlin heard the anger in Gage's voice. "I thought...."

"Nothing haunts these grounds besides myself. No nonhuman creature can enter the property without an invitation. Never extend one to any being, no matter how harmless they seem, or how much they beg for you to let them in, especially lost children after today. You've now seen firsthand what the more devious of vampires will resort to when they are after something. I'm sure today is only the beginning of my grandfather trying to get to you and me."

Reaching the bay gelding, Gage grabbed the reins dangling from the horse's bridle. The riderless thoroughbred happily plodded alongside the Friesian. Neither Caitlin nor Gage said anything more to one another.

Once inside the barn, Gage dismounted then reached up to help Caitlin down. "I apologize for being harsh. Antoine is just extremely dangerous. He will smile as he tears you limb from limb. Have a healthy amount of fear of him."

"You weren't harsh. You were protecting me, and I won't give him the opportunity now that I know better."

Gage kissed her. "Thank you for understanding, cher. So, what did you name these two?" He unbuckled the girth and pulled the saddle off his horse.

"I hadn't picked anything out yet." Caitlin handed him a bridle to hang on the wall. She patted the black horse who stuck his head out of his stall door for the treat she held. "Maybe we can call this guy Bonne Chance for luck?"

Gage pointed at the bay. "And this one?"

"He's yours. You pick his name."

"Maybe Cliché, in honor of your first encounter with Antoine."

Caitlin laughed. "Poor horse. I don't think he'd like being called that any more than Antoine did."

Gage grinned. "You're probably one of the first in a long time not to be intimidated by him. I think he was more angry at your laughing at him than he was at being called cliché."

"I'm sorry, but it is hard to be scared of him when he looks like a hipster Dracula. I was waiting for him to call me Mina. Do all old vampires dress that way?"

"You don't see me running around dressed like that. However, many of the older ones do, especially if they want to make a certain impression."

Gage watered the horses before they strolled together to the house.

Embracing Her Darker Side

⟨∽⟩

With Bonin watching the property, Gage wouldn't let Caitlin out of his sight, nor was she allowed to go anywhere alone. She grew restless after being cooped up in D'Orme.

Alcee watched Caitlin slide on a pair of heels and grab her briefcase. "Where do you think you're going?"

"To the office to get some work done." She checked her hair in the mirror then grabbed her truck keys off the hall table.

"Gage won't be happy about this. Let me go with you." Alcee followed her to the door.

"I'm a big girl, Alcee. I can take care of myself." Caitlin opened the front door.

"Bonin may be out there watching."

"Bonin hasn't been seen in two weeks."

Alcee blocked the doorway. "Damn it, ma dame folle! Stay here if you don't want me going with you."

"I will be fine without a vampire bodyguard hovering about. Life has to go on. Bonin or no Bonin." Caitlin pushed past Alcee and ignored the stream of French curse words coming from him as she continued down the porch steps.

Alcee followed her to the car. She kept her hand on the door lock button to prevent him from opening it. "Caitlin, I'll teleport into the car if needed."

Caitlin huffed but didn't take her fingers off the door lock. She didn't doubt Alcee was already warning Gage that she attempted to escape D'Orme without a vampire escort.

Let her go. I'll handle this. Gage's instruction confirmed Alcee indeed told on her.

"Vampires. Loyal to one another, but screw what the human wants." Caitlin put the car in drive after Alcee stepped aside. The glare Alcee shot her confirmed he heard her grumbling.

Freedom at last! her mind shouted as she pulled out of the driveway. It was a gorgeous day. She drove with the windows down, enjoying the temps and fresh air.

We aren't ignoring your wishes, mon coeur. We're trying to keep you safe. Gage's voice reverberated around her. *You really shouldn't be out without one of us with you.*

Caitlin rolled her eyes. "I'll be fine. I'm going to the office."

Don't roll your eyes at me. I'm only concerned about my wife.

Caitlin scoffed. "Concerned? More like smotheringly overprotective."

You win this round, cher. I'll have one of the conference rooms reserved for you. Just be careful on your way here, and don't pick up any strays.

GAGE SMILED at her after spotting her through his office window before giving Jim his attention again.

I made it safely to the office.

His eyes drifting back to the window along with the right corner of his mouth curving upward in an amused grin confirmed he heard her.

After two hours of working, Caitlin's stomach growled. Gage would still be in meetings for another hour, so she let Sharon know she was going to try out the new place that opened just a few buildings down from the office in case Gage wanted to join her once the meeting wrapped.

"I'd definitely ask for a table for two as I'm sure he'll head that way.

He didn't request his usual lunch order after you called and said you were coming in," Sharon said, smiling. "We're all glad to have the cheerful Evariste back again. It's nice to see him working normal hours and actually going to lunch versus sitting behind his desk around the clock like he used to."

Caitlin laughed. "He just puts in those extra hours at home. Can I bring you back anything?"

"No, cher. I already ate. Thank you for offering though."

CAITLIN WENT AHEAD and ordered once she reached the restaurant in case Gage's meeting ran late. She sat out in their courtyard, enjoying a glass of wine and some shrimp Creole.

Tristan walked up to her table. "Out without an escort, Mrs. Arsceneaux? I wouldn't have expected Evariste to let you out of his sight already."

"Tristan Dausan, shouldn't you be turning to ash walking around in the midday sun?"

"So you know what I am now." Tristan smiled as if he caught a canary escaping from its cage. "Your husband isn't the only one who is a daywalker. It is actually a somewhat rare talent among our kind."

"It's a shame some vampire passed on that trait to you." Caitlin went back to eating.

Tristan moved behind her. "No fear of me anymore, Cate? Maybe you don't remember the last time vampire me and mortal you met?"

"I remember all too well, *prefect*." Caitlin took another sip of her wine, not allowing the vampire to intimidate her.

Tristan noted the ancient title she used to address him.

"Do you really remember, *medica*?" he whispered in her ear. "How you begged for mercy as I tasted you?"

A twinge of fear ran through Caitlin, but she refused to show any outward signs of it. Tristan nor Antoine would frighten her any longer.

His fangs brushed her neck. "Your blood was so, so sweet, and your fear intoxicating, just as I desire in all my prey."

Caitlin ignored the proximity of his canines to her. "I'm not the woman you killed long ago. And I am certainly not afraid of you."

"What makes you so sure I won't kill you right now?" Tristan asked, his teeth once more raking her skin.

"Two things. Antoine Bonin won't take kindly to you sampling his entrée, and Gage knows you are here. He's en route as we speak."

Tristan hissed, pulling away from her. "I don't sense Arsceneaux, and I don't work for Bonin anymore."

"You may not work for him, but you still fear him." Caitlin swirled the wine in her glass. "You also fear my husband. Maybe, Tristan, you should start to fear me."

Her last comment sounded in stereo around them, echoing off the brick courtyard walls. An invisible force shoved Tristan backward. He fell into the chair behind him.

Caitlin closed the distance between them. "How's it feel to be the hunted this time?"

She smiled, running her tongue over one of the four new canines at the edges of her mouth. "Evariste's almost here. I suggest you leave."

Seeing Evariste turned her into one of them, Tristan's mouth gaped open in astonishment. "Arsceneaux doesn't fed on blood. How—"

Gage snatched Tristan by the back of the neck, lifted him out of the chair, and tossed him away from the table. "I believe my wife asked you to leave."

Dazed by everything, Tristan scampered off through the arched courtyard entrance.

Gage turned his attention to Caitlin. "Are you all right?"

"Ça va bien." Caitlin smiled, taking his hand and sitting down again.

Gage sat in the seat next to her. "J'aime quand tu parles français."

"I know you do. I wish I remembered more of it. Care to join me for lunch since you are here?"

"Happy to. Are you sure you're all right?"

"I'm fine. Tristan was just being obnoxious as usual and ruined a quite enjoyable meal."

"Don't let him sour your stomach, cher."

"He just claimed he doesn't work for Antoine anymore. Perhaps

Bonin's new hold on the area has weakened, which means you and Alcee can relax the guard a bit."

"The guard is staying as it is. You need to remain fearful of Antoine, regardless of what Tristan said, as Tristan is a damn liar. He's still on Bonin's payroll," Gage chided. "Even I am wary of my grandfather. And don't allow Tristan to get so close to you again, or I'll hire a full-time bodyguard to be with you, since I can't always be."

"I have a healthy amount of respect for Bonin." She returned her attention to her lunch while Gage perused the menu left on the table. "Did you sleep better last night? You were gone before I got up this morning."

"Not really. Still having strange dreams about the Roman empire."

"Did you watch something about Rome earlier this week?" Caitlin tried to figure out what caused him to have them.

"No."

"Then did you read something about it or related to it for Rome to be on your mind?"

Gage sighed. "Ancient Rome doesn't interest me in the slightest, so, no, I didn't read anything about it. All I've had time to read are proposals and vendor scorecards this week."

The waiter showed up and Gage ordered a shrimp po' boy. The sandwich was a quick entrée to prepare and eat. He needed to be back at the office in an hour.

No one disturbed their lunch other than the waiter periodically checking on them.

"Are you going to the office, cher?" Gage signed the bill. "We can walk back together if you are."

"No. I have some errands to run."

The look he shot her warned he didn't like the idea of her being out around town alone.

"Stop worrying so much. I'll make sure I'm home before the sun sets and the things that go bump in the night come out to play."

GAGE SNORTED, closing the check presenter. He briefly thought he imagined her suddenly straddling him with her white blouse partially open and her skirt pushed up around her waist. Her mouth pressing down against his and her unbuttoning his shirt made him realize he wasn't seeing things.

"Caitlin." Gage closed his eyes, trying to control the animal stirring in him. "We are in the middle of a restaurant courtyard."

She laughed, letting her hair down and pressed closer to him. He groaned as her lower body slid enticingly over the growing bulge in his lap.

"Would you deny your wife, who desperately needs your affection?" She slid the leather length of his belt through its buckle before her fingers pushed the button through the hole keeping his pants shut.

"Cate." Gage opened his eyes and noticed they were no longer in New Orleans. Hell, they were no longer in the twenty-first century for that matter. They were in the captain's quarters of the galleon he once owned. Several of the cabin windows were open, allowing the Gulf breezes to surround them. All Caitlin wore when he looked up at her again was a thin poet's shirt, which also once belonged to him. The front was unlaced, giving him full view of her as she sat on the table in front of him. He still wore his brown trousers, but his boots and shirt were flung on the floor a few feet from them.

"I would never deny you anything when we're alone." Gage's fingers sought the apex between those creamy thighs in front of him. Caitlin moaned as he continued stroking her until she lay quivering on the table.

"I need you inside me."

His tongue replaced his fingers, flicking out, lapping at her sex, repeatedly tasting her until she tugged at his hair. His name reverberated in his ears from how loudly she cried it as she came. Both the man and the vampire loved how she always surrendered to him. He nipped along her thigh, then led her to the bed.

Caitlin watched him as he removed his pants.

"Save your husband's tortured soul from this erotic spell you cast over him, witch." Gage pulled her on top of him. His hard shaft fit perfectly inside her velvety depths. She ground her hips against his, tightening and releasing around him, drawing him in deeper each time her body rocked. A growl rose in the depths of his throat. Flipping her onto her back, he rode her hard and fast.

Caitlin turned her head, offering up her neck. "Drink, Gage."

He happily accommodated her request. He'd never tire of the euphoria sinking his fangs into her flesh brought on. Dynamic vitality surged through him the more blood he imbibed. Visions flashed through his mind. Caitlin stood above him. Racked with pain, he thought he was dying. She whispered something to him, ending his distress. Images of other battles, her dressed in a long, green gown and robe similar to Morrigan's played out before his eyes. Now, she ran from Roman soldiers pursuing her. They caught her and forced her to the ground as their commanding officer approached. The legatus removed his helmet and knelt beside her. Gage didn't understand the Gaelic tongue she spoke in. The legate pushed her hair aside to reveal a small birthmark at the nape of her neck. The man laughed and turned so Gage could see his face. He recognized Antoine Bonin immediately.

A burning sensation in his shoulder ended the odd image. The same addictive rapture that had flowed through him when he tasted Caitlin returned. His fingers threaded themselves into her hair. He grinned and pressed her face closer, urging her to take more when the pressure of her bite lessened. Pure ecstasy consumed him when she complied with his unspoken command and greedily continued to feast on him.

"Oh, you truly belong to me alone now, ma magnifique femme."

Their souls merged as their bodies did. The jointly forged blood bond united them for all eternity. Once she drew back from him, he kissed her; the taste of his own blood lingered on her lips and tongue.

"My lovely bride." Gage brushed his knuckles down her cheek. She smiled, her eyelids drifting downward, concealing now royal purple eyes.

Exhausted and sensually sated, the Gulf gently rocked them to sleep.

Ancient History

G age woke with a start, his cell phone loudly ringing on the arm of the couch alongside the pillow propped against it. He ignored the phone and rubbed his eyes. *Was I dreaming?* He looked at his watch. It was almost four o'clock.

Sid knocked on the open office door and then walked in with a hot cup of coffee. "Late night last night?"

Gage took the coffee. "Yeah. How long was I out?"

"For only an hour. You fell asleep when you came back from lunch. With the way you were snoring, we figured you needed the nap. Are you okay?"

"Fine. Why?" Gage went to wash his face in the private restroom in the rear of his office.

"You haven't been yourself lately."

Gage grinned. "What makes you say that?"

"You're distracted, and I've never seen you sleep at the office." Sid paused, expecting a response. When none came, he continued with another example, "The surprise wedding last month."

"I'm sorry, Sid." Gage walked out of the bathroom. He must be confusing his employees with his odd working hours and the recent changes in his behavior. "While the wedding was a bit spontaneous, I've actually known Caitlin for a very long time. We went our separate ways a few years back, and as you know, ran into each other again with Giovanni being a pest then picked up where we left off. I couldn't see myself living without her again."

"Never pictured you as the spontaneous, romantic type. I expect an invitation to any future life events." Sid patted Gage on the back.

"Sure. No problem."

They walked back to Gage's desk together.

"Cut yourself shaving this morning?" Sid asked, sitting down.

Gage froze at Sid's words. "What?"

Sid pointed at his collar. "You've got a cut on your neck."

Gage went back to the bathroom, looked in the mirror, and pulled the collar of his shirt away from his skin. The white starched material concealed the three other puncture marks in his neck and the top of his shoulder. *What in the hell was going on today?*

GAGE COOKED dinner while waiting for Caitlin to come home. He and Alcee discussed the latest report from the shipping team. They stopped talking as the front door shut.

Caitlin set her laptop case down and tossed her keys on the hall table.

"Smells wonderful," she complimented Gage as she entered the kitchen. He smiled as she walked over to him then kissed him hello.

"I hope you enjoy dinner as much as you did lunch today." Gage waited for her reaction. Her cheeks flushed. Visions of the two of them in the captain's cabin flashed through her mind.

Alcee didn't miss the way Gage grinned and Caitlin blushed before turning away from him; their behavior revealing a new, intimate connection between them that wasn't present prior to today. "I take it the two of you met for lunch."

"We did. We ate at the new Burgundy Room off Esplanade. It was very good." Caitlin sat down on one of the stools by the island. "Gage even gave it his stamp of approval, and you know how picky he is."

Alcee now saw what was left of the bite marks on Gage's neck. By the smaller size of them, a female vampire bit him. "Unique cuisine?"

Gage didn't notice the older vampire studying him as he sautéed the vegetables in a pan on the stove. "No, traditional Creole cuisine."

"Moscato, madam." Alcee offered Caitlin a glass of wine.

She accepted the glass. "Merci, Alcee."

Gage brought the steaks and vegetables he cooked over to the table.

Caitlin smiled at him as he served her. "Thank you, Gage. You're going to have to give me a few more cooking lessons, so I can make dinner more often. I'm embarrassed to cook the few dishes I know for you."

"Your cooking is just fine, cher. I'd tell you if I didn't like anything you prepared." Gage gave her hand a squeeze from across the table.

She cut into the steak on her plate and savored the smokey taste of it. Gage always knew how to bring out the best flavors in a piece of beef. The room suddenly rocking interrupted her musings about dinner.

"Caitlin, cher, what do you think of the steak?" Gage tried to draw her attention back to the casual conversation he and Alcee were having.

"I'm sorry. I missed what you said."

The room spun again after she stood up to get a glass of water.

Gage caught her as she collapsed. "Caitlin?"

"What have you done?" she demanded. A hazy recollection of something similar happening to her before fueled her temper.

Her accusation flabbergasted Gage. "Excuse me?"

She glared over at Alcee and spoke in flawless French, "What have I done to deserve this, Roman?"

"You will be fine, Celt. I just needed to see for myself." Alcee tilted her head to the side, inspecting the faded bitemarks disappearing from her skin—damning evidence of her passionate encounter with Gage earlier that day.

"Mon Dieu," Alcee mumbled, gently opening her mouth to reveal four pointed canines.

Gage couldn't believe the change in her teeth. "I turned her into one of us."

"Non, you have not. She is mirroring your abilities due to the drug I put in her wine. A healer cannot become a vampire."

Sean appeared out of nowhere and knelt down beside Alcee. "Morrigan is not going to take kindly to you doing this."

"Probably not." Alcee shrugged. "Help me get her to the couch."

"What did you give her?" Gage demanded as Alcee and Sean pulled Caitlin out of his arms.

"Nothing fatal. She will be fine." Alcee helped lift Caitlin to her feet.

"I've got her." Sean swung Caitlin up into his arms. "Make sure Evariste is okay."

Alcee turned Gage's head to look at the marks on his neck. "How are you feeling?

"Angry." Gage kept his eyes on Sean as the guide gently laid Caitlin down on the couch.

"Besides that, mon ami? You've bound yourself to one hell of a powerful ancient."

Gage remembered the vision of her encounter with the Roman soldiers. "Ancient? How old is she?"

"Her soul is as old as yours," Sean answered, walking back over to him.

"Three hundred?"

Concern marred Sean's normally calm features. "You are much older than that, Evariste. We really need you to remember who you two are."

"Just tell him, Sean. Enough of these games. We don't have time for them any longer." A hooded man in black and gold armor walked into the dining room.

Gage couldn't believe his eyes. An immortal casually strolled through his house. "How in the hell did you get in here?"

"Death isn't subject to the same laws others are. War and I are always the exception to every rule." Death pulled back his hood, revealing his face.

"Dante!" Caitlin recognized the immortal calling himself Death.

She definitely wasn't happy about seeing him by the way she suddenly snapped something in Gaelic at him.

Dante chuckled. "You can berate me later, Rosso. For now, you and Mr. Inept-At-Hiding need to break through the haze the Fates cast over your minds."

"Inept at hiding?" Gage finally placed the man's face. "Giovanni, you're even more of an annoying ass in person than you are on a call."

Sean set his hand on Gage's shoulder, getting the vampire's attention. "Evariste, you know you are the grandson of Antoine Bonin. But that isn't his real name. He was born Antonius Baracus, and this isn't the first lifetime you've lived."

Memories hit Gage like a freight train. He and Alcee were the two soldiers who captured Caitlin in his vision earlier that day. He remembered wondering why Baracus was so hell-bent on capturing the woman. They had ridden hard to reach the coastline of Gaul then sailed through a maelstrom to reach Britannia in search of her. Antonius scoured the countryside like a deranged lunatic, searching for a woman who matched Caitlin's description.

Roman Britannia

Only a few days before capturing her, a soldier swinging a large mace knocked Gage from his horse. He lay on the battlefield, certain the mace shattered his spine, and blacked out. He woke to find Caitlin, in a forest green cloak, leaning over him. Gaelic words flowed softly from her lips. He didn't understand a word she said but was transfixed by whatever tune she sang and the soothing feel of her fingers lightly traveling along his cheek. The gold pendant that the voodoo priestess had given him hung from a chain around her neck.

"Th-thank you," he managed to stammer then drank cool, refreshing water from the clay bowl patiently held up to his lips. She smiled as she whispered something and whisked her fingers over his forehead before her hand rested against his chest. He could barely tell it was there through his cuirass.

She couldn't be real. She had to be a spirit sent to escort him to Elysium. "Am I dead?"

"You will live, Roman. Mars still has use for you on the fields," she responded as the wind blew the hood of her cloak back, revealing long locks of wavy red hair and eyes a pale shade of violet.

"Surely, you are wrong, dea. No mortal woman of your beauty

would tend to wounded men on the battlefield. You must be a hand-maiden of one of the gods. If not Mars, perhaps Venus or Minerva."

Mist swirled about the lovely creature tending to him. The rain picked up a bit more.

"Perhaps Asclepius is the one watching over you right now." She smiled before raising the hood of her cloak up to hide her face.

"Whichever of the deities are, I'm blessed by them to enjoy a moment in your company."

"You're a strange soldier to flatter a woman bringing you back from the brink of death. Most don't even realize I'm beside them."

The sound of hoofbeats racing toward them caused her to look over her shoulder and rise to her feet.

Gage gently grabbed her wrist to prevent her from leaving. "Wait!"

"Please. I must go." She glanced back in the direction of the five cavalry men headed their way before staring down at him again.

Something—sadness, maybe desperation?—flickered in the depths of those purple orbs holding his gaze. Whatever it was, it bothered him enough he relinquished his grip on her. She vanished into the mist. Had she been a hallucination from striking his head when he fell from his horse?

After Baracus heard the mysterious healer remained with his grandson for more than a fleeting second or two, he planned to use Gage to draw her out. All the men who saw her previously stated she vanished within a moment of appearing beside them. For whatever reason, she seemed willing to linger a bit longer with Evariste. If today repeated, he would finally be able to ensnare the woman.

Wanting to see her again, Gage agreed to his grandfather's plot.

ALCEE, three other men, and Gage lay alive and well amongst the so-called wounded in a staged battle a few days later. Once most of the men cleared the field, the mist arrived as it always did before the healer appeared. Almost as if the gods tried to conceal the woman they dispatched to help those in need. They all saw her now: kneeling and whispering as she checked the wounded Baracus intentionally had dragged from their tents and left in the damp grass to fool her into coming. Once or twice, they heard her sing, soothing some of the men's suffering. As she had done with Gage, her hands rested in various places on their bodies and her fingers caressed their faces while she offered them water. Today, she wasn't alone. Two other cloaked figures mirrored her actions and tended to the soldiers.

Gage hoped Fortuna favored him and the red-haired healer was the one who wandered his way. His grandfather was adamant that the woman they needed was the redhead. The others wouldn't suffice.

He couldn't help smiling as the woman they waited on turned in his direction. Strands of crimson and copper escaping out the side of her hood confirmed the identity of the healer approaching him. He laid his head back and closed his eyes.

Recognizing the armor and the man's face from just days before, Caitlin frowned. She briefly studied the four other men lying around them before kneeling next to Gage.

"Decurion, I am beginning to think you are not meant for your chosen profession. It amazes me you command a turma of men with being felled in battle twice before one full week passes."

He grinned but did not open his eyes. "Mayhap I allowed myself to be wounded in hope of seeing you again, dea, so that I may learn your name."

Caitlin looked him over. "You are neither wounded nor dying, Roman. You waste precious time bettered used to help those in need."

"My wound is not of a physical nature. It is one even more fatal and scarring, as it exists in my heart. I believe you are the only one who may heal it." Gage propped himself up on one arm, signaling his men to start closing in.

Caitlin snorted. "No doubt the wound is in your head. You've taken leave of your senses if you think I would fall for such childish flattery."

Gage laughed. "Such a sharp tongue lives in that tempting mouth."

A twig snapped behind her as one of Gage's officers approached. The other men who lay in the clearing were now on their feet. Alcee grabbed her ankle as she started to run. She fell into Gage's lap.

"You are not vanishing into the mists today, medica." Gage's arms locked tightly around her.

The sound of a heavily armored escort approaching caused Caitlin to turn her face away from him. The eagle emblazoned on a massive rectangular shield along with the standards carried by one of the other mounted officers identified the legate leading the small entourage. A sinister energy smothered Caitlin the closer the man came. She stared up at Gage. "I beseech you, Decurion, release me. You do not know what you do by keeping me here. You must let me go."

"I have orders from the emperor to bring you to Rome."

"Then take me to him. I will go willingly, but please do not turn me over to Baracus." Caitlin thrashed against Gage, trying to free herself before Baracus reached them.

"By the gods!" Alcee exclaimed as the hood of her cloak fell back, revealing flame-colored hair and the amethyst eyes which made her legend famous around Britannia and in Gaul.

There was no denying she was the healer they searched for. She was certainly the rarity described in local lore with her odd-colored eyes. She fought like a madwoman, hitting the shoulders and cuirass of the man who held her.

Alcee caught the arm she managed to free when she twisted loose of Gage's grasp.

"Hold her down. I need to inspect her for her mark," Antonius Baracus commanded, now standing in front of them.

"No!" she screamed and spat at Baracus. "Don't touch me!"

"Calm down, medica. No harm will come to you," Gage said, wishing she didn't fight them as she did.

Baracus slapped her, nullifying Gage's promise. Caitlin's face turned red from the handprint the Roman left and her fury at how she was being handled.

"Now that you are still." Baracus clutched her face and jerked her head sideways. He pushed her hair from her neck to reveal a small moon-shaped birthmark on her nape.

Gage only made out a few of the angry Gaelic curses she hissed at Baracus.

"This is the woman we need. Take her back to camp."

One of the centurions came forward carrying shackles.

"No harm will come to me. You're a lying, heartless bastard like the rest of your brethren! The gods will avenge the insult you pay their priestess."

Lavender eyes seared that vengeful promise into Gage's soul. Thankfully, he caught himself before he uttered that he'd endure any punishment the gods chose for a single kiss from those soft, full lips of hers. What in Hades was wrong with him today? The woman cursed him with damnation and justifiably called him a bastard, and all he could think of was how alluring her flushed face would look in the lamplight while lying nude with him in the blankets and furs he currently used as bedding.

Gage and Alcee released her once the centurion secured the iron bands around her neck and wrists.

"Stop your prattling, woman. Before we silence you." Baracus took a threatening step toward Caitlin as the guards hauled her to her feet.

"Legatus, she's frightened, and your actions give her reason to be." Gage didn't like how Baracus treated the woman who only wanted to help the wounded. "Be more respectful. She has saved many a Roman life."

"You're too soft on these heathens, Evariste. They must be taught to obey their betters. Even so, I must commend you on your excellent performance today. You have served Rome and me well capturing the healer." Baracus patted Gage on the back then led Caitlin off to a waiting wagon.

Setting Wrongs Right

G age and Alcee returned to camp after sunset. Caitlin sat silently on a log outside Baracus's tent. She shot them an angry glare as they dismounted.

"If looks could kill, I believe we both would be dead." Alcee nodded in Caitlin's direction. "She's probably cursing us to Tartarus or someplace like it."

Seeing the woman chained like an animal, guilt tugged at Gage's conscience. By the gods, she did not deserve such treatment. What was his grandfather thinking to treat an ally as he did? They did not have many in Britannia. Most would like to see the Romans hung from the white cliffs along the sea. He would be no different if some foreign military threatened his home or loved ones in Gaul.

One of the sentries heard Alcee's comment to Gage. "She's been staring daggers into us all afternoon. The witch refuses to speak or eat. She even started casting spells and threw the gruel we tried to give her onto the ground."

Alcee and Gage smiled at the soldiers' fear of her cursing them.

"Simpletons," Gage muttered, walking past them to the food left on a small table outside of his grandfather's tent until it would be taken inside when Baracus requested his dinner. He took an apple from a bowl then poured water from the pitcher beside the bowl of fruit into a mug.

"You waste your time, Evariste," the sentry warned as Gage started toward the prisoner.

Gage ignored him. The supposed witch glowered at him from her perch atop the fallen tree. Where had she gotten those amethyst eyes? They glittered with defiance when he stopped before her. He offered her the apple. As expected, she didn't take it from him.

"You must eat if you are to keep your strength, dea. The emperor nor Baracus will be pleased if the great medica dies on her journey to Rome."

She said nothing and changed the direction she faced, so her back was now to him.

Why were the barbarians of this country so stubborn? He scrutinized the firm set of her shoulders and the red tendrils cascading down to her waist before twisting along the curve of her rear. Forgetting about the woman's tempting, rounded bottom, he shrugged and sat on the log beside her. He wasn't the two weak-minded centurions she chased off earlier. With the slight turn of her head, the woman was startled that he didn't abandon his efforts to make her eat as the others had.

Gage unsheathed his dagger and started slicing the apple. "I do not blame you for being angry with me. I would feel the same way if our positions were reversed. Though I would eat and drink to maintain my strength to fight my captors."

He set the apple slices on the log in between them. Gage didn't miss how she cast a quick glance down at them and the mug of water before squaring her shoulders again. "These apples are very good. Better than any I have eaten in Rome."

Gage bit into a large slice he cut from the half an apple still in his hand. Her eyes flitted in his direction after it crunched between his lips. Once more, they returned to staring off in the distance, and she reset the stubborn posture of hers. He almost laughed at her tenacity in trying to resist the lure of the apple. Knowing the crunching sound tempted her, he intentionally chewed louder than normal. "Are you certain that you don't want a slice, dea?"

Caitlin's stomach audibly growled after hearing a second piece crunch as he bit into it. She wished she had eaten before journeying to the front lines that morning. Or ignored the calls for help. Damn the order and her vows for making her tend to both friend and foe! Look where it landed her. She twisted to face Gage as he drank from the mug he held.

He noted the way she longingly stared at the cup. Part of him wished she looked at him like that. He could easily imagine sampling the pouty mouth that now moved side to side as if she hadn't had water in months while running his hands through the thick, scarlet rolls of her hair. His eyes locked with hers as he took another deep drink from the mug. The woman's resistance definitely faltered.

"This is not as good as the emperor's Falernian wine, but I would trade a slave for it after a battle."

She rolled her eyes. Her facial features hardened with a renewed tenacity not to accept any form of charity from the Romans. "No doubt you would trade many lives for silly things like wine, Decurion. Clearly, life has no value to you."

"Believe of me what you will. I won't try to change your mind."

"Let her starve, Evariste. She will eat when she gets hungry enough," Baracus barked from the tent, interrupting the interesting scene between his grandson and the Celtic priestess. "I have been awaiting your return, so I may eat my own supper. It grows cold while you provide Roman hospitality to an undeserving philistine who cannot appreciate it. Come, join your grandfather in celebrating the success of today!"

Gage set the mug of water on the ground by Caitlin's feet and rose to do as requested. Prior to entering Baracus's tent, Gage caught Caitlin quickly sneaking one of the apple slices into her mouth. He grinned at his small victory in the battle to regain the woman's trust then stepped between the drawn flaps to dine with his grandfather.

"Why is Rome in need of a Briton healer's talents? Certainly there are many good healers and practitioners of medicine in Italia."

Baracus laughed and gestured for Gage to sit at the table. "That woman is a descendant of Morrigan."

Gage wasn't familiar with the name. "Morrigan?"

"The Celtic Athena."

Gage's face went ashen white. "She is the human child of a god? Have you lost your senses to risk provoking an immortal's wrath?"

"It is said that the Morrigan's abilities can be obtained by drinking the blood of one of her descendants. I could become more powerful than Vespasian."

"You are mad. What you speak of is treason against the empire and the gods. You break your ranks from Agricola's legions over a woman, who may just be a peasant, and absurdly ambitious plans to seize control of Rome via a long-distance coup?"

"If she is Morrigan's progeny, this is not absurd. Nor am I wrongly ambitious. Agrippa and Marcus are threats to the empire. By taking power into my hands, I ensure continued peace and stability for Rome."

His grandfather had finally lost his mind. Gage stood to leave the tent. "I want no part of this."

Baracus's hand on his shoulder stopped him. "I need an adopted son. Drink her blood with me. You will inherit an empire."

"I do not need or want an empire."

Baracus shoved Gage so he fell back into the chair he had been sitting in. "Then witness the birth of your new emperor."

He kept Gage pinned in the chair as he called for the guards to bring him the woman. "I will kill her quickly, since I know you have not the stomach for this, Evariste. A cup of her blood should be all that is needed to become a god of war."

Aghast at the thought of Baracus murdering the woman out of whatever insanity gripped him, Gage argued with his grandfather for the first time in the year they had spent in Britannia. "Do you honestly expect me to idly stand by while you slaughter an innocent woman?"

"You will do as ordered, boy. I don't give a damn what your conscience may think as you watch me ravage or kill any woman of my choosing."

Two guards brought Caitlin into the tent, ending their conversation. She reminded Gage of a wild, noble creature. She stood proudly in the firelight. Her chin titled upward in defiance. The two sentries removed her emerald cloak. Without the cloak, the simple emerald-green gown accentuated the curves of her body. Waves of crimson silk fell wildly down her shoulders with the weight of her hood no longer holding her hair back. Violet eyes smote them where they stood.

After the sentries departed, Baracus backed away from Evariste. He stared at the woman as if she was one of the steaks he had devoured for dinner.

Seeing the deranged expression on his grandfather's face, Gage looked around him for a better weapon than the dagger he currently wore. He wished he had not taken off his sword before entering the tent to eat. Baracus's own weapon lay only a few feet away.

"My grandson and I were discussing the importance of following orders." Baracus walked around her, inspecting the prize captured earlier in the day. "I wondered what your thoughts on the matter might be, Celt."

"I hardly believe that my thoughts on military protocol would be of importance to you."

Baracus laughed. "She is capable of speaking to more than you, after all, Evariste. Quite sophisticatedly too, compared to her tribesmen. It is rumored that you saved two of my men from death on the battlefield three days ago. I am told the past several months you healed many men, including my grandson, from injuries sustained in the fighting between Rome and your people."

Caitlin raised her shackled hands up to chest level. "If this is how you show your gratitude for saving soldiers of Rome, I would hate to see what you do to those who are your enemies."

"Those, domina, are a precaution. You also saved men that are my enemy. Therefore, I do not know if you are friend or foe."

"Is the great legate Baracus scared of a simple woman?"

"We both know that you are no ordinary woman, medica." He moved closer to her. "In the light of the torches, I can see why my grandson was so willing to play the part of the fallen hero this afternoon."

Caitlin shot Gage an accusatory glance then became a silent statue once more.

"It is a shame to waste such beauty. Death would not become a woman like you at all. Evariste, join me, and I will give eternal life to you, along with the woman as your reward."

Evariste's eyes shifted between Baracus and their prisoner, but he did not respond to his grandfather's offer.

Baracus grinned. "Think of yourself as her savior, Evariste. You will be the one who determines whether she lives or dies. Tell me, medica, is it true that if you drink the blood of one of Morrigan's descendants you obtain the goddess's powers?"

Caitlin warily watched Baracus. "I would not know, Legatus. I do not believe in the fables told by the locals."

"Evariste has no stomach for spilling a woman's blood to find out if these tales hold any truth. I, on the other hand, am very curious to learn if they do."

Caitlin winced as he spun her around to face Gage and placed a knife at her throat. The tip penetrated the skin on the side of her neck. Burgundy-hued liquid formed contrasting dark drops against cream-colored flesh. Tears welled up in her eyes. She stifled a scream as Baracus cut the wound a little deeper then licked the droplets from her skin.

By the gods, the woman was brave. Evariste knew well the pain sharpened steel inflected entering the flesh. He snatched Baracus's sword from where it sat and crossed the open space to stand face-to-face with Caitlin. His arm wrapped around her waist, jerking her forward into his chest. At the same time, he thrust his dagger into Baracus's exposed rib cage. A sharp pain ripped through his own chest when his grandfather plunged the knife that had been at Caitlin's throat into it, just below his shoulder. Gage pushed Caitlin out of the way, drawing Baracus's sword to confront his grandfather. Instinct drove his hand forward. The blade easily slid through muscle and the thin space between two ribs then pierced Baracus's heart.

ALCEE HEARD the sound of a sword unsheathe, followed by the thud of a body hitting the ground. He rushed into the tent to see Baracus lying in the grass.

"What have you done?" Alcee ran to Caitlin and unlocked her shackles. "Take her and flee, Evariste!"

"What?" Gage was still stunned that he had murdered his grandfather.

"Run! Ride south!" Alcee shoved Gage and Caitlin toward the rear of the tent. "Before someone sounds the alarm. More guards will be on their way."

"Evariste Arsceneaux!" Baracus growled, sitting up.

Gage could not believe his grandfather rose from the dead. "How is that possible?"

"He isn't what you believe him to be." Alcee swiped the sword from Gage's hand and cut an opening in the side of the tent. He handed the weapon back to Gage then pushed the two of them toward it. "You must go, now!"

As two other guards engaged Alcee, Gage helped Caitlin onto his horse. Thank the gods the horses were kept close to his grandfather's tent! They raced out of the camp and rode southward through the night in silence.

Absconding With A Witch

G age followed the coastline, knowing it would take them south. It
was late the next day before he slowed their travels.

"We must stop and find shelter for the night." Caitlin startled Gage
out of his erratic and confused thoughts.

"An entire century is more than likely pursuing us. We need to place
as much distance as possible between them and us."

"To do that, we need rest. Your horse is tired, and you are wounded.
There is an abandoned farm not far from here where we can take shelter.
It is difficult for even the locals to find."

"If I can reach Agricola—"

"Roman, we will be dead by morning if we do not rest. Your horse
will fail, and the men you fear are potentially following us will find us on
foot. You cannot defend against a legion, especially injured. I save both
your life and mine if you listen to my counsel."

Exhausted, Gage gave in. "As you wish, medica. Tell me how to get
to your farm."

Caitlin provided directions as they rode through the woods. Gage
wondered if she intentionally tried to confuse him as they traveled
winding paths long overgrown with ferns and fauna. It seemed like they

were riding in circles. A half hour later, a small cottage and dilapidated barn appeared in a clearing well concealed by the large trees.

"How did you ever find this place?" Gage asked, stopping in front of the cottage.

"I played here as a child. We will be safe for the night." Caitlin looked around at the abandoned farmstead. It had been a few years since she visited the place. The Romans bloodily expanding their reach in Britannia ruined the warm memories of gathering flowers and playing with the woman who once lived there. A mortal priestess murdered in the early days of Roman forces conquering the area.

Gage dismounted then reached up for Caitlin. He winced as he helped her down.

Caitlin touched his shoulder, causing him to grimace again. "You must let me tend your wound."

"After I untack and stable my horse. Go inside and see if the house is still habitable."

As soon as he removed the bay's saddle and bridle, the horse shook his head and let out a loud whiney. Gage laughed as the horse trotted a few feet away then rolled in the grass. He noticed Caitlin watching him from the dust-covered window. Half of him wished he had never encountered her. The other half reminded him a virtuous man didn't allow women, especially women who healed wounded soldiers at substantial risk to themselves, to be murdered. Like Caesar, he certainly cast the dye and crossed the Rubicon. There was no going back to Baracus. He hoped that his good relationship with Agricola and Vespasian would offer some form of protection against his grandfather's wrath. Baracus never turned a blind eye to a man who wronged him. He was a vindictive bastard who enjoyed decimating a rival in every way he could, from eroding their political standing to destroying their sources of income then finally dispatching the poor fool who dared cross him. *Unfortunately, I am that poor fool this time, and my slight as a relative is worse than that of a stranger.*

Wanting to be familiar with the area should they need to flee or defend themselves, he walked the perimeter of the property, identifying escape routes and looking for natural attributes they could use to stall an attack long enough to disappear into the surrounding wood. Once content he had determined the best exit and defensive strategies he could, he whistled loudly to his mount freely grazing in the clearing. The horse trotted up to him and followed him into the barn. After putting the bay inside the most intact stall in the barn, Gage found an old wooden bucket and filled it with water from the well. He hadn't even set the bucket on the floor before the bay dipped his muzzle into the cool water. Needing food, rest, and water himself, Gage walked to the cottage.

He dropped his saddle on the floor, announcing his arrival. Caitlin jumped at the unexpected noise behind her.

"Sorry if I frightened you." The apology came out gruffer than intended. He ran a hand through his hair, still not quite believing the events of the past day. *By the gods, he was a fool to handle things as he did! Attacking his grandfather may have spared her life, but for how long? And he most certainly condemned himself with his actions.*

The aroma of something cooking over the fireplace wafted over distracting him from his thoughts. His stomach growled at whatever Caitlin made over the fire.

Forcing aside his hunger, he sat on the bed and removed his armor and the tunic he wore underneath it. He looked at the cut where his chest and shoulder met. The wound was much deeper than he expected it to be. Thank Mars Baracus's blade landed where it did. Another inch lower and he'd no longer be living. Another inch to the right, and the tendons would have been severed, limiting the use of his arm.

Caitlin sat down beside him with a small bowl of water and a rag. He flinched as she gently washed the incision. "The cut is very deep, Decurion."

"Thankfully, the dagger pierced my shoulder and not my heart or lungs." Gage stared at it once more. "Do you by chance have a needle and thread, or will we have to sear the skin together to close it completely?"

"As all ladies should, I always carry my needlework under my tunic," Caitlin jested, pulling a vial from a pocket in her skirts. "I have something much better than stitches and less painful than searing the skin."

Gage leaned back from her before she could pour the contents of the vial onto the wound.

286

Understanding his distrust, she smiled. "I owe you my life, Roman. I promise it won't poison you."

"Do not disappoint me, dea. I will be very unhappy to awake in Hades." Gage turned sideways to give her full access to his shoulder.

"Perhaps it's the Elysian plains you will wake in as you are not filled with the hate that Baracus is." Caitlin slowly tipped the vial, allowing the thick liquid inside it to coat the gash. "This will sting."

Her warning came a bit late. Gage groaned and his breath hissed out of clenched teeth as his eyes watered. "What concoction are you using that burns so, witch?"

"A healing salve. You will thank me for it on the morrow. The burn is staving off the infection starting to set in." She carefully bandaged the wound to protect it and keep the salve from being rubbed off by his shirt. "There is more hot water in the pail by the fireplace should you wish to wash."

Gage started to offer her the chance to clean herself first when he realized she had already. Streaks of black and brown dirt no longer marred her face. Her hair was still slightly damp from the rinse she gave it. She must have cleaned up as he secured his horse. Gage wished for a bath, but that luxury would not be his again until he returned to civilization.

THE LIGHT in the cottage faded as the sun disappeared behind the horizon. Caitlin chopped up some turnips and carrots she found in the unkempt garden outside. Periodically, she watched the soldier as he cleaned himself with one of the rags she had found. His skin was almost golden; sun-kissed from long hours outside. While he was not the most muscular man she observed, his body was still defined and toned.

Gage grinned as he caught one of her curious glances. She immediately returned to chopping carrots after his eyes met hers.

"And what fine meal are you preparing for us?" He ambled over to her.

"Boiled carrots and turnips. They were all I could find in the garden outside." Caitlin dumped the freshly cut vegetables into the pot with the others already cooking, trying to ignore the half-dressed man standing beside her. Turning to retrieve some of the freshly picked herbs from the table to season the bland vegetables, her body collided with his. He took a step back. His arms instinctively wrapped around her, preventing any chance of her falling.

Her cheeks flushed due to their intimate contact and her hands slightly shook against his chest.

Gage softly chuckled. "Do I make you nervous, dea?"

"Why are you calling me that?" She looked away from the green eyes that probed hers.

He caressed her check with his thumb. "Is that not what you are?"

"I am far from a goddess." Caitlin's voice wavered as the soft brush of his finger sent a sudden spark of pleasure across her face.

Gage raised a brow, giving her a lopsided grin while playing with one of the red locks that rested on her shoulder. "How would you have me address you, medica?"

"My name is Caitlin."

GAGE ENJOYED the effect he was having on the woman; pleasantly surprised that she did not scramble away as he anticipated her doing the second his fingertips touched her skin. She had combed out the tangled copper and crimson strands so they floated freely around her shoulders. Her hair reminded him of the silk banners that hung in the emperor's palace gently swaying in the breeze. Her eyes closed as he tilted her face up to his. It had been an eternity since he held a woman against him as he did now. His lips brushed against the full mouth he regularly contemplated sampling since encountering her on the battlefield. He waited a second or two to see if she rejected his advances. When she neither objected nor pulled away, his mouth firmly covered hers, his tongue gently prodding her lips open, seeking to taste the woman in front of him.

She shyly returned the soft strokes. Desire overcame reticence. His arms tightened around her.

Calm your baser desires, man. She is no common maid or whore. Do not treat her like one, Gage scolded himself. He cleared his throat, running his hands down her back then released her. "I believe I may have something to contribute to our meal."

Caitlin took a moment to recover from the kisses they shared.

Gage grinned before walking over to the saddle bags he discarded on the floor. He reached into one of them and pulled out some dried venison and hard tack. "Here."

Caitlin placed them in a small bowl, which she set in the center of the table, then she filled two wooden trenchers with cooked vegetables. After placing a trencher on either side of the table, she selected two pieces of the venison from the bowl for herself, leaving the rest for him. "I could not find any utensils other than the spoon I used to cook with. We will have to use our hands."

"A meal fit for a king or emperor." Gage sat down at the table to eat what they were able to pull together. He broke the piece of hardtack and split it between himself and her.

"I am glad you are pleased, Decurion." Caitlin smiled at his comment before taking a bite of the venison. "My, this is salty."

"The salt preserves the meat." Gage doubted she had any experience with what a soldier's life was like.

"I realize you are Baracus's grandson, and that probably assisted in you obtaining your rank. But, I am still curious to learn how a man that seems to have a good heart becomes a decurion."

"Being Baracus's grandson has not assisted in my military career. While it ensured my entry as an eques, Baracus made it much harder for me to obtain any position of command. He more severely tested my valor and loyalty than any other officer I served." Gage paused to drink some water. "Many a soldier has a good heart, Caitlin. Not all of us enjoy the death and destruction that comes with war. Those things merely happen to accompany a soldier's life."

"Then why serve in Rome's legions?"

"Family obligation, and it is required of all men of age and ability." While not the exact truth, he gave her the simplest answer he could. He chewed a carrot, debating whether or not to share the full story behind his service to Rome. It had started out simple enough with wanting to prove his birthright and to seek adventure in foreign places. Over the years, it evolved into secret service as one of the emperor's eyes and ears in his grandfather's ranks. Not even Baracus knew of the oath he swore to Vespasian.

The emperor took a liking to Gage after watching him shoot in an archery contest. Gage met Alcee when he began his training as part of the elite team that served the emperor in secrecy. Vespasian sent he and Alcee with Baracus on his trek into Britannia. He doubted Baracus's reason for the venture of expanding the empire's borders in the island territory. After sailing from Gaul, Baracus chose to disclose that their mission was not only to claim the entire land for Rome, but also per the emperor's order, they were to capture a woman and return her to Rome. Gage knew Vespasian had not issued the second decree. He originally believed the woman to be the daughter of a king or warlord who Baracus intended to ransom or kidnap to cause unrest between Rome and the Britons, not a druid rumored to have powers that healed the sick.

She periodically stared at him while they finished their meager meal in silence. By the way her eyes quickly shifted with each movement he made, he got the feeling she was continuing to assess his character and whether or not she could trust him.

"If I intended to harm you, medica, I would have done so already."

Surprisingly, she laughed at him. "A man who intended to harm someone wouldn't have saved them as you did me. I'm not afraid of you, Decurion. I am merely puzzled by your actions."

"Perhaps I'm lulling you into a false sense of security, so I might ravage you once you fall asleep. You are quite the prize with those crimson locks and violet eyes."

Caitlin rolled her eyes. "Men, always looking for a concubine to warm their beds. You don't strike me as the type to own slaves or brutalize them."

"Normally, I wouldn't be. I abhor slavery, but I might make an exception when it comes to you, especially with how sweetly you kissed me before dinner." Gage knew he shouldn't tease the woman as he was, but couldn't resist doing so.

She actually blushed and looked down at her plate, not saying anything more to him.

"I meant you no offense, Caitlin. I was enjoying bantering with you. I apologize if I crossed the boundaries of propriety with my remark. " Gage wished she'd speak to him again.

"You didn't offend me. Others have said crasser things to me. Your remark about the kiss we shared reminded me of someone from my past. That's all. It's getting late." Caitlin picked up the plates then carried them over to the bucket she left near the hearth to wipe them down.

He noticed Caitlin yawning as she washed their dishes. "Take the bed and rest. I will fix a place on the floor."

"The bed is large enough for both of us to share. I trust you not to compromise me."

I do not trust myself not to do so. Gage untied his bedroll from the saddle. Late fall nights in Britannia were bitterly cold. The softness of the bed and the extra warmth she would bring sleeping beside him would be better than the reed and lime ash floor, a luxury for such a humble abode, considering most peasant cottages had dirt floors. "Shall we retire for the evening then? We will need to be on the move early in the morning. I want to reach Clausentum by midday."

Gage made a thin pillow for them with the tunic he wore earlier. Caitlin fell asleep only moments after lying down with her back to him. He drifted in and out of sleep for the next couple of hours. At one point, Caitlin rolled over in her sleep and curled up against him, resting her head on his chest. Feeling her shiver, Gage drew her closer, offering what warmth he could under the blanket that barely covered them. It was hell to lie so close to her, but sharing body heat would help them get the precious sleep they needed. He kissed the top of her head and placed his hand over hers, since it also rested right where he'd normally settle his hands. Closing his eyes, he willed himself to go to sleep.

RAYS OF SUNSHINE found their way through the dirty windows waking Gage. Caitlin had changed positions again. Her back was now firmly against his chest and her round bottom pressed into his thighs and groin. Still trapped between the land of dreams and consciousness, his arm tightened around her waist. He nuzzled her ear, breathing in the light scent of roses and lavender, rousing her now. He whispered in Gaulish as his hand moved down her hip. It continued its journey, sliding under her clothing and traveling up her torso.

Caitlin sucked in her breath. The light caress of warm fingers made her skin tingle. They both moaned as his hand cupped her breast. His fingertips danced across her ribs then down her belly, seeking out the flesh between her legs as he kissed her neck and shoulders.

Becoming aware of what he was doing and who was in his arms after she rolled over to face him, Gage stopped the intimate play. "Forgive me. I am not used to sharing my bed with a woman who is not my lover."

"There is nothing to forgive. Your touch is pleasing, Evariste."

Hearing his name whispered in such a welcoming tone, he couldn't resist the parted lips so close to his own. Passion ignited between them once more. He tugged her on top of him. His hands under her skirt and chemise grasped and kneaded the soft round globes of her bottom, rocking her against the erection he woke with. The delightful friction of her lower body moving along his tempted him to take her. She was willing, and the slickness of her sex when his fingers teased it earlier confirmed she wanted him. By Hercules, the woman practically rode him already. Her eyes closed and lips parted, her body swaying in time with the tempo his hands encouraged her to take up, clearly enjoying the pleasure doing so gave them both. All he had to do was loosen his woolen trousers to slip inside her.

Gage groaned. "Caitlin, you crimson-haired enchantress."

He flipped her onto her back beside him, stopping things before they led to something neither could reverse. Thank the gods the cooler weather had set in requiring the legions to don winter apparel, otherwise he would be seizing what was freely offered. "You shouldn't say things like that to a man nor should you sit astride one as you did me this morning. You do not know what you are inviting."

"Perhaps I know exactly what I was encouraging. What is wrong with a woman wanting a man to love her?" Caitlin asked, disappointed as he pulled his hands from under her clothing.

"Caitlin, stop tormenting me. A man can only take so much." Gage forced himself from under the covers. Most priestesses in Rome were virginal. He assumed the peoples of Britannia required the same of their holy women. "Have you ever made love to a man?"

Caitlin blushed at the question he posed.

"The color in your cheeks tells me all I need to know. I have no intentions of being the one to take your innocence, especially not in this place."

Between the cool morning air and the cold water he used to wash his face, he regained some sense of impulse control. "We need to leave if we are to keep a safe distance between Baracus and us."

He started to pull his tunic over his head but stopped as he realized his shoulder no longer bothered him. After he set his tunic down on the bed beside Caitlin, he unwound the bandages on his shoulder. The wound was completely gone, with no scarring left in its place. He touched the area where Baracus's knife had cut him. "Do my eyes deceive me?"

"They do not." Caitlin hung her feet over the side of the bed. "It is all I can offer as repayment for your protection."

"You owe me nothing, Caitlin. It was I who placed you in harm's way."

Once he finished dressing, Gage went to check on his horse.

CAITLIN BRAIDED her hair back after washing her face and straightened her gown the best she could. She threw the remaining water from the bucket onto the fire to try to hide any sign of their stay should Baracus's men discover the cabin then walked outside.

"Ready?" Gage asked as she reached him.

She gave him a quick nod and placed her foot in his hands so he could help her mount.

After settling into the saddle behind her, he turned his horse and continued southward. Two hours into their ride, they came upon a large estate with multiple workers tending to the fields.

"What a sight we must make," Caitlin said after the scattered group of people stared up at them.

Gage urged his horse into an easy lope. "Knowing how much you

Britons hate the Romans, they are most likely cursing me for absconding with one of their women."

Caitlin laughed. "Is that what you are doing, Decurion?"

"It appears so. Unfortunately, it is a much more common sight than you may realize between some soldiers forgetting their manners and raiders from the North."

"I am not sure which is worse, the Vikings or the Romans. How many women have you absconded with, Evariste?"

"You are my first, gleoite."

"You've learned some Gaelic. You also speak Gaulish in addition to Latin. I assume you are from Gaul, as not many Romans from Italia have your gift to speak multiple tongues."

Her observations startled Gage. "You impress me again. Most women do not make such a connection between languages and geography."

"Perhaps you should seek to encounter a different class of women."

Gage chuckled, enjoying the woman's wit. She was a refreshing change from many of the women in Rome's upper class who pursued him due to his status and wealth. "Perhaps."

"Where are we headed?"

"To Hispania then Gaul. It is not safe to stay here. I will figure out the rest of my strategy once we are somewhere we can fully disappear from Baracus's purview. Until then, I will focus on evading my grandfather and whoever he dispatches to find us. He will not rest until we are brought back to him."

"What happens if he finds us?" Caitlin was almost afraid to ask the question.

Gage shuddered at the thought of Baracus capturing them. The legate demanded absolute loyalty from his men and severely punished any treachery. "You do not want an answer to that query."

"I find it hard to believe you are a descendant of such an animal," Caitlin looked down at the strong hands holding the reins and resting on the horse's neck. "Why are you saving me, Evariste? Why not spare yourself by turning me over to your grandfather?"

Gage sighed. "If I turned you over, Baracus would kill me the second he had you. Perhaps I hope the gods will show me mercy and favor by sparing one of their descendants from a painful death."

A loud scoff left Caitlin's lips. "The deities that watch over us all only show favor when they feel it is merited, and by your own beliefs and laws, women are nothing. I doubt Mars would find you sparing one worthy of merit. Do your legends and tales not paint us as the cause of all woes that inflict man?"

"You truly despise us Romans."

"With just cause. You enslave and torment my people."

"I enslave no one." Gage carefully avoided the tormenting part of her statement.

"And why should I believe that?"

"My mother was a slave. My father purchased her to assist with household chores at his villa. After my father's first wife died, he fell in love with my mother. He had to petition the tribunal courts for her freedom. Thankfully, he was able to obtain it. But her life prior to his purchasing of her was miserable and not one I would wish on anyone. My grandfather reminds me of how much I owe to him and my father, for without their benevolence and prestigious family bloodline, I would be nothing. My father was a good man, and my grandfather once was. Baracus changed after a battle in Parthia. He became vindictive and ambitious, enough so to make many enemies throughout the empire."

Caitlin looked over her shoulder at him. "What brought on such a drastic change?"

"No one knows as he won't speak about whatever occurred there."

Clausentum

⚬~⚬

"Stay here while I secure us passage to Hispania." Gage left Caitlin at an inn after reaching Clausentum. The innkeeper agreed to hide her from anyone who might come searching for them. "I will return within the hour."

He walked to the waterfront and made inquiries into passage across the sea to Hispania. Luckily, there was a ship that planned to depart in the evening. The captain welcomed the extra fare two passengers brought. Upon returning to the inn, he found Caitlin sitting in the dining room, telling a legend of the land to a group of patrons.

Gage shook his head. "You do not obey my order to remain inconspicuous by entertaining those in the dining hall."

Caitlin smiled up at him. Her lavender eyes bright with excitement. "When do we depart?"

"Within the hour. The captain is only awaiting our return." Gage opened the inn door for Caitlin. She took two steps forward when he pushed her back against the wooden slab.

"What is wrong?" She wondered what caused his sudden retreat.

"My grandfather's men beat us here." Gage watched a centurion slowly walk the street, searching for familiar faces in the crowd.

Caitlin now saw the soldier. "Is he looking for us?"

"Not very well considering I found the two of you without much effort." A male voice from behind them caused Caitlin to jump and them both to turn.

"Alcee." Gage smiled at his brother-in-arms.

"I thought you might need some help making it out of Britannia. Come back inside. It's safer than standing in the shadows."

Alcee gently took Caitlin by the arm, leading her into the inn's dining hall once more while Gage slowly closed the door to keep it from slamming and attracting attention.

Gage and Alcee stood on either side of the window beside the door, watching the centurion several yards away from the inn. Gage worried about the opposition they'd face on the way to the wharf. If one centurion patrolled the street, there were more nearby. "How many men are here?"

"Only one squad of five."

"Tristan!" Gage recognized a prefect who joined the lone guard on the street. "My grandfather is definitely not happy to send Tristan after us."

"Not happy is an understatement, my friend. The flames of Hades do not burn like Baracus's wrath."

Gage chuckled. "I do not know if I should be honored or offended by his dispatching Tristan to track me."

"I'd choose the first."

"Who is Tristan?" Caitlin asked, causing both men to look over at her.

Alcee inhaled before answering. "The more accurate question is *what* is Tristan."

"Tristan is only let off his leash when my grandfather is out for blood." Gage wished someone other than the vicious prefect tracked them. He'd be hard to evade. "Does he know we are here?"

"No. He thinks he is here before your arrival."

Caitlin believed she had a potential solution to reach the wharf. "Would a group of druid priests catch his eye?"

"He would burst into flames if he ever came close to a holy man," Alcee remarked, entertained by the thought of Tristan spontaneously combusting.

Gage looked over at Caitlin. The way her lips pursed then relaxed as she stared out the window across the street conveyed she contemplated something. "What are you thinking, medica?"

"The merchant across the street sells robes to the local priests. The robes are full with large hoods which would easily hide our faces. We could walk right past the centurion and Tristan unnoticed."

Alcee liked her creativity. "Suicidal plan, but it might work if you keep those purple eyes focused on the ground. However, we are missing a priest for our procession as we need four, and we can't walk across the street to obtain the robes without Tristan seeing us."

Caitlin whispered something in Gaelic while touching a statue of the Morrigan that the innkeeper kept near the door.

Alcee scoffed at her actions. "Praying to a Celtic goddess won't help us at the moment."

"Do not doubt the power of prayer to any god you believe in." Caitlin gestured to the door. A robed priest entered the inn and came toward them. When the priest drew closer, Gage heard the soft clank of a sword against armor with each step he took. The man stopped in front of the three of them, black robes folded in his arms.

"Morrigan wishes you safe passage. I will escort you to your ship." The priest handed Gage and Alcee their robes. He then pulled Caitlin's around her shoulders. "Morrigan instructs that you are to go with the decurion. Others will deal with Baracus."

"I will do as she wishes." Caitlin raised her head as he secured a large gold and emerald brooch bearing Morrigan's crest over the toggle holding the cloak closed. "Know that I am not happy to be sent off with a stranger."

"She would not send you on a journey with someone who would do you harm. He saved your life; therefore, you are indebted to him."

"I healed his shoulder."

"A shoulder is not equal to a life, especially yours," the priest scolded, raising the hood to hide her face. "She also instructs not to reveal your talents, unless absolutely necessary."

"I would not be in this mess had I ignored her earlier request to do exactly that when she sent me into Baracus's clutches." This was the second time the goddess asked her to hide her skill with a sword and her powers.

Her voice raised at the end of her statement, catching Gage's ear. Concerned about whatever angered Caitlin, he walked over to them. "Is something amiss?"

"No, Roman. The good father was reminding me to be a faithful servant."

"Your faith will be well rewarded, medica." The priest bowed his head in reverence. "If you heed my counsel wisely, woman. Now, follow me."

Caitlin glared at the priest, not moving, further piquing Gage's interest in the matter.

"And what counsel might that be?" Gage inquired.

"That a woman should not travel alone with a man who she has not wed," Caitlin snapped, her fists clenched under her cloak.

The priest halted then turned to face her and Gage. He raised his head to reveal his amusement with the claimed counsel. "I do not believe that was my counsel, child."

"I have no intentions of defiling the woman. She travels under the protection of the emperor. I am charged with being her guard. No harm will befall the lady."

"Evariste is an honorable man. He would never take advantage of a woman," Alcee vouched for his friend.

The priest looked from Caitlin to Gage. "Still, perhaps a marriage might be a wise undertaking to protect Caitlin's reputation. If it is your wish, medica, to be forever joined to the Roman as his wife, I can perform the ritual before you depart."

Caitlin loudly gasped. "That is neither necessary nor something I wish. Priests of Morrigan serve as guides to her children. They do not perform marriages."

"You are mistaken, medica. We are empowered to do all things sacred." The priest winked at her. "Are we ready to continue to the wharf, Decurion?"

Gage walked beside the priest to the inn door. "Why is it a holy man, a man of peace, carries a sword and wears armor under his robes?"

"My service to Morrigan is not much different from yours to

Rome." The priest cast him a causal glance then opened the large door. It creaked loudly, swinging open.

Tristan and his centurion glanced over at the building. Not concerned by four druids leaving the inn, they looked back up the road anyone journeyed to come into town.

Caitlin kept her head bowed as the four entered the street. The priest led the group while Alcee and Gage walked on either side of her. People respectfully let them pass, especially with a high priestess among them.

"Medica! Medica, wait!" a woman called, running up to them. "Please, medica, heal my child."

The woman fell to her knees in front of Caitlin and offered her the toddler she carried. The woman's actions drew the attention of passersby and Tristan

"Please, medica! He only has a year of life and may die from fever. I am on my way home from the alchemist, who advises there is no hope for him."

Caitlin glanced over at the priest helping them. Knowing she sought his approval of healing the child, he nodded. It was the moral thing to do. Alcee and Gage watched as she knelt down and took the child in her arms. She rocked him for a moment then kissed his forehead.

"Take him home and place him in bed. He will wake in the morning fever free," Caitlin instructed the distraught mother, handing back her son.

"Thank you, medica. Thank you. We are forever in Morrigan's debt. May the goddess bless you as you have me." The woman kissed Caitlin's hands before disappearing into the crowd.

"Allow me, priestess." A hand extended in front of her. It emerged from the distinct wristbands and red tunic of a Roman prefect.

Caitlin's mouth went dry. She swallowed nervously, glancing sideways to see Gage's hand move to his sword hidden underneath his cloak. Alcee and Gage exchanged quick looks, prepared to defend themselves and Caitlin as needed.

"Thank you." Caitlin nervously accepted the hand of the man she instinctively knew was Tristan Cassius.

Tristan helped her to her feet. "Priestess, one of your sect may enter

Clausentum with a decurion. The decurion is wanted by Legatus Baracus for an attempt on his life and the abduction of the woman."

"I see." Caitlin kept her eyes focused on his boots. If she looked him in the face, she'd condemn them all. "How does this matter concern me, Prefect?"

Tristan smiled at the formal address. At least this heathen knew how to respectfully address one of her conquerors. "I fear for the woman's safety. The decurion will assassinate her once he is here, as she will no longer be of use to him. With being the high priestess of the local temple, the woman may seek your protection. For her safety, would you be kind enough to advise me when you see or hear from her?"

"Of course," Caitlin agreed. She bit her tongue; highly insulted that he assumed she, of all people, would need anyone's protection from a Roman officer.

"Sean," she addressed the tallest priest in the group.

"Yes, medica?"

"Please notify the prefect the moment the decurion and woman are sighted. I do not want any harm to come to one of Morrigan's daughters."

Sean bowed politely to her. "As you wish, medica."

"My thanks for your cooperation with this matter, high priestess. Allow me to extend Baracus's gratitude as well." Tristan set a small pouch of gold in her hand then half-bowed to her.

"Your kindness will not go unnoted, Praefectus. Morrigan thanks you for your donation, and for"—Caitlin paused, contemplating the right words—"for your vigilance in seeking out our missing priestess."

"We must hurry to the temple for the evening ceremony." Sean reached out for Caitlin and gestured to the stone temple on the hill just past the docks.

"Of course." Tristan bowed one more time then departed.

"That was too close for comfort," Alcee said once they were out of Tristan's earshot.

Caitlin hardly believed they walked away from Tristan unscathed. "Do you think he recognized any of us?"

"If he had, we would be dead or in chains." Gage's answer gave her chills.

Sean clasped Gage's wrist when they reached the ship. Gage returned the gesture. "Fair winds and following seas, Decurion."

"Thank you for your help."

Sean's farewell shocked Caitlin. "You aren't coming with us?"

"No." Sean smiled at her. He would miss the healer he had mentored since the day she was born. "I'm not intended to walk this path with you. The journey is yours alone. I will buy you time by sighting the decurion and you in the forest outside of town."

"Thank you, Sean." Caitlin hugged him.

The captain of the ship motioned for Gage to join him on deck.

Sean watched Gage escort Caitlin aboard. Morrigan had better be right with the reasoning behind her decision to let the Roman take Caitlin from their homeland. Alcee followed the two onto the vessel's deck.

Caitlin stared out at the open sea while Gage concluded his conversation with the captain.

When Gage rejoined Caitlin and Alcee, Alcee saluted his old friend. "I am afraid this is where my assistance ends as well. Baracus will grow suspicious if I am away from camp too long. I'm supposed to be on reconnaissance and scouting for you two. The gods protect you on the crossing."

Alcee descended the gangplank.

"Sean," Caitlin shouted to the man still standing on the dock.

He turned and looked up at them. "Yes, Cate?"

Caitlin suddenly sprinted off the ship to him.

Gage remained where he was, observing the exchange between Sean and Caitlin. Sean took her hand. He watched Sean's lips move but couldn't make out what he said. Whatever they discussed distressed Caitlin based on her body language. Caitlin embraced the man. Sean lightly kissed the side of her head before letting her go and gently pushed her in the direction of the ship. *What were the two to one another?*

Caitlin nodded her head then made her way up the gangplank.

The captain gave the order to make sail now that the woman was back on board.

ALCEE STOOD BESIDE SEAN, watching the sailors untie the mooring lines. The ship drifted away from the pier.

"Did she truly save that child's life?" Alcee asked.

"Yes. If it would not have given her identity away, she could have fully healed him and eliminated his fever entirely."

"No wonder Baracus is so interested in her."

Crossing Boundaries

G age woke in the middle of the night to find Caitlin missing from
their corner under the covered area that had been designated as
theirs for the journey. Even with the captain's assurances that the
woman was safe on board, he preferred to stay near her. When he
stepped outside the shelter, he saw her standing at one of the ship's railings staring in the direction of Britannia.

"What troubles you, gleoite?"

"Nothing of importance, Evariste." Her wistful gaze remained fixed
on the dark seas.

"To use my given name instead of decurion or Roman, it must be of
great importance. I'm sorry that you are leaving your home."

Caitlin looked down at her hands as the breeze caught her hair.
"Morrigan placed me in your care. I trust her judgment."

"Then share with me what causes such a sorrowful gaze and tears."
Gage gently lifted her chin and wiped a tear from her face. "Leaving a
husband or lover behind?"

"I am not married."

"You will see Sean again." Gage thought she pined for the priest
who aided their escape. A pang of jealousy twisted his gut as he spoke

Sean's name. Rarely had he been jealous of another, nor had he wanted to be the sole subject of a woman's fantasies until now.

Caitlin laughed. "Sean? You believe Sean and I are lovers?"

Her laughter confused him. "With your goodbye to him and finding you forlorn in the middle of the night, what else am I to think? I do not know many things, other than a man, which would make a woman weep like you are."

"Then you do not know much about women, Evariste. Sean is like a father to me. I leave no lovers behind. I'm merely saddened by the events of the past several days and for leaving the familiar behind."

AFTER REACHING the shores of Hispania, they traveled to a property near Tarraco to a trusted friend of Gage's seaside villa.

"Evariste!" An older Spanish gentleman greeted them as they rode through the gates of his estate.

Gage embraced his friend after dismounting. "Celio!"

"Welcome, old friend. And who is your lovely companion?"

"She is a ward of Vespasian placed in my care. Celio, may I introduce Caitlin? Caitlin, this is Celio."

"Welcome, Caitlin. Come inside. You must be exhausted from your ride and want to bathe before dinner."

Celio lived in a small palace with high ceilings and mosaicked floors. The home was located on some hills overlooking white beaches that separated the countryside from the blue-green waters of the Mediterranean. Celio instructed two servants to take his guests to their adjoining rooms on the backside of the house. He remembered well the days of escorting high-profile members of the Senate or the emperor's family with orders to never stray far from their side before retiring. Protocol required Gage to remain in close proximity to the woman. Vespasian would undoubtedly be furious if any harm befell her for him to assign her a military escort.

The two rooms opened to a single, large balcony overlooking the sea. Gage walked with Caitlin outside to take in the view.

"Are we safe here?" she inquired, noting the door that opened into his room.

"We are. Celio merely honors the tradition of a guard being close to the one they protect should anything happen. You should rest. Celio's dinners tend to be extravagant affairs lasting late into the night."

After a quick nap and a bath, Gage joined Celio in the atrium.

"So tell me how you became the guardian of a Celtic woman instead of leading cavalry on the battlefield?"

"Vespasian has summoned her to Rome. She is the daughter of a powerful Briton family that he seeks to strike an alliance with to bring peace to the province." Gage altered the truth somewhat.

"Ahh, and which of his sons is the husband-to-be of the girl?"

"Neither. They are both promised to others."

"Is she hostage then?"

"No. Her family asked the emperor to find her a suitable Roman husband in hopes a marriage between a noble house of Britain with an upstanding Roman family will calm things in the region they oversee. The woman is to reside at the palace until the emperor secures a betrothal contract on their behalf. Based on my discussions with the lady, I'm not certain she fully grasps why her father is sending her to Rome." Gage lied with such ease he surprised himself.

"Why not marry her to one of the Roman officers or provincial leaders in Britannia?"

Gage shrugged. "I do not understand the logic of sending her to Italia myself, but who am I to question imperial orders?"

Celio laughed. Their conversation shifted to swapping stories of life in the legions and making inquiries about old friends.

GABRIELLA'S VOICE coming from the hallway ended all discussion centered on political alliances and military life. Celio's wife hated the time she spent apart from her husband when he served in Rome's army and forbid any discussions of political topics in their house.

"The women are arriving for dinner." Celio could see Caitlin and Gabriella making their way into the atrium.

Gage turned. The vision that greeted him shocked him into stunned silence. Caitlin was beautiful in traditional Roman dress. She wore a green and gold garment. Two gold medallions pinned the material together at her shoulders. Her long hair fell around her in loose curls. Gold ribbons intertwined randomly in scarlet locks to match her clothing.

"Remember your duty to Rome," Celio whispered, noting Gage's reaction to the woman who accompanied his wife.

Transfixed by Caitlin as she stood speaking with Gabriella, Gage missed what Celio said. "Pardon?"

Celio laughed. "The look on your face tells me you would prefer feasting on your ward more than dinner."

The four walked to the dining room together.

Gage enjoyed the lavish meal a great deal. It had been a while since he dined on such exquisite cuisine and drank good wine. Several times during the dinner, Caitlin shyly looked away from him due to the how intently he watched her.

"With the way Evariste stares at you, I assume the two of you are soon to be married?" Gabriella inquired, having never seen Gage so taken with a woman before.

Celio also noted how Gage interacted with the violet-eyed woman throughout their meal. "I believe Vespasian would deem Evariste a suitable husband for his ward if Evariste petitioned for such a union."

"Ward?" Caitlin didn't understand Celio's comment and shot Gage a questioning look.

"What Celio means is that as a ward of the emperor, Caitlin, Vespasian will choose a suitable match for you. Is that not how marriage is handled in Britannia?" Gage clarified, not making eye contact with her.

"Not always, Evariste. Sometimes a bride and groom find one another on their own."

"Love matches can be doomed from the start. Most Romans believe marriage is for prestige, and love is reserved for the mistress a man takes outside the marriage bed." Celio chuckled as his wife hit him for making such a remark.

"I am now curious, Celio. Why would the emperor deem Evariste a worthy suitor for my hand?" Caitlin smiled and picked up her wine glass, wanting to learn more about the man taking her further into enemy territory.

"My many years of loyal service to Rome," Gage spoke up, preventing Celio from disclosing anything about him.

"Evariste, you are being modest. There is more than your years of service in the legions." Gabriella thought he merely acted humble as a virtuous man should.

"Gabriella, my beautiful wife, what is for dessert? I am dying for something sweet to end the evening with." Celio distracted his wife, understanding Gage did not want to share more information than necessary with the woman he escorted to Rome.

GAGE SIPPED sangria from a silver chalice while watching Caitlin stroll along the shoreline as he stood on the balcony. He could safely observe her from there while giving her some space to cope with everything occurring. The round blue moon illuminated the beach, allowing him to see her clearly. Her hair and her long skirts swirled around her in the breeze. He kept his eyes on her until she disappeared below the balcony. A short time later, he heard the door between their rooms open and shut. He didn't need to turn to know Caitlin entered his bedroom. When he finally chose to face her, she stood in the arched entryway leading onto the balcony.

"You should not be here." He tried to play the chivalrous guardian when all he wanted to do was take her in his arms and taste her lips again.

"I wished to say good night."

"Good night, Caitlin. May Somnus grant you pleasant dreams."

Disappointment swept over her face. She looked down then back up at him before spinning on her heels. "Good night, Decurion."

Gage grabbed her arm, halting her departure. He wasn't sure if it was the moonlight, sea air, or the wine, but he wanted her. He wanted her with such a ferocity the only thing that would keep him from her was Mars himself. Caitlin turned, standing taller so her lips met his.

Their mouths moved against one another; tasting and savoring out of pure depravation.

"Love me like a man does his mistress," Caitlin whispered between kisses.

"I'd rather take you as a I imagine I would a wife if I ever married." Gage smiled down at her. "I cherish you too much already for you to be a mere mistress, Caitlin."

"Take me however you please then, Evariste."

His fingers worked to unpin the two brooches holding her clothing on. Once the pins slid free, the green and gold-trimmed cloth tumbled down in a rolling wave then slowly pooled around her feet.

"You are perfection, dea." Gage's eyes swept down the nude form bathed in the soft light of flickering flames. Copper falls cascaded wildly over full rounded breasts then continued down to the tops of curvaceous hips. Where her hair stopped, long legs began. Legs he was anxious to feel wrapped around him.

He led her inside then disrobed himself. She lay back on his bed with him. "You are certain about this, Caitlin? Your virtue can't be restored once taken."

"War between our peoples robbed me of my virtue long ago. You're an honorable man. There's none other better to take what little I have left."

Gage caressed her until she begged him for more; his fingers stroking, prodding, and gently massaging, so it wouldn't be such a shock when he finally sheathed himself inside her. He continued his sensual assault until her body continually tremored then he slowly entered her. After one quick thrust to take her innocence, he returned to an easy gentle pace, teaching her how to make love and be loved the rest of the night.

Prophecy & Planning

ᏮᏮᎦᏪᎦ

S hocked by how long ago Caitlin and his paths had really crossed, Gage turned to stare at Alcee. "Why did I have no memory of this before now?"

"The Fates erased your and Caitlin's memories." Alcee frowned, wishing Gage's full past had come to light under different circumstances.

"The time separation was the only way to keep Baracus from tracking both of you," Sean expanded on why such a thing was done.

"So you suppressed our memories and my abilities?" Caitlin jumped to her feet with the drug wearing off. Furious, her face turned crimson after learning of what her supposed guardian had done to her and her husband. The house rattled and the chandelier swung above them all.

"Calma, Rosso. It was your idea—and Gage's too. The two of you solicited the Fates after Baracus tracked you to your home outside of Rome." Dante glanced up at the large, swaying light fixture above them then back at the woman causing the localized quake.

"What?" Gage and Caitlin asked in unison as the room stopped shaking.

"It was a choice you both freely made after the Council sentenced Baracus to death. Evariste had been severely injured when we clashed

310

with Baracus in Gaul. The injury and the two of you wanting a new start away from the trauma you incurred in antiquity caused you to set out for the New World. Caitlin traded her immortality and powers for a mortal life with you, Evariste. Everything was going well until Caitlin became pregnant. The unborn child inherited Caitlin's abilities, drawing a revived and recovered Baracus out of the woodwork. After he and Tristan attacked the two of you, Alcee and Sean managed to save you both. However, the child Caitlin carried was lost. With the brutality of the attack, Evariste's conversion to a vampire, and the loss of the child, you both went to the Fates and asked for a way to safely live out your lives. The Fates advised there was no other option than for you two to be separated. The cycle of violence from Baracus would repeat if you remained together. In hopes of staying alive and one day learning how to defeat Baracus, you two made the difficult decision to part. Your memories were altered, and each of you were assigned a guide to help you in your new life. Baracus stayed well-hidden until recently. The Council and Morrigan hoped to ease your memories back; hence Rayne and I posing as investors seeking to buy Evariste's company. We all wanted to prevent the shock you are undergoing now. Baracus's showing himself more frequently forces us down a different road." Dante paused, giving Caitlin and Gage time to absorb all he shared.

Gage and Caitlin stared at one another, jointly experiencing rapid glimpses of them heartbrokenly bidding each other farewell.

"Has a way to kill Baracus been found?" Caitlin's throat tightened while she spoke, fearful Gage and she would be forced apart again.

"Yes, but it won't be easy to execute," Sean said, concerned about the tears in Caitlin's eyes and the torment on her face. The woman rarely cried over anything.

Gage offered her an unsure, quick smile while taking her hand. He refused to continue the two-thousand-year-old cycle of violence which kept him from his wife. And there was no way in hell he was going to let a menace like his grandfather reign havoc on humanity again. "Nothing in our pasts appears to have ever been easy. I'm not giving up my wife a third time. We'll do whatever is needed to eliminate my grandfather."

"Battling Baracus is like fighting the devil himself. The conflict which drove you to the New World almost wiped out Europe." Alcee hoped the two were ready for what was coming. "Baracus is a first descendent of Lilith as I am. His tie to her is what keeps reviving him. We need to destroy that bond before he can be killed."

"Merde," Gage cursed. Lilith, the mother of all vampires, turned his grandfather. Many vampires in Louisiana thought of Gage as powerful, but he had nothing on his grandfather; a first-generation immortal might as well be a god. "Going after Lilith would start an apocalyptical war."

"We do not need to go after Lilith. There's another way." Alcee glanced over at Dante and Sean. "If we have Death and War's assistance, there is a chance of ending Baracus completely this time."

"You shall have it, Alcee, along with the assistance of my most powerful sorceress once she recalls who she truly is." Morrigan revealed her presence in the room.

Alcee stared at Caitlin standing next to Gage. "Sorceress?"

"What else would she be? Honestly, Alcee, how many healers do you know who can manipulate time and commune with the dead?" Sean confirmed the nature of Caitlin's talents.

The four men moved out of Morrigan's way as she approached Caitlin. "I warned you long ago of what type of evil you would face if you accepted the gifts I offered."

"How could I not accept them? My homeland was at war. You raised me to fight for my home and my people. I also had the ability to save souls from the war the Romans waged, along with defending against the raiders from the North."

"You truly are my granddaughter." Morrigan smiled. "Even with all the support I give you, I fear you are not prepared to do what is necessary to eliminate Baracus. Part of me wonders if reuniting you and Evariste is a poor error in judgement the Council and I will end up atoning for in the future."

Sean set a confident hand on Caitlin's shoulder. "She is more than ready."

"We shall see how well you trained her, guide." Morrigan arched a brow. Her lips twisted into a doubtful frown before her eyes rested on Gage. "And you, Decurion? Are you ready to face Baracus again? You struck him down twice in Gaul and Italy only for him to rise once more."

"I will finish him this time," Gage vowed.

"Centuries ago, prophecy warned a cursed droch-fhuil would seek vengeance against the one who betrayed him by returning a lost child of the Tuatha De Danann to her people. Not even the Morrigan could shield the lost child from destiny, so instead, the goddess sought to outwit fortune. She cast a spell gifting the spoken of child to whichever commander of the Ancient World the Fates deemed to be a worthy match for her. Wanting to limit the destruction the droch-fhuil would bring to the realms, the Fates expanded on the Morrigan's spell. They wrote in the Book of Life the droch-fhuil would be struck down upon the union of the commander and lost one. When the droch-fhuil learned of our disrupting the future he planned, he retaliated against all the Tuatha De Danann, seeking out the descendant with the power to heal and to commune with the dead. For by their blood alone, could he become the conqueror he desired."

Caitlin gasped. "No wonder the child frightened Baracus."

"Baracus assumed a child borne from you both would bring about his downfall." Morrigan took Caitlin's hands in hers, giving them a gentle squeeze. "Remember who you are, draw on the depths of the magic which flows through you, and you shall eliminate Baracus."

After Morrigan vanished, Dante finished delivering the message the Council instructed him to. "Baracus grows more powerful each time he reincarnates. We will need to be strategic in determining the best place and time to confront him."

Alcee's shoulders raised with the deep breath he took in, contemplating how deadly a strike against Baracus would be. "Baracus is most vulnerable in daylight. The sun weakens him very quickly. He only ventures out into it for an hour or two at a time. Our other option is to attack when he is sleeping."

"It won't be easy to find him or reach him once we locate where he sleeps. My grandfather more than likely recruited an army of his own for him to hide here among us for centuries without detection. His bodyguards always fiercely protected him, even Vespasian feared riling him outright with the assassins he employed." Gage briefly thought about fleeing instead of fighting.

"We aren't splitting again, Evariste. We stand and fight." Caitlin questioned her own sanity as she spoke.

"If that is what you wish." Gage stared at his wife, mustering his courage and calling on his combat experience from centuries ago. "Baracus obviously wants a confrontation here and now, which means he feels he has the upper hand in modern day. We need to get him to come to us wherever we have the greatest chance of victory."

"Perhaps Britannia, with Morrigan's stronghold hidden there?" Alcee half-heartedly suggested.

"I wish we could confront him on British soil. We would have a stronger tactical advantage there than other locations. However, the risk of divulging the immortal realm to the human one is too great," Dante shot down the idea. "We can't allow the veil to be pierced or expose the populous to our kind. That would create uncontrollable havoc. Humans don't handle coexisting with other species as well as immortals do."

"I say we fight him here, but in the eighteenth century." Gage disclosed where he believed they should make their stand. "The surrounding area was sparsely inhabited. The indigenous population remained farther north, as they avoided the swamps more than us settlers did. There's no risk of exposing the immortal realm, and we know the local terrain better than anywhere else."

Caitlin smiled at Gage. "Not to mention, we were both mortal and in hiding then. Baracus wouldn't expect us to attack him. We were nothing more than an annoyance and lost prize until we conceived a child. For him to learn of the child, someone either in the family or working for the doctor monitored us for him."

"That thought crossed my mind as well. As disturbing as it is, we need to quickly identify whoever Baracus's informant is." Gage briefly contemplated who exactly might be Bonin's mole, but no one came to mind. "We also have the High Council and Morrigan's support behind us this time. The local Vampire Council hates my grandfather as much as we do. He was ousted from the vampire community for failing to blend in as needed to ensure the community survived on top of several altercations with Jude Robicheaux before he supposedly died. It wouldn't take much to sway the Council to support us."

"Sounds like we have our time and place." Caitlin looked at the men standing around her. "How do we keep Baracus from learning of our planning if someone in our inner circle is one of his minions?"

"We set them up and entrap them when they run like the rat they are to Baracus." Dante grinned, liking the direction things headed in. "Then, with them safely out of the equation, we put our people in place and spread the miraculous news of the first Arsceneaux heir being conceived throughout the region, luring Baracus straight to us. Sean and I can coordinate the rumor spreading and bring those we need to the eighteenth century. How do we gain the assistance of the local vampires?"

Alcee looked from Gage to Caitlin then started laughing.

Dante didn't like the vampire's reaction. "I fail to see the humor in this."

Alcee smirked. "Gaining the assistance of the local vampires is the easiest task of all. We only need to convene the Vampire Council."

"And how do we do that?"

"The chair sends out a mass summons."

"Who is the chair so we can solicit his support?" Sean started to think setting the stage in the eighteenth century might just work.

"That is a closely guarded secret. To reveal their identity places the vampire in the position at risk. In-fighting amongst our kind, as you've seen, is a far too common occurrence." Alcee chuckled then continued. "Although, I have a feeling the chair is well aware of our conundrum."

Caitlin noticed how Alcee stared at Gage. "You're the Council Chair."

"Yes, cher. I am."

Sean smiled. The Fates lined things up to tilt the odds in their favor. "Sounds like we have a rough plan. Should we regroup tomorrow to start setting our trap?"

"I think that would be best. Gage and I could use an evening to cope with all we just remembered," Caitlin said, taking Gage's hand.

Everyone departed, leaving Gage and Caitlin alone. Caitlin went to the living room and slowly sat on the couch, staring out the window into the backyard.

Gage watched her trying to hide the inner churn of her conflicting emotions. "Are you okay?"

"I'm confused. As I imagine you are."

He smiled as she leaned into him, seeking the comfort only his embrace offered. "I can't believe Giovanni is Death in the immortal realm."

Caitlin snorted. "It's a more than fitting position for him."

"You don't seem to care for him. Do you trust him?"

"Oddly, I do. He can be every derogatory thing I think of him, but he's also a skilled fighter. Morrigan and the High Council wouldn't have made him the Horsemen Commander if he was untrustworthy. The rigor of the trials one is put through are arduous at best and near soul destroying at worst for an immortal selected to be one of the Horsemen. If rumor is true, Dante's proved his valor and loyalty on many occasions."

"Why do I get the feeling there is more to your animosity toward him?"

Caitlin shrugged. "I honestly don't know. I don't remember much about him, at least not yet."

"You once told me you were married before, but our night together in Spain was your first time with a man. Perhaps Dante is your ex-husband?"

"He wishes." Caitlin laughed at the suggestion. "The memories of my prior marriage are hazy; just like the ones of Dante and all the others who serve Morrigan. The face that comes to mind when I think of it isn't Dante's. That man has blond hair with caramel highlights and hazel eyes. From what I can recall, my prior marriage was arranged between my grandmother and one of the fae kings."

She did her best to concentrate on the jumbled images and muffled discussions she had with Morrigan centuries ago.

Gage patiently waited for her to sift through her thoughts.

"The immortal I wed was named Gaelin. He sought others' beds. I don't recall either of us being happy about the marriage; we only went through with it out of duty and to please our families. For whatever reason, we managed to escape the consummation requirement for our marriage to be recognized. You were very much my first lover." Caitlin brought a surprised smile to Gage's face. Even back then, a virginal bride of Caitlin's age was a rare thing.

"Do you recall what happened to Gaelin? Did you divorce if you were so unhappy?"

"No. Gaelin died the first time Baracus came to Britannia. Somehow, Baracus and several of his men crossed over the sacred barrier into Sasainn, the immortal region Morrigan lives in. Your grandfather attacked the temple several of us practiced in. Gaelin stepped in front of an arrow meant for me as Sean arrived with other guides to defend the peaceful healers of the order after I called upon Morrigan for help. I had to choose between healing Gaelin or saving the lives of everyone else. He understood the quandary I faced and encouraged me to use my powers to save the others. They were the greater good. I left him in the temple after giving him a potion to ease his pain, then fought alongside Sean, driving Baracus back into the mortal realm. Sean, Dante, and I sealed the opening Baracus made in the veil that divides our worlds.

When we returned to the temple, Gaelin lay dead on the stone floor, well beyond the limits of my powers to bring him back. I tried to revive him anyway. My attempt failed. We all knew it would. He died a revered martyr of the immortal realm, which he didn't truly deserve, but who speaks ill of the deceased, especially when their father is a powerful fae king? We let his family and the immortal community have their hero. We needed him to rally the ranks at the time. I would never admit this to Morrigan, but I was relieved I couldn't save him. I was finally free to live my life as I chose to, until you and your grandfather lured me out."

"I'm so sorry for your loss and capture. I didn't understand the harm my actions would cause at the time."

Tidings Of Ill Fate

C aitlin wandered through the French Market with Allister. Alli stopped to admire an amber pendant that was in the shape of a sun.

Caitlin saw the disappointment in Alli's eyes when the jeweler told her the price. She picked up the pretty stone set in silver. "It is a beautiful piece."

"It's more than I wanted to spend." Alli longingly stared at the pendant in Caitlin's hands.

"I handmade it myself. That's why I'm priced slightly higher than the other vendors," the man explained why his pieces cost more.

"Silver and stone are getting expensive, and your work is stunning. Well worth the price you are charging." Caitlin handed the man her credit card. When he finished ringing up the necklace, she gave it to Alli. "For always being there for Gage. He and I appreciate you."

Allister smiled, taking the bag from her. "His grumpy self doesn't deserve either of us. I'm glad he found you again. Even under the circumstances. You're a saint for letting him put a ring on your finger."

Caitlin laughed. "I think a lot of people would tell you I'm as crazy as he is, and there is no better reason than love to get married."

"Interesting remark, especially coming from one who found obligation and family honor strong enough reason to once go through with a wedding," a hooded man said, leaning against a nearby column, his arms crossed over his chest while watching the two women.

Caitlin recognized the blood red ruby ring on his right hand along with the gold crest on his chest. "Alli, I will catch up with you at Café Du Monde."

"Who's the weird guy in the hood?"

"An old acquaintance." Caitlin noticed the way Alli frowned, continuing to stare at their hooded visitor. "I'll be okay. He isn't a vampire."

Allister grudgingly walked off after snapping a picture of the man watching them.

Seeing Alli scroll through her contacts then bring the phone to her ear, Caitlin smiled. She most likely called Gage or Alcee to tell them about the wierdo at the market.

When Caitlin approached the being who interrupted her shopping, all she could see were white teeth between parted lips from under the black hood as he smiled at her. But she knew exactly who he was by the ring on his hand. "It isn't Halloween, Dante. You need to learn how to blend in, even if you hate modern times. Baracus and his men would spot you a mile away."

"Perhaps that is the point of my appearance," the Horseman replied, unfolding his arms.

"You never do play by the rules of engagement, do you? As far as I know, Gage isn't trying to provoke Baracus. What message are you here to deliver?"

"We located Baracus's hiding place in the eighteenth century and here. Amazingly, he's holed up in the same location in both time periods. A small home in the swamps, not far from D'Orme. He also has a small army of humans and vampires as Evariste believed. They're spread from Shreveport to Grand Isle."

"Grazie for the warning. I will let Gage know. I assume you briefed Sean and my grandmother before coming here."

"I didn't advise either of this, yet." Dante took Caitlin by the arm. "There is more, medica. Follow me. It is not safe to discuss such matters in the open."

Caitlin noticed how Dante's eyes rested on Alli still lingering within view. "She wouldn't leak information to Baracus."

"You do not know that she wouldn't, cara."

"Fine. Where do you want to talk?"

"This way." Dante guided her to one of the empty buildings across the street.

After closing the door and ensuring they were alone, he pushed back his hood.

In his Horsemen's uniform, Dante embodied every lustful thing Caitlin had heard whispered about him after they parted ways. She had thought the women in Morrigan's temple who sighed and cooed over Death while describing his chiseled features framed with dark brown hair and seductively piercing golden eyes exaggerated their descriptions of him, especially when talking about his muscular frame. When she had last seen him in Sasainn, he was tall and lean, almost lanky. Though his eyes had always been beautiful along with his face.

Even with toning down his otherworldly appearance when in the human realm, Death remained devastatingly handsome. Esther had immediately swooned over him, and so had she the first time she saw him in the coffee shop. Her reaction to spotting War beside him that morning had been the same. Maybe that was part of humanity's infatuation with the legend of the Horsemen. Whenever Dante grinned at her, she could still see glimpses of the young cavalry captain she dated. Did the romantic, kind soul he once had still exist somewhere underneath the older being's strapping exterior and cocky attitude, or had he completely died when he took the Horsemen's oath? Recalling the stories of Dante now being a notorious womanizer who left a trail of broken hearts and angry husbands in his wake wherever he went, she frowned.

"If you were not married to Arsceneaux, I would be more than happy to confirm what I truly am for you." Dante's brow seductively arched as he cupped her chin in his hand. He leaned toward her, his voice turning to pure velvet and holding the promise of carnal delight. "I have never made love to a woman with violet eyes. Perhaps I might have the chance to with your conflicted thoughts about me."

Caitlin slapped his hand off her face. "Doubtful, Dante. Even unmarried, I have higher standards for the men I date."

"I recall a time I met and exceeded your standards. Or have you truly forgotten Carthage, Rosso?" Dante reminded her of the nights she spent sleeping in his arms and the kisses they shared. Nothing more than innocent exploration occurred between them in their more passionate moments. He knew better than to take her maidenhead without wedding her. Sean and Morrigan would have drawn and quartered him had he ever taken her body without their exchanging vows.

"I think wine and battle caused a momentary lapse in my judgment."

"Then perhaps the later nights sharing my bed in Sasainn? You almost married me once."

"I was so naive back then to think you were more of a gentleman and honorable man than you actually are."

Dante laughed. "A dishonorable man would have compromised you. I never did, and I am always a gentleman to every woman I meet. I'm merely not interested in committing myself to one woman any longer when there are so many out there to love, especially after the one I contemplated marrying spurned me as she did."

"She only spurned you after you chose a promotion over her."

"You know damn well that is not true, Caitlin DeDanann." Dante restrained his temper after she flung that in his face for the millionth time. "I tried everything I could when I went to your grandmother and asked her to break your betrothal to Gaelin. She's the one who sent me off to the Horsemen. I never asked to become Death. I never wanted to be what I am now. Even with as much as I admired Raphael and the other Horsemen. And I never wished ill on you as you did me. While it goes against my better judgment to say this, I was disappointed when I learned you married Arsceneaux again. A small part of me was hoping for another chance to win you back after Morrigan disclosed you were the one I was being dispatched to assist. Who knows, I might have become the man you once thought I was if Morrigan hadn't forbidden the continuance of our romance. But peace in the realms and duty were always the higher call to you and her. Damn my feelings on the matter. I begrudgingly have to admit, Arsceneaux is certainly a more appropriate match for you than Gaelin ever was."

"What happened between us is long over, and my relationships are no longer any of your concern, Dante. Have you told me all that the Council commanded you to?"

"Struck a nerve, did I?"

"Everything you've said, you could have told me in the open. I no longer find you charming, Giovanni, and have other matters to attend to." Caitlin headed for the door.

"Evariste does not survive the battle." Dante's words froze her mid-step. "He dies when he confronts Baracus."

Caitlin shook her head, facing Dante again. "I refuse to believe the Fates would do that to us a third time."

"Why else would I be here, Caitlin? If the situation weren't dire, the Horsemen would still be in Sasainn. You know we are rarely dispatched to handle trivial matters." Dante walked over to her, needing her to understand he didn't toy with her. "Morrigan herself entrusted me with the message. She feared Sean would not share such upsetting news with you."

Caitlin's stomach churned. Dante spoke the truth. The Horsemen Commander always served as Morrigan's harbinger of ill fate if the goddess didn't deliver the message herself. "Can I stop Gage's death?"

"No. I will ride into battle with you both. I am under order to ensure you survive. You will be Baracus's main target once he dispatches Evariste. You will need Rayne's and my assistance to stay alive."

"You may ride at my side, but I will do everything I can to prevent Gage's death. My husband will not die, regardless of what the Fates say."

"His death is the only way of stopping Baracus once and for all. It will happen, Caitlin, no matter what you do." Dante put his hand on her shoulder.

Images of Gage dying on the battlefield played between them. She jerked free from Dante's grip.

"For what it is worth, I truly am sorry to deliver the message this time around." Dante grabbed her hand. "Evariste Arsceneaux is certainly worthy of your heart, Rosso. He's a much better man than Gaelin or I could ever be."

Caitlin recalled laughing at Dante when he told her Gaelin wasn't honorable. She had accused him of being jealous.

"Your laughter stung, Caitlin. As much as telling me you wished I wouldn't return from Egypt when Morrigan dispatched the Horsemen there. Your wishing me dead and then Raphael's being struck down in Alexandria changed all my plans for the future. I half wonder if your anger and wishing ill on me caused Raphael's death; that the Fates blindly took vengeance on your behalf, striking down the wrong Horseman. Qasim should have never been able to kill him."

"I had nothing to do with Raphael's death! Blame me all you like, but I didn't curse him or you. Thoughtlessly spoken words don't hold that kind of power. I never truly wished for any harm to befall either of you." Caitlin couldn't believe he held her accountable for such a thing. "I even came to you and told you I still loved you the night you returned with Raphael's body and the book! I apologized, and extended condolences, knowing Raphael was as much a father as a mentor to you. You are still the bitter child blaming everyone he can for his misfortunes that you've always been, Dante Giovanni."

"Allow me to finish speaking before you interrupt me again." Dante glared down at her. His tone terse as if he spoke to an insubordinate underling. "This discussion is difficult enough without your self-righteous indignation. I violate orders saying what I do to you. My torn loyalty between you and the Council is causing me to misspeak. What I am trying to say is I regret the decisions I made in my youth, Caitlin. I was a fool to believe I had no other option. You do not need to repeat my mistakes. We always have a choice in matters even when it seems we don't. Make yours very carefully."

Caitlin yanked her hand out of Dante's firm grasp when he opened his fingers. She was furious at her grandmother for the prediction and choosing Dante to be the messenger. "Tell Morrigan, when the time comes, I will take up the sword again. I will not idly standby following your orders or hers. Both of you can go to hell."

Dante grinned. That was the answer he expected from his Rosso. "Neither your grandmother nor the Council will be pleased when I share your response to them."

"Anything else I should know, Commander?"

Dante half-bowed to her. "No, medica."

The formal gesture and her old priestess title pissed Caitlin off more. Dante only followed old protocol to mock her calling him commander. She flung the front door open, raging off down Decatur Street.

RAYNE LOOKED over at Dante as he stepped out of the closed store. His conversation with Caitlin obviously didn't go well. "You always knew exactly how to infuriate her."

"She needs to be incensed. Her temper will be what saves her this go round."

"Will she fight or continue playing the pacifist holy woman?"

Dante grinned. "Il mio caro amico, do you truly need me to answer after that exit?"

"You better be right with this mutiny of yours. Both our asses are on the line if it fails. I can't recall a time previously where the Horsemen intentionally disobeyed Council directives."

Keeping Secrets

⟨∞⟩

"Gage!" Caitlin called for her husband as she rushed up the steps and into the house. "Evariste!"

Not finding him upstairs, she ran back down the stairs and out into the backyard. Concerned about her shouting, Alcee and Sean jogged outside after her.

Gage stepped out of the barn. He had been feeding the horses until he heard Caitlin yelling for him. "Over here, Caitlin!"

The panic on her face when she turned put him on edge. She sprinted to him. He pushed back the mass of red hair falling into her face after she reached him. "Cher, what has you so upset?"

"Baracus is nearby."

Gage still didn't understand how that was such upsetting news. They had suspected he wasn't far. "Did you see him?"

"I didn't see him." Caitlin paused to take another breath.

"Then how do you know he is here?"

"I told her, as I saw him." Dante walked toward them. "My men and I confirmed his location, only an hour's ride on horseback from here. He has about a hundred vampires and humans under his employ. Not a large force, but one that could be problematic, nonetheless. If the fight is to be in another century, you need to head there sooner rather than later. Caitlin and Sean can transport you and anyone else if time travel isn't one of your gifts."

"And here I thought Morrigan left Evariste and Sean in charge of matters. It appears I was mistaken," Alcee said, unsure of whether or not he liked Death's involvement in things.

Dante laughed. "I was sent to fix the mistakes Watchous and you are about to make, vampire."

"This isn't your fight to lead," Gage growled at the Horseman over-stepping his bounds. "Last I checked, you're here for support only."

Dante held up his hand, cautioning Gage to cool down. "Circum-stances are rapidly changing, Arsceneaux. I will assume whatever role is needed to fulfill my orders. Play general all you like, Decurion, but heed my warning to take defensive measures now. You're almost out of time."

Gage stared at the three men dressed in black and on horseback a short distance from them. When Dante's hand dropped, the three rode in different directions, leaving a lone riderless black horse, which Dante strolled over to then swung up into its saddle. "As it appears you and your little band of merry men are taking up temporary residence at D'Orme, my guest rooms and stables are at your disposal, Giovanni."

"Thank you for your hospitality, Evariste, but that is not necessary. We will handle our own lodging. You will see us periodically keeping watch. We are identifiable by the black and gold armor bearing Morrig-an's crest. Feel free to dispatch anyone you find around here not meeting that description. I wouldn't recommend challenging any of the Horse-men. It wouldn't end well for you."

Sean pulled Caitlin aside. "What other news did Dante bring?"

"You know exactly what he told me!" Caitlin glared at Sean. "How could you not warn me? This is just like Gaelin all over again!"

Sean hated the betrayal in her eyes. "Caitlin, I didn't tell you about Evariste as I cannot prevent fate from playing out. Morrigan should not have said anything either. It was better you not know."

"At least Dante gives me a fighting chance to save him." Caitlin jerked free then followed Gage and Alcee into the house.

Catching a shadow in his peripheral vision, Sean started toward it. "I know you're still here, Giovanni. You better damn well have a plan to clean up the mess you are making. And *you* are going to be the one standing in front of Morrigan if this all goes south, not me this time."

"You needlessly worry, General. I have things well in hand." Dante ignored the snort he heard and rode off to help patrol with the other Horsemen.

CAITLIN STAYED with Gage for the rest of the afternoon, never straying more than a few feet from him. Between the four shadows standing guard around his property and Caitlin's odd behavior, Gage's mood soured. He had enough to worry about without adding his wife being upset to the equation.

Just before dinner, two of the Horsemen met one another behind the house. Gage assumed the men rotated positions as was customary for watchmen to do. Caitlin scowled at the two before walking out the backdoor. Whatever she discussed with them wasn't well received by either immortal. She grabbed the reins of the Horseman she had words with when he started to turn his horse to prevent him from riding off. A strong gust of wind blew the man's hood back, exposing his face.

Seeing it was Giovanni, Gage frowned. "Dante and Caitlin seem to have some history."

"They served together several times in previous conflicts. Dante is only abiding by Morrigan's orders to protect her so you can face Baracus. He has no other motives for being here." Sean downplayed the interaction between Caitlin and the Horseman.

"I see the way he looks at her, Sean. He cares a great deal for her. Even with the two of you adamantly denying he does."

Sean sighed. Dante could conceal his emotions well, except when it came to Caitlin. Gage read them accurately. "They were kids when they courted. Her betrothal to Gaelin ended their relationship. And yes, Dante still harbors some romantic sentiment toward her. I suspect that is one of the reasons why Morrigan dispatched him here."

"And the other reasons he is here?" Gage wanted to know what Sean held back.

"Have you not heard the stories of the Four Horsemen? There is no other force on earth that can match the death and destruction they bring when commanded to do so."

"You said he and Caitlin served together? In what capacity?"

"She should be the one telling you this." Sean paused, slowly exhaling the breath he briefly held in. "But considering the circumstances, Caitlin was not always a healer. She was a military officer, trained in swordsmanship, magic, and combat, just as the rest of us are. Baracus isn't the only threat to humanity out there. A series of battles against another entity along with her forced engagement led to her resigning her commission after she had enough of following the High Council's and Fates' decrees. She took up the priestess's robes to honor her mother and escape anything more than marriage in name to Gaelin. The more Morrigan tried to talk Caitlin out of becoming a priestess and healer, the more determined Caitlin was to become one. Eventually, Morrigan came to realize Caitlin had chosen the right path. She was an incredible healer and saved just as many lives as she would have wielding the sword."

Hating the tragic life Caitlin led, Gage stared out the window at his wife. He didn't do much to improve things for her. "Until I lured her into the trap my grandfather set."

Sean sympathetically smiled. "Yes. But destiny always has a reason for things. You're the other half of her soul. The man she was meant to find. She is at peace with you, which I've never seen her be with anyone. She loves you. Don't ever take that for granted, Gage. Love like you two share is a very rare thing. Not many would be willing to endure all you have faced to protect one another."

Caitlin caught the last sentence as she entered the house. Irritation still creased her brow from her argument with Dante. "What are you two discussing?"

"How lucky I am to have you." Gage curled a knuckle under her chin then tenderly kissed her.

"I love you, Evariste Arsceneaux." Caitlin took in the way forest-colored eyes admired her before Gage whispered he loved her too.

Observing the two of them, Sean once more smiled. The Fates had chosen well in aligning Caitlin and Evariste's futures. The vampire handled the sorceress's temper in stride—and she, his. Sean vanished, gifting them a night alone before their world would crumble once again.

GAGE GROANED as his wife woke him a second time, stroking his cock until it hardened. "Caitlin, mon coeur, you are insatiable tonight."

"Do you want me to stop?"

"No. I'm enjoying this." Gage positioned himself between her thighs, taking her again as she wanted him to.

Waiting

"Where's your hood?" Alcee asked Sean as the Four Horsemen rode up to them shortly after dawn.

"No shame in what I do, so there isn't a need to hide my face," Sean replied with a smirk.

"He is not man enough to wear the black and gold," Dante fired back.

Amused by that claim, Sean let out a single, loud laugh. He had centuries of military experience on Dante and had bested all the Horsemen at least once during their preparation for the Council trials to earn their spurs. "Any trouble last night, Giovanni?"

"None. It was peaceful, almost pleasant for this vile century. We are going to see if we can stir up some hate and discontent in Baracus's ranks. Maybe get a few of his minions to change their minds about facing off with Evariste."

"Any weakening you can do will certainly be beneficial." Sean wondered how long it would be before Gage and Baracus came face to face. "I don't suppose you saw our informant milling around Baracus or his people.

"Unfortunately, not. But they are someone close to Evariste, most likely one of his sisters. It's definitely not the doctor who confirmed

Caitlin's pregnancy or one of his staff. We've been monitoring them closely for several days and no vampire has been near them. Considering Tristan is still lurking about, Baracus is gathering information on Caitlin and Evariste's modern-day habits to determine the perfect moment to go after them. Tristan watched Cate in the Quarter yesterday. He only left after spotting me; no doubt to report Evariste has more than the local vampires' support in this century as well. Until this evening, gentlemen." Dante grinned, reining his horse away from the two immortals he stopped to update.

Alcee frowned. "Is it wise turning them loose to rile Baracus?"

"Normally, I would say no. But there's a reason he and the other Horsemen are here. We need to let them do whatever it is Morrigan and the Council wants them to do."

"I'm surprised the Council made Dante such a powerful commander. He's reckless and full of himself."

Sean didn't disagree with Alcee's assessment. "And impulsive, and completely unpredictable, with questionable morals, which is exactly why they promoted him. As much as I hate to admit it, he is damn good at what he does."

"Give me a man like Evariste to fight alongside any day. He's loyal, reasonable, yet makes calculated quick corrections in the chaos of battle, and has all the virtues a commander at the head of a legion should possess. Had he been anyone else's grandson or assigned to a different position, he'd easily have become a tribune or legate."

Alcee and Sean walked back to the house.

Gage and Caitlin would be up soon. And Gage would most likely want to move forward with his own strategy against Baracus.

"General, your presence is requested in Sasainn." Arturo, one of Morrigan's and the Horsemen's aide-de-camps, appeared, halting the vampire and guide general.

Sean sighed. For him to be summoned with things escalating, Dante undoubtedly had done something to rile Morrigan or the High Council, and now he was going to bear the brunt of their wrath for the Horseman causing more trouble than usual.

Alcee laughed at the exasperated expression on the guide's face. "Good luck, mon ami."

Taking Up The Sword

C aitlin was still enjoying her coffee when Sean returned and tossed a saber on the table in front of her. Rarely did she see him look as annoyed as he was now. "What's the saber for?"

"If you are going to threaten the Council and your grandmother by 'taking up the sword again,' you better damn well know how to use one. If you don't recognize your old weapon, you certainly don't remember what to do with it." Sean walked across the room then held open the backdoor. "Come on. I won't be embarrassed by a former student of mine performing poorly on the battlefield after she stupidly tells the Council and her grandmother to pound sand."

"Sean, I didn't mean for you—"

"Outside, Caitlin. Now."

The furious stare Sean shot her warned he wasn't asking again. Caitlin picked up the saber and followed Sean into the backyard. "Did the Council honestly expect me to just shrug and say okay, I'm good with you killing my husband?"

"Of course not. They know you as well as I do, but to threaten retaliation as you did, that, that was careless, especially considering your abilities have not fully returned." A sword materialized in Sean's hand as he turned to face her.

"Let's see what you can recall." Sean unsheathed his blade.

Caitlin mimicked his actions and raised her blade. "Aren't we supposed to wear masks or protective clothing?"

"We aren't fencing, Cate. We're preparing for war."

Sean quickly disarmed her with only one swing. "Saints preserve us. You are worse than I ever imagined you could be if you can't even hold your weapon properly to manage one simple parry."

"I haven't exactly done this before. If you knew I was going to have to fight Baracus again, why didn't you put me in fencing lessons or something combat-related when I was a kid?"

Sean laughed at the idea. "You'd decimate your teammates on the piste once your instincts kicked in. Not to mention you weren't the best sportsman at a young age, especially when it came to taunting boys who said a girl couldn't do something. I can only imagine the calls I would have gotten from a fencing coach and how many black cards you'd have received in tournaments. Now, let's try this again."

The next three bouts lasted only seconds.

"Damn it, Caitlin! Stop resisting your instincts. You start to make the right response to my attacks then stop yourself. Remember who you are. You once decimated enemy legions. Focus, so you may do so again." Sean scolded then attacked her before she had the chance to anticipate his advance.

Ancient muscle memory finally kicked in. She readily deflected his strikes. Caitlin smiled as they parried and attacked one another until they locked blades, neither losing their weapon nor giving ground.

Sean gave her a second to try to overtake him. When she didn't do so, he shoved her back. Her free hand came around and her elbow collided with his chest. Had she been wielding a dagger, the blade would have dealt him a wounding blow on the bicep or side as her fist collided with him once her elbow landed. "Better. For a fleeting second, I saw a glimpse of the Defensore."

Sean spun the sword in his hand as he watched Caitlin catch her breath.

"I owe you an ass whipping for a few things in this lifetime, Sean." Caitlin raised her blade again, ready for the next round.

Sean laughed. "Arrogance is a weakness, Cate. One easily exploited like temper and fear. If you want to defeat a being like me or Baracus, you need to control both along with your mouth. Otherwise, an immortal can anticipate your next move." Sean teleported behind her and in two quick actions disarmed her again, holding her prisoner by crossing the two swords he held in front of her so that her neck rested between the enchanted blades. "Never give your opponent that kind of advantage. Shield your emotions and your thoughts."

Sean lowered the blades, letting her go. They only had a few days to teach her to defend herself.

Death Versus The Healer

Dante rode back to D'Orme. He watched Sean and Caitlin clashing in the backyard. Rayne glanced over at him as he stopped beside the captain. "How long has this been going on?"

"Three hours now. She's improving, but there's no way she'll be ready to face Baracus at this pace. We'll have to wear him down for her to attempt to take him. Or one of us will have to do it."

Dante scowled. "That isn't going to work. We merely trigger the cycle to start all over again."

After watching Caitlin and Sean for another minute or two, Dante unsheathed his own blade.

"Baracus won't be merciful as Sean is being, Rosso." Dante advanced on Caitlin, forcing her to fight him instead of the guide. Caitlin and he had grown up dueling and practicing with one another. Neither had went easy on the other when facing off back then. He hoped subconsciously she would do the same now.

Rayne walked off the back porch to stand beside Sean as Dante and Caitlin went blow for blow. "It appears the Defensore is still within after all."

Sean grinned over at War. "He's certainly bringing out the fight in her."

Unlike Sean, Dante refused to give Caitlin any sort of break. When Caitlin lost her footing and fell, the general expected the commander to backdown. When Dante continued his assault, Sean's fingers tightened around the hilt of the blade he held. "Enough, Dante! Let her regain her feet."

"Baracus won't allow her such luxury, nor will I!" Dante raised his blade, threatening to drive it down into Caitlin. "He will be unyielding once he sees her. He'll kill her if she doesn't fight back. Just like he did Gage in the woods."

Caitlin's leg shot upward, her foot slamming into his groin and her fist slammed into the side of his knee, knocking Dante off balance. She surprised everyone as she jumped to her feet. The commander stumbled but didn't go down. "You always were a cocky bastard, Dante."

Rayne chuckled and Sean grinned, both relieved to see the old Caitlin emerging to defend herself.

Dante was the only one not amused. Closing in on her, his eyes narrowed. Sparring turned to something darker as Dante continued his assault. For a while, Caitlin held her own then she began to tire.

"This is when Baracus will finish you. When your legs are weak and your sword heavy. Your fingers begging you to drop your weapon if only for a second. Your muscles wanting a momentary break. Doubt suggesting you surrender."

"Give her a moment to rest, Dante," Sean called, not liking how Dante behaved. "You aren't on the field. We have time."

"We're out of time, General. She needs to remember who she is." Dante attempted to strike Caitlin with repeated rapid flourishes of his blade, forcing Caitlin to deflect each blow and retreat from him. "Were you not once the Morte Defensore, mortal? The fiercest female harbinger to serve the Council."

Sean took a step forward, the warning in his voice louder this time. "Stop, Dante."

"Were you not the equivalent of a Horseman? The Defender Against Wrongful Death? My equal, Caitlin DeDanann." Dante disarmed her then rested his blade along the side of her neck.

"Stand down now, Commander!" Sean gave Dante one last chance to stop before he intervened in things.

Dante landed a kick into Caitlin's chest, sending her tumbling backward. "The blood of a goddess of war and a Horseman flows in your veins. You disgrace them both today."

Sean advanced toward them now. "Dante!"

"Remain where you are, General." Morrigan halted Sean. She hated Dante's tormenting Caitlin but understood what he was attempting to do.

"Evariste is certainly dead if this is the best you can do, Rosso." Dante struck her again as she tried to get up, sending her back to her knees.

Flashes of Tristan and Baracus attacking her in the woods played out in her mind. Her eyes searched for Dante after he suddenly disappeared. His voice came from her right then her left as he baited her by asking did she know where he was? As she started to stand, he seized her from behind.

"If you let him daze you like this, it's over. The second your blood is on his lips, you lose everything." Dante jerked her head sideways as a vampire would to get a clear area to bite.

His teeth grazed her skin, igniting pure fury and rage. She summoned a dagger and slammed it back toward his side.

He caught her wrist before the blade made contact with him and guided her hand slightly higher and a half inch farther back. "Here, Cate. If you wish to strike a wounding blow between the pieces of armor, you must be faster, placing more weight into the swing to force the blade through this sliver of weak area. But that is a risky move against a seasoned soldier when out of practice. Your blade will either strike a vital organ or bounce off bone if it makes it through. Neither fatal to a vampire, but it will buy you time to get free."

Dante let her go. Before she could fully turn to face him, he delivered a punishing roundhouse kick to her side. She yelped and stumbled but maintained her footing. "Fight me, Rosso. Or do you want to die?"

Sweat dripped down Caitlin's face and her side smarted as she lunged for Dante.

He laughed, teleporting to her other side. "Evariste is lost and so are you. You'll fail if you continue blindly charging like this. Just like you failed when the temple was attacked. You'll watch Evariste take his last breaths again as you did three hundred years ago, and before that, as you did with Gaelin."

"Fuck you, Dante!" Caitlin spat as images of flame and arrows along with shattering glass and exploding stone walls filled her mind. Gaelin rested in her arms, an arrow lodged in his chest. His immortality slipping away from the poisoned and enchanted tip forged from the same metal the Horsemen's and her blades were.

"I was there, Caitlin. You know I was. We saw one another through the flames after I responded to the call to arms. You let Gaelin die that morning. You'll allow the same thing to happen to Evariste when the time comes."

"I didn't kill Gaelin." Caitlin deflected another blow from Dante's blade.

"No. Your fear and inaction did." Dante seized her by the throat. "Had you not faltered, you could have healed him. You're weak, Caitlin DeDanann. I thank the Fates daily for your resignation. I can only imagine what would happen to me if you hadn't chosen the path you did. How many would have died due to your incompetence. Poor Evariste has no idea his loving wife will be his downfall."

"I made a choice to save those in the temple. Gaelin made his by deciding to step in front of the arrow coming for me. I always chose the greater good, you son of a bitch." Caitlin subconsciously called on powers she didn't know she had, sending Dante flying across the yard.

Climbing to his feet, Dante laughed. "The greater good or what benefitted you? There was no love loss with Gaelin's passing. You hated him as much as I did. The difference between us being I never abandoned my oath to you or the Council. I would have saved him *and* those in the temple because I have the mettle you lack."

Caitlin and Dante maneuvered around one another now; blade tips pointed at each other. Each holding a dagger and a sword. Power shifted in the air around them. Lethality returned to Caitlin's eyes and flowed through each step she took to counter his. He teleported and she traveled with him this time. The tip of her blade still tracked him when they materialized a few feet from where they had been.

"Your games no longer work, Giovanni." Caitlin made the wind swirl around them, creating a mystical barrier so he couldn't teleport again. The sky darkened above them.

The Horseman grinned at the woman no longer intimidated by him or anyone else. Death successfully reincarnated the Morte Defensore in all her glory. This was the Caitlin he grew up with: fierce, wild, powerful, passionate, and unwilling to surrender to anyone. "I can still best you, Rosso. You'll crumble as you always do since forsaking your oath."

"WHAT IN THE hell is going on?" Gage demanded, discovering his wife armed and fighting Dante. He cast a nervous glance skyward at the storm clouds.

"A sparring match. Things are perfectly under control," Rayne replied, impressed by what Caitlin had done to counter Dante.

"A hurricane in my backyard while Death threatens my wife suggests otherwise." Gage doubted Armageddon wasn't about to spontaneously begin in rural Louisiana.

Rayne grinned. "Dante is only seeing what Caitlin can still call upon if she needs to defend herself."

"I've never forsaken my oath to the Council, Dante." Caitlin's raised voice drew their attention. "The lives of the many always outweigh the one. You were at the temple when we were attacked, but you did not arrive in time to hear Gaelin's last words of protect the others. Your judgement of my actions and me is wrongly made, Commander. I also do not answer to you."

Caitlin attacked Dante. This time she outfought Death and sent him sprawling onto the grass. She slammed her saber into the turf just above his shoulder, her blade sliding through his hood, and pining it to the ground.

Dante laughed, yanking her blade out of his hood then extended a hand to her. "Welcome back, Rosso. Such an absolute pleasure to finally see your true self again."

Caitlin rolled her eyes, clasped his hand, and helped him to his feet. The skies brightened and the wind ceased. Once Dante was standing, they hugged one another as they had done after training together long ago. Noticing Gage now watching beside Sean and Rayne when she looked over Dante's shoulder, she smiled at her husband. He returned the smile as his voice whispered on the afternoon breeze, *Impressive work, cher.*

"Immortal weapons belong in immortal hands." Dante held out an open hand to take her saber and dagger. "They'll be returned to you when you need them again."

Caitlin shook her head but gave him the armaments.

"Well done, Cate," Rayne complimented her as she and Dante approached them.

She nodded to Rayne before embracing Evariste and kissing him hello.

Dante handed Sean Caitlin's saber and dagger. "You're welcome, General."

Sean took the two weapons. "I didn't offer my thanks."

"Perhaps it's time for you to retire with not recognizing what your student needed to bring out her best." Dante smirked as he spoke.

"Be thankful your assistance is needed, or I'd put my foot in your ass to remind you of your position, Commander. I don't have Raphael's patience for your shenanigans nor do I approve of your methods." Sean shot Dante a reproachful stare.

"She's ready. That's all that matters." Dante turned to Gage. "See you in the eighteenth century, Arsceneaux."

Gage nodded, unsure what to think about the Horseman any longer.

Dante looked over at Rayne then the two of them left D'Orme.

"Are we really leaving modern day?" Caitlin hoped Gage said no.

"Afraid so, cher. We'll test the Fates' favor tomorrow. Let us hope they like us more than they do my grandfather."

Generational Curses
❦

Sean joined them for dinner. Caitlin hardly spoke a word as they ate. Her silence and strange behavior the past twenty-four hours worried Gage.

Gage refilled her wine then settled an arm around her. "What's wrong, mon coeur?"

"Today, when Dante and I bouted, he said something...something strange."

"He says a lot of antagonistic and stupid things." Gage tried to make her smile.

She rewarded his efforts with a soft laugh and smile. "Yeah, but this remark was different. He said Morrigan's blood and that of a Horseman flowed in my veins. That can't be right. None of the Horsemen were ever married to my mother, and I only know of one who retired shortly after getting married."

Caitlin looked over at Sean. He frowned before his gaze drifted downward to the empty plates still on the table. "Is it true, Sean? There were whispered rumors of a priestess and a Horseman when I was in the order. I thought it mere myth."

"Some things are better left in the past, a mhuirnín." Sean wished Dante hadn't disclosed what he had today.

341

"Was my mother the priestess who had the affair with the Horseman? Who was cast out of the order for violating her vows and becoming pregnant out of wedlock?" The sinking feeling in the pit of her stomach cautioned she already knew the answer to the question she posed.

"Saoirse never violated her vows. Those with ill will toward your mother and Morrigan made up that portion of the story. Unfortunately, some of the elder priestesses wielded it as a cautionary tale allowing those lies to survive longer than they should. No matter how many times Morrigan and the rest of us have tried to silence those who enjoy speaking them." Sean struggled with how to tell Caitlin the truth about her parents.

"My mother was married. Didn't the law forbid a Horseman from marrying back then?"

"It did. And her husband wasn't a Horseman. But I can assure you, her husband loved her a great deal."

"How could you know that?" Caitlin's mouth fell open as she noticed the sadness in his eyes. "You, you were married to my mother?"

"Yes, Saoirse was my wife. I adored her, Caitlin. I loved her more than anyone else I've ever been involved with since her passing."

Gage's fingers closed around hers. His comforting touch and presence helped her absorb the shocking news. Their eyes held for a moment as Caitlin rallied the nerve to ask the remaining questions she had.

"But you're not, you're not my father, are you?"

Sean took a deep breath before answering. "No, I'm not. There are many days I wish I were. I'm exceptionally proud of the woman you've become."

Caitlin closed her eyes, trying to picture the faces of all the Horsemen. There had only been seven men to ever serve as the Four Horsemen if she included the two latest Dante selected to fill open positions. Dante and she were only two years apart in age, so he couldn't be the man in the stories. The original Horsemen Commander, Raphael Fiore, had always been present in her youth, but he was a strict rule follower and devoted to Council decrees as much as he was to Morrigan. She looked nothing like Michael or Rayne. She had spent enough time with them to have discovered the truth of one of them being her father long before now. That left only one person.

She focused on the hazy image she managed to conjure; him smiling down at her and telling her she would be an exceptional officer after she had passed the Council trials and taken the officer's oath. His hair was a lighter shade of brown with copper and red highlights. The red was similar to some of the darker streaks in her own hair. The warm copper shade of his eyes mirrored the warmth in his smile. He always lifted her up when she stumbled or held her when she cried in moments of doubt. He was at nearly every celebration in her life while he lived. She couldn't recall a time when he and Sean weren't nearby.

"Gabriel," she uttered the man's name before looking over at Sean for confirmation. "Gabriel was my father."

"Yes. Your mother and I married at a very young age. Our marriage was arranged by Morrigan and Dagda. At first, we had the ideal marriage, but over time, our duties eroded that. As we fell apart, she and Gabriel came together. I offered to divorce her once I realized how much she loved Gabriel, and Gabriel wanted desperately to marry her. We tried to keep things quiet, but your grandfather learned of everything despite our best efforts."

"Oh my god," Caitlin mumbled, horrified that her mother and Gabriel endured what Dagda had supposedly done to them. "Dagda banished the priestess to the human realm and took away her immortality. She died because of that. The Horseman was demoted and banished as well in the tale, but Gabriel wasn't ever banished, at least not from what I can recall."

"Dagda did all those things. Morrigan was furious with him. The banishments ended their marriage. She took those of us loyal to her and left Ireland for Sasainn to be near her now mortal daughter. She also reinstated Gabriel to the Horsemen ranks as all the Horsemen sided with Morrigan in the dispute. Considering what happened to the other Tuatha De Danann, Morrigan's leaving ultimately ended up being a good thing for us all. Sadly, Morrigan couldn't make Saoirse immortal again. Under Dagda's laws, humans and immortals couldn't be married, so her banishment nullified our marriage.

"Gabriel secretly married your mother. Those of us who knew of the marriage never disclosed it to anyone. Saoirse was pregnant with you when Dagda unleashed his wrath. I didn't want your mother to endure any additional hardship, and even though the affair had occurred, I genuinely liked Gabriel. I also understood how Saoirse and he could fall in love after our marriage deteriorated. I never made her happy. He understood her in a way that, even though I tried my damnedest to, I just couldn't."

Caitlin picked up her glass and took a long drink from it. She needed something to slow her racing heart. "I can't believe Gabriel did such a thing. That he had an affair with a married woman and risked a death sentence by taking a wife, and not just any wife, but a cursed daughter of the gods. He was always held up as a role model for younger officers to emulate."

"Gabriel was an outstanding officer and a loving father, as much as he could be, Caitlin. He's rightly held up as one others should strive to be like." Sean defended the Horseman Caitlin started to judge. "None of us are fault free."

"He engaged in an affair and got my mother banished on top of never telling me the truth. How could you possibly agree he should be held up as the shining example of integrity?" Caitlin snapped, angry no one had ever told her the truth before today.

"Gabriel split his life between being a Horseman and pretending to be a mortal blacksmith to be with you and your mother. He wanted desperately to tell you he was your father. Fear of what the Council might do and losing his daughter like he lost Saoirse prevented him from doing so. His fear was not unjustified. You weren't wrong when you accused the deities of being cruel and unjust after Morrigan announced your betrothal to Gaelin. If Gabriel had been alive at the time, the truth would have come out then. He wouldn't have allowed the marriage to proceed. He had high hopes that one day you and Dante might find happiness together. Morrigan and Raphael pushed the Council to alter the law forbidding Horsemen from marrying to prevent a repeat of your parents' experience after it appeared you and Dante might be following in their footsteps."

Caitlin scoffed at the thought of being Dante's wife. At least the Fates had spared her that. "Yet, none of you honored my father's supposed wishes. And what exactly happened to my mother since it sounds like most of what I've been told was only a half-truth or a blatant lie?"

"We did what was needed to protect you, Cate. There are a great many things you don't know and never will. As to what happened to your mother, there was an uprising in the mortal realm while Gabriel was in Sasainn. Your mother was killed in that conflict. Gabriel and I left Sasainn as soon as word of the fighting reached Morrigan, but we arrived too late. Your nightmares of monsters under the bed are from that day. We found you hiding under your mother's bed. Saoirse had told you to go under there and not come out until she came and got you or you could no longer hear fighting. I'll never forget your terrified face when I raised the blanket to retrieve you while Gabriel rushed Saoirse back to Morrigan in hopes of saving her."

Caitlin shook her head. "I can't believe after what happened to my mother Gram would have the nerve to send me down the same path."

"Morrigan wasn't sending you down the same path. She raised you to fight, in contrast to Saoirse's upbringing. She did everything she could to prepare you for your future, Caitlin. Morrigan fears you dying more than anything else and worries about you constantly."

"I find that hard to believe, especially with her marrying me off to Gaelin."

Sean sighed and leaned back in his chair. His fingers idly twirled his now empty wine glass on the table. "Morrigan never has fully explained her reasoning behind that to me. She only insists the Fates said it was the catalyst which would start you and Dante down the path to a greater destiny. While I severely question Dante's supposed prophesied future, the doomed marriage most certainly did when it comes to you. You never would have joined the Order of the Medica if Morrigan hadn't accepted the marriage proposal."

"I could have." Caitlin didn't want to hear any more about fate or destiny.

Sean chuckled. "We both know you only did that to escape Gaelin and to spite your grandmother. And I, for one, am thankful you did. Becoming a healer brought you Evariste, and I've never seen you happier with anyone else."

Caitlin stared down at her hands. *Happiness that would be fleeting.* She forced that thought into the recesses of her mind so neither Sean nor Gage would hear it. Everything she thought she knew was a lie, and she'd follow in her father's footsteps if what Dante said was true about Gage dying. "I think you should go, Sean. I'm tired and want to spend time with my husband after everything today."

"Good night, Cate." Sean left as she asked him to.

Transparent pear-shaped drops carved warm, glistening trails down her face when she could no longer hold them back.

"Caitlin." Gage drew her from her chair into his lap.

She wept into her his shoulder, wishing she was someone else, wishing Dante had never told her of what was to come, wishing Sean and Morrigan hadn't kept the truth from her.

"Whatever Dante shared, we will survive it." Gage held her tighter after catching that portion of her reeling thoughts. "We will get through all of this. If we've managed to find one another and start over in two other lifetimes, we will in this one."

His words brought on a fresh round of agony. It took every ounce of strength she had not to utter no, we won't. We're doomed like my parents. Dagda's curse follows us, too. A soul-wrenching sob fell from her lips. She collapsed into Gage's chest, needing his strength, his confidence to face a dark future.

Gage quietly sat with her until she could cry no more. "Go clean yourself up, cher. You're too beautiful a woman to have tear-streaked cheeks."

She sadly smiled at him. "As long as you stay right here."

"I won't leave my chair. Not even the Horsemen are capable of dragging me away." Gage pressed his lips to her forehead in a soothing kiss.

Caitlin went to the hall bathroom and washed her face and hands. She ran her fingers through her hair to try and straighten it a bit. Pulling herself together, she returned to the dining room. Gage still sat at the table as promised.

"I didn't even leave my seat to put the dirty dishes away since I promised you I wouldn't move."

Caitlin sat in his lap and drew his face toward hers. "Make love to me, Gage."

"Are you certain that's what you need right now?"

By the way he hesitated to kiss her, he must think she had lost her mind to go from crying her eyes out to wanting the one thing that made her forget everything she ever knew. And forgetting was what she wanted to do most at the moment. "Your love is exactly what I need, tonight, and forever."

The constantly simmering passion between them quickly flared into wild urgency the longer they kissed. Gage shoved the dishes off the table. They shattered against the tile. He laid Caitlin back against the mahogany top.

Caitlin pictured them naked; Gage pinning her down and thrusting into her. She opened her eyes when Gage huskily laughed, finding them exactly as she had pictured a second ago.

"My sorceress, if you are going to keep doing things like this, I can't promise to make love to you," Gage whispered, slowly drawing himself almost completely out of her; his lips curving upward in a sensuous smirk. "Not when your soul is crying out to be fucked instead."

A startled but pleasured cry left her lips as he slammed himself into her. Her nails raked across his shoulder; their bodies frantically collided against the table.

"Evariste!" she screamed, gripping a handful of his hair while her hand clutched his arm. "Yes, Gage. Yes, harder!"

A loud groan filled her ears. Gage more forcefully drew her into him while his hips bucked forward. The slapping of their bodies echoed through the dining room. She loved how Gage no longer held the vampire back anytime he took her. He let the beast freely rage. Tonight, her own lustful cravings equally matched his. He lifted her off the table as she neared climax, his teeth sinking into the spot her neck and shoulder met. White and blue bursts of light erased the darkness behind her closed lids, her body rippled and seized around Gage's. By the way his skin quivered then his muscles violently shook, he came with her.

"No!" she rasped against his neck, more firmly locking her legs around him when he set her backdown and started to withdraw. "Not yet."

Gage quietly laughed, bringing their bodies together. "Have I somehow turned you with as demanding as you've become the past few days, cher?"

"Maybe." Caitlin smiled as their noses brushed against one another.

"Maybe?" Gage's palm drifted down her back before settling in the curve of her waist. "Whatever is causing this, I hope it's a permanent thing. I'm enjoying the ravenous, lustful little monster you've turned into."

Return To The Past

〜

D'Orme – 1715

Gage held Caitlin's hand as they walked through their recently cleared yard toward their newly built house.

"Wow! Everything looks so different, so wild." Caitlin took in the endless expanse of trees surrounding D'Orme.

"The French are only just arriving." Gage smiled, looking around himself.

In all his years, he couldn't recall experiencing such a mix of dread and hope at the same time. He never thought he'd stand where he did again. Unlike Caitlin and Sean, he couldn't regularly time travel on his own. The best he could do was teleport fifty or so miles in any direction. Either Morrigan or the Fates sent them from Antiquity to the eighteenth century to escape Baracus after they made such a desperate bargain for a new beginning.

The first time he heard the name Antoine Bonin after stepping onto new shores he thought nothing of it. Surprised, when he met the elderly gentleman claiming to be his grandfather, Gage listened to the strange tale Bonin spun about searching for him. It offered enough evidence to convince Gage the man didn't lie to him. Six months later, malaria and dysentery from a contaminated fresh water supply swept through the small colony killing Bonin—or so Gage thought until fourteen years later when Caitlin was murdered and his own grandfather turned him into one of the undead.

"We aren't running again, and you aren't winning this round," Gage muttered under his breath, his eyes skimming the landscape for any sign of Bonin, or rather Baracus, lurking in the nearby swamps. Nothing moved, not even the wind blew the leaves on the trees. His ears picked up bird calls, the occasional croaking of an alligator, and the soft burbling of water from a stream flowing into the surrounding bayous, but not the odd fluttering sound of a vampire stalking through the woods. Baracus didn't know they were there.

"The house looks smaller than it did in modern day." Caitlin pulled Gage out of his current thoughts.

"I expanded the original floor plan two years from now and then again after a fire destroyed half the house in 1830." Gage lovingly ran his hand across one of the wood porch rails he had personally cut, sanded, and shaped.

"A fire?" Caitlin started at that news.

"Yes. D'Orme was set ablaze twice. The first fire I put out before it could do any damage. The second one, well, I wasn't fortunate enough to be home when the fire started. By the time it was discovered, we had lost the front half, but we managed to salvage the rear portion and the new wing I added."

"You make both fires sound like arson, not an accident of some type."

"That's because they were. The first attempt was to silence me after I challenged the introduction of slave codes in the state. The second time was because I harbored a group of runaway slaves that a bounty hunter was after."

"An abolitionist was a dangerous thing to be back then, especially in the South," Caitlin said, remembering her history classes and Gage's distaste for slavery in Antiquity.

"I would never call myself an abolitionist. While I loathed slavery once it was established here, the threats against my family and property for my beliefs caused me to stop publicly speaking out. I silently aided those seeking freedom instead. My continued private discourse with the governor and the state lawmakers trying to change things also earned me almost every vampire and human plantation owner's animosity from New Orleans to Alexandria. I can't tell you how many times my books were audited or ships inspected delaying deliveries as punishment." Gage stared up at the ornate decorations above the front door and at the tops of the columns. He hadn't replaced the ones around the front door after the second fire.

"You never embraced plantation life, did you?"

"No. How could you think I would after what happened in Britain to you or knowing what you do about my mother back then?" Gage's irritation at her asking the question caused a woman's face to appear in his mind. Her dark hair and brown eyes along with the kind smile on her face differed from Helene's, but he knew the smiling woman was his mother.

"What's wrong?"

"Nothing. Just a flash of memory. The past is still returning. I remember more and more each day."

"There's more to not liking slavery than your mother, isn't there?"

"She's the main reason I hate it." Another memory of him as a teen in chains being traded as a hostage by Baracus surfaced followed by a second of his father negotiating for his freedom. He would figure out these strange glimpses of the past after they dealt with the trouble Baracus caused in the present. "When it comes to my agricultural pursuits here in Louisiana, I only farmed enough land to feed my family and myself. I ventured into large scale farming once I could afford to pay freedmen and family members to grow a few things. Pierre turned the agricultural venture into what is today while Alcee and I focused on shipping the goods he and others grew. We also sold the timber from the land we cleared to grow crops turning a nice profit."

"I'm amazed at what you've done over the centuries."

"Having the good fortune of being willing to leave Europe for the New World and plenty of time to recover from my failures when I made them in this country enabled me to do more than many others ever really have the opportunity to do. But I'd give up D'Orme, the company, and my fortune for you, cher, as well as the child we lost, or rather will lose only a few months from now. I'd rather be a poor man who spent a lifetime with his wife and child than ever endure what we did again." He drew Caitlin to him, the raw wound of losing a child torn open again with finding himself back in the past and seeing Caitlin in period dress.

"Maybe the Fates will bless us with more to make up for the one Baracus took," Caitlin whispered, her own voice wavering.

"A child is out of the realm of possibility for us, cher. But maybe we can adopt if we survive this." Gage forced himself to let go of the unexpected grief gripping him. "Let's go inside. It's not often one gets to revisit the past or some deranged elf sends your past selves from your home on some random venture. Do you think we'll remember Sean doing so after all is said and done?"

"I don't know, and Sean wouldn't like you calling him a deranged elf. Fae are sensitive about that kind of thing."

"Then I probably shouldn't ask how he hides those pointy ears in modern day like he does." Gage opened the front door for them.

Caitlin lightly hit his chest and laughed. "You're just asking for it like Dante does by antagonizing him. I won't feel sorry for you if Sean slips holy water into your next drink."

Gage grinned and his eyebrows lifted, thoroughly entertained by the thought of Sean attempting such a thing. "I tend to like drinks that burn on the way down."

"How about a stake through the heart or a brick between the teeth?" Sean frostily inquired, eyeing the couple in the doorway.

"You are touchy about your ears, aren't you?" Gage intentionally tried to rile the guide that nothing ever seemed to phase.

"It was the deranged elf comment more than being touchy about 'my pointy ears', which heard every word you just uttered very clearly." Sean turned to rejoin the group sitting around the large table. "We've been wondering when you two would finally show up."

"Who's we?" Gage traversed the foyer to find Alcee, Dante, Pierre, and Rayne sitting around the wooden table inside the living room.

"The troops are in place and the joyous news of the next Arsceneaux being conceived is circulating. We need Caitlin to confirm it for your sisters. Or more accurately, your cousins," Dante said, spinning a dagger between his fingers.

Confused by what Dante said, Gage looked at Alcee and Pierre. "My cousins?"

"Perhaps, it's best he hears it from me since he doesn't remember yet." Pierre set a hand on Alcee's arm when the vampire opened his mouth to elaborate on Dante's statement. "Evariste, I love you like a son, but you know I'm not your father. Helene isn't your mother, she's your aunt. Alcee asked us to help hide you from Baracus. We agreed to do so. You have no siblings, by blood anyway."

Shocked, Gage sat down in the empty chair the others had left for him. "Do the girls know?"

"No." Pierre shook his head. "They were so young when this all started, they have no idea you're not really their older brother. I don't see a need to tell them otherwise, but I will leave that up to you. Truthfully, I don't think they'll care as their feelings won't change toward you. I hope yours don't toward us as we are still family."

"I need some time to digest this, but I'm glad to hear things most likely won't change." Gage managed to muster an uncertain smile for Pierre then shot Alcee an irritated glance. "But I may have a new business partner if I find out he has withheld any other information like this."

Amused by the threat, Alcee laughed. "No one else would want to co-own a business with such a moody individual who'd rather be outside fishing or sailing than in the office running things."

"Did we ever find out who is passing information along to Baracus?" Caitlin inquired

The angst that had temporarily retreated returned after Caitlin's inquiry. Gage couldn't bring himself to look at her with how close Alli and Caitlin had gotten over the past few weeks. "We're almost certain it's Alli."

"Alli? It can't be her. She'd never do anything to hurt you, Gage." Caitlin rejected the conclusion the men in the room had arrived at.

"She isn't doing it maliciously. She doesn't know who she's talking to. Remember the boy in the tree line? The one who cried for his mother in

French and led you astray?" Gage finally stared Caitlin in the face. Her lovely lavender eyes rounded in surprise, confirming she remembered her first encounter with Baracus at D'Orme. "Rayne spotted her chatting happily with a boy similar in appearance. There are no neighboring families with boys his age. Most likely, she innocently shares the news she is going to be an aunt in a discussion with him—or rather, Baracus. Dante will shadow her to confirm our suspicions after you have tea with the girls in an hour."

The troubled expression on her face warned everyone in the room she struggled with the news. "Should I caution her not to tell anyone?"

"No." Dante straightened in his chair. "We don't want to stop the information from reaching Baracus."

"Fine." Caitlin took a deep breath. "What day is it, Gage?"

"August twentieth of 1715."

Caitlin looked over at Dante. "This may not work. I don't find out I'm pregnant for another month or so. What if Baracus is smart enough to know that, or future Tristan or whatever his name really is warns him the rumors are false?"

"Let's hope neither have any type of foresight at the moment," Sean calmly said as Gage reassuringly settled an arm around her.

"Who's to say you're not carrying Gage's child? Medicine is drastically behind when it comes to women's health this day and age." Dante startled everyone at the table. "The babe could have been conceived recently or even a week or two ago. Did you summon the physician immediately after you missed your menses or did you wait awhile as I suspect you would as a mortal?"

"I waited to confirm in case my cycle was off." A smile slowly crossed Caitlin's face. "You're smarter than I give you credit for being, Dante."

Giving her a sideways glance, Dante's left brow shot upward in mock exasperation before the corner of his mouth curved into a lopsided grin.

Rayne chuckled beside his commander. "Don't tell him that, Caitlin. His ego is big enough as it is."

Dante scoffed and rolled his eyes, elbowing Rayne. "That was insubordinate. Be careful you don't find yourself on report, Captain."

Caitlin couldn't help chuckling at the two Horsemen. Something about their banter eased her nerves.

Dante's golden gaze turned back in her direction. "You, Pierre, and Gage need to leave for your tea, Rosso. Horse and carriage don't travel as fast as a car."

"I suppose we should go hitch the horse up." Gage stood, trying to remember how to do exactly that as he hadn't done such a thing in years.

Pierre winked at Gage. "Already done. We were just sitting around waiting on you and Caitlin to get here."

"Well then, let's go get the carriage and drive it round the front."

CAITLIN WAITED on the front porch with Rayne and Dante. She set a hand on Dante's arm, interrupting his conversation with Rayne. "Commander?"

"Si, Rosso?"

"A moment of your time." She crooked her head to her right, signaling she wanted to keep things between them.

Dante and Rayne exchanged puzzled looks before Dante gave her his attention again. The Horseman frowned but stepped away from Rayne. "Anytime you've ever spoken that phrase, I've regretted agreeing to it. What is it you require of me, Caitlin?"

"If I'm.... and we succeed in killing Baracus...." Caitlin couldn't finish her statement knowing Gage's fate. Her thoughts danced between it isn't possible and if we face Baracus and Gage dies, does past Caitlin become a widow who has to raise a child in Colonial Louisiana?

Dante gently grasped her arm. "Cara, you unnecessarily burden yourself. Stop doing so. What you imagine is highly unlikely."

"But what if the points you brought up a few minutes ago are valid. What if there is a child?"

"Then let us pray your past self will embrace the child as a welcomed gift."

"I need to know, Dante. Death can see, you can see if —" Caitlin pulled his hand toward her belly.

Dante shook his head, twisting his hand free from her grip. "No, Rosso. This time I am blind in the matter. Do not add more sorrow to your plate."

"I want what they took, Dante. What they are still planning to take." Caitlin looked down at the wooden planks beneath her feet, silently cursing the Fates, Baracus, and her own grandfather to hell.

Dante's fingers curled under her chin, lifting her face, so they gazed at one another once more. Golden eyes offered empathy for the difficulties she faced. "If it were in my power, I would gift you everything your heart desires. Unfortunately, it isn't. You're a strong woman, Caitlin. Call upon that strength in what is to come."

The creaking of carriage wheels and the jingling of a harness warned Gage and Pierre returned. Dante's hand fell from her face. He retreated back to stand beside Rayne.

"Ready to go?" Gage called, stepping out of the open carriage Pierre drove.

"Yes." Caitlin gathered her skirts before coming down the steps.

Gage set a wooden step stool down then offered Caitlin his hand to help her into the carriage.

"Thank you." Caitlin cast a quick glance back at the two Horsemen on the porch before climbing in.

Gage caught the perturbed look. "Is everything okay?"

"It's fine. I'm just nervous. We're in the open with no protection spell over D'Orme, and having the Horsemen lurking about isn't helping calm me any." Caitlin smoothed her skirts then looked over at Dante and Rayne again.

"We can always ask them to leave."

Caitlin smiled over at the vampire she had married in three lifetimes now. "Once my grandmother issues an order, those four won't disobey it. They'd just hide in the shadows."

History Repeats Itself

Fear steadily closed its wispy, cold fingers around Caitlin. Every slight noise from the wooden floorboards creaking, the wind blowing against the windows, to the random owl hoot outside sent her heart racing. Waiting for Baracus to make the next move was more nerve-racking than anything she had ever experienced before. Not even the protective armor and uniform Sean insisted she and Gage wear quieted the sense of foreboding whittling away her confidence to defeat Baracus.

You were once the Morte Defensore, a fierce warrior like your grandmother, and a sorceress like your mother. You can beat Baracus, Caitlin silently repeated over and over to herself.

Not liking how easily Caitlin spooked at everything or the phrases circling her head, Gage frowned. Nothing he said or did eased her nerves. "Caitlin, let's go to bed."

"He's right. Rest will keep you sharp for the fight to come." Sean set a fatherly hand on Caitlin's shoulder. "Find courage, *a leanbh*. You'll know what to do when the time comes. In the meantime, there is a small army watching over you."

Caitlin hugged Sean. "Thank you, for always being there. You didn't have to be." The soft laughter she heard and the shaking of his chest surprised Caitlin. She pulled back to look up into the glass-like blue eyes of the guide always there when she needed him.

"It was an honor to stand in Gabriel's stead. Perhaps when this is all over, we will pay him and your mother a visit. You did promise Gram you'd consider returning to Sasainn later this year."

Caitlin sadly smiled at the thought of visiting her parents' graves now that she knew who her father was. She always wondered why Morrigan chose to bury Gabriel beside her mother. "Good night, Sean."

"Good night, Cate."

Caitlin took the hand Evariste extended to her then followed him up the stairs to their bedroom.

GAGE HALTED at the top of the stairs. Something wasn't right. He pulled Caitlin closer to him, his eyes searching the darkened hallway.

"What is it?" Caitlin asked, after Gage's back stiffened.

"I'm not sure. I don't sense anyone here, but something feels off. Stay close to me." Gage cautiously pushed open the bedroom door.

No one was in the room. However, the balcony doors were wide open when they had been shut earlier.

Sean, he silently called to the guide downstairs before entering the bedroom.

Caitlin followed him through the doorway. "It's fine, Gage. I think we're both on edge and our imaginations are running wild."

"Hello, Evariste. I've been wondering when you'd finally come to bed." Baracus stepped into the bedroom from the balcony.

Tristan slammed the interior door shut behind them.

A maniacal smile etched itself across Baracus's face. "Congratulations are in order based on what I heard whispered today."

Gage pushed Caitlin behind him. She could fight off Tristan easier than she could Baracus. "Consider them extended. Now, leave."

"How did you even get in here?" Caitlin naively asked.

Baracus snickered at the inquiry. "Evariste extended an open invitation to his dear old grandfather before he passed. Why do you think Lachesis enchanted the property to keep me out? You should have chosen another century to confront me, Evariste. Now, turn over your wife, and she might live this time."

Sean shattered the bedroom door, startling them all. He shoved Tristan aside and headed toward Baracus.

"Run, Caitlin!" Gage shouted, throwing the hurricane lamp in his hand at Baracus. A line of flame shot up forcing his grandfather back onto the balcony.

"The house, Evariste."

"Forget the house, cher. Get out of here! I'll find you shortly."

Gage crossed the wall of flame to confront his grandfather.

Sean restrained Tristan so Caitlin could safely make it to the stairs.

Her lungs felt as if they would burst between inhaling smoke and sprinting down the steps, through the woods, and into one of the nearby cane fields.

"Find her and bring her to me," Baracus barked the order at Tristan before leaping off the balcony.

Tristan vanished from Sean's grip. If he had a second longer, Sean would have hexed Tristan so the vampire couldn't teleport.

Evariste swung a leg over the balcony rail then yelled to Sean, "There'll be more of them hunting Caitlin. Help her get to the Horsemen. I'll take care of Baracus!"

TRISTAN and several other vampires methodically swept through the woods and headlands, searching for the woman. Not seeing any sign of her, Tristan entered the closest cane field. He smiled as he discovered Caitlin crouched down in between the rows of tall stalks, silently creeping toward the bayou.

Hearing a loud crunch as he stepped on an old piece of cut cane, she scrambled backward, hoping to escape him. He pounced on her. Unlike the prior attack where she was too frightened to effectively defend herself, tonight, she brought her knee to his groin. His body instinctively recoiled enough that she was able to shove him off her. He reached out and caught her ankle, tripping her after she regained her footing. Without thinking, she slammed her free booted foot into his face, shattering his nose and busting his lower lip.

"Didn't expect you to fight so viciously this time around, Cate." Tristan ignored the blood pouring from his nose. "I'm going to enjoy this much more than I thought I would."

Caitlin flung dirt in his face, hoping to blind him before climbing to her feet. Instead of running, she pulled the dagger hanging on her side and backed into an open space between the fields.

Tristan laughed at her determined expression as she countered each step he took. "What does a healer know about wielding a blade?"

He lunged at her. Caitlin anchored herself for the impact she knew was coming. At the last second, she twisted, so his teeth missed her neck, driving her dagger into his stomach then yanking it up his sternum, cracking bone. "I'm no helpless healer or mortal tonight." Her elbow collided with his jaw, sending him sideways. She jerked her knife free from his torso.

Hearing racing hoofbeats approaching on her right, Caitlin shifted position, regrouping for Tristan's next attack. A short, sharp whistle only a few feet from her brought a smile to her face. Dante tossed her saber to her as he passed. The Horseman riding by distracted Tristan long enough for Caitlin to unsheathe the blade. She again drove her dagger into his heart, almost enjoying the disbelief on the dying vampire's face, then swung the sword in her other hand, beheading him. His body collapsed to the ground.

A hand clamped down over her mouth. She found herself drawn back into a strong chest. A welcoming calm fell over her.

"Shhhh...you're okay, cher," Gage whispered in her ear, thankful he found where she ran to before Baracus did. He smiled when she embraced him. Not wanting to lose track of the other vampires moving around them, he quickly glanced down to make sure she wasn't injured. Grateful she wasn't, Gage offered a quick prayer of thanks to the deities watching over them.

Two Horsemen appeared on either side of Caitlin and Gage, bracketing them in a wall of lethality to keep those hunting Caitlin at bay.

Dante wheeled his horse around, watching the outlines of several vampires he could see in the moonlight. "We'll take care of the hunting party to even the odds a bit. Protect Caitlin and yourself, Arsceneaux."

The Horsemen blended into the night. Ancient magic muffled their horses movements. If it weren't for the periodic thud of a body striking ground and the random cry of a vampire being skewered by their blades, no one would know the harbingers rode the edges of the field.

Caitlin and Gage fought any vampires that managed to slip past the Horsemen silently decimating their numbers.

Sean materialized beside her and Gage. "We need to keep to the Horsemen's center. The damage they're wreaking is keeping the majority of Baracus's minions back, but Baracus will rally them sooner or later. Hopefully, he will come out of whatever hole he's crawled into soon."

Gage spotted his grandfather observing the chaos from the far end of the field. "He's trying to wear us down. I'm ending this. Now."

"Gage, wait!" Caitlin tried to stop him, but he vanished into the night.

One of the more powerful vampires in Baracus's ranks managed to get past the Horsemen and grabbed Caitlin from behind. She grasped his forearms, caught him with her hip, and flung him over her head. Startled, the vampire lay in the grass blinking up at her. She slammed her sword through his heart before he could attack again. With her attacker dead, she scanned the field for Gage. He shouldn't have gone after Baracus alone. They had promised to confront him together. She found him and Baracus dueling on the opposite side of the field. Alcee was the closest to them.

"Alcee!" she screamed, hoping the vampire could hear her.

Thankfully, Alcee turned in her direction. She pointed at Gage and Baracus. The older vampire ran to assist Gage in fighting his grandfather.

Another vampire barreled into her, sending her to the ground. He jumped on top of her, trying to pin her down.

"What is it with vampires wanting me on my back so much?"

"Isn't that the position women belong in?" He laughed; his fangs protruding only an inch or so from her neck.

Caitlin thrust her dagger into his abdomen. "I'm not a get down to

361

business kind of girl. I need some type of foreplay." She twisted the blade. "At least take me to diner or something."

Sean's sword separated the vampire's head from his shoulders. "If you are done messing around, we have work to do."

"What type of bodyguard are you to let a guy other than my husband get that fresh with me?" Caitlin shoved the vampire carcass from her then took Sean's hand. He pulled her to her feet.

"Been a little busy fighting off your other suitors." Sean grinned as two more of Baracus's men approached them. "You do attract the strange ones, don't you?"

They stood back-to-back, watching the new vampires.

"How are Gage and Alcee doing with Baracus?" Caitlin asked, not trusting herself to take her eyes off the vampire before her.

Sean looked over to see Gage, Alcee, and Baracus still engaged.

"Holding their own," Sean responded as the two vampires finally attacked him and Caitlin.

"Go help them!" Caitlin shouted as she locked swords with one of the immortals. She cried out as something stung her from behind in the small gap by her shoulder where the armor protecting her chest and back slightly separated.

ALCEE AND GAGE had Baracus pinned on the ground when the arrow struck Caitlin. After hearing her cry, Gage turned his head to make sure she was okay. Relief flooded through him as she looked toward her side then yanked out the arrow.

Baracus took advantage of Gage's checking on his wife and sprang to his feet.

Gage cursed at the error he made as he blocked his grandfather's sword an inch from his face.

CAITLIN THREW the arrow on the ground. *Where had it come from?* The wound it left behind hurt like hell but wasn't fatal. She looked up to see Gage fall under Baracus's relentless pummeling strikes.

"Gage!" Caitlin screamed, running toward Baracus and her husband.

"Caitlin, wait!" Sean yelled, finishing off the man he was fighting.

Hearing Sean's warning, Dante glanced up from the vampire he just killed.

THE WORLD SEEMED to be in slow motion as Gage defended himself from the ground.

Baracus ruthlessly dealt blow after blow, trying to kill his grandson. "I need the sorceress, Evariste. All you had to do was stay out of my way, and I would have let you live."

"You cannot have my wife!" Gage used the bracers covering his forearms to deflect another blow from Baracus's blade.

Baracus drove his sword through Gage's armor, piercing his heart and lungs.

Lilth

D ante grabbed Caitlin's wrist and yanked her backward, speaking to her in Gaelic, so she did not turn her blade in his direction. He wrapped his arms around her, holding onto her as she fought for her freedom.

"Release me, Giovanni!" Caitlin ordered, horrified at the scene unfolding in front of her.

Baracus brought his sword down through Gage's cuirass a second time.

The bloodcurdling wail escaping Caitlin's lips sent an urge to let her go to Gage through Dante's entire being. He struggled to keep her against him. "You cannot engage Baracus. He is still too powerful."

"You told me I had a choice, but you keep me from helping him!" Caitlin stared down at her hands, unable to use the magic she possessed any longer. Dante had syphoned her power away. "Let me go, Dante! Please!"

Dante hated the pain he caused her. "Forgive me, Caitlin. I cannot let you face Baracus alone."

She stared up into iridescent golden eyes. "I'm not alone. You're with me. We can take him."

Dante's eyes widening after drifting to hers caused her to look in the direction of Gage and Baracus again. Baracus jerked his sword out of Gage's chest. A red river streamed from the wound, weaving its way down Gage's side into dark soil; the volume of the rapid flow making the dirt liquescent beneath the right side of the dying vampire.

"Gage!" Caitlin threw all her weight against Dante's arms.

Dante grimaced, refusing to loosen his hold. "Only a moment longer, Rosso. The others are coming. Trust me."

Baracus looked in their direction. "You are next, witch."

GAGE TURNED HIS HEAD, his eyes searching the night for a last glimpse of his wife. A fleeting smile curved his lips once they locked on her fighting to get free of Dante. She was safe; surrounded by the immortals who always watched over them. Baracus's days of terror were at an end with him having to confront the Horsemen and Sean if he wanted Caitlin.

I love you. He hoped she heard the faint words he sent to her.

"DAMN IT! LET GO OF ME!" Caitlin slammed an elbow back into Dante's side. "While there's still a chance of saving him!"

The hard blow sent a smarting thwap through Dante's rib cage. He cursed, glancing over at Sean then released her as she wanted.

Finding herself free, Caitlin bolted forward. The five other immortals on the field surrounded her, charging Baracus as a unified group.

Vampires poured from the trees after Baracus called for reinforcements.

"Keep them all back!" Caitlin directed, sliding on her knees the last foot to Gage.

While the Four Horsemen eliminated the new vampires, Sean and Alcee forced Baracus back, so Caitlin could tend to Gage.

"We're not parting this time, Evariste Arsceneaux. We promised one another we wouldn't." Caitlin cut the straps to his cuirass, yanked it off then ripped open his shirt. The white shimmer of bone shone through the wounds in his chest. A wide gash ran the length of his neck. The way he wheezed with every breath warned fluid filled his ailing lungs. She whispered in Gaelic and brought his hand to her face while placing her other hand over his heart, willing his body to heal.

"Caitlin, finish him," Gage weakly whispered.

She shook her head, slipping her hands under his shoulders to reposition his body. "We will finish him together."

Gage closed his eyes as she lifted and pulled him into her lap.

"Medica, you can't save me from these wounds. I've lost too much blood to heal."

"You will be fine, Decurion. I refuse to let you go." Caitlin drew her dagger from its sheath on her side.

"Kill Baracus, so we have a chance in our next life." Gage struggled to sputter out the words, the forcing of air through his lungs caused him to cough up some of the blood now slowly drowning him.

Slicing her wrist open, Caitlin winced. "Drink, Arsceneaux. I'll never forgive you if you don't."

Gage took the wrist she offered to him. He stared up at her briefly before latching onto her. The viciousness of his bite brought a pain-filled scream from Caitlin. Memories of the two of them together flowed through her until his jaw loosened and his canines slipped free from her skin.

"No, Evariste! We fought so hard to overcome." She cradled his lifeless body against her. He was gone.

A tormented cry left her lips.

Earth and air trembled, reverberating her wrath and grief from being torn from her soulmate again.

Sean looked back over his shoulder, concerned that she might take her own life with how long she sat staring down at Gage's body.

"She is stronger than that," Dante yelled at Sean then glanced over at Caitlin.

Searching for strength, Caitlin rocked back and forth, clutching Gage to her, weeping into the dead man's chest.

"Come on, Rosso. Fight for the both of you," Dante mumbled, willing her to stand, to go after Baracus as they all had hoped she would.

Sean signaled Rayne and Dante to prepare to execute Baracus since it appeared Caitlin wouldn't do so.

Give her another moment. Dante silently argued with Sean. *She needs to do this.*

She's faltering, Dante. Your plan failed. Now do as the Council originally instructed and finish Baracus. Caitlin and Gage will earn the chance to break the curse of being ill-fated in another life. Sean raised his sword, walking toward Baracus.

Dante teleported between Sean and Baracus. "Don't, Sean. Don't put her through this again."

"I told Morrigan you were the wrong one for this tasking. Your heart always came between you and your better judgement when it came to Caitlin. Now stand aside, Commander. So I can do what you won't."

Sean's words roused Caitlin out of the haze of grief and anger.

"Baracus!" she growled out in an inhuman voice, standing up and stopping everything in motion around them.

Vampires and the other three Horsemen stood frozen like statues created to depict an ancient battle. The breeze no longer blew, the cicadas no longer sang, and the earth no longer even spun. Time itself stopped. Only Sean, Dante, Alcee, Baracus, and herself remained free of the spell.

"You are more powerful than I thought, witch," Baracus said, amused by what she had done.

Caitlin picked up Gage's sword and spun it once, learning where the weight was to balance it properly as she fought. She turned to face Baracus. The vampire from Gage merged with her own powers. Neon purple eyes and distorted features locked on the Roman responsible for all their suffering. Without saying a word, she lunged at Baracus. He barely had a chance to bring his weapon up to block the blade sailing toward him.

She fought him with more strength and skill than he ever anticipated her having. They went several rounds alternating conqueror and conquered.

Baracus didn't understand how she switched between the fighting technique of a Roman soldier and however she had been trained. The woman was supposed to be a healer and sorceress, not a swordsman. "How is it you fight with the same technique as my grandson?"

"We share a blood bond, and I was once the Morte Defensore, the female equivalent of Death, you fool. Did you learn nothing about me or Morrigan while you were in Britannia?" Caitlin swung at his legs. The blade collided with the side of his knee, dropping him to the ground. "To think you were once called the most feared man in Rome. Look at you now, bested by a heathen."

Baracus regained his feet but found his sword heavier and heavier to lift. "What trickery are you using on me, witch? At least defeat me in a fair fight."

"No trickery, Baracus. No spells. You're merely tired. I wouldn't use magic against you. I want the world to know a Celtic woman defeated the great Baracus."

Caitlin locked swords with him again. Despair fueled her merciless blows. She gradually overtook Baracus as his attacks slowed and weariness made him falter. "Yield to me."

Baracus fell to his knees again. "Kill me, witch. I won't surrender."

Caitlin sinisterly smiled, dropping her sword and grabbing a handful of Baracus's hair. "You'll die soon enough."

She jerked his head back as he had done to Gage and her long ago; ensuring his jugular was exposed.

Sean realized what she intended to do. "Caitlin, no! There's another way. She'll decimate you!"

Calling on what part of Gage remained within her, Caitlin sunk her teeth into Baracus's neck. An orange glow came from under her lips.

Baracus shrieked. The sensation of heated iron burned his skin then molten energy flowed into his veins. "What in Hades's name are you?"

Caitlin searched his memories until she found the exact one she wanted: an image of a female vampire with wine-colored hair seducing Baracus. Taking Baracus's blood connected her to Lilith as she hoped it would. Lilith's eyes opened and locked on her as she watched Lilith feed from Baracus. Past and present intermingled in the temporal plane only souls and dark magic walked.

Caitlin threw her head back from Baracus's neck. "Lilith! Your throne for a soul!"

The earth tremored again as the oldest vampire in creation emerged from beneath the dark soil of the field.

"How dare you challenge me, daughter of Morrigan!" Lilith hissed, enraged at being dragged across the expanse of time. This foolish sorceress interrupted her feasting on her favorite blood slave.

Caitlin yanked Baracus's head up so Lilith could see his face. "Give me back my husband, or I'll slay this pathetic excuse of a vampire you call a son then you."

"I cannot give you what I do not have." Lilith stared at the rings on her hand as if bored by her.

"Return my husband's soul, or I will hunt down each of your children and butcher them one by one until there are no more left to feed you. We both know it is their lives and your feeding combined that sustains you. Without them, you die."

Lilith's icy gaze locked on Caitlin. "You do not have the courage, little one. Not even you are foolish enough to invoke my wrath."

"You leave me no choice, Lilith." Caitlin swung Gage's sword, intending to behead Baracus.

Dante caught her wrist, halting her blade mere inches from Baracus. "You do not have sanction to take his life."

Caitlin's arm shook from straining against Dante's grasp and the weight of the blade in her hand. For a brief second, the Horseman's face went out of focus as furious tears clouded her vision. "Gage is dead, Dante. Let the Council damn me to Tartarus for executing a viable threat to the realms."

Dante's fingers slowly crept over her hand then wrapped around hers and the sword hilt clasped tightly in them. "Protecting the realms is no longer your charge. It's mine. Allow Death to perform his duties."

Dante's eyes shifted to their right, warning Caitlin of danger from behind. The Horseman seized a hold of her waist then pivoted with her, so they changed places. Stunned, Caitlin found herself staring at Lilith over Dante's shoulder. She hadn't sensed or heard the vampire's coming upon them.

"Move aside, Horseman. If the foolish priestess wishes to test me and the Council by doing as she threatens, let her do so. She forgets she surrendered the Defensore's rank centuries ago." Lilith's gaze remained locked on Caitlin, but she didn't attempt to circumvent Dante.

"I forget nothing, Lilith." Caitlin came around Dante's left side and shoved the vampire queen. With her powers and Gage's strength combined, the hard push sent Lilith across the field. She summoned an orb of fire in her empty hand, prepared to go to war with the mother of all vampires. "If my fate is to be continually tormented, yours will be no different."

"So be it," Lilith said, her nails extending into jagged, black blades; her face distorting.

"There is no need for—" Dante started to warn the two female beings to stop escalating.

Ignoring Death, Lilith sprang forward. Caitlin stepped up, intending to meet her in the center of the open space before them.

Dante cursed, snatching a hold of Caitlin again. He unfroze the other Horsemen to prevent the clash about to occur.

Teleporting between Caitlin and Lilith, Rayne halted Lilith's attack. The vampire froze in mid-air before him. "Lilith, back away, or I will cut you down. You know I will. The Council has given me the discretion to finish this anyway necessary to preserve the realms."

Lilith slowly descended until her feet met the ground. War was the only Council harbinger she ever hesitated to challenge. The two shared a hard-earned, mutual respect of one another. Both had fought together against enemies of the High Council. Both harbored an equally powerful blend of white and black magic they could call upon in conflict.

"She threatens to annihilate a species within the realms, Captain. That gives me valid claim to defend my kind."

Rayne's hand moved back to the hilt of the blade hanging on his side. "Caitlin is grieving the loss of her husband. A vampire. One of your direct lineage, Lilith, forcefully created by the animal you failed to eliminate centuries ago when the Council asked you to put him down. Anger causes her words and actions this night. In a clear state of mind, she would not utter them."

"You're loyalty to Morrigan blinds you to the slight I am paid." Lilith remained where she was. The fury dancing in her eyes warned there was no retreating from the fight Caitlin provoked.

"Your ego and wrath impair your judgement," Rayne calmly countered. "We are not enemies, Lilith, do not make it otherwise. The

Council only wants Baracus. Withdraw and return Evariste to the realm of the living, and I will ensure Caitlin does no harm to your progeny."

"War speaks the truth. Give me Evariste, and I will leave you and your kind alone." Caitlin stepped in front of Rayne, not carrying if Lilith killed her. "When your children were slaughtered by Senoi and Smmangelof, did you control your wrath? Did you not seek vengeance against those who murdered them? I loved Evariste. I, too, lost a child; one Evariste fathered. Baracus and one of his minions, another vampire, killed my son. I demand a life for a life, Lilith. As vampiric law allows when one is wronged. See the truth behind my rage tonight for yourself." Caitlin cut open her healed wrist then extended it to Lilith.

Lilith took Caitlin's hand. A skeptical expression covered the vampire queen's face. "How do you know I won't drain every drop of blood from your veins?"

"I'm taking a blind leap of faith. With the loss of Evariste and my child, I have nothing left to live for anyhow. Do what you will."

Lilith's tongue snaked out, sampling the burgundy torrents descending the length of Caitlin's arm. Taking in the ancient energy from the woman's blood, Lilith's lids closed. Intoxicated by the rare sampling of an immortal's life essence, the vampire sensually purred. Like a drunken cat, she rubbed her cheek against Caitlin's arm, smearing blood across her face. Her tongue lapped up another mouthful of sanguine streams to invoke visions of Caitlin's past. Lustrous black filled her almond-shaped eyes when they opened again to stare at Caitlin and Rayne. Lilith smiled, shamelessly displaying fangs that had turned and killed thousands over the years. "The Fates hid the truth of your existence well. Immortality still thrives within you, Caitlin DeDanann."

Not amused by Lilith's antics, Alcee yanked Caitlin's wrist free, then ran his thumb over the knife wound to close it. "Enough, Mother! That small taste more than adequately confirms the knowledge you already possess and should belay your fears. As your eldest living son, I will vouch for how much she loved Evariste. The Morning Star corrupted Baracus long ago. I've done my best to limit Baracus's havoc and to protect Evariste from him for centuries. Your choosing to let Baracus live was a grave mistake. Now give Caitlin what she requests."

"A woman who threatens to slaughter my children cannot possibly love one of them" Lilith stared down the length of her nose at Alcee in a haughty display of royal indignation.

Alcee scoffed, not intimidated by the being who sired him. "If she had asked politely or cried out to you for mercy, her pleas would have been ignored, as they were before. This isn't the first time she's come to you. But unlike last time, I will assist her in taking her vengeance against the more dastardly of our kind."

"You side with one who would see all vampires dead?" Lilith took a threatening step toward Alcee.

"If you cannot see there is little difference between your plight and hers, yes. I will annihilate those who cannot obey the laws and risk the rest of our lives."

"We have nothing in common!" Lilith shot Caitlin another sinister glare.

Caitlin inhaling behind him sent Alcee's hand upward, silencing whatever retort she was about to utter. Now that Caitlin was quiet once more, he focused on dealing with Lilith. "You share many similarities, Mother. Baracus wanted Caitlin beneath him; to serve his every whim as a slave similar to what Adam expected of you. He murdered her child because it was a threat to him. He forced her to go into hiding, hunting her as you were once hunted; he forced her apart from the man she loves because like the creator protected Adam, you protected Baracus. You are no better than those who dealt you the unfortunate hand that makes you what you are. Will you show her the mercy you weren't allowed, or be no better than Adam, Senoi, and Sammangelof?"

Lilith looked from Alcee to the Horsemen standing around them then back to Caitlin. Her dark eyes studying the redheaded sorceress fighting for the return of a soul; a soul which had become hers the moment Baracus sunk his teeth into Evariste's neck.

Caitlin heard the whispering deliberation taking place in Lilith's mind. The vampire's insulted dark side clashed with her empathetic lighter side. The longer it took for Lilith to recall Gage from the under-world, the greater the risk he wouldn't be able to return. "Lilith, I give you my oath as a descendant and priestess of Morrigan, give Evariste back to me, and Baracus's life is the only one I will take from your progeny."

Lilith huffed but remained silent.

Humility would never win over a vampire nor would Caitlin lower herself to groveling. If Lilith wouldn't listen to Alcee, she wouldn't listen to a grieving widow either. Caitlin needed Lilith to view her as an equal or a threat. Remembering an old legend that in punishment for Lilith's taking of human lives, she had been subjugated to the most powerful of demon kings, Caitlin called on the one being Lilith feared, a being who would happily bargain over a soul. "Iblis!"

"By the gods," Rayne muttered after Caitlin called for Lucifer to come forth. "Let us pray he does not answer."

A loud crack of thunder followed by a jagged chasm opening between Lilith and Caitlin caused all of the Horsemen to draw their weapons. Silver and gray streams of smoke and steam poured out of the opening, covering the ground in a murky fog. Heat rose with it, followed by a rapidly expanding fiery glow, warning them all Iblis prepared to make his entrance.

Lilith's eyes flared then rested on Caitlin, narrowing again. A new round of fury marring her face. "Leave me and my children be now that I return your husband to you."

"You drive a hard bargain. Remind me to never cross you." Gage set his hand on Caitlin's shoulder to let her know he was beside her: alive and well. She spun and threw her arms around him, tears streaming down her face. Gage brushed his lips across her temple. "It's over, cher. It's all over. We won't be parted again anytime soon."

Gage and Caitlin turned together to look at Lilith. The vampire queen inclined her head to them. Before Caitlin could thank her, a swirling black mist enveloped Lilith. The vampire dissipated into the night air.

A deep chuckle echoed around the field then a gravelly voice came from the gaping earth, "As my assistance isn't needed, medica, I'll take my leave. Tell your grandmother my debt to her is settled this night."

The separated sections of earth sealed themselves together as if there had never been a rift.

Baracus snarled and attempted to rise against the magic holding him in place. "I'll have your sorceress, yet, Evariste."

Like a lightning strike separating a tree limb from its trunk, Dante precipitously beheaded the Roman. Not even Caitlin had caught how quickly the Horseman drew his blade to address the unwisely voiced threat.

"With Death claiming him, Lilith can never accuse you of breaking your promise." Dante kicked Baracus's corpse, confirming the monster who terrorized Caitlin and Gage was dead. "The curse he and Dagda placed on the two of you is broken. May the Fates restore everything wrongly taken."

Thankful the worst was past, Caitlin shook her head, watching Dante drag his blade across his thigh, cleaning off Baracus's blood before sheathing it. Her hand trailed down Gage's back as he moved away from her toward where Baracus's head had landed. She worried about the sullen expression on her husband's face. "Gage?"

He didn't answer her. He just stared down into his grandfather's open eyes before picking up the severed head. "Burn the body and this, Giovanni. To ensure he doesn't return again."

As if throwing out a random piece of junk, Gage tossed Baracus's head toward his grandfather's lifeless form.

"Do not worry, Evariste. No being returns when killed by a harbinger's blade." Dante nodded to Rayne.

Rayne extended a gloved hand. Baracus's body combusted. Orange and red fingers of flame shot upward as if futilely seeking assistance from the night sky before surrendering to nothingness.

"Well done tonight, medica," Dante complimented Caitlin.

"Thank you for your counsel and help, Commander." It was the best she could put her gratitude into words for his encouraging her to rebel against Morrigan and preventing her from damning herself so she could have another chance with Gage.

"Until the next time our services are required." Dante bowed politely. The two Horsemen standing a few feet behind Dante and Rayne vanished. Dante whispered something to Rayne before the two walked away together. Their forms fading into the night.

"May that be the last we see of them," Gage loudly remarked, smiling at Caitlin.

"You won't be that fortunate, Arsceneaux," Dante said as he and

Rayne took on solid form once more. "Not with her grandmother being our employer. Morrigan asks we relay one other thing, Rosso."

"Which is?" Caitlin eyed the Horsemen. Morrigan better not be sending anymore tidings of ill fate after everything she just went through.

"Now that things are as they should be, no more battling vampires for you. At least not for a few months. Morrigan is most anxious to meet her great-grandchild growing in your belly and doesn't want to risk losing such a precious gift."

"What?" Caitlin couldn't believe what he said. In the dim moonlight, she could make out the grin on Dante's face before he pulled his hood over his head and disappeared with Rayne.

"This one will be your ward!" Sean yelled into the night sky.

"Too dangerous a job for me. That's a guide's role, General, and last I checked, it was your job to protect Morrigan's descendants, not mine." Dante's voice echoed around them

Caitlin and Gage laughed, their eyes meeting before Gage scooped her up into his arms and kissed her.

"Blessed be Morrigan and the Fates," Gage whispered once the kiss ended.

Warm tears escaped Caitlin's eyes. Joy overwhelmed her. A child grew within her, an immortal one at that. Fate gifted her a child and another chance with Gage. This time without any threats looming in the shadows to tear them apart. "The curse really is broken. We're going to get our happily ever after."

"Appears so, cher." Gage stole another kiss from her.

Alcee clapped Gage on the back, interrupting the intimate moment. "It's a damn good thing she was able to bring you back."

Gage offered his old friend a bright smile. "I'm just grateful Dante's plan worked as expected. Let's head back to the house"

Caitlin grabbed Gage's arm, preventing him from taking a step forward then shot Sean a glare. "Dante's plan? What plan?"

"Forget he mentioned that," Sean said, starting to back away from the group.

"Freeze, guardian." Caitlin cast another spell, preventing him from moving.

"That is not fair, Cate," Sean complained as she strode toward him.

"Life's not fair. Dante, return to me." Caitlin summoned the Horseman Commander back to their realm.

"In need of my services again already? Or have you chosen to reward my valor with the one conquest I have yet to complete, Rosso?" Dante leisurely ambled over to her.

"Neither, Commander." Caitlin faced Sean again. "Now, what was this plan my husband mentions?"

Sean tried to muster an apologetic expression for keeping her in the dark. "Cate, we would have never put it into play if we didn't already know the outcome."

Caitlin almost laughed as the glamour over him faded and a stoic-faced elven fae stared at her instead of a human Sean. "Start speaking the truth, guide. Or do I need to ask Dante to reveal everything?"

"Caitlin." Gage hooked an arm around her waist, bringing her flush against him. "Let Sean go and send Dante back to wherever he came from. One of us had to temporarily leave the other to finish Baracus. You are the more powerful of the two of us. It only made sense for me to give my life. Besides, Lilith would have never answered my call. I've tried summoning her to no avail previously."

"What if I had failed or Baracus got the upper hand?" Caitlin stared at him as he pulled slightly away, so he could rest his hand on her belly.

"You failing never crossed my mind. You're too stubborn a woman to let evil win. Now, release the men who saved us today, so we can return home to celebrate the news of our first child and the curse being broken." Gage nuzzled the side of her face. Images of them making love played out in her head.

"Because my husband is alive and well, the two of you are off the hook. Unfortunately, my child needs a guardian, and I wouldn't want them to have anyone else watching over them."

"God help you if it has dad's temper and mom's powers." Alcee smirked as he spoke.

The Six Month Mark
❧

D'Orme - Present Day

Caitlin laughed, lying beside Gage as they snacked on strawberries and cheese in bed. She admired the handsome vampire who smiled much more than he ever had in the past. "I bet you regret all those times you hung up on me and declined my meeting requests now."

Gage grinned. "Not in the slightest. If I hadn't done so, you wouldn't have been so curious about me once you learned who Chef Gage really was."

"Oh, you're still such a stubborn ass at times." Caitlin rolled her eyes then watched the sheers hanging from the canopy above them dance in the wind.

"And you love when I am," Evariste whispered in her ear before his lips drifted to the sensitive spot beneath it.

Caitlin sighed, delighting in how his teeth lightly scrapped her skin. While he was no longer technically a vampire, he could still take on the attributes of one. "Only when it comes to playing in the bedroom."

Gage scoffed and propped himself up on his elbow again. He picked a slice of his favorite cheese off the plate between them then topped it with a slice of strawberry before popping it into his mouth.

The way he silently stared at her while he slowly chewed the mouthful of food made Caitlin wonder what today was really about. He had taken off work for a second time that week. They spent a good part of the morning making love after a sumptuous breakfast in bed. "What's on your mind, Decurion?"

"It's been six months since we married. I promised you that you could divorce me if you weren't happy being Mrs. Arsceneaux."

The reminder of his promise startled Caitlin. "I'm more than happy being your wife. Is there something in particular that makes you think otherwise?"

"Well, cher, you never answered my question about whether we stay here in Louisiana or go elsewhere? Not to mention, you keep putting off moving all your stuff to D'Orme."

"I'm pregnant and don't feel like packing up a bunch of stuff, especially if it means missing too many of your omelets and dinners. They're much better than what I make for myself." Caitlin couldn't believe the fact she hadn't rushed to move in with him bothered him so badly.

"I offered to go with you to Virginia."

"I didn't want to pull you away from your family as everyone transitioned into their new lives. They needed you here. Deciding whether or not to remain immortal or live a normal, human life had to be a difficult choice for each of them to make. I'm kind of surprised the Fates allowed them any say in the matter. Plus, my lease still had a few more months left on it. It's not like I'm in a hurry to pay the extra month's rent to break it early."

"So does that mean you've decided we should continue living here?"

Caitlin smiled at the hopeful ring in his voice. Even though he offered to move wherever she wanted, he obviously wanted to stay at D'Orme. "I don't know. I mean I really do like it here, but I am also a big fan of Williamsburg, and I haven't seen this villa outside of Rome you supposedly own.

Genuine surprise covered Gage's face as she draped an arm over his shoulders.

"I hadn't thought about reclaiming the property in Italy. I suppose I could do that, if it's something you'd like me to do, but that would mean resolving a few things in the first century with Vespasian."

"I hear he's a reasonable man and can be quite generous to those who suffered calamity under his rule. I think being persecuted by Baracus would more than qualify for leniency if you plead your case correctly. We can plan for that discussion and figure out where we'll live later, Decurion. We have all eternity to figure that out. For the moment…" Caitlin impishly smiled before sliding down underneath the covers. Her lips skimmed his belly then teased the inside of his thigh. The deep groan rumbling from his chest as she ran her tongue along the length of his cock confirmed she succeeded in distracting him from needless worries about where they should live or getting divorced. There's no way she'd ever dream of doing so.

"Eternity looks promising, wherever we live, if this is how every day is going to be with you." Gage curled his fingers into her hair in response to her pleasuring him.

Epilogue
6∾9

Rome - 70 CE

Caitlin watched her son and daughter play in the courtyard of Gage's Roman villa. Her oldest, a daughter with red hair and green eyes, laughed as she sat in front of one of the stone benches entertained by something no one else could see. Who visited her daughter?

The three-year-old giggled again bringing Caitlin over to her.

Recognizing the Venetian-tinged accent of the voice that softly whispered on the breeze, Caitlin smiled. "Turned in the Horsemen's laurels to become the guardian of my daughter, Dante?"

Dante now revealed himself to her. "No, Rosso. I heard a rumor that Evariste Arsceneaux was restored to favor with Vespasian and once more took up his seasonal residence outside of Rome. I was also curious to see if this one inherited her mother's eyes."

"Thankfully, Saoirse has her father's beautiful green eyes." Caitlin sat on the bench beside Dante. "Lower your hood, so you don't frighten my children."

Dante laughed but pushed the hood back. By the dust on his boots and the gloves he wore, it was evident he stopped in Rome after completing an assignment somewhere. "Neither of them had any fear of

380

me. In fact, they laugh at me a great deal. I was going to take offense then I thought about who their parents were. The three of us had quite the conversation about their legendary father and mother. However, your son grew bored and wandered off. I think the two of them believe I am making up tales that couldn't possibly be true."

"Undoubtedly, as they have not seen that side of Gage or me. How have you been, Dante?" Caitlin wondered if there was another reason he was there.

"Va bene. Truly, I am well, Caitlin. And stop worrying. I'm merely checking in on the Arsceneaux family. I have no messages to deliver. I can see you are well by the smile on your face. How is Evariste?"

"Gage is good. He should be home shortly if you want to stick around and say hello."

"Unfortunately, Morrigan is expecting me. I may return this evening if not dispatched again. I haven't harassed the decurion recently and know how much he misses Sean's and my company."

"Morrigan promoted him to general for protecting her bloodline a month or so ago. But I suppose you know that."

Dante stood. "I am not going to lie, Rosso. It was disappointing to learn he officially became one of us. We didn't need any more cantankerous guides in our ranks. Give him my regards."

"I will, and you are welcome here anytime you wish to stop by."

"Does that invitation extend to when I am in need of a woman's touch?" Dante cupped her chin in a gloved hand.

"No chance of that ever happening. I hope you find your guiding star one of these days, Dante. I hate for anyone, even you, to wander through eternity alone." Caitlin always sensed loneliness more than anything deep down in Dante. Underneath all of his audacity and mischievousness, a good heart existed that deserved someone who would treasure it.

Dante hated her sympathy. He was fine with things the way they were. He had accepted eternal bachelorhood centuries ago. It was safer not to be attached to anyone with the duties he assumed when Morrigan promoted him. "While I may have lost out on you, I certainly do not spend my nights alone."

Not doubting the truth of that statement, Caitlin smiled. The

Horseman made even Morrigan's high priestesses and handmaidens debate breaking their vow of celibacy. "Keep any sons you may have away from my daughter, Dante. Same for your daughters with my son."

"No need to worry about that, cara. There are measures one may use to prevent unwanted offspring."

Returning home, Gage overheard the last half of their conversation. "Keep your manners about my wife, Commander. I would hate to have to call you out."

"Rest easy, General. I merely enjoy teasing her." Dante smirked, watching Gage stop beside Caitlin. "I'm surprised you still worry about my luring her away."

"Oh, I don't worry about that at all. As I have something you never will."

Dante's brow rose as he shot Gage a cynical look. "Fangs?"

Gage laughed, allowing his elongated canines to show. "While those come in handy at times. I have something much better"—Gage brought Caitlin's hand to his lips—"her unending love and fidelity."

"You need to not enjoy the pleasures your wife offers so much, Arsceneaux. Since the first two didn't wear the novelty of it down, the twins will certainly curb your appetite."

Gage smiled at Caitlin. "Twins? Are you pregnant again?"

"Not that I'm aware of. Dante is just stirring up mischief this afternoon."

"Maybe we should see what we can do to fulfill that prediction later when the children are in bed," Gage suggested, giving her a come-hither grin. "We don't have a daughter with her mother's eyes yet."

Dante loudly laughed. "Careful what you wish for, Evariste."

"You aren't one to lecture anyone on carnal appetites, Giovanni. You were summoned to Sasainn over an hour ago." Sean materialized in the courtyard and grabbed Dante by the ear as he used to when Dante had gotten himself into trouble as a teen.

"Release me, guide. I have killed beings for lesser offenses than the one you pay me now." Dante squirmed as Sean tightened his hold on his ear.

"What's he done now?" Caitlin put her hands on her hips, giving him the same scolding stare she did her children when they misbehaved.

"It's more who than what," Sean stiffly advised.

Gage shook his head. "There was a rumor circulating around the Council Chambers that Sanjur chased a cloaked, dark-haired man through the center of Ephesus this morning after catching him in bed with his wife."

"And Hera is demanding Morrigan give her his head for the offense paid to her son," Sean added, confirming the cause for the summons. "Honestly, Giovanni, at your age I would expect better."

Dante sheepishly grinned. "In my defense, she didn't tell me she was married and appeared in disguise. If I had known it was Clio, I would have never touched her."

"Dante! Really?" Caitlin couldn't believe he did such a thing. "You were stupid enough to sleep with a muse married to a djinn, and not just any djinn, but one of Hera's sons?"

"Oh, he's done much worse. Between his and Destahn's antics, I'm surprised we still have four Horsemen. Let's go deal with the latest bit of chaos you've brought upon yourself, Commander." Sean vanished, taking Dante with him.

Gage laughed at the disbelief still on his wife's face. "Thank the Fates you two never married. You'd be dealing with a mischief-causing delinquent every day for eternity."

"I thank them for that and you regularly." Caitlin kissed him.

NINE MONTHS LATER, Caitlin gave birth to twins: a son, the spitting image of his father and a daughter with gold hair and lavender eyes.

Sean held the tiny girl in his arms. "The gods help us, as you are a miniature version of your great-grandmother."

Caitlin laughed, rocking her new son. "I think we will have to worry more about this one. He has Gage's looks and the mark of Morrigan." She gently brushed the baby's dark hair back, revealing the small moon on the back of his neck.

Sean smiled, seeing the tiny birthmark. "A future guardian like his Uncle Sean."

"Let us hope not. A soldier like his father, or perhaps a future

Horseman," Dante disagreed, taking the little girl from Sean. She gazed up at him with her mother's eyes and grasped one of his fingers. "Isn't that right, mia carina? No guardian work for your brother. Though you might make a great guide with those violet eyes. You don't miss a thing just like your mother."

"You're both wrong." Caitlin smiled at her husband. "Alessandro Evariste will become the next Defensore should he choose any mystical role over normal career callings." Caitlin gave her second son an Italian name with him being born in Rome.

Gage gently lifted his son from Caitlin's arms. "Protector of men. It is a great name for him. What shall we call his sister?"

"Aria. She has her mother's lungs with the way she cries," Sean suggested as the little girl started crying when Dante handed her to Caitlin.

"He is not worth your tears, little one. Don't tell me we have to worry about you crushing on handsome faces already," Caitlin whispered then softly sang an old Gaelic lullaby trying to calm her.

Aria quieted when Dante knelt down beside Caitlin and offered Aria his finger to grasp again. "Your mother is right, carina. I am much too old for you."

Gage snorted at the way his daughter calmed in the Horseman's company. "She and I will have a long talk about you and the trouble you Horsemen bring later. Hopefully, that will cause her to steer clear of the four of you."

Dante chuckled, staring at the tiny hand clasping his finger. "Careful what you tell her. You may feed her infatuation and have her searching us out."

Hearing his eldests' voices in the hall, Gage strode toward the nursery doorway.

"Are you ready to meet your big brother and sister?" Gage asked Alessandro, who stared up at him with wide eyes. "It sounds like they are anxious to meet you."

"Saoirse, Dante, come see Alessandro and Aria." Gage invited his older children into the room.

Dante started at the name Gage spoke. "Dante? I thought his name was Sean."

"Though it went against my better judgment, we named him Sean Dante after the two men who protected his mother all these years. As you're rarely around and the guide always is, we call him Dante, so everyone knows which Sean we are calling." Gage sat down on the floor to let his children meet their new brother. Both older children crowded around their father, fascinated by the newborn he held.

Dante watched the two asking Gage questions as they stared at Alessandro. He was touched by Caitlin and Gage's decision to honor him and Sean as they did.

"Come over here, Dante Arsceneaux," he called the young boy to him. The boy cautiously walked over, starring up at the Horseman. "You have a great name, which means you will do great things."

He took the medallion he wore and placed it around the boy's neck. "As the oldest, you are the watchman for your brother and sisters. Take good care of them."

The boy lifted the gold emblem from his chest to look at it. He ran his small fingers over the laurels on either side of the crest.

"Say thank you," Caitlin reminded her son of his manners.

The little boy mumbled thank you before running over to his mother's bed to see the infant in her arms.

D'Orme - Present Day

THE SETTING SUN filled the Louisiana sky with an orange hue and cast a flamelike glow across the gardens. It was nice to be back at D'Orme after Gage's assignment in Rome came to an end. While Italy was lovely, Louisiana would always be home. The warm spring night reminded Caitlin of when she first met Gage several years ago. The mix of roses, honeysuckle, jasmine, and magnolia embraced her like a long-lost friend, welcoming her back to her favorite chair on the balcony. Her eyes found the rose bush with dark royal purple blooms starting to open by the fountain that Gage had planted in her memory. No longer did it sit alone in its special place; alongside it was a freshly planted friend with newly opening lavender blooms rimmed with a dark fuchsia.

Caitlin had never seen the color combination tinting the velvety petals before.

An arm settling around her waist then drawing her into a warm side drew her gaze from the garden to the green eyes of her husband.

"I see we have a new addition to the garden."

"You said the rose bush seemed lonely, so I gave it a friend."

Caitlin softly laughed at the remark. "Do roses get lonely?"

"If soulless vampires do, I assume roses can long for company too. I think you'll like the name of this one. I know I do. It makes me think of how long I will love my wife." Gage handed her a rose he cut earlier from the new bush. A small white card dangled off a golden ribbon tied around its stem.

Caitlin smiled as she read the name of the rose *"for eternity."*

Thank You For Reading!

If you enjoyed *House of Arsceneaux*, please consider posting a short review on the website where you purchased the book, Goodreads, Story-Graph, or on Caterina's website shop.

Reviews are an important tool to help new readers discover a books. Even a simple one or two line review helps raise awareness about books and I truly do appreciate when someone takes the time to leave one.

Language Glossary

Cajun, Creole, and Louisiana Slang
Alors pas – Of course not!
Cher – term of endearment
Comment ça va! – How are you or how's it going?
Couyon – stupid, crazy, or foolish person (derived from couillon)
Dat - That
Kaw – Come on!
Laissez les bon temps rouler! – Let the good times roll!
Ma petite sœur – my little sister
Mon ami/mon amie – my friend
Pirogue – a wooden boat primarily used by Cajuns in shallow swamps.
Possede – mischievous or possessed
Sha – phonetic spelling of cher to show regional dialect differences
Tête dure – hard headed/stubborn
Vay ya or veiller – gossip, talk, or chatter
You jokin', right? – Are you serious?

Traditional French
Bête jalouse - Jealous beast
C'est vrai? – Is it True/Is that true?
C'est vrai. – It is true.
Ferme ta bouche – Shut your mouth/shut up
La chasse commence. – The chase begins.
Je brûle pour mon amour. Toujours. – I burn for my love, always.
Je t'aime. – I love you.
Je t'aime de toute mon âme. – I love you with all my soul.
Je suis vraiment désolé. - I am truly sorry.
Ma ange – my angel
Mon coeur – my heart
Ma magnifique femme - my magnificent woman/wife
Ma petite amie – my girlfriend
Ma petit choux – my little cabbage or dear
Ne me laisse pas seul! – Don't leave me alone!
Tu es mon âme soeur. – You are my soulmate.

Italian
Calma – Calm down, relax
Cara – dear, feminine
Il mio caro amico – my dear friend, masculine

Mia carina – my little cutie, feminine
Rosso – Red (Dante's nickname for Caitlin)
Mi Scusi- Pardon me or I'm sorry when a person is at fault for something.
Va bene. – It's good or if answering how are you doing – slang for Things are going well. Or I'm good.

Latin
Dea- goddess
Legatus – legate
Medica - healer
Preafectus – prefect

Gaelic
A mhuirnín – my darling
A leanbh – my child
Droch-fhuil – evil blood, a type of vampire
Gleoite – pretty, lovely, or gorgeous

Acknowledgments

I wanted to thank everyone who helped me create and polish this book. Louisiana holds a special place in my heart, so it was important I get this one right out of the gate.

First, a big thank you to Beth for the developmental edits and Tori for the line, content, and copy edits.

Thank you to the Silver Quill Writers, the Williamsburg Writers, Glenn, D'Artagnan, Etana, Tracy, and Tierra for helping spot plot holes and providing feedback from a reader's perspective on where additional work was needed. You guys are amazing critique partners and beta readers!

Rachel D, Sarah T, and James G - You guys might recognize this one. All your feedback offered way back when I first tinkered with this storyline was all incorporated. You guys are the original alpha readers for my hot messes when I was trying to figure out my writing style and how to write. Thank you for pushing through all those years ago.

Kathleen with Book Brush - Thank you to you and your team for creating such a lovely cover!

Amy and Kim with RMWB - Thank you for helping whip the blurb into shape!

Ka-lynne Art and Wavyhues - Thank you for bringing Evariste and Caitlin to life through your artistic eye. The illustrations are stunning!

As always, thank you to my friends and family who offered thoughts and ideas to be incorporated into the book along with your continued support of my author-ly journey.

About the Author

Caterina is passionate about history, music, romance, old languages, and travel. She regularly intertwines these subjects in her writing.

When not traveling or working, Caterina finds time to sing classical music, make soutache jewelry, write, paint, shoot archery, and fence. She is always up for trying something new so the list of hobbies is ever expanding.

If you would like to contact her or learn more about her and future works, you can find her on Twitter, Facebook, Instagram, and at her website, https://caterinanovelliere.com.

You can also sign up for her Random Musings Newsletter or catch her podcast, Cat-astrophic Ramblings on your favorite podcast app.

Scan the QR code below for Cat's linktr.ee profile and to easily follow her on multiple platforms.

facebook.com/CaterinaNovelliere

twitter.com/chantueserouge

instagram.com/chantueserouge

amazon.com/author/caterinanovelliere

bookbub.com/authors/caterina-novelliere

youtube.com/@catnovelliere

Also by Caterina Novelliere

Servants of Morrigan: Four Horsemen Series

Mark of The Night

When The Moon Bleeds

War Rising

Servants of Morrigan: Immortal Creatures Series

House of Arsceneaux

Stand Alones:

Tale Of Rouen

Novellas:

The First Encounter - Releasing Summer 2023

Made in the USA
Coppell, TX
15 September 2023

21583369R00236